BLOOD DEATH AND SALT

***

A JOHNNIE KING NOVEL

by

Jan O'Kane

First Edition, published 2015
Available in Softcover and on Kindle

ALWAYS REMEMBERED PUBLISHING
Durham NC 27705

Cover design by Michael O'Kane
Copyright © 2015 Jan O'Kane
All rights reserved.

ISBN-13: 978-0692464427
ISBN-10:0692464425

Acknowledgments

I thank, honor and praise God for the talents He has graced me with in this life. I trust writing has been one of the many abilities, as it has been my lifelong dream to be a writer.

To my husband, Michael, who has been my rock and support throughout this entire process of writing, as well as my first and third editor.

I am privileged to have a supportive family, especially my brother Stan, who encouraged me and kept me working even when my goal seemed so far away.

To Traci Hall, my editor, who took her valuable time to not only edited my manuscript, but also provided me with excellent advice and critiques. Hopefully, I followed all her constructive points to improve my efforts.

I also want to thank Joe Clemente, retired FBI, who provided me with details and assistance concerning the FBI.

To Mac McGovern who deserves a huge amount of gratitude for his enormous help in bringing this book to publication and market.

Thank you,
one and all.

Disclosure

This is a work of fiction and imagination. Actual names, characters, places, or incidents either are the product of the author's imagination or are used fictitiously, and any resemblance to actual persons, living or dead, business establishments, events or locales is strictly and entirely coincidental.

Dedication

To our law enforcement personnel, who serve and protect us with integrity.

Thank you.

Introduction

Meet Johnnie King, former FBI agent, settling into a mundane life is now working at The First National Bank of Ackers, WV.

Vandalism strikes Johnnie's office, leaving a body in her office closet. Johnnie and Detective Terry Nichols attempt to tackle the case.

Things change when the state attorney Mirah Anderson and her traveling companion FBI agent John Erickson insists on coming to Ackers.

Now bodies are accumulating. Who will be next?

Johnnie, Terry, Michael, Johnnie's husband, and her former boss from the FBI, Noah Drake and his team find that this case will take more than their efforts to unravel. How many entities are involved in this dark and dangerous small town and its bank?

**Watch for more adventures of
Johnnie King and the team.**

***

The night brought cold winds early this year and Johnnie King could hear the wind blowing outside her office window and almost feel the gusts as it rattled the windows in the old bank building.

The architecture of this place amazed her. Built around the turn of the century, six floors to its structure and her office was perched on the top floor. She loved just roaming around the building when she was first hired. She told Gary Percy, her supervisor, about her wanderings in the open places. Continuing a habit she developed when she worked for the FBI, Johnnie wanted to know her surroundings.

Johnnie liked having a desk in a private office. An office was never going to happen with her previous employment. She was either working in the field or in a cubical. She did enjoy the challenge of fieldwork, but there were times when she would be away from home for several days. This job was different. She worked at a bank before the bureau, and liked the idea of closing the day with a completion of the day's work in balance.

She knew she was fortunate to have landed the job at the bank. She never expected to be in management when she applied since her expertise was far from banking, but things had worked out well like having her own office.

She certainly did not start out in the position of processing manager. She went through a few other positions while working through the ranks before attaining this position. Johnnie did not think she would exceed this level, and she was content with staying in this position.

She loved the job and her co-workers. Well, for the most part that was true. Some were vain and some just had to have their eyes and nose into everything. That was true no matter where you worked. She sat back in her chair and looked around. It was a nice office with two windows, bookshelves and a huge desk. Most people thought it indulgent but the truth about the matter it was an old wooden desk with a larger top attached. The oversized desk was more about the work, getting involved in tracing outages or doing research made it necessary to have room to spread the work out on a large surface.

The walls were some sort of unusual grass wallpaper painted white before she was hired. Blue being her favorite color, she loved the azure border along the ceiling that matched the drapes over the windows and the glass panel by the door. She rarely closed her door during working hours. She wanted her co-workers to feel welcomed. She even kept a bowl of candy on the corner of her desk for the employees.

Johnnie referred to the people who worked in her department as co-workers. She wanted the department in her care to be a team. In the bureau, being a part of the team could be the difference between a good ending and something else.

Johnnie already put in 10 hours of this eight-hour day. "Banker's hours" where are these perks, and who gets such a thing? Such glories went to the big boys.

Before leaving every evening, she checked with the night crew to see that things were moving along well. If they had the slightest problem, she would stay. She felt it was her duty to be as much a part of the work team as anyone.

Walking into the confirmation department's room, she asked if there were any problems. Mary Edgington leaned back in her chair. "Things are going well and we should be wrapping up in just a bit. After I film the work, the day will be history." Mary always saw the best in every situation. Johnnie often wondered how she was able to stay so cheery even on the most difficult days.

Walking into the computer room, she found Karey Cousins. "How goes it Karey?" Karey was busy sorting checks and arranging them in the proper trays. "Okay, should be out in good time tonight, about seven." Johnnie loved it when the days went smoothly. "Great, but you have my number if you need anything." Karey smiled, "You say that every night."

Johnnie grinned as she waved good-bye to the night crew, before returning to her office to collect her things.

Back in her office, she secured some of the files she had been working and locked her desk and credenza. Wow, it was finally Friday, walking to the front of her office; she went to the closet in the corner and gathered her coat and purse. It was her habit to close her office door every night before leaving the bank. She never locked the door, if someone wanted to get into the space, there was always the full-length window next to the door.

Walking through the parking lot in the crisp fall air, she found it invigorating and chilling. Late September in West Virginia could definitely put a nip in the air. Wishing she had worn a heavier coat and scarf, she could only pull the collar up around her neck as she walked the across the lot.

***

Getting into her car, she locked the doors, secured her seat belt, and took out her phone. "Hey honey, I am on my way home. Do you want me to pick up anything on my way?"

Michael Joseph King, Johnnie's husband of just over eight years, normally did the cooking for the two of them.

Michael, standing six foot one weighing in at 176 pounds, with black hair and gorgeous green eyes was a man comfortable in his own skin. Some people never do achieve the sense of self that he possessed.

"No sweetheart, I have everything under control. I think you will like tonight's dinner. How about your favorite Italian white bean soup served with hot bread and those no bake cookies you like so much?"

Johnnie was more than ready for dinner and soup on a blustery night was perfect. "I am really ready for the soup. Do you know how cold it is tonight?"

Michael laughed. "Why do you think I made the soup? Besides it is so easy and quick, I had no choice. I only got home about a half an hour ago."

Johnnie had to ask. "If you got home a half an hour ago, just how did you make bread?"

This banter back and forth between the two was pretty much normal for this couple. "Did I say I made the bread? You know there are these things, called bakeries. I picked up two loaves and they are in the oven waiting for you. Those little ciabatta loaves you like so much. "

Johnnie was ready to pull out of her parking spot. "I guess I will just have to hurry home to enjoy dinner. I have to ring up now, getting ready to drive." She never used her phone when she drove.

As always, dinner was perfect especially since they ate sitting on the floor in the family room in front of the fireplace. The room had a raised hearth and it was easy to use the inglenook as a table of sorts. Well, until the fire truly started to roar.

After the meal, Johnnie said she was going upstairs to put on her snuggie, as she called the lounging nightwear, and come back down. She had scrubbed her face, used her night moisturizer, and brushed her teeth. She was ready for bed. She knew the fire would lull her to the stage where she fought to keep her eyes open.

Although the kitchen was very large, more than enough for the two of them to work together, Michael would rather work in the kitchen on his own.

Johnnie walked in the room with a huge smile. She recognized the bottle of wine that Michael had opened. Together they sat comfortably on the floor with the large pillows pulled from the couch, and the wine was Johnnie's favorite Australian red.

Johnnie loved this old house, the family room a wood burning fireplace, and dark stained hardwood floors. The walls were the palest shade of salmon and well matched to the brick of the fireplace.

After a glass and a half, Johnnie knew something was up. "Okay what is going on here, dinner, roaring fireplace, and now my favorite wine. What gives?" Johnnie snuggled a bit closer, and Michael put his arm around her.

Michael took on a very serious tone. "Are we ever going to talk about adopting? I know finding out that we could not have our own children has been a devastating setback, especially since you left the FBI so we could start our family. Moving to Ackers was because we decided it was the perfect place to raise a family. However, we have to face the facts. If we are going to have a family, don't you think we should talk? I don't claim to know what you went through or what you are still going through, but I am trying. I really am. Give me some sort of idea what you want."

Johnnie dreaded this subject. Finding out that she could not have children really shook her to the core. She remembered as a child she told her mother she wanted six kids, and now she would have none. "I know we need to talk about it, but I was thinking if we waited, we could always adopt an older child. You know; give a good home to someone who really needs love and care. Don't you like the idea of an older child?" The despair in Johnnie's eyes said everything. "Do we really need to discuss it right now?"

Michael took a deep breath. "How long do you think we should put off our plans?"

Johnnie felt like her emotions were welling inside. She could handle armed gunmen, talk down a volatile hostage situation, she could keep up with any man in the FBI training, but this topic came close to breaking her. "I just want more time, I don't want to seem selfish; but I really am not ready. Michael, I have thought this over a hundred times in my head. My dream of being a wife and mother always came first, The FBI or the bank just secondary. Now, I just don't know. To be very honest, I don't know if I will ever be ready. I think I would like to go to bed now."

Before she got off the floor, she gave Michael a kiss that said she was not upset with him, only the subject, and the circumstance. "Are you coming up?" She said with hope in her eyes.

He just smiled and got up, taking the wineglasses to the dishwasher; he then followed her upstairs.

Friday night was a night to remember. She may not be able to have a baby; but there was nothing wrong with trying.

***

Monday morning, how did it roll around so fast? She didn't even remember enjoying her weekend.

In the morning, Michael brought Johnnie's tea up as usual. He told her he was going to Clarksburg to meet with a prospective customer, but his meeting was not until mid-afternoon. He would be home until one o'clock. He asked. "What are you planning today? Do you know what time you will be home?"

Johnnie really didn't like the vault days. "Ugh, I have vault day. I don't even like to think about a day in the basement. Guess I can't put it off, so better get started. The lower vault is full of dust, dirt, and worst of all spiders. How did those creatures get into a sealed vault? I shouldn't be too late tonight, once I prep the film for shipment that is about all I can do for the day."

"I could see by your outfit you weren't planning on being in your office today." Michael always noticed the little things.

The dress for the day needed to be casual and yet professional. Jeans would have been nice, and much more sensible, but still she needed to be able to meet with a customer should the need arise. Her obligation is to the bank, she needs to appear at all times as a proficient and organized employee. Her outfit for the day was her favorite pair of black leggings with a long black tunic. She did have to dress it up a bit with some jewelry. Although when working in the vault she would tuck her ornamentation inside her tunic, she never did wear rings other than her wedding rings on heavy workdays. She did not want to lose a finger or a ring. Therefore, she would turn the engagement ring to the inside of her hand and even tape it in place. To play it safe, in case she needed to meet with someone, she kept an apron in the lower vault for such workdays.

Johnnie always tried to think of every possible scenario, even personal safety while working in out of the way places like the lower vault. That must be why Gary Percy, her supervisor and senior vice president of the bank assigned her the contingency plan.

It was part of her job to review the organization of the lower vault, which she did on a semi-annual basis. However, today's review would give her a good opportunity to pull the microfilm she would need to continue the project assigned to her by Tom Midland, Executive Vice President of Lending. She didn't know why he assigned the project, but she always carried out instructions.

Giving Michael a kiss goodbye, she started her day. The morning air was chilly so Johnnie grabbed her heavier coat. She did not want that night chill to catch her again. The scarf she wore matched the collar of her coat and wide enough to keep her neck warm. The weather reports called for falling temperatures. She knew West Virginia's eastern panhandle got some cold weather, but this early?

Pulling into the bank's parking lot, Johnnie took her favorite parking place. The first row of parking after the drive in teller lane was for the employees. Johnnie chose to park in the section under the street light. Leaving the bank at odd hours, she preferred to have her vehicle in a well-lit area. It certainly wasn't to show off her car. She was still driving her old station wagon, which she loved regardless of Michael's opinion. This green monster may be out of style today, with all the SUVs on the road, but she loved this vehicle and its power.

Don greeted Johnnie at the door. Don Phelps was the maintenance man for the morning. He usually started at seven in the morning and left about three in the afternoon. He was a pleasant chap who just took care of the bank's maintenance mainly because he loved the old building. He knew every nook and cranny in the place. He was probably the only one besides Johnnie who knew where to look for the unusual items one might request. He lived close so it was easy for him to walk to work. Don was a man of stocky build with a rough complexion, average height, and thick graying hair. He always had a smile from ear to ear, as he greeted the employees. It seemed as though nothing could destroy his mood.

"Good morning, Don. How goes it today?" Johnnie greeted every employee she encountered.

"Pretty good day so far, but then it is only 7:25 on a cold Monday. Glad to see you dressed for the chill."

After her brief encounter with Don, she crossed paths with Harrison. Harrison Magers was a good-looking man, six feet tall, black hair and blue eyes, very symmetrical features. Too bad, he was the bank clown. He could really go beyond his present position customer service manager if he would just take his job more seriously.

"Hey Harrison, how's your day looking?"

Harrison was standing by the partition separating his office from the lobby. "I don't have much planned, but I see this must be vault day. You are dressed for rough work."

"What makes you think I am working in the vault today?" Johnnie smiled.

Harrison laughed at her comment. "Come on, you are known for your high heels and today you are in flats, a sure give away."

"Okay you caught me, it is a dirty job; but somebody has to do it." Johnnie waved as she headed to the steps. She always took the stairs. She wanted the small bit of exercise that the climb to the sixth floor provided.

Half way up to her office, she encountered Tom Midland. "How is the research project coming along? You have been able to keep it secured and away from any prying eyes, right?"

Johnnie found Tom's concern about the assignments he gave her almost brotherly. "All is well, not to worry. Today I will pull the microfilm I need along with several other rolls as a part of my semi-annual lower vault inspection."

Tom again slowed her down, and looking in both directions in the stairwell before speaking. "You do realize this research is centered on Victor Andropov. He is dangerous, and if he knew you were gathering this for the state's attorney general, he just might try to do something none of us want to see happen. He can be a violent man, and he has his, shall we say, body guard near him every second of everyday"

"Not to worry, I have not told anyone, except Michael, of the project. I am doing all I can to keep the research project secret. I have no desire to turn this into an encounter with the likes of Victor Andropov or his bodyguard."

Johnnie arrived on her floor. As she neared her office, she noticed the door. The door standing open, was not a good sign. She knew she closed the door Friday night when she left. It was still early so only the morning computer operator was on the floor at present. If Silva had been snooping, she would have been smart enough to close the door.

As she drew nearer to the door, she could see files scattered and opened on her desk. She noticed her credenza drawers opened. Her heart sank, not only would this change her entire day; the potential of danger to her co-workers could become real. She needed to get Frank Ridges from security up to her office now. This was important and needed to be on record.

After calling Frank, she called Tom to keep him up to date. "Tom, someone has been in my office and broke into my desk and credenza. Don't worry, the materials for the project are not kept in my office; all is well. It remains secure. I do, however, want to know if someone from the attorney general's staff has been talking about this project."

Tom was very concerned his first question was if she called Frank.

"It's okay; I called Frank as soon as I saw the files lying on my desk." Johnnie knew Tom was truly concerned for all concerned.

The security officer, Frank Ridges, came up to her office. Frank asked if she had entered or touched anything in her office. Explaining that she did not, but thought it was necessary to have a record of the invasion. As former law enforcement, she knew not to touch the scene.

Frank went into the office. His hand on his gun, ready for use should the need arise. A bit melodramatic, this did not seem like an event that would require such action. At least until he used his radio to call for backup.

Unaware of what was going on in the office, she did her best to keep the employees from getting too excited. She asked all but her assistant Ana to go on with their day. She needed to keep the atmosphere calm. People in the state of chaos make errors, so it was important to proceed as though it was a normal day.

Johnnie could hear Frank on his radio. "Chuck, I need you and Pete up here on six at Johnnie King's office now. I have put in a call to the police department, but I want this door secure. We will need to have the employees come through the back lunchroom door."

Chuck and Pete came up to her office, they kept a perimeter around her office cleared. Johnnie stood near the elevator and stair area to instruct employees to enter by way of the lunchroom side door. Word spread through the bank like wild fire. Having security to any part of the bank apparently caused anxiety. She didn't know what was going on and it was her office. Calling security was just for a matter of record. What was Frank thinking?

Soon other officials started showing up on the floor. This was a secured floor, how could anyone have gotten to her office in the first place? The elevator had a code in place. This just did not seem like a simple snooping job, not the way Frank and his crew were acting.

When Johnnie turned her door station over to one of Frank's men, she sat at Ana's desk just outside her own office for the moment. Johnnie was still sitting at Ana's desk when a woman in a navy blue suit, raven colored hair, cut in a simple easy style, approached her. This woman had uniquely violet colored eyes.

The woman introduced herself as Terry Nichols a detective with the Akers police. "You can call me Terry; I prefer to keep things casual. You are Johnetta King and I understand it is your office that has been broken into?"

Johnnie could see the cool confidence of this woman. Her eyes had an intensity to them that made the violet all the more noticeable. Terry Nichols stood approximately five foot eight inches and wore a shoulder holster. Most would not notice the telltale sign of a gun, but Johnnie noticed everything.

"Yes, I am Johnetta King, you can call me Johnnie. I don't understand why the police have been called in for a vandalized office."

"I would appreciate you accompanying me to the police station." Johnnie knew whatever happened she had no part in the event, but apparently; her office was a crime scene beyond simple vandalism.

The woman was pleasant, but she was rather insistent that Johnnie come with her. "I need you to accompany me to the police station, now."

She asked the detective, "You want to tell me exactly what is going on, after all it is my office that seems to have caused a fuss."

"Mrs. King, Johnnie, I would much rather discuss this at the station. I will tell you everything we know once we are at the precinct."

Johnnie observed the woman's face and body language. "I know you are attempting to create a casual atmosphere in an attempt to get me to talk to you. You don't need to worry, I would be happy to tell you everything. Although I can't tell you what you want since I don't know what is going on in my office."

"Please, Johnnie, let me explain everything at the station."

Johnnie did not want to cause a problem so she picked up her coat and purse and went along with the detective. As soon as they got into the car, the detective turned to her. "I know this is out of the norm, but I know of your law enforcement days. You have quite a reputation among the law enforcement community. When the papers announced you chose Ackers as you home, I did some checking on you. I am guessing it would be useless to ask you if you touched anything in your office? I know you would have kept the scene pristine."

"I am confused, why would you check up on my FBI days?"

"Well, you are like a celebrity here in Ackers. To have a FBI agent chose to move to our little hamlet is the most exciting thing to happen in a long time. We are after all, a small town and you are accustom to big city living. The newspaper article was rather vague about your reason for coming to Ackers, but here you are in the flesh"

"I didn't know about a newspaper article. Back to your question, as I got close to my office I saw the mess the office was in, and I knew something was wrong. Locking my desk and credenza is a part of my standard operating procedure. I know better than to touch or disturb anything. So I did not go into the office."

"Why lock your desk?" Terry asked.

"I hate to say that some of the employees have prying eyes. When I first came to work at the bank, I didn't lock anything. I simply cleared away my desk and that was that; but then it seemed as though someone was interested in employee payrolls. Grudgingly I started locking my desk and filing cabinets. I hated the idea that it was necessary to lock everything. Whoever broke in put things away just not in the right files. This was so different it looked like someone was searching for something. Someone wanted me to know they had been in my office."

"So your office has been broken into before." The detective was very interested in this news.

"I would not call it a break in at that point since I didn't and still don't lock my office door. I simply close the door." Johnnie could tell this was going to be an interesting meeting.

Terry pulled into the parking lot at the police station. As Terry continued with the personable approach, they chatted about nonsense as they walked to the detective's cubical.

Bullpens and cubicles caused an instant flash back for Johnnie. The detective took off her coat and hung it on the hook on the corner of the cubical. She put her purse in the drawer, and took her gun off and put it in a drawer and locked it.

"So, why do you lock your desk drawer?" Johnnie parroted.

Terry laughed, "Old habit. When I was a beat cop there was an individual brought into the station. He was higher than a kite and he went for one of the officer's gun. From that point on, I take mine off and lock it so that can't happen with my gun. The poor guy was only brought in on a minor charge that quickly grew to a felony."

Terry walked Johnnie down the hall, and opened the door to a conference room. Johnnie walked into the room.

"What? No one way mirror?"

Terry explained. "You are not a suspect. I just wanted you away from the bank and others so we could talk freely."

"Is there anyone you would like to call?" Terry asked.

Johnnie raised her eyebrow. "Is this where I call my attorney?"

Terry repeated. "As I said, you are not a suspect. Nor are you under arrest. I just thought you might want to tell someone where you are. However, if you think an attorney is necessary."

Johnnie reached for her cell phone. "I will just call my husband. Although I don't know what I can explain to him."

"Hi Honey. This day is off to a strange start. Someone has been in my office and disturbed a number of files. I am with Detective Terry Nichols of the Ackers police department. If you could delay your meeting and come to the station, I would appreciate it. My car is back at the bank."

"Johnnie, we can wait for Mr. King, or would you rather we get started now. It is up to you." Terry did seem like the type of person who would be easy to work with on a case.

"I think I would rather start now. I want to know what happened and why am I here away from the rest of the bank employees?"

Terry took the seat opposite of Johnnie. "I first would like to know your feelings about Herb Jennings?'

"Herb, what does he have to do with the reason for my being at the station? Has he accused me of something?"

Terry raised her left eyebrow. "Why would you ask such a question?"

"Honestly, I can't think of a reason why you would have me here and ask me about Herb. So, did he say something, does he know what happened or who was in my office?"

Terry again referred back to the question. "I need to know your feelings on Mr. Jennings."

Why was the detective asking such a question? Johnnie thought she best respond as any employee would when asked. "Mr. Jennings is the Exec VP and a valuable employee of the bank for a number of years."

Terry watched Johnnie as she sat straight and secure. "Johnnie, the reason you are here is that I need the truth about your impressions of Mr. Jennings. It would also be helpful to know the general sentiments of all the employees."

Johnnie knew that she needed to answer the inquiries as to her true attitudes. "Okay, if you need to know the truth. I am not fond of Herb Jennings. I believe him to be a bully. He enjoys his authority and uses it to intimidate employees."

"Thank you. We also need to have some insights as to the opinions of the staff. This is not about you or your opinions of Mr. Jennings. This is about his death." Terry watched for Johnnie's reaction, but as seasoned former law enforcement, she remained calm.

"Herb is dead? How? When? Has anyone notified his children or his ex-wife?"

"His was a violent death, and for some reason was dumped in your office closet. Can you tell me why he would have been dumped in your office?"

"I am at a loss to think of a reason why such a thing would happen. I admit that we did not get along, but he stayed on the executive floor and I stayed on my floor for the most part. When I did to go to the administrative floor, it was to Gary Percy's office. Gary is my boss. He is much easier to work with than Mr. Jennings. Still I don't know of a reason why anyone would kill Herb and then leave his body in my office."

Johnnie and Terry were discussing what few details Terry had at present when Michael, escorted by Sergeant Will Hastings, came into the room where Johnnie and Terry were sitting.

"Hi Sweetheart, what is going on here? I noticed the floor directory, why the homicide division." Michael was still standing by Johnnie when Terry approached him with an extended hand.

"Mr. King, I am Detective Terry Nichols, we prefer a casual approach here, so please call me Terry. Your wife and I have been discussing the discovery made in her office today."

Johnnie could see that Michael was concerned and responded in a cautious nature. "What was discovered in your office?"

Johnnie looked up at her husband with a weak smile. "Herb has been found dead, apparently murdered. He was in my closet, but since I saw files scattered on my desk, I didn't enter. Actually, because of the disarray on my desk, I called Frank from security. I wanted it on record that someone had been in my office because of the research project I have been doing."

Terry interrupted. "What research project would that be? Was Mr. Jennings involved in any way with your project?"

"No, Herb was not involved in the project. Tom Midland assigned the inquiry. He is Herb's counterpart at the bank. I am to examine all records and transactions that Mr. Victor Andropov has made over the last four years and report my findings directly to Gary Percy. Tom wanted the task to be done so that no one would be able to determine what I was doing, or who I was assigned to examine."

Terry seemed to find it very interesting just now learning of this development. "Shall we discuss this venture of yours? I would like to know more about what exactly you have been doing for Mr. Midland and why this was requested in the first place."

"The project came through the office of the state's attorney general. Tom asked that I do most of the work outside employee hours. That meant the early morning computer employee and the late night crew should not be in the bank or at least not able to see the work. I did a lot of late nights and weekends to progress to the point I am currently. If whoever broke into my desk and credenza was looking for the result of my efforts, they were disappointed. I don't keep the work in my office. I keep one copy in the main vault and the working copy in a lock box inside the upstairs vault. The lock box is behind trays of signature cards. The cards being stored in the vault will be microfilmed later. In addition, to get into the vault it requires two keys. I keep one, as does Gary these are the master keys and the second key is kept in the computer room. I will admit that I have accessed the upstairs vault. When I have finished a portion of the research, I use my master key and the one from the computer room. I do however, register my access on the roster. I have mixed feelings about accessing the upstairs vault at odd times, so as soon as possible I have Gary initial the roster reflecting my access. It isn't like there is anything of true value in that vault. It is used for maintaining a rotating stock of computer disk and the signature cards, nothing else. Then once a week, if I have had the opportunity to work on the project that week, I update the copy that is in the main vault."

Terry still had questions. "Have you found anything of interest in your assignment?"

"To be honest, I haven't found anything that would warrant interest by anybody. Let alone the state's attorney office. At first, I thought they were looking for money laundering activities; but there is no indication of such doings. I understand this Victor Andropov is a person of interest in several unresolved crimes." Johnnie was now looking to Terry for answers.

Michael wanted to ask a few question. "Excuse me, do you know anything about this individual, Terry?"

Terry was ready to answer the questions she could. "Andropov has been in this area since I can remember. He owns The Flames Steak and Pasta Restaurant. He has his hit man, slash, bodyguard with him almost constantly. His name is Sebastian Osis."

The name got a reaction out of Johnnie. "Sebastian Osis, the man suspected of about a dozen murders? Wonder who his hidden angel is, it has to be a person with power? He appears to be untouchable."

Terry retorted. "Whoever it is must be higher than we will ever deal with in this life. If he were not a killer, he would be a nice guy. He talks like an educated man, not bad looking. Unfortunately, he is on the wrong side of a badge."

Michael commented on the topic. "I don't know this Sebastian person."

Terry slipped into police mode again. "Can you tell me what it is that you do Michael?"

"I have a security company called Security Now. I supply personal security, armament, investigations and premise security. I have had the opportunity to meet a lot of people, but I do not recall a Sebastian Osis."

Terry grinned. "I guess you don't deal with the criminal element."

"Oh, I am exposed to the criminal element; I just don't do any work for such enterprises or persons. On the rare occasion, if something that doesn't set right with me, I call the authorities that are best suited to handling the circumstances."

Terry still had questions. "Have you ever been approached by what could be deemed as a threat? I would think with your company it could happen."

Michael preferred to keep this part of his operation quiet. "I was a Navy Seal. Our training included the ability to recognize questionable episodes and I know the right people to contact in such cases. It is something I would rather keep off-the-record."

Terry agreed to the need of secrecy.

***

Terry's cell phone rang. She stepped away from Johnnie and Michael to take the call. It seemed to distress her.

"That was Debbie Hughes. She is the medical examiner. The autopsy has barely started, but she did find one factor she wanted to report. Mr. Jennings had a substance in his nasal passages. Since this particular signature is familiar to us, we believe it to be the work of Sebastian Osis. The substance is a particular salt that comes from Soledar in the Ukraine. Soledar actually means 'gift of salt'. We know this signature, even in our little state. Again, this makes us think that Sebastian is a hit man for Andropov since the salt is from the area where his parents lived before coming to the States."

Johnnie was on her feet. "Andropov? How would he know I was involved in the research? Outside of Michael and Gary, my boss, I have not shared anything with anyone else."

Michael spoke up. "Have you given any thought to a leak coming from the general attorney's office?"

Terry wasn't comfortable with that thought. "If the leak is from the AG's office, then we don't know how far word has spread."

Johnnie wanted to get back to the bank. She was concerned for the employees. This was going to have a devastating effect on everyone. "Terry, I don't believe at this point I will be of any help. I would like to return to the bank. By the way, have all the other employees been accounted for now?"

Terry said that she would call her partner, Murphy O'Shea and get an update.

Again Terry stepped away to call Murph. "Murph, how are things at the bank? Has everyone been accounted for at this point?"

"Hey Terry, things have calmed down a great deal since the body has been removed. Her office is sealed. We had a hard time finding the morning computer operator. Finally found the woman in a small room off the computer room. We didn't know about the room, but Don Phelps found her. He said he knows every nook and cranny in this building. You can tell Mrs. King her office is sealed. Maybe she will be more help answering questions." Murph was the one in the team to work the scene of any situation while Terry was great at working with the subjects.

Returning to the couple Terry asked them to sit down. "According to Murph, everyone has been accounted for. Your computer operator was hiding in a little room inside her workspace. Don Phelps was the one that located her.

"Johnnie, they have sealed your office until the crime scene techs can do their magic. I would like you to stay a bit longer. We could cover some more details." Terry explained.

"I don't know what other details I could provide. You know everything I know. I would like to get back to the bank. I had planned to work the lower vault today, so I won't be in my office. It will remain as is for the techs to do their thing."

"Terry, I will agree Johnnie and Herb were on different ends of the spectrum when it came to management style, but you don't kill someone because of management differences. What other information could you possibly need?" Michael didn't know if Johnnie had explained this point, but knowing her insistence on details, Terry most likely knew this already.

Terry motioning to the table for Johnnie to sit down again continued with her thoughts. "Management styles aside, what other differences were you aware of regarding Mr. Jennings?"

Johnnie sat down. "I know that Herb likes to be the center of attention, he will be front and center at any function. He often times overshadows Ernie Compoto, the bank president. There are rumors, but I don't like to take part in rumors."

Terry pursued the topic. "What have you heard regarding Mr. Jennings' drug use?"

"That's the gossip that I don't like to spread. I have no proof of his partaking of drugs of my own observations." Johnnie recognized Terry's style, more conversational than questioning.

"Those are the rumors we are looking into. Did you know Grammar Jonas?" Terry asked.

Johnnie had to think for a moment. "I have never met Mr. Jonas, but I have seen pictures of him from attending various bank conferences. Most of those pictures contained Herb you think he and Herb were partners in crime?"

Terry pulled up a file on her computer tablet. "Mr. Jonas has been mentioned as a part of a drug ring involving high ranking bank officials."

"Not this bank official. Besides, I am not high enough on the food chain for him to include me in anything. Guess that sounded a bit self-effacing, but we are in two different leagues when it comes to banking. Can I ask how is it that you have access to information regarding a banking drug ring?"

Terry continued. "Mr. Jonas had definite ties to a drug ring and money laundering at his bank. As far as his death the same foreign substances was in his nasal passages. The same signature was reported involving two boys from near this area."

Johnnie looked Terry straight in the eye. "The salt found was the same kind exactly?"

Terry said that it was and they were trying to make the connection. "You had never seen Mr. Jonas visiting your bank?"

"I have never actually met Mr. Jonas. As I said, I have seen pictures of him with Herb from the picture boards displayed at the cocktail parties at various conferences. I believe he had already passed away by the time I came into banking. I will admit that I have heard of such a signature as you described, but with different substances being used in different areas."

Terry half smiled. "Yes, it does seem that Sebastian Osis has been around. I know you want to get back to the bank, but we have plenty of questions. Some you can help with, and some you may not be able to. At any rate having your input will be quite helpful."

"How does lunch sound?" Michael chimed in. "Would you ladies like to join me?"

***

Terry and Johnnie agreed to lunch and left for a restaurant known for their steak sandwiches. The establishment had great onion rings as well. Terry and Michael enjoyed the sweet and crispy morsels. Johnnie however, had cottage cheese with her meal.

Lunch was a pleasant escape from the questions about Herb and his death but it didn't stop Johnnie from thinking about him or the bank.

Back at the station, Terry was anxious to move forward with her questions. "Johnnie, you mentioned you had made some observations regarding Herb, what type of observations did you make that lead you to believe in Herb's alleged drug use?"

"I think everyone knows the same signs. Herb had become increasingly hyper over the time of my employment. He was losing weight, constant sniffle, as well as sudden nosebleeds. I am sure if encountered on a regular basis you would detect the same symptoms. My contact with Herb, however, was limited to bank meetings or product development planning. We did not socialize, and I spent as little time with him as possible." Johnnie was thinking back on the few times she did work with Herb. She knew he was not a well-liked man, but no one deserves murder. She could not believe that after her time with the bureau, she still found the death of anyone disturbing.

Terry continued with questions, but Johnnie was lost in her own thoughts. "Johnnie, did you hear me? I asked you if you had ever noticed anyone coming into the bank that caused you alarm?"

"Sorry Terry. I can say the only person besides Herb that caused discomfort was Logan Ferns. Again I did not have dealings with him, but he had a sulking way that always made me think he was hiding something."

Terry found this very interesting. "What do you mean sulking? Did he spend any time with Mr. Jennings?"

Johnnie's expression was somewhat of a frown. "No, I never saw him with Herb. Just around the bank. If he was there to see

Herb, he did so without me noticing. Again, my contact with Herb was very limited. What do you know about Logan Ferns?"

The detective blew out a puff of air that made her bangs lift in the air. "Logan Ferns is one of those small time hoods that want desperately to make it to the big time. You know the saying 'he's a big fish in a little pond' well Ferns is a little fish in an even smaller pond. There have been suggestions that he has made connections with someone who will make him at least move up to medium fish. He doesn't realize he will never be a criminal mastermind. He is not the brightest bulb in the box, but I will have to say he is loyal. At least as far as the criminal factor is concerned. It will probably get him killed one of these days."

Johnnie was taking all of this information in but providing little in return. "I am sorry Terry, I am not as helpful as I believe you would like. It is just that I had my area of expertise, and it did not intersect with Herb, Ferns, Sebastian, or Andropov. Well other than Andropov's research I am working. I would truly like to be of assistance. I know there has to be some way in which I can be of help."

Terry was grateful for Johnnie's candor, and she knew that they would be talking again. "Well, I guess that is all we can cover for now. I would like it if you could give the situation some thought and maybe we could talk a bit later."

"I think that would be advisable. Right now I am drawing a blank, but in the past I have always found that I do better when I step away for a while then come back to a situation."

With that, Johnnie and Michael left the station. "Do you want to go back to the bank? Or we could go straight home?"

"You know home sounds good to me. I want to cuddle up in my favorite snuggie and just think about the day. I do have to say I am glad I didn't go into the office. I would have hated to have anyone see Herb's body. As it was, with Frank's team they kept the employees at bay. They did a good job I guess not all rent-a-cops are inept."

"Hey, watch it you are stepping on my business now. We employ lots of what you would call 'rent-a-cops' and you know most of them have had training beyond the average contracted guardians. They have been in the service, many from specialized forces or military police. It is a requirement for my company. The security business is not what it used to be, but I have to admit I do find it more challenging and definitely more intense." Michael was grinning. He knew Johnnie did not mean anything negative with her comment. It just wasn't in her to be derogatory about most things.

"Sorry, Husband, I know your company hires only the best, and apparently Frank has handpicked his employees as well. The same cannot be said for everyone."

Michael and Johnnie pulled up into their driveway.

"Be it ever so humble, there is no place like home." Johnnie smiled.

***

Johnnie and Michael entered the house and Michael turned off the alarm. As Michael joined Johnnie in the kitchen, he found her making a pot of tea. "Are you sure you are not English? I think you drink enough tea for all of the British Empire."

Johnnie turned around and greeted Michael with two cups in her hand. "Join me? I started a pot of spiced Christmas tea."

"It's not Christmas but you do know how to tempt a guy. I can smell the cinnamon from here."

"I wanted something to relax me. Today has not been my best day. Might even break my diet and have some of those cookies you keep buying."

Sitting at the table, they broke open the package of cookies. "You know I think I could eat this entire package. Do you want any more?"

The doorbell rang just as Johnnie got up from the table. "Who could that be, I wasn't expecting anyone."

Michael told her to stay at the table he would check the door. As he walked through the hall, he stopped at the side table and opened his gun box. Loading a magazine, he put the gun behind his back in his waistband.

Johnnie saw him and she cocked her eyebrow as her heart skipped a beat. Michael just turned and motioned for her to sit down.

As he opened the door, he was surprised to see Terry on the porch. "Terry, why are you here, is something wrong?"

"No, I just really needed to talk to Johnnie and you too. I need to clear a few things in my head."

"Well, come on in, we have been enjoying a cup of spiced Christmas tea. Let me get you a cup." Johnnie was up to get the cup and a dessert plate for more cookies.

"I am sorry to just show up like this, but I really wanted to talk to you both." Terry took the cup and sat down. "Christmas tea, aren't you a bit early for the season."

"It is my favorite tea for when I need to relax. Today, I think I could drink the entire pot." Johnnie could not help but wonder what more she could tell the detective.

"In that case, you may need to make a second pot." Terry seemed to be more unnerved than she was at the station.

"Terry, what has upset you so much? I thought we were doing okay with the investigation. I don't know what else I could tell you."

"Johnnie, have you met Mirah Anderson?" Terry again seemed unusually uncomfortable.

"I know that she is the state's attorney general. Why?"

"My captain told me she heard of Herb's murder and she was coming up to Ackers. She will be here tomorrow." Terry seemed upset by the news.

"Is there a reason why it is so upsetting for you?" Johnnie and Michael were both a bit uncertain of what to make of Terry's reaction.

"I take it you have not had dealings with her in the past. She is every law enforcement officer's nightmare. She will nag you through the entire investigation and then she will step before the cameras and she will do the press conference. It is not that she takes the glory for whatever the incident may be, it is that she paints the police in an entirely incompetent way. It is as though the investigation was in need of her personal attention."

"Terry, I can't say as I have had the occasion to meet Ms. Anderson, but I think we will do just fine with or without her in the middle of the investigation." Johnnie placed the plate of cookies in front of the detective.

"Here's the thing." Terry continued as she sipped her tea, "she is not going to be involved in the investigation. She will just impart the impression of this being her investigation to the press, and in the process will discount any efforts made by the police. It is not a matter of pride; it is a matter of having our citizens loses faith in our police department. We haven't had a murder here for a long time, and this one is very frightening to everyone. We all know you're an extremely capable investigator, Johnnie, and well, we thought if you were involved with the investigation it might keep her off her game."

"Whoa, I don't want to become a pawn in the political atmosphere of the local police and the attorney general. What makes you think it will be any different if I were involved?" Johnnie and Michael were both dismayed with this development. Johnnie had played with the idea of returning to the bureau, but she did not want to become involved with an attention-seeking attorney general.

"I was hoping you might know John Erickson. He is an FBI agent that travels with Ms. Anderson. Do you know him?" Terry was unhappy with the development and she wondered about this traveling FBI agent. "It isn't like I can tell her not to come. She is after all the State's Attorney General."

Johnnie was sympathetic, but had no idea what she could really do. "I don't actually know Mr. Erickson. I know he came into the bureau as I was leaving, but that is about all I know about him. That would mean he has some experience. Do you know why he travels with her?"

"No one seems to know why she has her own personal FBI agent. Is he a bodyguard, or an investigator, or is this duty some sort of demotion?" Terry was trying to relax and let the tension drain from her. Just sharing her tension with someone seemed to calm her.

"Do we know where Herb was murdered?" Johnnie was slipping into police mode. She also did her best to get Terry to talk of other things.

"All we know at this point is he was not killed in your office." Terry knew the response would be a bit of good news for Johnnie.

In an off-handed way, she asked Terry about her years growing up in West Virginia. "Have you always lived in Ackers? Ever think of moving away?" With this effort, Terry became more relaxed and let go of her misgivings about having Ms. Anderson at the bank.

The early evening continued with just mundane conversation. Still the conversation would drift back to the arrival of the attorney general and her traveling companion.

"I don't want to wear out my welcome. I believe I should be heading out and allowing you both your own time. I most likely will be at the bank tomorrow. I will see you then, Michael it was a pleasure to see you again and I am sorry I invaded your personal time." Terry stood to shake Johnnie's hand. "Hope you don't mind, but I am a hugger." Johnnie embraced Terry rather softly.

Michael walked Terry to the door, as he bid her good bye. Johnnie stood at the door with Michael and waved good-bye to Terry. "Terry is a rather trusting soul. Never approach the home of someone involved in a case for a personal visit. I am surprised by her actions."

Michael put his arm around Johnnie. "I think she senses in you those reasons why I fell in love with you. You have a habit of being so naturally inviting." "So says you." She leaned her head on Michael's arm as they continued to watch Terry proceed down their street. Johnnie was feeling the effects of the day. "I know it is early, but how about an early night?"

"I think I had better send an email to the client I was to meet this afternoon. I will need to set up another appointment. But I will join you as soon as I can." Michael went to the study upstairs.

Once Johnnie had gone up to the bedroom with a book to read, Michael called Josie. Josie Callow was Johnnie's niece and he knew she would want to know what was going on with her aunt. "Hi Sweetheart, I am sure you have heard about the happenings at the bank today."

"Oh, Uncle Michael, I have been worried to death about Aunt Johnnie. I wanted to come over; but I was afraid she needed her rest." Josie was the only daughter of Johnnie's older sister Angela. There were many years between Angela and Johnnie, almost 16. Result was that Josie was closer to Johnnie's age. Johnnie being only five years older, it seemed as though they were more like cousins, or even sisters, than aunt and niece. Still Josie had a great deal of respect for her aunt. She even moved to West Virginia when Johnnie and Michael relocated.

"Honey, if you are not tied up tomorrow morning I would like for you to come over and sort of look after your aunt."

There was never any doubt that Josie would immediately respond. In fact, she asked if it was all right if she came over and spent the night.

Michael was more than happy to have Josie spend the night. That way she would be there when Johnnie woke.

***

Johnnie woke on Tuesday morning with a blearing head as Michael came into the room with her tea. He noted her complexion was somewhat pale. "You look a bit worn out this morning. I am sure that Gary would not mind if you were late today"

"I feel like I was on a binge last night, and I didn't have a drink of anything other than tea and water. Go figure. As for the late arrival, I would love that, but it would not provide a good example for the rest of the employees. I have a job to do just like everyone else. I need to be there to provide stability for everyone. Well, I don't mean me, personally, but it is necessary to keep things as normal as possible." Johnnie sipped on the tea and recognized it as ginger. Michael always knew when she needed a pick-me-up.

Michael sat on the edge of the bed as he continued his conversation with Johnnie. "What are your plans for the day? I would think that your office is still off limits or covered in dust from the CSI crew. I thought you and Josie could spend some time together to get your mind off of the situation."

"I don't want Josie involved in this. We don't know who or why Herb was killed. Face it, I may be drawing unwanted attention. Josie being near me, well; she could get caught in a crossfire. Besides I need to be there, remember the attorney general is coming today. I am still not sure of the reason she is coming. I honestly do not believe there is any. We could send her emails and keep her informed if necessary via Skype." Johnnie placed the teacup on the nightstand. "I need to get started on a day that I am sure will be a challenge."

"Well, then you won't like the surprise in the family room. Josie is here, she came over last night. She is as worried about you as I am."

"Did you two forget that I have been known to handle situations far more volatile than this one? I can handle myself. Besides, if anyone is in the limelight, it will be Ms. Anderson. So don't worry." As she tossed back the covers, she reached up to Michael and hugged him. "The sooner I get there, the sooner I will know what I will encounter today."

"Well, I will be downstairs, what do you want for breakfast?" Michael enjoyed cooking and he had been spoiling her since the day they got married.

Johnnie showered and picked out one of her favorite blue slacks and a white blouse. A bit underdressed; but she didn't feel like being Ms. Banker today. She finished adding the final touches, putting on the earrings that Josie had given her for Christmas.

Johnnie stopped in the doorway of the kitchen. Michael was making her favorite, French toast. "Hey chef, if you are trying to spoil me, it's working." "That is only because I love you." Again, the right words at the right time. "Why don't you let Josie spoil you today?" Michael smiled as Josie came out of the family room.

Josie helped Michael finalize the breakfast. Michael finished the French toast, and Josie warmed the toasted pecan syrup.

Johnnie sat down at her favorite seat at the kitchen table. "I imagine I will be spending some time with Gary. Herb's death is most likely going to add a lot more pressure on him. Maybe I can help him out in some way."

"That's my girl, always planning on a way of helping someone else. Just don't let yourself become overburdened." Michael placed her plate in front of her as Josie placed the warmed toasted pecan syrup on the table.

"Come on, you two sit. I would love a few sane moments today." Johnnie wasn't exactly sure what she would find when she got to the bank.

Josie sat down with a plate and added a piece of French toast to her own plate. Michael said he was rushed. He went upstairs to the study to collect some contracts.

"Aunt Johnnie, Uncle Michael said for me to take the day and keep you occupied. So why don't we do something fun?" Josie was normally very good at sidetracking her aunt. Today was not going to be one of those days.

Johnnie finished her breakfast and was getting ready to leave. Michael came into the kitchen with his jacket. "Guess the day needs to start." Michael gave her a kiss on the cheek and started out the door. Michael stopped to say, "You best be careful today. They still don't have very many answers and it could be dangerous for any one at the bank." Johnnie reacted as though he had not warned her, she simply blew him a kiss.

"Aunt Johnnie, are you sure you need to go in at your regular time? I would like to hear about yesterday."

"Nice try Sweetheart, but I will let you drive me to work. I left my wagon at the bank yesterday."

***

Johnnie instructed Josie to vary the normal route to the bank. The standard operating procedure was to keep your routine unpredictable. Johnnie followed the rules, but never envisioned it as something that was necessary in this quaint little town. Now with Herb's death, she was taking these precautions very seriously.

Josie brought her all the way to the back steps so that Johnnie could use her key and enter by way of the back stairs. She was not looking forward to meeting up with anyone today. She knew there would be so many questions, and she didn't know enough to answer. Besides, if she did she would not discuss an ongoing investigation.

Johnnie decided to stop on the executive floor and talk with Gary. She found him at his desk with several files sitting around his normally cleared desk. "I see you are already overburdened. I thought maybe there was something I could do to help you."

Gary smiled and asked her to sit. "I will be more than willing to give you some of these files. It seemed that Herb had more going on than he ever shared with me. I could use some help just going through these files. I need to find out what they are and if we can determine what he was working on recently. Maybe we can find a clue as to what happened to him."

Johnnie picked up two of the stacks from his desk. "I will be more than happy to help, but I may just have to work in the board room. I have no idea what my office will look like after the techs finished up yesterday. I will let you know what I find upstairs." She said good-bye to Gary and stopping in the boardroom to leave the files before continuing up to her office.

Johnnie found Terry already standing in her office doorway. "Hello, is there any news?"

"The only thing I can tell you is that the techs made a mess in your office. I am sorry about its condition. Just so you know Murph stayed with the techs last night." Terry was concerned about the bank's exposure.

"Please thank him for me. I wish I knew what Herb had gotten himself into, whatever it was most likely got him killed. I doubt it had anything to do with the bank or me. However, it is a good way to stymie an investigation. Leaving the body in my office puts me in the spotlight; I know it was just a tactic for distraction."

Terry leaned back on the desk in front of Johnnie's office, trying to stay clear of the finger print dust on the desk. "Well, I doubt you will want to work in your office. Is there somewhere else you are going to work?"

"I mentioned to Gary that I would work in the boardroom. In the end that just might be more convenient. It may just keep Mirah away from the employees." Johnnie knew her weak point was always thinking of someone else.

Terry told Johnnie, "It will be okay. After today, most of the investigating will be interviews. I don't know when she will be arriving?" Just then, Terry's phone rang. Again, she excused herself and stepped away. Terry returned to Johnnie. "That it was Murph who called. Ms. Anderson had called the station to say she would be in Ackers around 11 tomorrow."

Terry and Johnnie were both glad to hear that she was not heading up from Charleston immediately. With the body removed, and the crime scene techs finally finished, now the interviews that Terry spoke of would begin.

Mirah Anderson would be available for interviews to the press, but as the state attorney. She does not do investigative work. Because of the research, it gave her a viable reason to come up from Charleston. There had been rumors that she wanted to be the US Attorney General, so she must have had someone in the FBI that owed her a big favor.

Johnnie was anxious to get her office back in order. She asked if Terry knew of any cleanup crews in either Virginia or Pennsylvania. Terry told her she would have her office email over a few contacts and give her a list. Terry called her office and Murph answered; he said to wait a minute and he would email the list over to her. Terry asked if it was okay to forward the list, she had just received to Johnnie's email address. Johnnie said she appreciated the help, and would take the list down to Gary. After the quick email, Terry said she would be at the station and if Johnnie needed anything, call. To be certain that Johnnie had her number, she gave

Johnnie her business card. Then she asked if she could leave by the back steps. Johnnie told her it was okay, but that the bottom door would lock when she exited.

Johnnie went to Gary's office to talk about hiring a crime cleanup crew. Gary looked up from whatever he was working on asked her to come into his office and pulled out a chair for her. Instead of returning to his place behind the desk, he sat next to her. Gary was definitely one of the good guys in the bank.

Johnnie looked at Gary; he was not as tall as Michael was and his hair showed signs of graying already, and his gray eyes looked very tired. He always did his best to soothe every situation, but this one was going to be a bit harder to soothe. "Are you okay?" This time he was in her court. "I am fine. I have had a lot of experience with various crimes, just never thought I would be in the middle of one myself here at the bank. I am more concerned with the employees. I have a list of cleaning services and would like to get the office back to normal."

She gave him the list that the detective had provided. She asked if he had a preference. She knew he would not, but he was her boss and she wanted everything done properly. She wanted nothing coming back to haunt her in this case.

As expected, he had no preference. She told him she would check out the companies. Going into a bank where there was sensitive information she did not want to just call anyone; but she did want it done as fast as possible.

She was ready to leave when Gary spoke up again. "Do you want some time off?" Johnnie smiled. "No, I have seen worse. All I want right now is to get a crew in here to clean up the office. I am planning to come back to the bank when we can get a cleaning crew in here; hopefully that will be done quickly. When the office is cleaned, I think the employees will feel more comfortable."

Returning to the boardroom, she got online with the computer in the room. She did a check for complaints and service records of the various cleanup crews. Then she called Luke McGuire of Taking Your Crime to the Cleaners, who promised he could have a crew there by early evening.

Johnnie filled Gary in on who was coming to do the cleanup. She told him she was going to make it a short day. As soon as she sorted the files she had taken from him into priorities, she was going to take off. Reviewing the files took a fair amount of time, but she felt better having something to do. With that completed, she was ready to head out. She was glad she had left her car in the lot the night before.

Returning home, Johnnie was able to sleep for a few hours but now she was hungry. She called to see if Michael wanted to go to lunch at one of her favorite restaurants, a crepe restaurant. Their menu was great for when you needed to eat, but didn't want anything heavy. Michael said he would be by to pick her up.

She called Josie and invited her to lunch with Michael and her. There was no doubt that she would take the opportunity to see her aunt.

The atmosphere of the restaurant was very fresh and upbeat. The place used round tables, and the tablecloth had the appearance of the green ivy climbing on latticework. The top of the table was glass so their trademark tablecloths stayed clean.

Johnnie always felt refreshed when they came to The Ivy Crepe. Her favorite dish was the Bananas Foster crepe. The delicate pancakes topped with a luscious cream that added to the richness of the dish. Michael decided on a heartier dish, while Josie followed suit with her aunt; but she favored the strawberry crepe with cream cheese filling and warmed strawberries on top.

Afterwards Michael took Johnnie to the bank, and told her to call when she was ready to come home. He did not want her walking the lot.

Johnnie would have preferred to go home, but work was work. She had told Luke that she would be waiting for him. Luke said he and his crew arrived about 6:30. She did not want strangers in her office with her not there to protect bank information. As she went to her office, she found Grace Harvest, the bank's auditor sitting in at Ana' desk. "Hey, Grace, I did not know you would be here tonight, but I can say I am glad to see you. I was uncomfortable leaving my office unattended and now we can keep each other company." Grace was a shy girl approximately 26 years old; her green eyes were large and very expressive setting off her beautiful auburn hair. Both ladies were dressed for comfort. Jeans with a T-shirt for Johnnie, while Grace enjoyed wearing dresses. She must have been fun growing up. Johnnie wondered if Grace had a room filled with a variety of dresses.

Grace came to the bank near the same time as Johnnie. She did her job well. "Gary told me about the cleanup crew. He thought you would need more rest, so he asked me to come into the office."

The cleanup crew arrived with Don escorting them to the secured floor. Johnnie thanked Don and he returned to the first floor. Johnnie and Grace sat outside her office with the curtains opened so they could watch the crew while continuing their conversation outside the office.

Around 7 o'clock, Terry arrived. Don had returned to the bank, he did not like the idea of strangers in the bank. So he was able to let Terry in and take her upstairs to Johnnie's department.

"Hi, Terry, have you met Grace Harvest? Grace is the bank's auditor. She wanted to be here the same as I did, and apparently the same as you wanted." Johnnie rolled another chair over to the desk where she and Grace had been sitting.

"Hi Grace, I am relieved to see several of us here. I don't foresee any danger tonight; but with the added people here, I am sure nothing will happen."

Grace looked at Terry. "Thanks for that. I had not given the idea of danger a thought."

Johnnie put her hand on Grace's shoulder. "If I thought for one moment there would be any danger, I would have sent you home as soon as I saw you sitting at Ana's desk."

The cleaning crew did a great job and soon they were packing up to leave.

Johnnie said she needed to call Michael to come and pick her up. "You know sometimes I think he is ridiculous, I can take care of myself. Hey, what's a gal to do with a sweet guy like him?"

Terry spoke up. "I can take you home." Johnnie responded. "That would be nice, but I have to call Michael and do one other thing before leaving. Grace, let's meet in the lobby and we can all leave together."

Terry did not want to say anything about the state's attorney in front of Grace, but she wanted to talk to Johnnie about Ms. Anderson. Johnnie called Michael and told him that Terry would bring her home, so he could stand down.

Grace said she would see them in the lobby and returned to her office on the executive floor to collect her coat and purse, and then wait for them in the lobby.

"What else do you have to do? I thought you wanted out of here as soon as possible." Terry stood by Johnnie's office door as she spoke.

"Little trick." Johnnie went to her office and pulled a strip of tape from the dispenser in her office. "Oh, I get it, your own little private alert system." Terry grinned.

"I just want to make sure no one else goes in the office until I get back tomorrow." With the tape placed, Terry and Johnnie went to the lobby to meet Grace. Johnnie told Don that he should go home too, and would he like a ride. He said he was content to walk the two blocks to his apartment and he wanted the exercise.

The three women left the bank together. The cars were parked side-by-side making the walk more comfortable for Grace. She felt better going out in a group.

Once Terry and Johnnie got in the car, Terry immediately locked the doors and secured her seat belt, as did Johnnie. Johnnie looked at Terry. "What is worrying you about the AG?" Terry felt a bit sheepish about asking, but she really needed to know. "Before she gets into the middle of the investigation, is there anything else you can think of that I should know." Johnnie laughed. "This is where you say, any detail could be helpful, right? I told you everything I know about Herb and the research. You won't get any surprises out of me." Terry said she felt terrible asking, but she wanted to make certain. Johnnie reminded her that she knew how it felt to be blindsided during an inquiry.

Johnnie asked Terry if she would like to come in, but she said she was meeting Will Hastings. "Isn't that the sergeant that was at the front desk?" Terry smiled. "You don't miss a trick do you?" Johnnie bid Terry good night and to enjoy what was left of the evening.

Johnnie was glad to be home, she just wanted some tea and toast, and Michael to snuggle with tonight. She did not want to think of the bank, Herb, or Ms. Anderson, just alone time with Michael.

Michael must have read her mind, he had the teapot sitting on the hearth in its little cozy, and even the empty cups were warming by the fire. "Want some toast?" Johnnie could not believe how he knew her every thought.

She answered in the affirmative, and he went into the kitchen. Returning moments later with a plate of six slices of cinnamon toast. "Do I look that hungry to you?" Johnnie took the plate as Michael sat down on the floor. "Well, I know you do tea and toast to unwind; but I thought you just might let me have a slice or two."

"You can have all you want, I just want you near me tonight." Johnnie said. "My thoughts exactly" replied Michael.

***

Johnnie was beginning to hate mornings. It had only been a couple of days, and she could feel the stress. If she had more control of the investigation, she would do much better. However, she is not in the driver's seat for this one and it was frustrating. She was watching and covering every detail of a situation. This standing on the sideline was maddening.

Johnnie arrived at the bank early and went directly to her office. Checking the tape on the bottom of the door by sight only she was satisfied that the place was secure. She did not want anyone to know she had placed this little alert on her office door. Since the tape was undisturbed, she went down to the boardroom where she found Terry waiting for her.

Johnnie and Terry worked well together. It seemed as though they fit together like a hand and glove.

Johnnie decided to continue working from the boardroom to keep Mirah Anderson away from the employees. It was not long before Don called from the lobby. He told her he would be bringing Ms. Anderson up to the boardroom.

Don knocked on the door and brought in the new arrivals. Johnnie and Terry exchanged glances knowing there was nothing either could do about the additional law enforcement involvement.

Ms. Anderson and John Erickson joined the detective and Johnnie in the boardroom. The detective thought it better to meet behind closed doors. If they were in Johnnie's office, there would be lots of attention and speculation to the gathering.

Ms. Anderson was right to the point. "What can you tell us about Monday morning?"

"Okay, we will jump right in to the matter. Monday I thought I would have a busy day since I was planning on working in the lower vault. However, as I drew closer to the office I could see that the door was open. That's when I called for Frank from security."

"Okay, but why call security? Was there something of importance in your office?" Ms. Anderson had assigned the research project so she no doubt wanted to know if the materials were safe.

"This is a bank, we have lots of confidential information, and then there is the research project that you assigned that was not meant for the others to see. I maintain a lot of such information in the office. As far as the research project, it is not in the office. I keep it in two different secured locations"

"Yet you had no trouble having the security officer going into your office?" It was obvious that Ms. Anderson had never worked an actual crime scene. Johnnie just wanted to groan, but she stayed professional. "Mr. Ridges, our security officer, has been with the bank for many years and to be truthful if he wanted he could have seen anything in my office without leaving such a mess. I asked for security more out of making a record of the invasion. I totally expected him to come out and ask if I wanted to call the police for a crime scene detail. When he came out and called for backup, I was surprised. I had no idea what he found in there other than my disturbed desk and credenza. I was not expecting trouble."

Ms. Anderson then asked about the research project she had ordered on the Andropov group. "I had all the details for that research locked in a box inside the upstairs vault used for keeping the backup tapes for the work of the previous days. The second copy remains in the vault downstairs. If that is what the individual was looking for, they didn't find it." Johnnie could almost see relief come into Ms. Anderson's eyes.

"Why did you keep it in this upstairs vault? Would this not have made the employees inquisitive?" Ms. Anderson must have thought the research had something to do with the murder. "Have you ever shared your findings with Mr. Jennings?"

"I was told the research was confidential and to only return the research findings to Mr. Percy. I would not have shared it with Mr. Jennings. I am not in the habit of ignoring my instructions. As to the upstairs vault, my instructions were to keep it secured. Keeping it on the floor allowed me to work on the project when I was alone in the office. If the only copy were kept in the main vault I would not be able to work it after hours." Johnnie had seen the attorney on TV with various news conferences in the past and understood that this was just Mirah's way. She did have a reputation as being abrasive.

John Erickson on the other hand was a very low-key man. He sat quietly listening to the exchange. Johnnie still didn't know why John was with Mirah, but she found that she liked him, in spite of not knowing his story.

"Okay, let's leave the research details alone. Was there a reason for Mr. Jennings to come to your office at night?" Johnnie knew that interviews go on repeatedly looking for any discrepancies in the story.

"I have no idea why he was up there at any time. He pretty much stayed away from the floor. Only on holidays, he did make an appearance in the lunchroom. That is when a covered dish lunch by and for the employees of the bank is held." Making direct eye contact with the state attorney general Johnnie continued explaining. "Herb never came up to my office. He preferred to call people to his office. It would appear that my office was chosen for the dump site and I have no idea why."

Ms. Anderson then asked how Mr. Jennings died. At this point Detective Nichols responded. "Mr. Jennings had been shot in the back of the head twice. Some take that as a professional hit, but we are not prepared to say that or to release that detail. There was the same signature we have seen before and typically associated with Sebastian Osis. We know he was killed somewhere else and moved to the office, it was a dumpsite. We don't know if it was in the building or if he was killed and brought into the bank. On the other hand, who would have been able to get into the bank after hours? Although the crime scene techs have been over the bank and haven't found any evidence of his being killed in the building. We too still have questions."

A professional hit. Johnnie thought moving to a small city would prevent her from encountering such a situation again. She preferred not to divulge rumors of Herb's life. But then again, they would find out in their investigation, so she hesitatingly added the suspicions involving Herb. "I don't like saying this, but it had been rumored that Herb had a drug habit. Rumor was he was involved with cocaine. I don't know if that it is true, and I have never spoken about it to anyone other than Michael, my husband and Detective

Nichols. To do so would damage Herb's reputation, and the bank would suffer as well."

"That could explain why a hit, but still does not tell us why your office." Mirah questions needled Johnnie. Johnnie was far more comfortable talking with Detective Nichols; she just didn't understand why Mirah Anderson came to Ackers. Maybe she had heard that Herb was involved with drugs and she was waging a war on drugs. Who knows what goes through the mind of political people?

Ms. Anderson continued with the drug angle. "You have heard of Logan Ferns I would assume?"

"Yes, I have heard the rumors and I have read the papers, but I don't know the man. He lives in a different world than mine I don't know him personally." Johnnie just had answered the same questions to the best of her ability and hope that Mirah would get tired of asking questions.

Detective Nichols entered the conversation. "Logan Ferns has been investigated recently. I wish we could find a way to put him where he belongs, but he seems to have powerful friends with money and lawyers and even politicians. Every time it looks like we have a case, someone makes waves. He seems to be untouchable; but we will get him on something someday."

Ms. Anderson seemed a bit put off by the detective's comments and she did her best to continue the conversation without taking obvious offense. "What evidence have you collected on this Logan Ferns? Have you sent it to my office? Have you shared your investigation with any other law enforcement agencies? Did you send it to the FBI?"

Terry said. "Whoa, so many questions, yes we have evidence on the man, yes we have sent the materials to your office and as for the FBI unless I can bring them into the investigation or he crosses his enterprises over state lines, I am not sure what to do about the FBI. My one attempt was met with, shall we say, negative reactions."

Johnnie hated the dog and pony show Mirah was putting on for someone's benefit. She no doubt knew who had received the information and who did not; she was just showing she was the alpha.

Johnnie was glad to return to her office in hopes that Mirah would find individuals on the executive floor more interesting. No doubt, she would find Gary. Mirah decided to stay in the boardroom the remainder of the day.

Johnnie had encountered so many types in her law enforcement days, but Mirah Anderson took the cake. Johnnie was never so happy to see five o'clock come but before she could leave the bank, she wanted to continue her routine as she had done before all of this happened.

She checked with the employees in the back, confirming the day was going well and she felt comfortable enough to leave the bank. She then returned to her office and followed through with her closing procedures. She cleared away everything, collected her coat and purse, and continued to use the tape routine on the door. She was able to put fresh tape on the door without anyone seeing her.

Exiting by way of the back steps, she felt the cold air blow through the stair well. If it is this cold in September, she hated to see what this year's December would be like.

***

Her night felt short. Thursday morning came far too quickly. It seemed like Johnnie had just fallen asleep when she woke at 6:30 as usual. Michael was stepping out of the bathroom, "Hey, thought you were not going to rush into the office?" "Well, that was my plan; but my internal clock didn't seem to know it was allowed to sleep in today. Besides I am concerned that Mirah will question employees and I am not comfortable with that idea."

Michael came to her as she sat up in bed; he kissed her on the forehead and asked if she wanted her tea. "I think coffee might be more the order this morning, but I will come down with you and enjoy your morning company. I would much rather spend time with you than Ms. Anderson."

Johnnie was not one to sit when she knew something needed attention. After one cup of coffee, she told Michael she really did need to hit the shower and get moving for the day. The morning computer operator, Silva, was already at the bank and Johnnie did not want her alone for too long.

Silva was a short woman, with light brown hair and of Eastern European decent. She had long slender fingers that provided her with extra income as a hand model. Silva was using the extra income to pay for her son's trip to the National Swim Competition.

This morning Silva was nervous about needing to talk to someone about Monday morning. She was not going to tell Johnnie or those detectives. She wanted someone up the ranks, and when the attorney general and that FBI man came to the bank, she knew whom she wanted to tell.

With Silva's habit of being the bearer of news, she was excited. This was biggest news she had ever uncovered. She went downstairs to get some copies. It made for a good excuse for being on the executive floor. As she just happened to pass the boardroom, she saw John Erickson. He may not be the state attorney, but a FBI agent would be someone special.

Stepping into the room, Silva asked if he had a moment that she could talk to him. John's first reaction was to ask if she remembered something about what happened.

Silva said, "I don't know if you know it or not, but I was a good friend of Herb Jennings. I want whoever was responsible for his death to pay. I did see someone Monday morning. I didn't think it was anything to worry about until I saw him go into Johnnie's office. He was not an employee. He was tall, white and had red hair, and wore a window washer's security harness and he was carrying something big into her office. That could be how her office got out of order. He could have been very innocent. I did see window washers here the same day, but I only saw him once. I think it was too cold and windy on Monday to do the exterior of the windows. It seemed strange that he would be in her office and it scared me. I figured I would lock the computer room door and turn off the lights and hide somewhere safe."

John seemed very interested and he wanted all the details. This was perfect, she may lead them to the killer, and afterward she would be like a hero. Who knows, maybe there would be a reward in it for her. It could be enough to pay for Aces trip for the Nationals. She could definitely become the hero that Johnnie was not, the way she called for security. Silva gave it some more thought. Yes, this was just what she needed; this could end up being a career move for her. Herb's death did sadden Silva, but she knew he would be the first one to take advantage of any given situation.

John asked Silva who else she had spoken to regarding what she saw. She said she had not spoken to anyone else. He suggested she inform the local authorities about what she observed, and he would be happy to take her written statement. He told her they were all working together; but he would make sure that Mirah Anderson would hear of her information. This just put Silva in seventh heaven. She liked the idea of the attention from an authority figure like an FBI agent and even more so with the attorney general. She could maybe someday cash in a favor.

By the time, Silva left the boardroom employees were coming into their offices. Quickly she took her place by the copy machine. She did not want anyone knowing what she had really been doing on the executive floor.

"Hey Silva," called Helen Flint, "We don't get to see you too often on this floor. You are always so busy in the computer room".

Silva did not want to attract attention so she started making copies of the papers she had brought along as a diversion.

"I know it seems like a treat to get out of that room. It is either too hot or too cold in there. And they say that it is climate controlled." Silva was quick with her response.

Helen walked over to Silva and continued with small talk as she finished copying the papers. Silva knew the distraction of the papers would allow Helen to believe that was the reason for her being on the executive floor.

Silva returned through the front, since the back door locked when it closed. Darn, she forgot to put something in place to hold it ajar. She had to knock on the back door of the executive floor. Since she was still holding her copies, she hoped they would assume she needed another copy. To play it safe she stopped at the copier again and made one more copy.

She took the elevator up making a show of holding the papers she had copied. She returned to the computer room and continued her work without another word of what she had seen.

Employees were settling into quiet conversations. Johnnie knew this meant they were still talking about all the commotion, but it was only natural, so she did not try to curtail any talk. Besides, everyone needed an outlet to express grief and emotions. Herb might not have been a favorite, but he was still a bank employee. He did interact with the employees at the Christmas party, and the occasional bank breakfast the bank catered for the employees, as well as the holiday covered dish lunch.

Johnnie needed to speak with Tom. She wanted to ask Tom if he had a minute. However, before she had the opportunity to ask. Tom spoke first. "I don't want you doing any more research until this is all resolved. As it is now, the situation may solve itself. Gary tells me you are not finding anything out of the ordinary in your efforts. So let's just put it on hold for now." Tom was a considerate person and he did not want her staying late. He wanted her home and safe until all this murder business was finished. Tom had a demanding way about him; but if you did your job, he was appreciative. This time Johnnie was the appreciative one; she did not want to be working late hours until this was resolved. Just playing it on the safe side, Tom arranged for Frank Ridges to escort her to her car in the evenings. She had strict instructions not to come in early. She was to arrive at normal time and park in the first parking place; no more back lot until this was finished.

Johnnie did not like preferred treatment. She wanted the same for the employees of the morning and night crews. She even voiced her concern for the cleaning crew. Tom had told her he would put out a notice to all the employees.

The remainder of the day was uneventful. Johnnie was glad to be leaving at regular time. She walked out of the bank with the last employees from the day shift on her floor. In an effort, not to draw attention to the crew that was leaving, Johnnie told Frank she could walk out with the employees. Still he stayed until he saw the last employee drive out of the lot.

***

Johnnie's night at home was a whirlwind of thoughts and scenarios. It seemed like all she was doing was thinking about how the investigation was proceeding. It made for a very quick and stressful evening. At night, she turned to Michael. He was her rock.

"How long do you think it will take the press to stop running stories on Herb?" Johnnie asked. Michael thought about it for a second, "I suspect it is probably the most exciting thing that has happened in this little community. I guess it will take something bigger for the press to drop the stories and speculations. You know how a major political scandal becomes old news when some celebrity gets married or has a baby, or a bigger scandal comes along. Johnnie, you know how the press works. As long as it sells newspapers, they will continue to carry the story. It's just the nature of the beast. You have seen it before, so you should not be surprised. I know since this one seems personal you are feeling it more than you did when you were working a case." Michael and Johnnie both knew it was true, but it did not make it any easier.

"I know I am lousy company tonight, so if you don't mind; I think I will just get ready for bed and curl up with a book." Johnnie was an avid reader, and it took her mind off current situations. Her favorite topic in her reading material would naturally be crime stories. Sometimes it would be medical thrillers or action stories; but she would always return to the crime stories.

"It's okay Honey. I have plenty of paper work to do, not to mention the design layout for a new project up in Wheeling. You go ahead, I am going to the study to work. I will be in later, most likely much later." Michael really had little to do; but he knew Johnnie needed her time.

Johnnie went to the upstairs study to look for a book to read. The shelves were overflowing with her crime novels; but she did have one section she reserved for earth sciences. Once read, she would mark the tops of her books so she could find one to read. Tonight she just wanted something to absorb her mind. She did not want a murder mystery book tonight. She opted for a book for strictly entertaining. Strangely enough, entertainment to Johnnie was to read about geology.

***

Johnnie was determined to have a good day. Michael was there at the bedside with a fresh brew cup of coffee.

"You can read my mind, can't you?" Johnnie smiled.

Michael handed her a cup of her favorite coffee. "T.G.I.F. and I thought you might enjoy coffee with hazelnut creamer, I know it is your favorite."

"I am glad someone is on my side. I have to get to the bank on time so I can meet up with Mirah. Not looking forward to the day, but what can I do, it is out of my hands. I don't think Gary likes Mirah being involved; but there isn't anything he can do either. So I guess the sooner the day gets started the sooner I will get back home."

Johnnie arrived at the bank at the normal time. She went to her office to check the tape. Once she was comfortable that the office was secure, she went in and put her coat and purse in her closet. She was so grateful that the traces of the tragedy were gone.

Afterwards she went to the computer room, no Silva. Where was she? Maybe she could be down stairs. No, she did not remember seeing her car in her parking place. She immediately called Frank. "Frank, have you seen Silva this morning?" He told her no; but he thought that maybe she got a ride to the bank so she would not have to walk the lot so early in the morning.

Johnnie returned to her office, and called Detective Nichols. "Terry, maybe I am over reacting; but Silva isn't in yet. She should have been here at 6:30 and that makes her two hours late. She is a punctual employee, by 8:30 she should be in the computer room. I will not be able to work today until I know she is safe. I tried calling her; but no answer."

Terry did not like the sounds of this development. She told Johnnie that she would send someone to Silva's house and make sure everyone was okay, and would call her back as soon as she knew the status. Terry's partner, Murph, went to Silva's house using an unmarked car.

Johnnie tried to stay busy and keep things normal, but then she looked up to see Terry at her office door. "I didn't expect you to come in because I called. I don't want to overdramatize her absence. People around here are still shaken over Herb's death."

"I know you didn't expect me; but I am as concerned as you about Silva. I told them to call me on my cell as soon as they knew something." Terry sat in one of the guest chairs in Johnnie's office. "I thought I would just wait with you, if you don't mind."

"Of course not, I will admit I am worried. This is not like her to be late. Even if something held her up, she would have called and left a message."

Terry and Johnnie sat in the office nervously talking.

Terry wanted to ask Johnnie about her name. "Just how did you get a name like Johnnie? It is very unusual for a female."

"My mother wanted to name one of her children after her father. His name was Nicolai John. My sister was named for my dad's mother Angela. Mom wanted to name one of her children John. She thought Nicolai was a bit too old world. I guess being a girl I ended up with Johnetta Lynn. I do have to admit, I kinda like it, believe me no one else in my school had a name like mine."

The detective's phone rang, and they both stiffened. Terry answered and Johnnie could tell by the color draining in her face that the news was bad.

"What happened?" Johnnie held her breath waiting for Terry to tell her the details.

Terry hated telling Johnnie the news. "I asked my partner, Murph, to go over to Silva's house. When he arrived, he could smell smoke and attempted to ram the door down; but it was open. He found her on the floor with a head wound. I am so sorry. She didn't make it. She was already gone even though the EMTs kept heroic measures going all the way to the emergency room."

Johnnie sank back into her chair. This cannot be happening she thought. First Herb's death and now Silva's

This was more than she ever thought could happen in a small city bank. All bank employees received the same safety talks, especially officers. Vary your morning routine outside the house. Don't put any identifying marks on your house or your curb. No house numbers, no names on the mailbox. Granted they always figured these rules were for the officers, but Johnnie always tried to impress upon the employees the need for their safety as well.

"Do you think this is related to Herb? She could have seen something or someone that morning. Maybe someone spotted her before she turned off the light and concealed herself in the wire room. Did she tell you anything?" Johnnie's mind was going a million miles an hour.

"Oh Heavens above, was her son home? She has two sons; one is in the service in Iraq and her other son is in high school. It is always so hard to tell children." Terry could tell that Johnnie worked with the employees on her floor as though they were a team. "You know, when I was at the bureau, I had my share of sad news to impart. Law enforcement officers dread the duty of notifying loved ones. However, here at a bank, who would ever think it would be necessary in this job?"

Terry told her that the police would handle the notifications. Terry suggested she should come downtown to the office and that would keep people from asking too many questions.

"No, I will have a department full of frightened people. Please let me know as soon as the police notify her son, I think her youngest is Harold, but he goes by Aces. He is a great swimmer. After the news release, then I will tell my employees or maybe Gary will. Oh, I need to call Gary. He will want to know this as soon as possible. In the meantime, I will send Sarah in to work Silva's duties. I will have to work up a schedule on the floor and do some employee shifting."

Johnnie was trying to talk out the details with Terry before she left. She was hoping for some sort of information for when she told Gary. "Silva did not tell me anything of what she did or did not see, but she told Frank she thought the police had been sent to get her for skipping out on jury duty. That's why she was found in the wire room Monday morning. Do you think you could check out the jury duty story? No court starts before nine in the morning."

"Yes, I can check it out but are you sure you don't want to go into the station."

She asked Terry how the announcement would come about. Was the police department handling a news conference, or was the local media going to report it on the morning news?

Terry was not certain how it would come down. "Why don't you give Gary a call and I will go down and tell Mirah. Let's just hope the news isn't released via Ms. Anderson. She could put a spin to the incident that could make people think Herb and Silva's deaths were connected."

Johnnie assured her no one would make an attempt on an employee in the bank; but just the same, she was going to ask Gary about the bank sponsoring lunch today. She did not want any employee out of the building.

Terry made her way to the boardroom as slowly as she could so that Johnnie could break the news to Gary first. Mirah she was the only one in the boardroom. She didn't know where John had gone; maybe he just went to the restroom. She would let Mirah tell him.

Johnnie dialed Gary's extension. "Gary, I have some distressing news. Terry's partner found Silva, her house was on fire, she had a head injury and, Gary, and she didn't make it." Johnnie's eyes filled with tears as she told Gary the news.

"What? When? Have you told Mirah?" Gary was stunned.

"This morning I realized Silva wasn't here, and I didn't react well. I contacted Terry. She sent her partner to Silva's house. I'm sorry, I should have told you first, but I guess I was just too worried to think straight. Terry informed Mirah. It is a police matter, so we decided it would be best if she notified the family. Gary, Terry has gone back to the station. We are not sure who will release the news, the media, or an official from the police department. I just hope it is not announced from the homicide division. I know it is far too early for autopsy but with the head wound. Well, speaking from my old life, homicide is the first thought. Do you want to come up here and wait for the mid-morning news? I have that small TV in my office I can turn it on and we will at least know what they release."

"Yes, but I want to come up quietly. Does anyone else in the office know what has happened?"

Johnnie was speaking in her normal friendly voice so as not to have any of her co-workers pick up anything out of the ordinary. "No one knows, and they won't until the news is released. I would like for you to be up here when the news runs the story on Silva's death."

"Okay, I will be up just before the mid-morning news. Is your TV set up so the employees don't see it broadcasting?" Gary wanted everything as low key as Johnnie did. He knew it would be tough once the news did get out.

Johnnie tried to go about the morning as if nothing had happened, but there was no denying that tragedy had struck the bank twice in one week. It was almost 10 AM and the local news would be doing an update on stories. Gary came upstairs and quietly sat in front of Johnnie's desk.

"I am glad you have that TV. Once we know how this is released, then we can proceed." Gary tried to make small talk.

The morning news was about to start; a reporter from the local news station was standing in front of the burned remains of Silva's house. "The mother of two sons died this morning in an early morning fire. Police and fire officials are not able to report much other than her name was Silva Ames and she worked at the First National Bank of Ackers. This is the second death of an employee from the First National Bank of Ackers in recent days. At this point an investigation is ongoing and no further details are available."

Johnnie shut the TV off and looked at Gary. "So how do you want to handle the situation? It would have been a lot easier if the report had not mentioned Herb's death. That is going to cause for too many questions. I think we ought to have lunch brought in today. It might make the employees feel better if they don't have to leave the building. We should have employees leave in pairs tonight, including the night shift. If need be I will stay tonight and make sure the employees get to their cars safely. Gary, I think you should be the one to tell the employees. It is going to be important that they see that we both are supportive during this time." Johnnie always wanted to show teamwork.

Gary told Johnnie that she should not be the one to walk out the night crew. He lived close enough that they should call him when they are ready to leave for the night. Probably would be a better idea if he just stayed in the bank. That way the employees would not be alone in the building. Johnnie agreed.

"Can you gather the employees from the confirmation unit? Let's meet in the central processing area. There are enough tables and chairs there for everyone. Let's try to make this as easy as possible for everyone." Gary stayed in the office as Johnnie went to gather all the employees from the other department.

As Johnnie entered the computer room to tell Sarah that there was a meeting in the central processing area, she was the only one to ask. "Is this about Silva? Has something happened to her?"

Johnnie knew that some of the employees would probably figure it out before the announcement; these people were intelligent. "Let's just meet and see what is going on all together."

Johnnie returned to her office. "You ready to do this?" Johnnie knew it would be as hard for Gary as it would have been for her.

"I wish I could talk with everyone like this floor. Just cannot close down the teller line. I will send a memo out to the officers and managers, if I can't talk to them personally. We will draft a notice for the employees. We need to do this as quickly as we can, can't afford to have someone come into the bank and tell one of the tellers."

With the employees gathered in the central processing area, Gary did his best to tell everyone what had happened. Without a script, his message was heartfelt and emotional. "I know it is unusual for me to be up here to talk to all of you, but I have news that I want you to hear from me. Today, when we noticed Silva had yet to arrive, we called the police. They went to her home. Murph, one of the detectives that has been around here lately, went to her house. He got to the house to find smoke and Silva unconscious on the floor. Unfortunately, she did not regain consciousness. The police have notified her son Harold, Aces. The media has mentioned that two employees of the bank have died in recent days. Just remember we have no proof that they are related. Nevertheless, you know how the media can make a mountain out of a molehill. We wanted you all to hear this from us first and not the media. I should also mention that Herb's services are going to be private at the convenience of the family in Virginia."

The room fell to a hush for several minutes. The switchboard rang, bringing everyone out of their stunned state. The questions started immediately, all talking at the same time. Gary looked at Johnnie noting she was going to have her hands full with a million questions. These were Silva's co-workers; many of them knew her from personal outings and social gatherings.

Kelly seemed particularly unnerved. "Is the bank going to do anything to protect us?"

"We will do our best to protect everyone. In fact, we will have lunch catered in today so that no one need leave the bank. We will also make sure Frank is here in the morning to guarantee your safety walking through the lot. Everyone is to walk in pairs, for the night crew I will be driving the employees to their cars. No one is to be walking through the lot alone. We have no reason to believe any of us are in danger; but we are taking every ounce of care." Gary said he needed to go break the news to other department heads.

Before he left Johnnie asked Gary if he could stay for a bit. She needed to talk to someone about the situation. Gary complied and said he needed someone to talk to as well.

"I just don't understand. Why Herb? Was he involved in something dangerous? I know we don't discuss the case I am researching, but you and I both know it is in a secure place and not in my office. So I have no idea why anyone would ransack my office."

Gary thought for a minute. "I don't know what Herb might have been up to; but I can tell you it could not have anything to do with the research. I never told him about the project to start. In fact, as far as I am aware; he did not know of the project at all."

"Well, that sort of puts us totally back at square one. I can think of nothing else that is in my office that is not available to anyone. Why kill Herb, and how does this relate to Silva, if it is in fact connected?" Johnnie sat there truly disturbed by the entire event. However, she decided she had better turn her attention to the employees.

Gary returned to his office. He started notifications with Harrison, knowing that Harrison and Silva were friends he wanted to tell Harrison in person. It was only fair to give him time to absorb the news before the memo circulated throughout the rest of the bank. He called the officers in each department to give them the news. It would be important that they were ready for the questions that would follow.

The day was a total loss in departments on the sixth floor. People were too shocked to put themselves back into a working frame of mind. Johnnie understood. It was human nature and this was news that truly was shocking to everyone. She was no exception. She had dealt with many difficult deaths before, but not with 21 people coming at her so fast, looking for the same answers she was searching for at the same time.

Johnnie told everyone she would try to help in any way she could, so she encouraged them to talk. She wanted everyone to talk but not get overwrought. As a licensed psychologist, she knew the need to release feelings and emotions were very important. She also knew some could not talk now, but would need to at some other point in time.

The first visitor to her office was Kelly. "Johnnie, I feel like a major coward; but I want to take my vacation now. I have a sister, Kassandra and her husband Corey who live in St Petersburg Florida. I have already called her and told her I would be coming for a visit."

"I will need to check the vacation calendar. You know how it works, if someone with more seniority wants the same period, they get first choice. This late in the year, do you have vacation time available?" Johnnie could see the dejected expression on Kelly's face.

"I have seniority now. Silva was the only one that had more seniority than I did. Besides Sarah can cover the job, so it will not interfere with the operations of the central processing unit. That would make it okay for me to take my vacation now. Please, I need to get away. I can't take all these deaths." The dejected look turned to more of desperation on Kelly's face.

Johnnie knew that the vacation schedule was clear. "Okay, I will inform Gary you will be taking your vacation. Do you want to start on Monday?"

"No, I want to start it immediately. I will call my brother Augie to come and pick me up."

"Okay, Kelly I am sure it will all work out." Johnnie did her best to calm Kelly, but she left Johnnie's office in tears.

News of Silva's death circulated around the bank like wildfire. Johnnie dreaded the response it would bring. In addition to dealing with distraught co-workers, she had many members of departments coming up to talk to her. Harrison approached her first. He came up to her office daily to raid her candy dish but she knew he wanted to talk about Silva when he closed her door.

Harrison had been friends with Silva since he came to the bank. Odd friendship, he was a customer service manager and she a computer operator. It wasn't as though they had much in common. Their work never really crossed paths.

Harrison was impeccably dressed as always. He made a striking appearance normally. He never had a hair out of place, well at least not until today. With his eyes red and misted, he was a walking shell of himself.

"Harrison, I don't like closing my door especially now. The employees are jumpy enough." Johnnie knew he would not pay any attention to her, so she got up from her desk and opened it part way.

"Do you want to talk about Silva?" She asked him.

"You know I liked Silva, she was so much fun to be around, and she seemed to have her finger on the pulse of what goes on in this place. Do you think that is what got her killed? I know she and

Herb went to lunch together. There is all this talk about Herb and drugs. Do you think Silva was involved as well?"

"Harrison I am still digesting the news, but I just can't imagine Silva having anything to do with drugs. As for Herb's involvement, I have no idea. Are the deaths related? I have no idea. I am sure the police will do an excellent job with the investigation."

"Come on Johnnie, everyone knows you were FBI. Surely you have an idea of some kind." Harrison was pressing for any tidbit he could get out of her.

"I am as mystified as you are about these happenings. I haven't had much time to absorb everything, like I said I am still digesting the news."

Harrison stood up and reached into her candy dish. He opened the door the rest of the way trying to act casual. "You know I guess one of these days I will have to refill your candy dish."

Johnnie knew that Harrison was doing his best to act normally; but he was failing miserably at the effort.

Johnnie thought next would be Harvey. He was always good for trying to get the scoop on everything. Harvey was a member of Frank's crew, but like Silva, he did his best to stay on top of the rumor mill. He normally stuck to the gossip on the first floor. Of course, recent events were happening on the sixth floor.

To her surprise, Harvey did not enter her office. She did like Harvey when he was just being Harvey. No gossip, no digging into employee's lives, just a good guy. He was of average height, about five foot 10 inches, he had a beautiful crop of blonde hair and brown eyes. His hair was always styled to look professional; but he did wear it in a longer fashion than most.

Johnnie called Gary, "I had a few visits from employees bet you have as well. Wonder if a staff meeting after the bank closes might not be a bad idea."

"I was going to call you. There is an emergency meeting of the board Monday night. I am sure that they will cover many of the recent happenings." By his voice alone, Johnnie could tell that Gary was as worn out as she was, and the weekend was going to be needed rest for both.

"I don't envy any of the board members. Waiting until Monday is going to keep everyone in a frantic state for the weekend." Johnnie knew what she was talking about, with her background at the bureau she knew the people would be afraid to answer their doors, let alone go out of the house over the weekend.

Johnnie tried to forget about the board of directors. They will have to appoint someone to Herb's position, most likely Gary. It seems the logical step. There was so much to think about she wondered what Mirah and John would say about these happenings. With the deaths of two bank employees, she knew that Mirah would somehow try to influence any decisions made. She could not help herself from slipping into investigation mode. What was happening at the bank seemed, to her, something like an iceberg. There was far more to this than anyone could see at this time but it was out of her hands.

***

Johnnie wasn't sure what would happen in the next couple of days; but since it was Friday, she hoped everyone would take the news and let it process over the weekend.

Johnnie left the bank with the normal day crew, as per her orders. She wasn't a custom to walking out during daylight hours. She exited the bank with Ana and Frank. Frank was walking everyone to his or her cars. It was a small gesture but the employees were very appreciative.

Johnnie got home and all she wanted to do was soak in a warm tub of bubbles with a cup of tea. Since Michael wasn't home yet, she was going to take the opportunity to do so. After making her tea, she selected her favorite scented candles, lilac, and she ran the water. As she stepped into the claw-footed tub, she moved the reading rack to the bathtub so she could read in peace.

She didn't get much time to settle when she heard the front door open. She could hear Michael's voice saying something about go home.

"Johnnie are you home? Did those media people bombard you?" Michael knew Johnnie could handle herself, but didn't stop him from worrying.

"Up here, Michael. I decided on a warm soak to help melt away today's happenings."

"Did they get you when you got home?" Michael was amazed to find she was able to get past the hoard of media people out front.

"I went to Josie's after work and had her bring me home. The alley seemed an easy way to get inside the house. We moved to the alley at our first opportunity. Since I wasn't in my car it was easy to escape their detection."

"Why didn't Josie stay instead of going home?"

"I think she had plans for tonight. She didn't tell me what her plans were; but I suspect she has a gentleman of interest. I told her to do a fast drop and keep going. That way it would be less obvious. If she were seen, it would look more like a curious neighbor. I am so glad you put that back door on the garage. It made my escape from the hoards much easier."

Michael cocked his left eyebrow. "Do you think it was safe for her car being seen close to us?"

"Nah, I had rented a car and had Josie drive it. I seriously doubt anyone could or would suspect it was my method of reaching the peace and quiet of our home." Johnnie seemed to sink lower into the tub.

"Okay, do you have any preference for dinner tonight?" Michael was heading back through the bedroom as he spoke.

"Oh if I could, I would love some sushi; but I am not going out there and I am not asking a delivery person to fight their way through the crowd."

"Well, it is good for you that I know your favorites. I picked up enough sushi to feed the entire block. I thought you might want something quick and easy, plus I know sushi is among those quick meals you like most. Sorry we can't go out to the restaurant. You sure you don't want another covert maneuver." Michael knew she would not, but he wanted her to know that the evening and probably the weekend was going to be an indoor adventure.

"You know if you would have told me when you first came home, we could be eating already. You know you can't let fish sit out too long." Johnnie was reaching for the towel to wrap around herself. She dried her feet before going to the bedroom to dress. What a waste of bubbles and candles she thought as she dressed in her snuggie.

"I didn't expect you to fly down the steps, can you leap tall buildings in a single bound as well?" Michael was grinning, as he opened a bottle of bubbly for them and had just finished laying out the sushi. He knew to take the wasabi portion that Johnnie would eat and water it down until it was a thin paste. He liked his more in the somewhat firm presentation. "Your dinner awaits my queen."

With dinner over, Johnnie was exiled to either the family room, the study, or the bedroom. She could have her pick. Michael took care of the few dishes and glasses from dinner. Johnnie decided on going to the study. It didn't have a fireplace, nor did it have a huge patio window.

Friday night was an evening spent in quiet conversation with only a few candles lit. She didn't want to turn the lights on and give their position away to the throngs of media. Besides, she wanted the lilac candles she had lit earlier. Lilac was one of her favorite fragrances. Before Michael came into the study, she was watching an old TV program on her tablet involving crime solving.

Michael came in and settled next to her, they talked almost in hushed tones. Johnnie told him about Silva, which she knew he was already aware, and she told him about Kelly's abrupt almost demand for a vacation.

Some of the media had finally given up by the time Johnnie was tiring. Michael told her to take her tablet with her into the bedroom and watch her FBI programs. He was going downstairs to lock up. He not only checked the doors on the first floor and the one to the garage, he even went out to the garage to make sure the back door was secure; and then he checked all ingresses within the basement as well. He would watch TV from the study and leave Johnnie to her tablet.

***

The rest of the weekend was very quiet. Sunday Josie used the rental car again to drive through the alley and pick up Michael and Johnnie for Mass. They parked the car as close to the church as possible: Johnnie wanted to avoid any questions from interested parishioners following the Mass. As the three entered the church, they spotted Pat Cates standing in the back, almost as if he were waiting for someone. Michael and Pat were in the Navy Seals together. The look between Pat and Michael said this was not an accidental meeting. After Mass, they went to Josie's house for luncheon. Josie knew her aunt would be going stir crazy by this time. Since restaurants were still problematic, the luncheon at Josie's was a welcomed outing.

The day was gone before they were ready for it to end, but Michael reminded Johnnie they still needed a ride home. Pat came to their rescue, offering to take them back to the house.

He used the same procedure as Josie when she brought Johnnie home on Friday.

Johnnie offered a nightcap to Pat, if he dared. He said he would come in, but first he would go over to the next block and park in the old school parking lot. It was doubtful that anyone would pay any attention to him walking through the alley.

Johnnie was tired and dreading what the next day might bring, so she visited with Pat and Michael in the study for a bit before retiring to the bedroom.

She had the distinct feeling that Pat and Michael had some issues to discuss. Those two were so much alike.

Monday at the bank is going to be a bit tough with all the questions. She really didn't want to think about how terrified the employees were going to be, knowing there were unsolved murders that involved people they knew and socialized with on occasion. Johnnie did not blame them for their anxiety, she was feeling the same way.

Still she wondered if the research project had anything to do with Herb's death. Maybe Herb could somehow be involved with the research. However, she had not seen anything in her research that would even hint of Herb being involved. What of Silva, she could not imagine how her death tied to this mess. Would the rest of the employees be safe, something had Kelly terrified. Would others want to take an immediate vacation as well? Would any of the employees consider quitting because of the deaths? What a predicament this was going to be and what would the board think?

She decided there was no value in worrying about what was going to happen until it did. This may not be her case or investigation, but these were co-workers of her's. This wasn't the same as working with her team at the bureau. These were untrained frightened people.

***

Johnnie was too preoccupied to think of breakfast. Something Michael did not appreciate. He knew she wanted to get involved, and he understood why. Unfortunately, she would have to conduct her life like the rest of the employees. He also knew with her it was going to be near impossible. He decided, for this week, he would let their routine slide.

Johnnie took the back stairs down to Tom's office on the fourth floor. She poked her head in his door and asked if he was busy. "No, come on in, I was going to ask you to come down this afternoon anyway." She went into his office and took a seat in front of his desk.

"I have to tell you, Tom, not only has the bank lost two valuable employees but the talk among the employees is raging. I am afraid it will get worse before it gets better. No one outside of you, Gary and I know about the Andropov research, at least among the employees."

Tom sat back in his chair. "No doubt you are correct. How many people have been quizzing you about the Andropov research? No doubt Ms. Anderson has had questions."

"Yes, she has, but not about the findings, just where the results were stored." Johnnie did find it strange that Mirah seemed to have no interest in the actual research. "Detective Nichols knows about the research. That has been about it, I keep the findings in two secure places trying to protect the information in every way possible. But again, I find it odd that Mirah was more interested in its location and not the research findings."

Tom frowned. "It is strange. After all, she is the one that ordered the research. Has she asked the location of the keys?"

"No, it seems like the entire project is not on her mind at the moment. I just wanted you to know that everything involving the project is secured. No one has asked to see the research. I expected Detective Nichols to ask to see the contents; but she asked me what I found. I told her that there was no evidence of any irregular or illegal activity."

Tom knew Johnnie would protect the information. "I knew when I gave you the assignment, it was in good hands. I do want you to know I do not expect you to withhold any findings regarding the matter. I want you to give it to the law enforcement personnel if they requested."

"Okay, I just wanted you to know what has happened so far. I haven't been really asked to produce the material; but I do feel better knowing you want to comply with any request." Johnnie was glad she came down to talk to Tom. "I appreciate your understanding about law enforcement questions. So far, they don't really seem interested."

"Has anyone hinted to your involvement in Herb's death? If they do, you let me know." Tom was a good person to work with and did his best to be fair and caring. "Well, if they do, I will stand for your character. We know you had no involvement in the unfortunate happenings. They probably know that you and Herb had differences, but considering Herb, who didn't." Tom grinned. "I had differences with him myself."

Johnnie thanked Tom and returned to her office.

Gary circulated the announcement to all the departments, informing the employees of the meeting scheduled the following morning in the lobby. This of course, brought about more questions. This day was emotional for so many. Silva's death really affected the employees and they continued to ask what Johnnie knew about the deaths, and the morning meeting, Johnnie was so busy answering her phone, she was not aware of Mirah standing at her door. Mirah interrupted by clearing her throat. Johnnie finished her conversation and hung up the phone.

Johnnie's surprise was evident. "What brings you up here? I thought you wanted to keep a low profile, isn't that why you wanted to stay in the boardroom?" Mirah came into the office and sat in the chair in front of her. "I know you have heard the rumors about Herb and his drug habits. What else can you tell me about him?"

Johnnie realized that Mirah knew about the difficulties she had with Herb. "I truly don't know much. He was divorced and considered a bit careless in his personal life for a banker. Beyond that, I do not know anything else about his life. I can't tell you if the drug rumors are true or not. I suspect you have heard about the differences he and I had. As it was, I kept to my regular work and stayed in close contact with Gary. The differences sort of lost intensity and died out about a year ago. I do not like bullying, and Herb was known for his intimidation schemes. I am sorry he is dead, but as to where he was killed or why I have no idea. Even worse, I have no idea why his body was brought up to my office, or how the perpetrator got into the bank as it had to be early."

"Well, you can understand why we had to look in to your history." Mirah seemed as though she enjoyed putting her on the spot. Johnnie knew how to respond to such an attempt to alarm. Apparently, Mirah was not listening to Johnnie, and she must have forgotten about the expertise Johnnie had in psychology and human behavior. "You can look all you want. I can tell you my life is pretty much an open book."

Mirah straightened her posture. "I did look in to your history with the bureau. Everyone holds you in high regard. Why did you leave?"

"I would think you already know the reasons why I left the agency, it was strictly for personal reasons." Mirah was doing her best to rattle Johnnie.

Mirah left her office as quickly as she came. Johnnie was annoyed with Mirah's clumsy attempt to unnerve her.

She was glad that she would be leaving at the prescribed time with everyone else, as she did not want to encounter Mirah or John Erickson at the end of the day. So she was ready exactly at the end of the day's work schedule.

***

"Hey, there's my girl. I called your office, guess I am not use to you being home on time." Michael picked her up and swung her around.

"Hey, careful! I do have a knife in my hand." Johnnie was surprised with Michael's enthusiasm to see her. "Why are you home so early? I thought you would be working a bit late."

Michael took a deep breath. "Today, after you left the bank, Gary called me. Someone made an attempt on Harrison's life. They tried to run him off the road as he was coming down 29th street. He did go over the curb and seemed to be a bit shook up. Anyway, Gary wanted to know if you had made it home safely. That is why I told the office I would be out for the rest of the day. So why did you come home?"

"Remember the orders I got from Gary and Tom, no late hours. Is Harrison okay? Why him, why our bank, what is going on? It makes me wonder if someone at the bank is keeping too close of an eye on me. Harrison came to my office earlier. He was fishing for information as he always does, but first off, I don't gossip and secondly, I would not tell him anything if I did know something. On the other hand, I can tell you I will find out what is going on. I have a few contacts from my other life back at the bureau. Funny, at this time, that other life is looking safer than being a banker."

She went on to tell him she just was tired and wanted to start some notes of her own outside the bank. She would talk to Terry tomorrow and provide her with a copy of her notes. She had to wait until after the employee assembly then she wanted to meet with Tom and Gary, and later with Terry.

Michael had always suspected Johnnie missed her bureau days. She worked in the field, but she truly shined in the investigative department. She was also an excellent profiler considering her background, but there wasn't enough information to do any profiling.

Johnnie had put down the knife she was using to cut a bagel and sat down in her spot at the kitchen table.

"Want some tea?" Michael was already preparing the kettle.

"Oh you know me too well." She replied.

He gave her the tea, and pulled a chair up beside her. "So where do you start? It has been some time since we did a case review."

"I am going to start with the most obvious. I think the research project is at the bottom of all this; but I don't know how Herb fits in the picture let alone Silva and Harrison." The events had Johnnie stymied. "However, I am not going to wait for any more unfortunate things to happen to the employees. I am going to tell Gary and Tom, I plan to be in and out of the bank from time to time. I hope it won't be obvious; nevertheless, I need to do this not just for me but for the bank too."

Johnnie and Michael were absorbed in their efforts to sort out why these events had happened. They were too involved to stop and fix dinner. "How would you like some Thai delivery? You can get that seafood dish you like so much." Michael smile. "And yeah, you just might order some Pad Thai."

The food was delivery and they enjoyed their favorite Thai dishes. Now it was back to reviewing what little they knew. "Johnnie, this seems to be going nowhere fast. Do you want to call Noah and see if he can provide any insight?"

Johnnie was eager to call Noah. However, she knew just talking to her old team would bring up memories she tried to let go of in order to step away from law enforcement. "I would like to call him, but I will do it tomorrow. I am somewhat mind numb now. Thank you Sweetheart."

"For what, I am just helping you find some answers." Michael knew how much Johnnie was chomping at the bit to get involved in this case.

***

Johnnie was having trouble sleeping. After a night of cat naps, she gave up and decided to go down to the family room. She always found it helpful when working a case to sit quietly with a tablet and just write every thought or word that came into her mind. Right now, that is what she needed to do.

Michael woke and not finding Johnnie in bed, he went downstairs. "I thought I would find you here. I see you are reverting to your old methods. Find anything helpful yet?"

Johnnie looked up at Michael with a sigh. "I don't know if it helped or hurt. I don't know enough of what the police have found. It could be that after this morning's staff meeting I will know more, or at least be able to think. Maybe my mind is being pulled in too many directions."

"Well, I know one direction that will help, how about your favorite tea and a bit of toast? I know you are not going to want to eat a real breakfast, but I would feel better if you had something." Michael was always trying to get Johnnie to eat a decent breakfast, but today it would be hopeless.

Johnnie shook her head yes. "I am dreading this staff meeting. I figure Gary will take Herb's place. He deserves it, and he is the most qualified. I am just praying that the recent deaths are not made the center point of the meeting."

Johnnie arrived to find most everyone in the lobby. It looked like everyone wanted to know what was happening. By the activity at the front of the bank, it looked as though the meeting was about to start.

Gary stood up front with the bank president Ernie Compoto. As usual, Ernie stepped back to give Gary the floor. Ernie avoided public speaking. "I know you are all anxious to know what is going on with recent events. Truth of the matter, we don't know, it is too early in the police's investigation to know. The only thing that many of you may not be aware of, would be Harrison's accident yesterday. I would like to caution everyone to be wary. Let's everyone play it safe."

Several knew the news; but others were surprised to hear that someone else could be in danger. It was not certain if the episode was an attempt on his life or not. It could have been just an accident. Johnnie could not help but think the worst and she feared for Harrison.

Now Ernie stepped forward. "You all know that we have a vacancy in the executive division. To resolve that situation will be Gary Percy. In order to keep the bank running smoothly, we have already decided on a replacement for Gary's position. Johnnie King will fill the position of Senior Vice President." Johnnie's gasping stunned reaction to the announcement made heads turn. She did not want to take his job. She had plans of her own.

After the meeting, Johnnie went into Herb's office, now Gary's. Not waiting for an invitation to sit down, she just sat. "I don't understand. Why take me out of my office? You know I don't want to work on the executive floor."

Gary sat back into his chair. "Is there a particular reason why you find this so distasteful?"

"Well, to be perfectly honest, I had plans of spending more time reviewing the deaths of Herb and Silva. I need to know why someone went after Harrison. I don't want anything more to happen to the employees. No danger and no stress, working under this kind of tension will result in errors. For the sake of the bank, I think it is important to find the answers and secure the safety and peace of mind of the employees." Johnnie was set on getting involved in the investigation.

"No surprise, you can take the girl out of the FBI, but you can't take the FBI out of the girl. Actually, you will be working from two offices. You won't need to be on the executive floor all day, you will also continue with your duties on the sixth floor. Besides, with this arrangement, you will be able to leave the bank when you feel it necessary without being under constant observation by the employees on your floor. The board thought with this arrangement you could come and go without the employees feeling deserted." Gary's explanation made perfect sense.

"I understand the concept of the decision, but you caught me totally off guard. I guess you can tell by my reaction I was not expecting being part of the announcement." Johnnie was somewhat embarrassed by her gasp when the announcement was made to the staff. "You are right I will want time to slip away on occasion. I am sure Detective Nichols and her team can handle the investigation, but I want to know what has been determined at this point. I am worried about Harrison, if something can happen to Silva and Harrison I want to make sure the employees are safe."

Gary knew that Johnnie had the best intentions. "I know you will work together very professionally with the local law enforcement. Just remember you are not carrying the burden of these problems by yourself. Do you intend to keep Ms. Anderson and John Erickson informed?"

"I had plans of asking Terry, Detective Nichols, if she would be offended if I called my old section chief. The resources of the bureau are greater than local law enforcement departments. As for informing Ms. Anderson and John Erickson, I will leave that to Terry." Johnnie was hoping that Gary did not voice any objection.

Ernie seemed to materialize out of nowhere. "So you are going to start your own personal investigation. Is there any reason why you think the locals can't handle the situation?"

Johnnie did not appreciate Ernie's comment. "I know that the local law enforcement is making use of their resources, but the resources of the FBI may be of help."

Ernie continued. "Do you think you will be able to bring the FBI into the investigation?" Johnnie looked at Ernie with some confusion. "I wasn't thinking of them being involved in the investigation. I was thinking of borrowing some of their assets. I see no reason for the FBI to become an active part of the investigation."

Gary sensed the tension that was suddenly in the room. It seemed as though Ernie was baiting Johnnie for some reason.

"Well, I guess I have taken up enough of your time, I should be getting upstairs. I am sure there will be questions waiting for me." Johnnie did not want to start her new responsibilities with tensions between her and Ernie after all he is the bank president.

Returning to her office, she found several messages on her desk. Ana approached her door. "Are you okay? You seemed so surprised by today's announcement."

"Surprised is putting it mildly, but I will do what is necessary to keep the bank operating at its most efficient and accurate levels. Have you been overrun with questions from the employees on this floor?"

"No more than you would expect, assuming you are anticipating being hit with a barrage of questions. I know that the employees have questions about what happened with Harrison, and when will you be moving off the floor." Ana always did her best to cushion Johnnie, although Johnnie never understood why she did so.

Johnnie explained that she would be dividing her time between the offices. Assuring Ana, she would not have to face the questions on her own. "Why don't we gather everyone in the central processing center, and I will do my best to answer some questions, and hopefully put their minds at ease."

Johnnie looked through the messages. The only one she wanted to respond to was Michael's call. "Hey Husband, how is your day?" Husband was Johnnie's term of endearment for Michael at times.

"How did the meeting go this morning? I thought you would call me right away."

"I guess I would have if I hadn't been in shock. Gary is the new Executive VP, but the big surprise was when they announced me as the new Senior VP. I was not ready for that and really don't want the job."

Michael was not surprised. "What did you tell them?"

"I didn't call you right away because I was talking to Gary. I told him I was going to ask Noah about using some of the resources of the bureau. He was okay with the idea, but Ernie stepped into Gary's new office. He seemed too antagonistic for some reason."

"What made him so? Is he opposed to utilizing different resources?"

"That is the thing he just suddenly seemed to be annoyed with the FBI making their resources available. He did not provide a reason for his dissent. It is so out of character for Ernie. He has always been so easy going." Ernie's behavior truly stunned Johnnie.

"Maybe he is just feeling the stress of the deaths. After all, he is the bank president, and I would bet this makes him somewhat worried about the community's faith in the bank. He probably thinks having one FBI agent in the bank is enough. Have you talked to John Erickson about any of this stuff?" Michael always tried to look at any situation from as many different angles.

"No, I don't think I have said 50 words to John Erickson since his arrival. I still plan to leave that part up to Terry. I suppose the situation is stressing Ernie. If I were in his position, I would probably be as testy. Gary is not opposed to me approaching Noah, but I am sure he wants me to run it past Terry first, which was my plan at the beginning. I am just going to offer Terry additional tools. Anyway, I have to run, there are so many questions, and I am going to talk to the employees and see if I can put their minds at ease."

Michael laughed. "See you tonight. For some reason I am expecting an FBI agent to be coming home."

***

Johnnie took the next morning to go to the police station. She got her visitor's pass and went up to see Terry, who had just come back to her office with a cup of tea. She offered a cup to Johnnie, who opted for a soda.

The two sat in Terry's cubical, and finally Terry pulled out her tablet and asked how the employee meeting went and were there any surprises.

"Things went pretty much the way I had expected. Gary Percy will take Herb's position, and I will take his office for the present. I talked to him about that, and he said it would allow me more freedom to come and go without the employees of the processing division noticing. Lord knows I don't want Gary's job."

Johnnie looked directly into Terry's eyes. She wanted to see her reaction to what she was thinking. "Terry, if you don't like what I am about to suggest; please tell me. Noah Drake was my section chief when I worked with the FBI. Now I am not suggesting that the FBI step into the mix. I was thinking more along the lines of using some of their resources. If you think I am stepping into something that I should not, please tell me."

Terry listened and wondered how this was going to succeed with her and Johnnie working together. She was pleased to find Johnnie would call her old section chief. The resources of the bureau would be a definite help.

Terry had to voice her thoughts. "I have to be honest with you I just don't feel comfortable with the way John Erickson and Mirah Anderson stepped into the picture. It would be nice if we could find out why he travels with the state attorney. Is this something you think your former section chief can help us with on the QT?"

Johnnie assured her that Noah could be trusted to do some checking without raising red flags.

She and Terry talked about the morning and she told her how Ernie wanted to know why she wanted to bring the bureau into the investigations. She also told her in the past he never really got involved in much; but these recent events must have him somewhat scared.

Terry tossed some question out for Johnnie. "Okay, so the research has to do with Victor Andropov. Everyone believes he has his hand in drug trafficking but to tell the truth; I never did believe such a thing. What else do you know about him?"

Johnnie considered the question for a moment. "Well, if Herb was into drugs; it could have gotten him mixed up and on the wrong side of Victor or someone else dealing drugs in the area. However, it could be someone entirely different. It is far too early to know for sure. Nothing in my research indicates that he is doing anything wrong, no money laundering schemes, nothing. That is like the major red banner for drug dealers. His banking activity is what I would expect to see for someone who has a restaurant. Now if he has activity at other banks, well, it is something I have no way of checking."

Johnnie was at a loss for additional information. All she knew was that she was to gather up all activities on all the Andropov's accounts, including any cashier checks or money orders he may have purchased during a given time. She explained that the details were finished. Now she would have to find the film and have it developed to track every transaction. What kind of time that would take she had no idea. Johnnie also told her that for the present Tom did not want her working the project.

Johnnie told Terry the details were in the vault on the sixth floor and that there was a second or duplicate set of the current research in the main vault.

Terry was amused. "So you have the detailed project in two places. Do you have a watcher watching the watcher too?" Terry couldn't help but laugh at the duplication. "Seriously, why do you have two sets of the research?"

Johnnie laughed with her. "I just like to have a backup, like the extra gun some law enforcement officers carry. You need to be ready with a fallback plan in the event of an unforeseen problem."

From the police station, she went home. This had to be the longest week of her life, and it was only Tuesday.

***

The next morning Johnnie was back at the bank and went to the executive floor to check in with Gary. She told him about her meeting, and relayed to him the same thing she told Terry, with a few exceptions. She did not want to say that Herb had been involved with drugs until there was proof. She did tell him, in case he didn't already know that Herb and Silva had lunch together on several occasions, but that didn't mean she was involved in anything more than brown nosing. She also told him that she did not know about the lunches until recently when Harrison told her. It seemed strange that he had his accident that same afternoon. She confided in Gary that she was going to have Terry come into the bank and quietly sweep for listening devices. She suspected her office might not be secure.

She left Gary's office and went to her secondary location in the bank. She did not like this office; too many individuals stopping by, and she knew the reason why. These people were just being nosy. She decided if she wanted to get anything done, it was going to be in her own office. The executive floor was like being in a fish bowl with people stopping by to hear what she had to say. These same people never came to her upstairs office.

Johnnie returned to her office on the processing floor. Harvey Thompson, who never went any further than the lunchroom, was now walking up and down the floor trying to catch her eye. Johnnie had hoped that since he did not come into her office earlier he was going to keep his distance. She felt terrible, but every time he came through, she picked up the phone. She needed to keep her attentions on her work.

As she did in her FBI days, she started a casebook and thought it would be a good idea to add a flow chart, a trick Noah had used when she worked with him. She detailed everything she knew; at the top of the list was Ernie as the president, then Herb as executive vice president. Tom Midland was the executive vice president of the lending division. Gary Percy was the senior vice president, and Johnnie's boss. On the same level with Johnnie would be Harrison. She tried to list the entire staff right down to Frank Ridges as the head of security. She did take the time to outline the department affected by Silva's passing. She had Ana Deacon, her assistant noted, since Silva reported directly to Ana, and Ana reported to her. Johnnie noted her various co-workers that worked on the floor with her and she charted accordingly, Sarah Oxford as the floater was pretty much the end of Johnnie's main co-worker staff, and she was the employee now covering the morning computer function. Some employees although she was ultimately responsible for them, she did not have as much direct contact.

Johnnie detailed everything she knew. She wrote up questions she wanted answers to, and she even used a code for particular people, it made it easier for others to follow the order of the staff.

As she thought about the new faces, Mirah Anderson and John Erickson, she had to wonder what they were bringing to the table. She knew John was FBI, but she thought him too inexperienced to follow such a case. Of course, that could be unfair; she had no way of knowing his past case involvement. She decided this was something she and John should talk about if they ever had private time. She decided to return to her new office in hopes of catching him alone.

Johnnie walked into the boardroom to get coffee. At least, that was her excuse. John Erickson was sitting at the first seat opposite the door.

"Hi John, how are you doing? Have you had any luck lately with your investigation?" It was plain he did not want to give her any information; nevertheless, she was former FBI, and she was at the center of the happenings in a way it seemed.

"Have you worked very many of these type cases?" Johnnie did her best to sound interested but not pushy in her asking.

"Nothing quite like this situation, I have worked a few kidnappings. We got the kids out of harm's way, and we put the people responsible away. We were fortunate with the successful conclusions. Not all kidnapping cases end that way. I also worked a few drug cases. I worked the case of Grammar Jonas death in Reston VA. Johnnie, were you involved in the Jonas case?"

"No, I was just leaving the agency when that happened. What was the result?" Johnnie was interested in this bit of information, but did not want to seem overly interested.

John was nervous about telling her, but she could always just Google the case online, so he had no real reason to avoid telling her.

"Grammar was one of those characters that liked big showy things. His house was in the elite area of town; he drove a sports car, and he flirted with every lady who made eye contact with him. He was obvious about his wealth. Actually, we all thought he was living a bit too large for a banker's salary. That is how we believe he got involved with Victor Andropov. He started playing fast and loose. Most likely, he stepped out of line. We did not get the person responsible for Grammar's death, but we believe it is tied to Andropov. Now we are hoping we can tie Andropov to this case."

Johnnie was satisfied that he had some experience. As they continued to chat, John wanted to know why she left the agency. "I guess I wanted a bit more stable hours. We hoped to start a family; however, that hasn't happened. I love the bank, but there are aspects of the agency that I miss."

Now it was John's turn to ask about her cases. "So what was your most memorable case?"

"Well, I worked in the field, but loved to do the investigative work. I guess that is why I like the job I have now. I loved the research and details of a case. I think the most challenging case we worked on was probably the Crystal Jenkins kidnapping case. They shuffled the poor girl back and forth between West Virginia and Virginia; then for good measure, they took her to Ohio on one occasion. Crystal was never hurt, just held for ransom by some young men. At least it was a happy-ending. That was before your time. In fact, that is how I came to be in Ackers to begin with, and I loved this little town. So after we closed the case, Michael and I decided this was a nice place to live and raise a family."

She believed she had gotten a feel for John, and now she needed to continue with her own quiet investigation.

How long could a day be? The day seemed to go on endlessly. Johnnie knew she wasn't making the progress she wanted with her casebook; however, she did note some thoughts she had picked up while talking with John.

She remembered attending a banker's convention and hearing of Grammar's murder. Was there any possibility that the deaths of Herb and Grammar could be related even though the events were years apart? It was hard to tell. Most of the bankers at the convention heard of the case. Unfortunately, it all seemed like gossip and at the time did not interest Johnnie.

Johnnie decided that she needed to go home and concentrate on her notes. As she got into her car, Frank called to her. "Are you taking some time off? I was wondering how long you were going to try to carry all this on your shoulders."

Johnnie knew that Frank was being considerate, and she appreciated his concern. "I think I need to relax with a cup of tea, and let this sink in or maybe out of me." With that, she started the car, and she heard a strange noise coming from within the car. "Hey Frank, can you take a listen to this thing. It looks like I have car problems. Not exactly what I need today!" Frank was standing by her car. "I have to tell you, I am no good with cars. Let me call a service station for you, we can do it from the guardhouse." As they walked over to his outdoor post in the middle of the parking lot, there was a loud explosion and shattered glass was flying everywhere.

"What the hell!" The boldness of the perpetrator stunned Johnnie. Frank put Johnnie in the guardhouse, thus avoiding any fuel to the media circus they wanted to avoid.

Harrison was the first to reach Frank, "What happened?" Frank was as confused as Harrison. "I don't know! One minute Johnnie and I were talking, the next thing her car starts making funny noises, and we were going to call the service station, and then this happened."

Gary came out to see what happened. "Where's Johnnie?" Frank told him that she was in the guard building.

Gary immediately went over to the door of the small building, knocked on it, and then opened the door. Gary took charge, and walked her from the guard building into the bank, they returned to his office. Some of the exploding glass hit her, leaving some lacerations. Gary called Michael and told him to come to the bank as soon as possible.

Johnnie sat alone in Gary's office she was relieved that he closed the door. Harrison was the only one who dared to open the door. "You okay?" Johnnie smiled and told him she had just a few cuts and thanked him for asking. Then he closed the door and let her to her own thoughts. Detective Nichols was the first to arrive. Gary told her that Johnnie was in his office.

Terry knocked on the door and opened it to find Johnnie sitting back with her eyes closed. "You okay? Any idea of what happened?"

Johnnie opened her eyes. "I am not an alarmist, but I think it was a bomb. Not to kill me, but to scare me from doing any personal investigating I suppose."

"Just who did you tell you were doing your own investigation?" Johnnie thought that Terry's tone was harsh; nevertheless, she understood what it was like to work a case like this one.

"I don't know anyone who would bomb my car. I did talk to John Erickson today; however, we just kept it to comparing experiences sort of conversation. Nothing in the conversation that would arouse anyone's interest. I wanted to know how much experience he had with the FBI."

"Did his answers satisfy your questions or did they create new ones?" Terry remained in her role as detective. Regardless of the bond she and Johnnie were developing, she needed to do her job or they both could end up like Herb.

"Look Terry, I know you need to do a job here, and I am going to do what I have to do to protect the employees. The way I see it I can investigate this as well as the next FBI agent. However, I would rather work with you than the current FBI presence. If you don't want me to work with you, then I guess I will work it myself." Johnnie suddenly realized she was the harsh one in the room.

Terry sat down in the chair next to Johnnie. "It is not that I don't want you helping us investigate this matter; I know we can use all the help we can get. However, we get a report about an explosion at the bank, and I was scared to get the details. I thought maybe you..." She did not finish her sentence.

"I thank you for your concern, and I truly do appreciate your friendship. You know when I talked to John earlier today he mentioned he worked the Grammar Jonas case. I know a bit about that case. I was just leaving the agency when Grammar died. I never read his file or anything it was handled by another team. However, I remember the next year, at a banker's convention Grammar's death remained a hot topic. I mean it had been a while, but still it was the center of gossip at the conventions. Of course, Herb's presence was what started the talking. Most of the bankers at my mid-level management avoided him like the plague. But for others, I guess he did have a certain charisma."

Terry walked over to the window and said. "Michael just arrived; he is talking with Gary Percy." She waved from the window, and Michael waved back. "How about I walk you down to meet him?"

Johnnie gathered her things, and they started down the back steps. As they cleared the door, Terry told her she would like to come over to the house tonight if she thought she would be up to it this evening. Johnnie agreed that she would be fine, in actuality she had been in tougher spots in her law enforcement days.

Michael came over to Johnnie, embraced her like a bear and kissed her. "Are you okay? Do you know how lucky you are?"

"Look at the car Michael, the damage is all in the back. The fact that it did not start gave me a reason to get out before anything happened. It was not a death threat it was a warning. There may have been a delayed fuse. That would explain why it did not go off until Frank and I were clear. Of course, that would hint that whoever planted it was close and watching the bank. Think of it this way, now I have to get a new car. You have been after me to do so and now I guess I will."

Michael turned from looking at the car. "Okay, I see your point, but still, do you know how lucky you are? We are going to the hospital. I want you checked out and have those cuts attended. You are going to need some glue."

Johnnie did not want to go to the hospital. "I can handle the cuts myself. Just a bit of glue and I will be fine. I have it in my first-aid kit."

Michael was standing his ground on the issue of the emergency room. "You are going to the emergency room. End of discussion."

Terry watched the two argue about going to the emergency room. "As the police on site, I am agreeing with Michael. You really need to have yourself checked out. I am going to suggest that Frank go as well to be check. He has some nasty cuts that need attention."

Johnnie was trying to talk them out of her going to the hospital. "Terry you are coming over tonight and we can all have dinner together." This caused Terry to make a new suggestion. "How about we meet at Tomas'? We can have dinner after the emergency room, and I can expense it out."

Johnnie had been in many situations over the course of her career, but hospital visits always rated low on her list of favorites. She spent more energy trying to get out of going than just going and having it finished.

"That is very generous of you, but it is not necessary. However, we will have to get through the emergency room first." Michael really wanted to keep Johnnie out of the public's eye. He was very appreciative of Terry's offer of dinner at Tomas'.

"Yes, it is very necessary. So take her to have her glued and then home for some rest. We can meet at say eight. I will have Tomas hold a back dining room for us."

"You can do that? Just call him at the spur of the moment and get a special dining room?" Michael was surprised that such a well-rated restaurant would accommodate them with so little notice.

Terry explained. "Tomas' father was on the force years ago, so he is family so to speak."

Johnnie and Michael met Terry outside of the restaurant. "Wow, they did a great job with those cuts. I think it is funny that they now use glue instead of stitches. Tomas has the room set up, and we can enter through the kitchen so no one will see us."

Terry was right. Tomas himself met them at the kitchen door and took them to their dining room. He was going to wait on them so that everything was perfect, and they enjoyed their privacy. "This dining room looks like it is out of a movie set, it is beautiful." Johnnie knew the place was the best place in town and could even put the country clubs to shame, but this is more than she expected.

"Yes, Tomas keeps this room open for just such occasions. Now, I know you all want to know what is going on and why I didn't want to go to your place. We found a bug in your office Johnnie and we don't know how long it has been in place. It contains a code key; although we are hoping to break it without getting John Erickson involved. Maybe it will lead us to who killed Herb and why. It explains the attempt on Harrison's life. We are going to play it safe. While we are here, with your permission, I will have someone go over and sweep your house and make sure there are no bugs planted at your residence."

After Michael and Johnnie digested the news, they agreed to have someone go by the house. Michael said he could unlock the back door from his cell phone. However, he insisted that the house was clear. After all, security was his business, and he knew that he had used the latest in technology to secure his home. He wanted to change the topic. "Any idea what is good on the menu?"

Terry said there wasn't a bad thing on the menu, and that they can prepare a dish to order.

Johnnie's relief was obvious as she had so many food sensitivities. "I would love to have an order of wonderfully rich cheesy lasagna. Trouble is I can't eat onions or garlic, and most Italian restaurants use a lot of onions and garlic."

Terry smiled. "Tomas will make your dish to order. He will use the herbs and spices you want. He is an amazing chef. He normally keeps a base sauce ready for special orders anyway."

Michael asked for a menu. Terry told him just tell Tomas what you want, and he will see to it that you get exactly what you want. Michael thought about what he would like to eat since this was his chance to enjoy garlic and onions.

Tomas smiled at the group and said. "We are ready to serve everything from Calamari to Osso Buco or soup such as Italian Wedding Soup or Modenese Pork Chops. He told them to feel free to ask for anything. Additionally, the bread served is a delicious ciabatta and bunyaculta, which is a creamy garlic dipping sauce. It would be easier if you just named a dish and we will do our best to make it for you."

Terry could not help but grin. "See I told you he could provide just about anything."

Johnnie decided on an order of calamari and lasagna, while Michael ordered the Osso Buco. Terry said they made the best Carbonara, and that is what she wanted for the evening.

"I don't know how we will keep Mirah or John from finding out I am involved in the investigation. However, I think the longer we can keep them in the dark the better. I plan on checking with Noah and see what he can tell me about those two." Johnnie learned long ago to trust her instincts.

Terry's phone rang and they all drew a quick breath. Terry answered and by her body language, they were able to relax. She hung up the phone and relayed the details. "No listening devices, and your place was dusted in the most obvious places to see if anyone had searched your laptop. The house and the computer are clean, and yes, I gave instructions for them to clean up any trace of their work. However, I still want you both to have a detector. Before any conversations, check and make sure there are no bugs. I know I sound melodramatic, but I would rather be on the safe side. The bomb tells us that they think you are a threat."

"I'm the threat? Whose office did they ransack? Whose car did they detonate? Whose co-workers died? Yes, I am the threat. I am the threat you never want to deal with! And I am going to keep on being a threat. No one is going to scare me off my own case." Johnnie was adamant.

Michael looked at her "Your case? I think not."

Johnnie rolled her eyes, "I am not trying to be difficult, and I am not pushing you aside Terry; however, I can and I will help on this matter. Besides, you know I can handle myself. I will call Noah Drake. He has a couple things that we can use. Oh, Terry I need to let you know I plan to carry my gun. I am licensed in this state and my gun is registered, so it should be okay with the department."

Terry took the topic to the dinner they would soon be enjoying.

Tomas could not have been more helpful, bringing the meals himself. He said he wanted to provide them with all the privacy. Terry just smiled at the sounds of enjoyment from Johnnie and Michael. She knew they would all enjoy their dinner. Tomas was an excellent chef.

Terry decided they should make plans for other meetings; but maybe they should be at out of the way places, so they could talk of any progress that Johnnie made on her side of the investigation.

Tomas returned to the room. "Who would like dessert?" They all agreed that his desserts would be too wonderful to pass up. They ordered a variety of things, coconut custard pie, chocolate mousse, and Tiramisu. Tomas brought the desserts with extra plates and forks and a knife. "I have a feeling you will be sharing." Then he left them alone to their desserts and coffee.

Johnnie and Michael got back to the house and even with the coffee and desserts in them, they were exhausted enough to head for bed. "I can't remember when I was this weary." Johnnie muttered." "I don't know." Michael replied. "When was the last time someone tried to kill you." Johnnie just smiled, kissed him on the cheek, and headed for the bathroom.

"What are your plans for tomorrow?" She asked him. He said he had to be on the road for a meeting, but he should be home in time for dinner.

Michael, being a security consultant with several satellite offices, traveled from time to time to work with his various offices, but it just felt wrong to leave now.

"You will be careful." Johnnie shouted from the bathroom. He laughed and said yes, he would watch for bombs. "I am not kidding! If they want to stop me, they might go after you or even Josie."

Michael grinned, "You might be former FBI, but I am a former Navy Seal. As for Josie, we might want to have a friend happen by to keep her company."

"Yes, maybe we could get Pat Cates to visit for a while. He could keep an eye on her. I do believe she likes him. I would definitely feel better if there was someone looking out for her. Do you think Pat will be available? You know he seems to have a special interest in Josie, and I think she is interested in him as well."

Pat had been in Michael's Navy Seals unit, even though he was several years younger. He knew how to take charge of any situation. He also worked for the government, so he had resources.

Michael could tell how tired Johnnie was by her nightwear. Tonight would be her night for flannels. When she got tired, she was always cold. It was no surprise to him to see her dressed as if it were winter already.

When she finished up in the bathroom, she came into the bedroom to find him sitting in the chair with the evening's paper. "Looks like your car didn't make the news."

"That is fine by me. I would rather the event stay out of the news. It is a good thing that Frank is as protective as he is. He kept the news crews out of the way. He told them it was just a small car fire, nothing serious. He didn't let them get close to the car, and the explosion blew the license plate off of the car so they wouldn't have a way of checking ownership. The news people would go crazy with a bomb at the bank right now. Frank found the plate and he gave it to Terry when she came to the bank."

The two watched a little TV until Johnnie was no longer interested in the program. Michael turned down the lights, and he got ready for bed. He knew Johnnie needed the rest. Nevertheless, that didn't stop Johnnie from rolling over to face him, and start talking. She actually talked herself to sleep. He knew he would have to let her talk it out, or she would not get any sleep. He was right.

***

Johnnie felt better when she woke the next day, maybe because she decided to avoid the bank today. She called Gary to tell him she was not going to come in today and she wasn't sure about the following day.

She had to get a rental car and it probably would be good to be out of sight, out of mind. Then she called Terry and told her she was going to be available by cell phone.

Johnnie pulled out a project notebook and listed everything she knew about Herb. Unfortunately, it wasn't much. He was the executive vice president of the First National Bank of Ackers. How long had he worked for the bank? Who interviewed him and hired him? She could get access to his personnel file. Where did he work prior to the FNB? Again, the personnel file would be useful for this information as well. She knew he was divorced, and knew he had three children, twin girls, and one son. They stayed with their mother after the divorce. Did he have shared custody? Did he have supervised visitation rights? Details on the custody could reflect other problems.

She sat for a long while just staring at the paper. She had been at the bank for three years and her knowledge about the man was not much. She never recorded any thoughts on drug usage. If there was no evidence against the claim, then it stayed out of what she referred to as her casebook.

Johnnie knew Silva had been with the bank for five years. She had two sons. One was serving in Iraq and the other was in high school. She was married and divorced twice. As far as she knew, the divorces were not a problem. Johnnie knew the first marriage occurred when Silva was very young, too young to be married. The second one lasted about three years; but she did not know the reason for the divorce. She always figured that if an employee wanted her to know something, they would tell her.

Silva had been one of those nosy employees, and did her share of gossip, but why did they kill her? Did she see something that she didn't tell the police?

The fire starting after six in the morning and her due at the bank at six thirty, it all happened so fast. Her house had to be under watch to have happened as soon after Aces left for his swim practice. At least, she was thankful that whoever murdered Silva waited until Aces was gone.

She would have to call or maybe set up an appointment to see Terry. She wasn't a cop; she couldn't just show up at the station when she wanted. She also knew this was not the only case Terry was handling.

She then thought about Harrison. Using the same casebook as she did with Silva, she noted everything she knew about him. He came to the bank about the same time as Silva. He was manager of the customer service area. He seemed to like his work. He and Silva shared the same interest, mainly gossip. He visited Johnnie's office a lot to grab a few candies from her candy bowl, and ask about the happenings in the bank; something Johnnie would discourage him by just saying she did not know.

Then she started a new casebook on herself. She had to be honest about all the things she was involved in for a long time. For all she knew, this was something out of her past. During her time with the FBI, she was instrumental in arrests and convictions. She had to start from the beginning.

She went into the bureau after obtaining her Ph.D. in psychology with a minor in criminology. She actually was a licensed psychologist, but never set up a practice of her own, but she did work for three years with a hospital in DC. She acted as a counselor for hospital employees. So many times, particularly the ER personnel needed someone to talk with after a bad emergency case. The experience made her an excellent profiler. She did field work with the Behavior Analysis Unit, however, she was always talking to the forensic team, was excellent with firearms, and was as good as any man in physical combat. She continued to stay in shape. She and Michael would spar to maintain their skills. She was glad that she had such skills. Her training for the FBI never left her. Very few people knew of her degree, and she preferred it that way. Yes, psychology does help in any field, but with a Ph.D., some people are intimidated. She had to consider all the cases she was involved with to see if any could possibly come back to haunt her. She would have to call Noah. They always had a good working relationship and he was easy to talk with, probably because their backgrounds were so similar. She knew he would talk with her about the old caseloads. She made a note to call him but only after, she got her ducks in a row first.

She noted her date of employment at the bank, and listed her various positions. She loved the reconcilement department; she learned so much. When the processing manager position opened, she was pleased to have the job awarded to her. She loved doing research and making sure the bank was always in balance. She did well with paper trails and she often times would help with teller outages. Most of the time large outages traced back to the paperwork. Even the research project was nothing more than detailing a paper trail. She even liked the challenge of working with the banking software. In addition, she learned from the bottom up; but her rise to middle management was meteoric.

She put the casebook down. Her best bet was to use her PC Tablet with Excel and her tablet pen. She could then write in notes and the Excel program could put them in date order.

Now she felt like she could call Terry, and used a burner phone to leave a message on Terry's voice mail. Due to Michael's security agency, he had a few burner phones in the safe in case he needed to connect with a client or if a client needed to talk to him or his office. She remembered that when she called Terry earlier she said she would be available by cell; but failed to tell her it was a different number. She now had to call Terry to supply her with the number of the burner phone.

With all that done, she decided she needed to get out of the house for a while. She rarely went shopping; but today she was going to test her powers of observation. She would go to the mall, and just watch to see if she could detect anyone following her movements. She normally would call Josie to go along, but should there be anyone following her, she did not want to create a potential threat for Josie.

She didn't like having to carry her gun again. Nonetheless, she needed to error on the side of caution.

Johnnie wasn't one for carrying a purse or bag, but since she wanted her tablet with her, she had no choice today. The jacket also zipped in the front, which was a good way to keep her firearm concealed. She loved the new shirt holster; it was big enough to carry her Glock 23. This was virtually the same weapon as the FBI used, but not government issued. To play on the extra safe side, she carried a smaller gun in her purse. She also carried Detective Nichols cards with her both in her purse holster and in her shirt holster, along with a copy of her gun permit.

She was ready to go, but she first checked all the doors and windows. She even used a small piece of wire across the doorframes that would alert her if anyone entered. She checked her street looking for any cars that were different and parked along their street, and then she headed down and out to the garage through the mudroom.

Her first stop as always was the bookstore. She loved books and was always buying several. She loved going to the café within the bookstore to get a wonderful cup of honey latte. She also bought a magazine or two so that she could sit at the café and have her coffee and just people watch.

She knew what to watch for and kept her eyes roving over the people in the store. The thing she had to be most careful about was the potential tail from whoever bombed her car.

She sat in the café at one of the windows with her magazine in front of her and watched every person that passed within eyesight of her table. She noticed a woman with a shopping bag. She was muscular and wore her hair pulled back in a long ponytail. She wore a pair of knee-high boots and jeans. She also had a turtleneck sweater and a sleeveless vest. She walked past the café a few times. However, when she came into the café and got herself a cup of tea and a muffin, Johnnie lost interest in her for the moment.

She continued to watch the people mill around the store. She decided to move on, so she cleared her table and put her things back into her bag and started for the area with the cookbooks. She walked casually so she could still watch the crowds, then she spotted the woman from the café. She was following her, and now Johnnie had to lose the tail.

Johnnie lazily walked to the geology section then to the music and movie section, watching the entire time as she moved from area to area. Too many stops would alert the tail following her. Johnnie knew she was a rookie and she wondered if an additional observer was also watching. Johnnie did not see any sign of a second observer. She just wanted to be careful, and decided it was time to move to the front to be where there was more traffic. Any tail would be hesitant to do something openly; they would want to catch her at her car or moving to another store. The training never really left her, even if it had been awhile, procedures came flooding back to her. As the old saying goes, it is like riding a bike, you never really forget.

Johnnie returned to the café, ordered another honey latte, and sat back to watch. She took a window seat to watch the cars noting who was arriving and departing. She pulled out her laptop as a ruse, to disguise her purpose of sitting there. She wanted to appear to be just enjoying her latte.

She pulled up her casebook on herself and added to the information about her day of people watching. She did as much looking around as she could without giving away her true purpose.

It wasn't long before her thoughts proved valid. A young man came into the bookstore and approached the new release section. He immediately locked eyes with Johnnie. Any one sent to keep an eye on a mark would never make immediate eye contact. The young man wore jeans and a hoodie with a denim jacket over the top of the hoodie. She was certain he was there to observe her actions. This young individual was not at ease with his responsibility. He even came and sat down at the table next to her and started a conversation. He was either fumbling or he was in tuned to what was going on with her.

"Hi, I saw you with your laptop, wondered if you were a writer. You seemed so intent on writing at a feverish pace." The young man tried to bring her into the conversation. Johnnie looked over at him and smiled. "I have an article scheduled for the magazine I write for and it is due by the end of the week. So please excuse me, I really need to stay on top of this article."

The young man smiled, excused himself, got up, and walked back to the newly released area near the café. He picked up a book and glanced through it while facing Johnnie's direction. Johnnie could not help but think to herself that good help was hard to get these days. This person was not FBI; these had to be private employees. Professionals were far more careful about their tailing.

She knew it was okay to go ahead and leave. She would return home by the main roads. She did not know why they were following her, but it was not the time to travel back roads.

Johnnie walked to her car full of confidence, prepared to play cat and mouse. As she pulled her rental car out to the road, an oversized Hummer came screaming around the bend. Johnnie had to slam the breaks to keep from hitting the monster vehicle. The driver looked directly at her. Logan Ferns, his activities have always interested the police. This was trouble and she knew it could be very dangerous. She thought he had to be behind all this activity. She knew enough of Logan's reputation that she did not want to be caught anywhere in a quiet spot with him in the picture. She definitely was not heading home. It made no sense to invite trouble. This was going to call for a quick change of plans, on the spot thinking. She would get her nails done at the salon just a few blocks from where she was now. It would help relieve some tension, and it would give Michael time to get home and her time to think about what she wanted to do next. Why Logan, she expected the threat to come from Andropov? Now who could she trust, John Erickson and Mirah Anderson? This would take more investigating, but for now, she would stay close to people.

She was armed, and she was good at hand to hand; nevertheless, she didn't want to invite trouble. She had to stay in control and if that meant staying in a public place longer then she would do just that until the potential threat was resolved. These were not the bureau days where she worked with a team, and she had others who knew the plan.

Since she needed to drive this rental, it was possible they would not recognize the vehicle she was driving. Still she wished she had her station wagon. Since the bomb damaged her car, she was stuck with this rental, and had no idea of its pick up power.

Parking in the lot at the salon kept Logan's people from following her. That didn't indicate he had given up on watching her, it just meant he wasn't the only one doing the watching. He had his guys also watching. Johnnie needed to be vigilant, watching everyone she came into contact with that she didn't already know. Unfortunately, she did not know many of this town's residents. She was attentive to every motion around her.

Once inside she asked if Lotus had an opening to do her nails. She was in luck Lotus did have an opening if she didn't mind waiting a while. This was as good a place to wait. Logan would not come in here so she felt herself slipping into a comfort level. She asked for some quiet time to rest until her appointment time. She sat back in the small private room for relaxation; the reclining contour chair and soft music were so relaxing and she started to drift off. That is when she realized that she needed to lock the door. Since she knew the owner from her previous salon, she just called her on her cell. Johnnie told her she had a bit of a hard week and would like to lock the door to the relaxation room, and asked Stella not to tell anyone she was in the room, but Lotus.

She locked the door and returned to the recliner to lie back relaxing while listening to the quiet music and nature sounds. Someone knocked on the door and woke her from a wonderful nap. She listened for someone to identify who they were, and when Lotus asked if she was ready, she responded that she was and would be right over to the nail room.

Johnnie opened the door to find the woman from the bookstore standing in front of her waiting. Johnnie could not believe she had slipped up so easily. How did this woman know where to find her? How did she entice Lotus into calling her?

"We are going to walk down the steps, and I will be helping you along. You will tell the girls at the desk that you don't feel well, and that you called me to come and pick you up. Do you understand? Don't try to reach for your gun under your jacket, and I will take your purse." Johnnie was angry with herself and wondered if Michael would ever know what had happened to her.

Outside Johnnie tried to free herself from the woman's hold but to no avail. She was holding tight until she walked Johnnie to her car.

"Allow me to introduce myself, my name is Jasmine West."

Johnnie was still frustrated and surprised that this woman could find her. "What? Am I supposed to know my kidnapper?"

Jasmine laughed. "No, but you might want to know one of your husband's employees."

"Are you saying Michael put you on my tail?" Johnnie could not believe that Michael would put a watchdog on her.

Jasmine suggested they get into Johnnie's car. "You would have never known I was there, but I saw one of Logan's men approach you in the bookstore, then to see the near miss with Logan, that was a good thought to come to the salon. Sorry you were not able to get your nails done."

"Okay, you say you are with Michael's company. Then you have to know that I spotted you in the bookstore, and I knew the man that approached me was also watching me. What I want to know is just how did you find me here at the salon?"

"That was the easy part; Michael arranged for a bug to be planted on your rental. It has been in place since you picked it up from the lot."

"I am going to strangle him when he gets home tonight." Johnnie blurted.

"Actually, he is home, and I think he will want a report on how today went. Don't take this personally, I am in training. He said the day would be easy because it was a simple surveillance." Jasmine tried to explain.

"If that is the case why show up here?" Johnnie was very confused.

Jasmine explained, "I moved to the other side of the bookrack where the young man was standing. Then Logan came in the store. He was talking to the man and told him to find you and finish it. That is when I went from trainee to abductor."

Johnnie had to laugh, although just to be safe, she wanted to see Jasmine's identification and then she said she was calling Michael. She told Jasmine the one who assumes is usually doomed.

"Where did you pick up that little jingle?" Johnnie laughed and said, "Criminology classes."

Michael answered his phone. Johnnie didn't know to be angry, or just laugh. "So you think I need a babysitter?"

Michael was puzzled, "What happened that Jasmine had to give herself away?" Johnnie asked if he was home, and he confirmed he was; so she said she would be there in about 20 minutes.

"Do you want to ride with me since you are already in the car?" Johnnie asked.

"That would probably be best. Logan's people will be looking for you alone. Having a second person in the car will only help to confuse them." Jasmine smiled and Johnnie grinned and agreed.

Johnnie and Jasmine walked in the front door. "Honey we're home." Michael answered "We, who's with you?" Johnnie was being playful. "I'll give you a guess."

Michael came around the corner. "Jasmine! You were supposed to watch her, not come home for supper."

"Don't be fussing with her, it is me that should be fussing with you." Johnnie loved that he cared and wanted to protect her; but she objected to him taking action, she was capable of taking care of herself and he knew it to be true.

Johnnie said they should sit down in the family room and just spend some time discussing this afternoon's events.

After getting everyone a glass of lemonade, Johnnie ran upstairs to change her clothes. She came back down in her favorite running suit. "Okay Jasmine, explain to Michael why you followed me to the salon, and yes I know about the bug. That being said, please remove the devise.

Jasmine related the comment she overheard in the bookstore and how she thought it was time to step in and get Johnnie out of potential danger. She knew that Johnnie was armed, but she also knew it was going to be at least two against one.

Johnnie looked at Michael and said, "I spotted Jasmine following me. I figured the man who approached me in the café was definitely watching me, too. Then I saw Logan, well more like almost crashed into Logan. I knew I needed to go somewhere they would not think to look. Since going to get my nails done was a Monday evening event, if they knew my schedule, they would not think to go to the spa."

"How did you figure out Jasmine was on your trail?" Michael looked at his trainee. Jasmine spoke up too. "How did you catch on to me?"

Johnnie smiled and answered. "How many ladies like the geology section as much as I do? Besides, you followed me from the cookbook area, to the music section then back to the café! I have to say, after seeing Logan nearly smash my car I thought you were working for him. That is why I probably turned pale when you appeared in the salon."

Now Michael had questions. "Why did you ask Jasmine to ride with you instead of driving her own vehicle?"

"That part was somewhat of a guess. I figured Logan might be looking for cars that were familiar. Meaning if he saw you driving a car that was at the bookstore, he might try to eliminate you. Michael, I am guessing Jasmine's vehicle is a company car. I suggest you park it for a while and not let anyone use it. Logan just might think he had competition in the reconnaissance business."

Johnnie thought that now was a good time to discuss the happenings of recent days. She pulled out her casebooks. She explained that she spent some time on them that morning, starting with Herb's death and his body in her office. She was convinced Grammar Jonas' death had a connection to Herb's murder. They had to be involved in some nefarious activity that got them both killed. She did not know if it involved banking, her research she was working on, or something different. If it was the banking, then that meant both the Mother Company and her bank could be involved since Grammar worked for the mother company. If it was something unrelated to the bank, she had no idea other than the potential of it being drugs. They all three got involved with the discussion, but Johnnie did not divulge what her project was at the bank. Being a banker meant keeping information confidential. She had been given an 'eyes only' order.

Soon they were all hearing their stomachs talking to them and decided to order a pizza.

When the pizza came, they took their notes and sat at the kitchen table. They continued to talk as they ate the pizza and had a beer. While Johnnie was not much of a drinker, she decided today was one of those days when a beer just might be good, besides pizza almost demands beer.

They tossed around different possibilities. They went through all the details about Herb, Silva, and even Harrison. How did all three become victims?

Johnnie spoke up. "I hate the idea that my office was bugged. Harrison was in asking questions about what I thought of Silva's death. I told him I couldn't even begin to understand and was too shaken up about it to talk. The next thing you know somebody tries to run him off the road.

Johnnie was exhausted the three of them had been at this for hours. Johnnie suggested that maybe Jasmine should spend the night. She thought it would be better in case Logan's people were somehow on to Jasmine. She was too tired to think anymore and wanted to go to bed.

They agreed that it was probably better, and Johnnie took Jasmine up to the guestroom. Since it had its own bath she would be comfortable there. Johnnie always kept extra toothbrushes, shampoo, and nightclothes so Jasmine could at least get ready for bed and freshen up in the morning.

***

Morning came quickly, Johnnie made breakfast, and Jasmine helped in the kitchen. Michael sat at the kitchen table reading the newspaper. Michael normally did the cooking but today was an exception.

After breakfast, just before Michael was preparing to take Jasmine home, they heard on the news that a car in the parking lot of Stella's Spa caught fire. They did not have immediate details, and no one had come forward to claim the car. Now, Johnnie did not want Jasmine to go home just yet.

"Michael, we can't let her go home now.

To error on the side of caution, Johnnie called Terry and asked her to come over to the house.

Terry came as quickly as she could. "So you want to tell me everything that happened so I can keep current with you?"

Michael was the first to speak up. "I had Jasmine follow my wife. It was more for training purposes for Jasmine. I know Johnnie is a good field agent, and I know she can look out for herself, so I thought this would be an easy assignment."

Terry looked to Jasmine. "I suppose you are Jasmine. What can you tell me about your training?"

Jasmine admitted it did not go as well as it should have; but the result was a blessing. She explained Johnnie was on to her, and she thought she would stay around the bookstore a bit longer. She saw Logan Ferns practically crash into Johnnie, and she watched where he went after the near miss. By that time, she had already positioned herself on the other side of the bookrack. When he came into the bookstore and started talking to the man who had attempted to engage Johnnie in conversation, she knew it was not good. That was when she heard Logan tell the other man to take care of Johnnie. She made her purchase and left. Michael had a locator in Johnnie's rental car, and she followed her to Stella's and had her nail girl tell her she was ready for her, to get Johnnie to come out of the secured room. From there they left the salon and came back to the house, deserting Jasmine's car in the salon's parking lot for a pick up later.

Johnnie spoke at this moment. "We aren't sure if it was the car Jasmine drove or not; but we decided to play it safe and call you."

"So nice of you to let me know of your adventures. You do understand, I am a cop, right, and I am on your side." Terry was not happy with what had transpired. She did agree to call the office and ask about the car. She got the license number of the vehicle and asked Michael if it was from his fleet. Michael admitted that the car was from his fleet after checking his computer. He decided that he would take Jasmine to the office to get her personal car and suggested she take some time off to visit some relatives. He said he would keep her on payroll and cover her travel expense, but that she needed to book a flight immediately.

Jasmine called her sister Chloe, who lived in Philadelphia and said she would be coming for a visit of indefinite time.

Michael and Jasmine left. Jasmine made reservations from her phone and got the next flight to Philly, which was not easy in these days of post 9/11. Michael went into Jasmine's apartment as she gathered her things and put them in her suitcase and a carry on. He secured her apartment making sure all accesses were impenetrable; then he took her to the airport. He took her to the security checkpoint and from there she was on her own. He doubted that Logan had figured out who she was and where she would go.

Terry and Johnnie remained at the house to finish their coffee. "While you are here Terry, I need to ask you something. I believe my office has a bug again. Can you come by some time and quietly check it out? I don't want anyone else to know about it. I am not comfortable, telling Mirah and John if you find a bug. It could be their bug, or it could be Logan's work. What I don't understand is how they keep getting into my office with all the activity and police presence. Harrison had been in my office earlier in the day before the attempt to run him off the road. Someone knew he was asking questions. Maybe he knows more about things than he should. He and Silva were friends, and he seemed stressed about her death. Of course, everyone was upset about what happened, but it was more than just upset. He actually looked scared."

Terry asked a surprising question. "Do you trust Harrison? It would not be the first time that a co-conspirator had an accident to cement their innocence."

"I guess anything is possible, but I honestly think he is truly concerned. He could be involved with Logan and trying to pump for any information I might know. However, if you saw how pale and fidgety he was, but I guess that could all be an act. Heavens, it is all the bank needs is a twist like that. We would certainly lose creditability in the public's eye. Maybe Michael can run a background check on him. Better yet, I can have an old friend from the FBI do the search. I would imagine that with John Erickson in the bank, they have already done searches. So I can get Noah to share what has been searched."

"I hate the idea of Harrison being entangled." Johnnie knew without proof, they could not make a move against him. It was going to be necessary to ask Noah for help.

Terry and Johnnie waited for Michael's return. It seemed like it was taking him forever to get back from taking Jasmine to the airport.

Johnnie was watching out the kitchen window. "I will feel better when Michael gets back, but you don't have to stay Terry."

Terry explained she could not stay. She had to find a gift for her Uncle Joe, who was turning 70. "What do you buy for the person who wants nothing and needs less?" She asked. She said she needed just an hour or so, but she could come back.

Johnnie insisted she would be safe in her own house. Besides, it would give her some quiet time to check out some online details she needed to put together for the casebooks.

Terry told her to secure the house after she left and call 911 if anything out of the ordinary happened.

Johnnie took a cup of tea with her upstairs to the study. She loved this room. It had large windows that let in great light. She had several plants in the room, and her computer was near a window. The room had cherry wood bookcases on every wall, and she had them filled. Johnnie could never discard the books she read. The room was a nice size with a cream and mauve large area wool rug in the center.

She settled down and started her online research. She wanted to do a check on Grammar Jonas and see if she could find any ties to Victor Andropov or Herb. She scanned the photos of various society events where she found a picture of Herb and Grammar with each other at a charity event sponsored by the mother company. It was not a surprise to see them with each other. Bankers mingle at these varying events. She needed something more, so she kept looking. If there was anything else, maybe she could find it in business licenses issued. Not that Victor's name would be out in the open but one of his companies could be in an article involving both Herb and Grammar.

One of the many benefits of owning a security service was that Johnnie and Michael's house always had the latest security toys. They had cameras situated so that all entrances were covered. While Johnnie worked away on the computer, she would occasionally check the security monitor built inside the desk. She never worried about intruders before, but things had changed and she knew she needed to be vigilant.

As she glanced over to the monitor, she observed two men approaching the back door. One was the man from the bookstore. She continued to watch to see if they were going to attempt to enter the house. As they neared the door, she saw the gun in one of the men's hand. Time to take cover, she thought.

She gathered her casebooks and her laptop and turned off the monitor for the security system. She then walked over to the bookcase that butted up next to the fireplace. Pushing the third brick from the left on the fireplace, the bookcase popped open. She could take everything inside, including her tea. Once inside there was a closing trigger. She settled into the room that was sound proof with specially padded walls, floor and ceiling. She had never actually used the safe room before, but it did give her a great sense of command in this situation.

The safe room also had the ability of Wi-Fi, and phone activation as well as another monitor for the security system. Sitting at the desk in her secured area she watched as the men moved through the house. They were not necessarily destructive, but they were not careful either.

When they started up the steps, she placed a call to Michael. She told him that she was in the safe room and was watching as the man from the bookstore and another man progressed through the house.

Michael wanted to know if she could tell what they were looking for in the house. She told him her guess would be anything that she or he might have collected on Logan. The funny part was she was not sure about Logan until yesterday at the bookstore. Now she was going to make it her business to find out everything she could about Logan Ferns.

After the call to Michael, she contacted Terry and told her what was going on, and that she need not worry, as she was as safe as a babe in its mother's arms. Terry did not have to return, but she would like Terry to send over some crime scene techs and check for fingerprints.

"Where are you that you know they are still in the house? Are you sure you are safe?" Terry was concerned for this enigmatic lady who she admired.

"I am in the safe room. Our house is always the guinea pig when it comes to Michael testing new equipment. I probably won't complain about it anymore after today. It never occurred to me that we would actually need this room."

Johnnie sat and watched the two men rummage through their belongings. She was definitely glad that the security monitor resembled a leather insert on the desk, and the cameras in the room were well camouflaged. There was no way of them knowing they had become film stars. Johnnie admitted to herself, this was fun!

The man from the bookstore made a comment to his partner. "Where do you think she would keep records of her work, or even of that guy's death? There isn't anything here but household bills and books. Hey, wait a minute. Did Logan say anything to you about this broad being former FBI?"

Johnnie leaned in closer to her security monitor. She was glad this was all recording. "Hell no, he never said nothing. Do you think he knows?"

His partner said. "I don't know; but we are out of here now!"

Both invaders took off out of the study and down the steps. They were in such a hurry; they didn't even notice Terry's car pulling into the driveway. Before she could get out of the car, they ran through the backyard and over the fence. She could hear the car start up and speed away.

With the outdoor camera, Johnnie saw Terry's car arrive. The camera mounted on the back of the house's cable captured the license plate of the intruder's vehicle, as they left.

Johnnie released the lock from inside the security room and shut the door as she exited her safe cocoon. She went downstairs to meet up with Terry and her partner. Johnnie could not remember his name. She had mainly worked with Terry and realized she had not yet met her partner.

Terry came to the door as back up arrived. Johnnie greeted the two detectives, and they went into the kitchen and on through the mudroom, so she could see the point of entry. "So you say you saw them coming, and you still stayed in the house?" Murph remained silent up to this point.

Johnnie again explained the safe room. She would have volunteered to take them upstairs to show them the workings of the security system, but she found herself not as comfortable showing Terry's partner the space. She just really felt better dealing with Terry alone.

Terry was supposed to be shopping for her Uncle Joe. How did she get here with her partner? "I thought you had shopping to do today?" Terry replied that she decided on a gift card to a bookstore. Her uncle loved Civil War stuff, maybe they had a book he had not already purchased. "Like I said, what to you get for someone who wants nothing and needs less?"

She approached Terry's partner and said she was sorry that she did not remember ever meeting him. He introduced himself. "Hi,

I am Terry's partner, Murphy O'Shea, just call me Murph." Murphy O'Shea how anyone could forget that name, but those early days seemed to be such a blur. "I am sorry Murph that I have such a bad memory of that day." Murphy was a complete gentleman in his response. "You don't remember me, because we thought it better for you to work with Terry, and I would work the scene."

Terry spoke up. "Did you see them touch anything that might render a print?"

Johnnie laughed. "They were touching just about everything in the study. They must not have a record, or they are not well versed in how to do a search. No gloves. I have to think, it is a case of no record, and they were amateurs."

"Look, the best way for me to provide you with all the information, is to let you have a copy of the DVD of the entire episode. Then you will have all the answers you need. I will also be recording the event in my casebook. We know that Logan is somehow connected to at least this break in, so I plan on continuing my search for a connection between him and Herb." Johnnie was glad to have the recording, and this would provide evidence that they could use later.

"I was wondering if you would consider taking up police work again, I know you are doing your own investigation; but maybe it is time to remind people of your abilities. I think you have the inside track being at the bank already. No need for undercover work that your bosses might be opposed to; but I think it is important enough for you to get back in the game. Too many things have happened, and I don't want to see another accident or murder." Terry suggested.

"For the time being, I think we will keep this from Mirah and John. I still do not know why those two arrived so quickly. I could understand an FBI presence being here if there was a suspicion of a financial miss handling, but why the state's attorney general?"

***

As Terry and Johnnie were talking, Michael pulled up to the scene of multiple police cars in the driveway.

"What the hell?" Michael slammed the car into park and exited the vehicle without closing the door. "Johnnie! Johnnie! Are you okay?"

"I am fine I was in the safe room. It would seem that Logan sent a few of his youngsters looking for information that I might have collected on Herb."

"Hey, is everyone okay in here?" Pat Cates walked in the front door. "I had to close your car door Michael. Were you in a hurry or something?"

Johnnie smiled at Pat, he was a good friend and her niece Josie had a bit of a thing for him.

"Johnnie, I wanted to talk to you and the authorities about the little I could find out concerning Mirah Anderson. From the limited information I could pick up, she is not a Washington favorite. She is well known, just not well liked."

Johnnie sat down at the kitchen table and Pat sat down across from her. Johnnie just shook her head. "That isn't a surprise. What do you know about John Erickson and why he travels with Mirah?"

"Strangely no one is talking about John. They seem to be ignoring him for some reason. I do not understand it myself. Normally I can pick up rumblings and details; but not on this one. Have you called Noah?"

"I had planned to call him tomorrow, but so many things happened today, I would like to talk to him tonight. I hate to bother him at home. Then again, I do not want this to be official, so maybe home is best. I can talk to Pam that way too."

Michael brought Pat a cup of coffee as he added to the conversation. "Johnnie, its not like you are a stranger to him. Besides him being your old section chief, he married your best friend and roommate from college. I think he would welcome your call."

Pat continued his comments. "He may know something about John Erickson. Heck for all I know John just drew the short straw, or those two have a thing, or well, who knows. All I was able to determine was that Mirah finds every camera near her, and she takes every opportunity to be at the big events within the Washington circles. I suggest you call Noah."

Through all these exchanges, Terry and Murph were sitting at the kitchen table just listening. Terry spoke up. "Hi, I am Terry Nichols, homicide detective and this is Murph O'Shea my partner. Can I ask how is it that you have your finger on the pulse of the DC crowd?"

"Sorry, I should have introduced myself, but our entry today was not our normal social interaction. I could say I work with the Department of Defense, and as such I am required to attend many of the same events Mirah attends." Pat took a sip of his coffee before he continued with his explanation. "A lot of what I do with the DOD is somewhat, well let's just say not everyone knows what I do at the DOD. I also have some dealings with Homeland Security."

Terry looked at Michael. "Is that how you know Michael? He told me of the information he sometimes provides to Homeland Security."

"No, Michael and I have a history from before our current contact. This ole guy was my commanding officer in the Seals."

Michael laughed. "He thinks that because there are four years between us, he can call me the ole man."

Murph spoke up at this point. "So Michael you supply information to the DOD or Homeland Security?"

"Actually, I have a backdoor connection to both agencies, but as I told Terry earlier, that is not something we discuss in open conversation." Michael was looking at Murph with intense eye contact.

"Believe me, I understand. Before joining the Ackers police department, I spent time with the National Reconnaissance Office. It has been awhile, but I believe in protecting my country and the freedom of our citizens. You have nothing to fear from me divulging anything of a delicate nature, or any of your involvements with any other agencies. You never know when you might come across information that could be very vital. However, to be totally honest, I never thought Ackers would be a place of interest to an element such as may be in our fair community." Murph wanted everyone to know the information was safe with him.

Johnnie spoke up. "With all the experiences we have had with specialty law enforcement or agencies, I think we are in safe company." Knowing whom to trust is important in any form of law enforcement. Trusting the wrong people could cost you your life.

"Well I would like to drop the topic of security agencies. Josie is coming over and I would rather Josie didn't know everything that I get involved in with the government." Pat was looking at Johnnie.

"I agree, Josie has not been involved in any intelligence work other than being office manager for Michael, so it is better we drop the discussions along such lines." Johnnie was delighted that her niece would be coming over.

"I think maybe I would rather she not see all the techs, are they close to wrapping up?" Johnnie always wanted to protect Josie. "Terry, Murph, would you guys like to go to dinner with us? I think an evening away from all this talk would be nice for all involved. Or do you two have to work tonight?"

"Sounds good to me, Paige and I seldom get a chance to go out for eats." Murph was on his cell calling his wife.

"How about I call Will Hastings? We have been dating for some time and I think he would enjoy meeting all of you. He is on the force, you might remember him; he is the desk sergeant. He took a bullet and it has caused some minor problems. But he doesn't want to endanger any partner assigned to him, so he has opted for a desk job."

Terry and Murph had covered just about everything they could for the time being. So, they were going to return to the station and wrap up for the day. The plan was to meet back at Johnnie and Michael's within the hour.

Johnnie stepped away to make a copy of the DVD of the break-in. She knew Terry wanted their report.

Josie walked in the door, and put her purse and coat on the love seat in the foyer. She walked on to the kitchen. "Hello. Why is there a police car pulling away? It might be unmarked, but I could still see the light that they use when necessary on the inside."

"That was Terry and Murph. They are the police working with your aunt on the murders at the bank. You know how she is; she just can't sit on the sidelines. You will get a chance to meet Murph O'Shea. Murph and his wife are joining us for dinner tonight. Terry and her gentleman friend Will Hastings will join us as well." Michael knew that Johnnie did not want Josie to know about the visitors they had earlier. Johnnie would tell her in her own time.

She would have to tell Josie eventually about the break-in and the incident with the car, actually both cars, but not tonight. Johnnie returned to the kitchen and saw Josie. "Hey, Sweetheart, how was your day?"

"I had a simply boring day. I just worked on cleaning out closets. Doesn't that sound exciting?" She laughed.

Pat walked over to her and gave her a hug and kiss. "Depends, who do you keep in your closet?" Pat had a way of making her turn a dozen shades of red.

"Pat, do you have to embarrass her like that?" Johnnie was smiling as she made the remark.

"Sorry, it is the only way I know how to embarrass her." Turning to Josie and taking her hand, he squeezed it. "Besides, I don't think she really minds."

Josie by now had turned several shades of red. "Aunt Johnnie, I hear we have two new couples joining our crowd. Uncle Michael told me you are working with them on the bank thing."

"Yes, Terry and her partner Murph are working the cases of Herb and Silva. I think you will like them both. Both have been great to work with on this case."

Michael laughed. "Your aunt will pick the restaurant, and as if you don't know, it will be the roadhouse."

"No surprised there." Josie winked at her aunt.

"Before we go, I want to put in a call to Noah. I want to see if he can check out Erickson and if Erickson has done any checking up on of his own." Johnnie was off to the family room to make the call.

The voice at the other end was not that of Noah, it was his wife. "Hi Pam, how are you? Haven't heard your voice in a long time. Miss you gal."

"Johnnie King, what are you up to? I heard you liked that little town so much that you moved there after you left the bureau."

"Well, this is supposed to be a nice little town, but lately I am thinking it belongs in a soap opera. You would not believe all the things that can happen in a small town. Eventually I will need to talk to Noah, but tell me what happening with you and Noah."

The two women talked for a few minutes before Pam turned the phone over to Noah.

"Hey girl, what are you doing to that little town? Read in the paper you had some trouble."

"I guess you could call it trouble if finding a dead body in my office is considered trouble, then yes. I am up to my eyeballs in alligators. What do you know about John Erickson?"

"Can't say as I know anything about him, should I?"

"He is an agent with the bureau. For some strange reason he travels with Mirah Anderson, the West Virginia AG. Is there any reason why an agent would be traveling with a state official? I would have thought the state police would offer protection, not the FBI. Would you be able to check him out on the QT for me?"

"Yes, I could do that, but since I have you on the phone what is all the rest of this stuff I am hearing about Ackers? There was another death from what I read." Noah was genuinely concerned.

"It is okay. I promise to tell you all I can when you call me with what you find out about Erickson. Right now I have a hungry tribe waiting on me to go to dinner." Johnnie was avoiding voicing anything until she had the chance to tell Josie what had been happening. Besides, she didn't want to talk about it on the phone.

"Anything else you need? When are we going to get together? We really should do it over the holidays at least. I know they are still off always. Honestly, Ackers isn't that far from Quantico." Noah did miss Johnnie and Michael they had become good friends over the years.

"No to answer your first question, John Erickson is who I am most interested in at the moment. Well yeah, there is one more thing, could you check to see if he has checked out anyone himself. I just find the situation very odd. I can't ever remember having heard of an agent assigned to a public official. It has me wondering." Johnnie could be honest with Noah.

***

Terry and Will arrived at the same time as Murph and Paige. They all piled in the minivan that Johnnie and Michael drove on trips. It allowed them to carry all sorts of things with them, but tonight it served as a friendly bus.

All eight of them agreed on one of those steakhouses where they had pails of peanuts on the table per Johnnie's suggestion. They even had a table for all eight in a quiet corner separated from the other diners.

As to be expected, the laughing and joy of just being free of the stress was a major lift to all. Johnnie ordered her favorite dish, ribs, baked potato, and a salad no onions. She never varied.

Pat never understood why she would go out to dinner when she got the same thing all the time, and with her and Michael's cooking abilities, no doubt, they could make the identical dish at home. Pat never let a chance to tease her pass him by. "So I see you still are entree challenged. Have you ever ordered anything else when you come here?"

"I don't think I want any surprise today. I have had enough to last a lifetime. Besides, I happen to like this particular dish."

"How did you ever become so flexible in your jobs when you are so rigid in your food choices?" Pat continued to tease her.

"To begin with, I love change; but I do have food allergies and I have to be careful. I stick to my favorites because I know they are safe for me to eat. Although I ordered a BLT at one restaurant, and they put an onion on the sandwich. Onions and I do not get along. That's why I ordered a BLT, not a BOLT!" Everyone laughed.

The evening continued with conversations of getting to know everyone. It was nice to know something about the person who had been working on the bank's situation with her. Johnnie found out that Terry and Will as well as Murph and Paige were all Catholic. Pat spoke up. "Is this where we say we don't discuss religion or politics? Except it looks like we are all in the same boat."

"So, Johnnie, Terry tells me you were an FBI agent. What is your story on the bureau?" Will was very inquisitive.

"I don't know that I have a story. Sometimes I miss the life. Recently, I miss the quiet of a running gun battle. Who would have thought banking could be so dangerous? I guess I should not joke about it; but yes, I do miss some parts. I did like the profiling, but life goes on, and we adapt."

Will still seemed to push the topic "So maybe someday you would go back?"

"Right now I just want to get through this ordeal." Johnnie smiled.

The dinners came, and everyone enjoyed the meal. Soon the topics drifted to police and security matters.

"Michael, do you use your house for testing all your security measures?" Terry was interested in the safe room.

"Well, it is helpful to know how each addition can be used when clients ask. You would be surprised how many people nationwide have similar rooms. Since 9/11, I have limited our work to the US. With today's possibility of terrorists, I just think it is easier to deal with people who are inside the country."

"Does that mean you check out your clients?" Terry asked.

"I do. I don't want my company working with an element that could be on some watch list. Our work has taken on a new complexion since 9/11; we just exercise caution. It is the prudent thing to do."

Michael mentioned some of the unique features that his company offered in a secured area. "Believe it or not, people in tornado alley want such a room; but they want it built to protect them from storms. With the storm structures, I really prefer to put them underground, but that isn't always an option. If we can work with the builder, it makes the entire process much easier. Meaning we can plan an access from within the house. Do you know how many people go outside in dangerous conditions to get to safety? We have retrofitted a few houses even afterwards, but it is not always possible."

The evening went along rather well, and it felt great to put the problems of the bank out of their minds for a while. Even if there were discussions about police work, it wasn't concentrated on the bank and the recent murders.

"Did any of you hear that Mirah is looking to make her way to US Attorney General? I thought she was doing a decent job and was satisfied in her current position. However, I am not privy to the politics at that level." Terry's comments apparently were not common knowledge among the group.

Michael looked to Pat. What do you hear in the Washington circles?"

Johnnie spoke up saying, "Pat you have already said that Mirah wasn't well received in some circles? Perhaps she ruffled someone's feathers in Washington. Maybe she was investigating someone up the food chain, but I don't know how that would lead to her interest in Herb's death. Does she think this case will be a feather in her cap? Maybe this drug thing is bigger than we know."

Paige spoke up for the first time since their introduction to everyone. "I don't know much about this lady; but at work I have heard she is a real bear to work with. She likes the camera, and the credit for every case solved; but rarely works on anything helpful."

Terry grinned. "You got that right. We are doing our best to avoid her whenever we can. Refresh my memory, where do you work?"

Paige said that she worked for a group of lawyers and none of them really appreciated Mirah.

Johnnie spoke somewhat in an absent mind sort of way. "From what I encountered, John seems like a nice guy; nevertheless, the reason for him being with Mirah is bothersome. I would like to find out what the story is on that front. I never heard of a federal agent assigned to a state official."

Pat commented on potential theories. "She has been taking on some high crime characters. Maybe Ferns or Andropov were the reasons for his presence, still she could have had a state police detail. Besides, in the big picture Logan and Victor are not exactly the biggest game in the field."

Johnnie was not so sure. "If Sebastian Osis is working for Victor Andropov, I would think he could be someone to consider."

Paige was feeling more comfortable with the group and spoke up again. "I have heard some unpleasant things regarding Sebastian Osis; but Victor Andropov doesn't ring any bells."

Terry commented. "The story is that Sebastian Osis is a hit man of the worse kind. We don't know about Victor Andropov. He apparently is an extremely private person with his own bodyguard, enter Sebastian Osis."

Changing topics Murph asked Johnnie if she enjoyed the change to a small town.

Johnnie thought for a moment before she answered. "I cannot deny, working with the bureau was exciting, but strangely enough working at the bank in the last week has turned out to be a test as well. I know you have heard about the body that was found in my office. Things like that don't stay quiet in a small town." Johnnie was slowly building up her nerve for the rest of the comments. "I did have a problem with my car having caught fire in the parking lot. Didn't seem too serious, but then I found myself being followed the other day."

Michael chimed into the conversation. "Now I know I will finally be rid of that old station wagon and get something more modern. That thing had power steering; okay I will give you that, but an 'eight track'. It is a wonder it was still in operation, I swear it must have been 16 years old."

Johnnie was aware of Josie watching her. "Didn't I tell you about the fire? It is no big deal, but I had to get a rental, which your uncle thought it would be fun to put a tracking device in the car without my knowledge. Worse than that, he assigned a tail to me!"

Michael told Josie there was another reason for assigning this particular person to tail your aunt. "You know her, the new hire in the office. Her name is Jasmine. She needed some field experience, so I had her tail your aunt."

"Okay, now you tell her the rest of the story." Michael knew he was putting Johnnie on the spot, but he was going to get it all out of her for Josie's sake.

"I had already left the store; but came face to face with a party of interest in the death of Herb. Well, Jasmine overheard their conversation. Once I saw who was driving the vehicle that came screaming around the corner, I didn't particularly want to go straight home. No sense in giving him details he didn't need to know, so I went to have my nails done. That is when Jasmine caught up with me. Again, your uncle was playing the overprotective spouse. As a result, Jasmine and I came home in my rental and the car she was driving stayed at the salon's lot. Someone likes to play with fire because somebody torched her vehicle the next day. She is safely out of town, so all is well."

"Not quite, finish the rest of the tale." Michael had Johnnie between a rock and a hard spot.

"Continuing on; the house was broken into this afternoon by the same man that was tailing me at the bookstore. I never thought I would ever use one of those safety rooms Michael has been installing in every house we ever lived in; but I do have to admit it came in handy. I will also admit it was somewhat fun too. I got to watch everything they did and said and they had no idea I was watching."

Josie gave her aunt a very serious look. "So that is why I saw the police leaving as I came up to the house. Were you ever going to tell me?"

"Of course I was; especially since I want you to be extra careful. If necessary, brush up on your safety room supplies. Make sure your phone is working from the room and that you have a comfortable environment, in case you have to stay in there for a bit. Surprisingly it gives you a great deal of peace of mind. I am not saying anyone in here is in danger, just let's not throw caution to the wind. Okay? Does that cover everything Michael?"

"Thank you, it does pretty much. I just have to protect my girls. It is my job. Josie, your mom would have my hide if you were ever in real danger. That is why you have that room. Angela made me promise to put one in your house since you insisted on living in your own place." Michael followed that comment with a very simple request. "Who wants a drink? I think I could use one."

The waiter took the drink orders, but Johnnie passed in favor of ginger ale, and Josie stayed with her club soda, everyone else indulged in a beer. Johnnie did break over for just a moment and took a long drink from Michael's beer. "Ah, do you want one of your own?" He asked her.

"Nope, but you might want a second one just in case this one evaporates. Not that I drank that much, but you might want to top it off."

Michael just shook his head. "You all wonder why I am going gray."

The remainder of the evening was just a matter of the group enjoying each other's company. Johnnie and Michael were both interested in Murph's career, and Paige said she was happy to report she worked in the legal library at the firm. To which Murph added. "It isn't a simple librarian job she has her masters in library science." Paige smiled at her husband. "He is right, I always wanted to work in a library, but with the way of electronic publishing is going it could be a dying profession."

"I doubt that, libraries are just fascinating and I think everyone should take advantage of their local library." Josie had gotten her love of books from her aunt.

"I hate to be the first to suggest it is time to leave, but tomorrow is going to be a busy day. I think we should call it a night?" Murph knew it was so easy to get lost in conversation and he was expecting a busy day.

Johnnie looked at her watch. "Oh dear, I had no idea how late it had gotten. To be honest, I like to be in my jammies long before now. So I think Murph has the right idea."

With that acknowledgement, they all called for their bills to settle and agreed that it had been a pleasant night. Since they all arrived in the same vehicle, they would have to leave together.

Once in the house Josie turned to Johnnie. "Were you going to tell me all those little details?"

"Yes, I was and for the reason I said. You need to be alert, just for caution sake, and mine too. If you notice anything out of the ordinary, get to your safe room. Call us from there and we will come and get you." Johnnie tried to ease the tension she saw in Josie's face.

***

Johnnie wanted to lay low. So, she had Michael drop her off at the back stairs. Without her car in the lot, maybe Mirah would think she was out of the bank and not come upstairs.

"Johnnie, there was a man here looking for you. He said to tell you Noah Drake, and you would know him. He said he would be in the board room." Ana wondered who the man was; but she knew better than to ask. If Johnnie wanted her to know, she would tell her.

Johnnie went to the boardroom and found Noah and several other FBI agents present. These guys were from her old team, but she could not help wondering why they came to the bank.

"Surprised to see me, Johnnie?" Noah said grinning.

"You could say that, maybe more like stunned. I just wanted you to get some information. You know I love seeing you guys again, but you did not have to make a trip to Ackers."

"Well, about that request I would like to cover some things with you." Noah wanted to speak to her confidently. He simply said. "We need to talk."

Johnnie suggested that they go to her office. She swept the room before their conversation started. Johnnie and Noah settled in the office. "This looks serious."

Noah sat down took a deep breath. "We did some general looking at the deaths of Herb Jennings and Grammar Jonas and found they were linked. You probably know that they were into drugs, and it would appear the source was one in the same. Meaning these incidents crossed state lines, opening it to a FBI investigation. We also did some looking into the death of your employee Silva Amos. She herself is clean, but her autopsy report is a problem."

Noah continued to explain their findings. "We reviewed Silva's autopsy report. No smoke or soot in her lungs, and a head injury was from blunt force, bringing the number to three individuals related to banking all being murdered. We figured it is time to step into the scene. We want Victor Andropov and Logan Ferns to know this is not going away quietly."

Johnnie was surprised and she wished that Terry were with her to hear the report from Noah. "How did you get the autopsy report before Terry? She and I have been waiting for the results. We figured the report wasn't going to be pleasant. I don't even know if her sons know the results or if they want to know." Johnnie was concerned about word leaking before Silva's boys were informed.

Noah told her not to worry about the word leaking before the locals were ready to talk to the boys. "It might be a good idea to talk to their aunt before presenting the report. She may prefer that the boys not know at this time." Noah finished by telling her that he and his team did not intend to interfere with the operations of the municipal authorities.

"So what is the connection?" Johnnie was interested in what the agency had found. Noah continued to tell her the details and suspicions involving the three. "You have heard of Victor Andropov? We have photos of both Herb and Grammar with Victor. He can be ruthless and murder is his resolution of choice. It would seem that Herb and Grammar might have crossed him in some way. The general thought is they helped themselves to a product shipment. It looks like some of their banking expeditions were more or less a delivery service cover for Victor. They both had Osis' signature, and we know he has a direct connection to Victor. Victor's reputation for violence makes him the prime suspect. Of course, Victor was not the actual perpetrator. He hires out such activity. His select agent for these jobs has been Sebastian Osis."

"Do you have anything on this Sebastian Osis? I have only heard of him by word of mouth." Johnnie wanted to know as much as she could learn since she really hadn't spent any time checking these men out other than what Terry told her.

"He has a distinctive signature he includes on his victims, that being a mark that is unmistakable and definitely out of place in the crime scenes. The salt used on and in the bodies is consistent with Osis' signature since he started working for Victor. Even Silva had the same salt coverings in her eyes and in her mouth. If she saw something and spoke out of turn, then that would result in such a signature. In other areas, he finds different items for signatures. Heck, he even had pizza dough in one poor chap's mouth. He is notorious in the law enforcement communities. That is why when reports of salt in Herb's nasal passages and on his hands, we knew it had to be Osis. Grammar had the same salt on his hands and in his nasal passages when discovered in his hospital bed after he suffered a severe allergy attack. No one realized he had a connection with Victor up until that time. The signature had been flagged, so if any other such murders happened, we would know." Johnnie was surprised that Noah knew so much about her adopted town and its characters.

"I have heard the rumors, but I have no real evidence of their drug use. I don't know much about Grammar at all. He was deceased before I came to the bank. I cannot believe Silva was into drugs. She was trying to be the best role model she could be for her boys."

Noah flipped through the pages in his clip workbook. "No, Silva had salt, just in her eyes and her mouth, not at all like Herb and Grammar. Consensus favors more likely she saw something rather than being involved with drugs."

"Thank the Lord. I have held her in high regard for her efforts in raising her boys. I really would be disappointed to discover she was involved. She did have lunches with Herb, but I think it was more for checking on personnel and adding to the rumor mill. Sad to say, those two kept eyes on everyone and shared what they knew. I am sure Silva supplied more information than she got out of Herb. He would have asked more questions rather than volunteering anything of true value. I told you that Silva has two sons. Charleston is serving in Iraq while Harold, who goes by Aces, is still in high school. He is on the swim team. From what Silva has said he is the star of the team."

"Do you think your detective friend could come into the office? I would like to share with her everything we know. What do you know about Herb's death?" Noah was being very helpful and he wanted the locals included in the investigation.

"You mean other than him being discovered in my office. I really didn't even see the body. I just came as far as the door of the office. I had been working on an investigation concerning Victor. I was alarmed that someone was looking for that information. I keep two copies of the research. One is here in the upstairs vault, hidden behind some old signature cards in a locked box. The second copy I keep in the main vault, in a safe-deposit box. That way, I know it will remain safe from prying eyes. Victor could have thought that Herb knew something about the research. However, why would Logan be following me, and putting a hit out on me when this case involves Victor?"

"What do you mean Logan was following you?" Noah hadn't heard about this incident.

"I went out for a day to clear my head. You know how I love going to the bookstore. Well, I went and noticed a tail. Of course, Michael had a tail on me as well. He said it was a training exercise, I guess in a way it was a good thing. Jasmine, Michael's employee, stayed behind when I left the bookstore. I nearly ran into Logan in front of the store. Anyway Jasmine overheard Logan say to the man who was tailing me to finish me."

Noah paced her office for a bit. He turned to her and said. "Let's take this one event at a time starting with Herb. He was found here in your office; it is a good size space, and unless the cleanup crew was excellent, I don't see any signs of salt remnants. Did you see blood when you came into the room?"

"It would seem that my office is a dump site, not the original crime scene. I never saw blood or salt. I couldn't. I never came into the office. However, Terry or Murph could tell you more about that discovery. The only thing that I was concerned with was the disarray of my office. There were papers and files all over the place. To me it looked like someone was trying to send a message, and I figured it had to do with the research I was doing on Victor." Johnnie tried to explain everything she could, but so much had happened. She knew her report was coming out as piece meal.

Noah sat back down in front of her desk. He knew Johnnie would want to present what she knew in a more concise manner. So he changed the subject. "You must be spoiled having a private office compared to the cubical you had before. I noticed not all the officers have individual offices, how did you rate one?"

Johnnie laughed, "One? How about two? I have another office on the executive floor. Remember how we were always talking to ourselves when working on a case. If we didn't converse with ourselves, then we talked to whoever was closest. Well, here at the bank they prefer the work to be quiet. Maybe they got tired of me working problems aloud."

Noah just shook his head and laughed. "I remember you talking to yourself. I think you started that trend."

Noah was such a nice-looking man. He was not the heart stopper as Michael was for her, but he was a distinguished looking gentleman. That distinguished look could disappear in a heartbeat if he saw his team in danger, or if a suspect tried to do anything hinky. Hinky seemed to be his favorite word when he was suspicious of a person or situation. "This is interesting, but we need to get more organized to keep all the details in order. If we don't we could miss something important. I don't want anyone in trouble or danger because of a slip."

She did miss working with Noah. He had a cool manner about himself; but he expected topnotch work from his team. At the bank, they seemed more laid-back than the bureau. No wonder Gary thought she worked too fast. Still, her work methods developed long ago and she didn't want to let them change just because it wasn't a matter of life and death. Well, in this case maybe it was a matter of life or death.

Noah backed off a bit. "How has Michael been lately? We use to see you two on occasions, but it seems like it has been a long time since we last saw you both." Noah and Michael had developed a trusting relationship, and he liked Michael.

"He's doing well. I wish he did not travel as much, but in the big picture, he is not on the road as much as he once was with opening the new offices. Of course, he still opens an office from time to time. It just depends on the market. Since I am not traveling myself, I miss him being home when I am." Johnnie was proud of Michael she would beam when she spoke of him.

"How long have you two been married now? I think you got married a year or two before or after me and Pam." Noah asked in a casual manner.

"Would you believe we have been married eight years already? How is Pam doing; have the doctors been helpful?" Johnnie was not one to circulate with the team on a social basis. Noah was her only exception. She and Pam went to college together.

"They believe it is fibromyalgia, and they had her on that biologic medicine; but she said it did not help. So she has changed her diet and quit working at the youth center. She does work out, but it has to be low impact. With her immune system questionable, we didn't think the youth center was the right place for her to work. She has found a new hobby to keep herself busy. She has become a freelance editor. It works out for her, and she loves it, even talks about writing a book someday. Her biggest problem is her inability to pace herself." Noah was proud of Pam, even with her pain she went forward with her plans.

Johnnie knew that Pam would love to write a book. She talked about it back in their college days. Now that she married an agent, she was hesitant to follow her dream. "We talked about her writing a book the last time we saw you guys." Johnnie commented. "I told her to use a pen name, and go ahead and write a book. I suggested she work through a publisher who dealt with political or law enforcement personnel before. They would know how to keep her identity guarded. I think she should go ahead and write. It is not as though she wants to write a revealing book about cases. She isn't close enough to the action to do something along those lines. She had always longed for a suspenseful romance. I think she would be good at doing so too."

***

Johnnie's phone rang, it was Terry calling from the boardroom. She came in today to discuss some of the case only to find many more agents in the building. Johnnie said it was okay, and that she should come up to her office and meet her old boss.

Terry came up to the office, and Johnnie introduced her to Noah as Detective Nichols. Terry requested that he call her by her first name. All three sat in Johnnie's office. Noah explained the extra agents as being his team he identified them as Smitty, Rob, Vince, and George. He then went on to explained how they discovered the connection between Grammar and Herb, and the results of Silva's autopsy. It all pointed to Victor Andropov. Noah asked Terry if she had ever seen a murder victim with a foreign substance in a victim's body.

Terry thought for a moment. "I do remember one case, it was a nasty death. The body was found in a 55 gallon drum with coal burning on top of the body."

Noah perked up when he heard about the case. "Was the case solved?"

Terry explained that it happened before she made detective, and she did not know. It could be a cold case; she was trying to remember the victim's name.

Johnnie saw the look in Noah's eyes. "Okay, I can see you are thinking. What is going on in your little crafty mind?" Johnnie inquired.

Noah smiled and said. "Sounds like signature for one of Sebastian Osis' hits. Furthermore, it was probably a hit for someone who really stepped over the line with Victor. He uses different substances for various areas. Coal, huh interesting. That makes me wonder why he switched to salt in these deaths. Any chance he has more than one client?"

"Doubtful, these types don't play well with others. They want the full attention of their, well let's say bodyguard for now." Terry did not think Sebastian would be working for anyone else he is always with Victor.

At this point, they started a brainstorming session. They talked about several cases, and wondered how many cases connected to Victor and Sebastian.

Before they knew it, they had been talking for over two hours. Sarah knocked on the door to ask if anyone wanted coffee or tea. They asked if she could just bring in some cans of decaf diet soda. They really didn't want to take their conversation to the lunchroom. Johnnie knew how easily conversations carried to the hallway from the lunchroom. "Thank you, Sarah that would be most appreciated." Sarah collected the various request and went on her way.

Sarah brought back the cans of soda and plastic cups then she excused herself from the office. Both Terry and Noah commented on how Johnnie's staff handled themselves. Johnnie was particularly proud of Sarah. She always seemed to rise to every occasion.

"Terry, would it be possible to meet at the police station tomorrow. I don't want the employees getting the idea that we are keeping secrets. We do however, have a lot to discuss and I know you have a lot of questions yourself, Terry." Not only did Johnnie not want the details leaked, she didn't want Mirah and John to ask any questions.

"I think that would be more effective for covering all the information that could be related. Noah do you know where the station is located?" Terry was interested in Noah's details and findings.

"I just need an address; these new cars all have GPS units built into the dash so no problem."

It was almost five, Johnnie told Noah and Terry that she had orders not to stay late. "This is just about as late as we should stay. Terry, do you want to come to the house? Noah, what about the team, you all came so fast, did you have time to book rooms at a hotel?"

Terry responded that she and Will had plans for the evening. "We don't get much of an opportunity to get an evening out. So if you don't mind, I will skip tonight."

"Enjoy! Tell Will I said hi. Before we do break up, Noah, did you find any information on John Erickson?" Johnnie wanted answers to her original inquiry.

"I wasn't able to get much in the way of details on Erickson's current appointment. I did find out he works in Leo Links' division. Leo is out currently, but I left a request for him to get in touch as soon as he was in his office. However, I did find that John did some investigating of his own. I have to say this is some report and there are parts here that I don't like. Terry, you and Murph have been included in the inquiry. No stone unturned, Michael and Johnnie are also included, no surprise on that one. He has investigated every one of your coworkers on this floor."

Johnnie was glad to have the report, and she wondered if Erickson would find out that she had a copy. Not that she cared. "Please tell me Josie was not included. I was hoping she could be left out of any of these things."

"Whatever is going on, it is kept under wraps. I don't know if she requested his presence or if Leo assigned him to her detail for some reason. Sorry, we are going to have to wait for Leo on that discovery."

***

Noah drove Johnnie home that evening. He knew Michael held everything in the strictest of confidence. "How does a pizza sound? I'll treat." Noah was happy to foot the bill for dinner.

The three pizzas came; Johnnie did not eat pepperoni, so she ordered a deep dish with extra cheese and pineapple. As they ate and sat around the kitchen table, they talked about old times when Johnnie was in Noah's unit. They talked about the various cases they had solved. It was stimulating to think back on all the old days when they worked together. Michael knew of some of the cases. One was a result of his security work. When a client requested certain items in their safe room, he knew it was not just for security. He made a call to Noah, so as not to involve Johnnie, and told him about the client. Many times, it turned out these individuals were on a watch list. Michael did not want his company connected with the arrest that would come because of the information. He even passed on some jobs. Some things are just not worth the money.

Eventually the conversation moved from old business to a more personal nature. Michael inquired about Pam's health. "Noah, what are they doing to help Pam? Is she getting better?"

"We have been to a dozen doctors. Finally found one that could help. He has diagnosed it as fibromyalgia as well as RA. However, I told Johnnie already that we have seen marked improvement in her condition. She is not working at the youth center anymore and she misses it a great deal. Johnnie would like to see her write a book, and I think she would like to do so, if her joints would agree."

"Well, I know Pam would really be a great writer. Writing has always been her passion. She worked on the college newsletter. Darn near ran the entire thing. I think the next time I see her I am going to encourage her to follow her dream. Maybe she could get a ghostwriter or something like that for the typing part, or even one of those voice activated programs that do the typing. It would be her story and I think that would make her happy. Besides, it might be good therapy for her both mentally and for her joints." Johnnie missed her good friend.

As always, when they got together, time got away from them. Johnnie was beginning to feel the results of a long drawn out day, and tomorrow would be even longer. She wanted to be at her best tomorrow when they met at the station.

Noah called the hotel where the agents were staying and asked one of his team to pick him up at a local restaurant. He wanted to safe guard his relationship with Johnnie and Michael. You just never know who would notice things. Michael drove him over to the local steak house and left before Noah's team member arrived.

"I can tell you certainly enjoyed seeing Noah again. To tell the truth, I have missed him and his wife. Hope when this is done, we can get together like old times." Michael always did like Johnnie's FBI team members, especially Noah.

***

Even though it was Saturday, Johnnie wanted to check on a few things before going to the station. She never liked leaving things unattended. At least, her office on the executive floor didn't have time to gather materials for an in-box. She followed up on bank business, and then she headed for the police station. She was in and out of the bank in less than 15 minutes. Ana and Sarah were keeping everything moving along.

It was just after 11 when she arrived at Terry's cubical. Noah was already waiting for her. Again, Terry gathered the information that she had, and they went to the conference room. They needed space to spread out. The conference room was the best place for the three of them to work.

Terry brought in three copies of the case with the crime signature that had shown up during her search. If this was Sebastian's work, it wasn't obvious.

Terry explained this involved the assault on a young girl, and that there was another party involved. Rumors flourished that he moved to avoid the same fate.

The point surprised Johnnie and Noah. "Just because the other party was gone, does not clear him. Did anyone do a follow up on him?"

"We communicated with the California authorities, but the unfortunate was already dead. His name was Jim Sonderson."

"I am sure something would have been put into the file, but I suspect it was a small part of the investigation. It does seem as though things in our little town are rather dangerous. If we can find a connection with Jim Sonderson and Victor, then we could spend more time on the case." Terry could see what Noah and Johnnie were thinking, but it didn't seem to make sense, and she told them so. "I would like to take a look at the Sonderson notes."

It took Johnnie a few minutes to find the report. "No autopsy report, only a death notice. We need more information than just a death notice. The file is incomplete. The autopsy report could identify a signature. Might not be Osis', but it still should be reviewed. Terry, I know this is a small police force, and you have limited resources, so let's see if the FBI can get some information." Johnnie asked Noah if he had any information about the case since it crossed state lines?

Noah called the FBI office in California asking for a copy of the autopsy report. California's office told him that it was still an active case. Now everyone was interested.

"He was found in Diamond Bar California, not the sort of place where a gruesome murder would take place. According to the LA office, the autopsy indicated that coal dust was all over the body." Noah said as he sat back down.

Terry was the first to speak. "My guess is he crossed Victor Andropov. Is there any way to trace the whereabouts of Sebastian Osis at the time?"

"The LA office is going to email the file over. Would you believe I didn't give them an email address for them to use to send the file?" Noah normally would have someone in his unit take care of these details. Here he did not have the personnel for such things.

"No problem. I can just call them back and give them my email address here at the station." Noah thanked Terry for making the call. The details in the report could somehow connect in some way to their case, especially since Sebastian Osis appeared to be involved. In this case, it was coal not salt. Maybe it was a matter of two separate issues.

It seemed like all other work sort of came to a halt as they waited for the report to be emailed. "It is possible that Sonderson tried to cut into Victor's drug trade and when he knew he was in trouble he fled the area. Too bad, Victor is not one to let things slide. He would make an example of Sonderson no matter where he went in the world." Terry hated to see all this happening in her little town.

Noah said the bureau had been trying for years to nail Victor with something that would stick. They even thought they could get him on tax evasion or something small. It could grow from there possibly.

Johnnie continued to look through the file. "So Sorderson ticked off Victor and decided to leave Ackers and head for a bigger area."

Terry liked the idea of getting Victor out of her town, but that still left them with the question, were Victor and Logan both in this game.

Terry excused herself to go to her desk and check her email. She came back with a 20-page report. "Well, looks like we have enough to work with so maybe we will find a connection."

Johnnie asked. "In all this discussion I never got the name of the unfortunate in the drum."

Terry told her the man's name was Blake Colton. He did not grow up in Ackers. He moved here when he was in his early 20's. He always had a knack for creating trouble. He was a known addict and that is probably what crossed him with Victor.

Johnnie was thinking aloud again. "This was more than being an addict, or even an addict with a secret, this murder was over the top. There has to be something else going on to cause this level of brutality."

They were all sitting around reading the report. Noah was the first to notice. "Go back a couple pages. Did you see the mention of a foster home run by a couple by the name of Colton? That could be the connection between Blake and Sonderson."

"Do we know where the Colton family lived?" Johnnie asked.

The trio was determined to find the answer to what happened in these two cases. Was Victor responsible for these murders?

They concentrated on just the cases involving the two men killed with a common factor. The coal factor made it probable that the cases were connected.

"Okay, let's see if we can pull this case together. What kind of history do we have on Sonderson and Colton?" Noah had his tablet out ready to make his chart. He was always working a case with what looked like a chain of command chart.

"Neither Sonderson nor Colton grew up in Ackers. So that is something we need to know." Noah made a side sheet with questions that would need to be answered.

Terry continued with her comments. Colton was a real hard nose she told them. It seemed he was in the middle of every problem. She could easily see him crossing Victor.

There were just a few notes on Noah's chart. One was Blake Colton the other Jim Sonderson and a question mark connecting them to Victor Andropov. They continued to read looking for any details other than the signature that could connect them together.

"We need to locate the Colton family. Social Services might be able to help with finding where they are at present. Of course, this was some time ago considering the age of these men when they died." Noah just shook his head. "You still work out details out loud I see." Johnnie just blushed.

The three worked on through the day without a break. Finally, a return call from Social Services came into Terry. After thanking the caller, she relayed the information to the others. "The Colton family lived in Vienna West Virginia. I know that area. Unfortunately, the foster parents passed away several years ago. I know it isn't much, but it is Saturday and we were lucky to get any information."

Terry said that Vienna was in Wood County and she would contact the Sheriff there to see if there were any records on these men.

The Wood County Sheriff was helpful and it came as no surprise that the men had a police record. He also confirmed that Jim Sonderson did grow up in the Colton household. Sonderson and Colton were as close as if they were blood brothers. They did everything together, including crimes. Charges included several breaking and entering and a record for drug possession. Another crime involved the assault on a young girl from Ackers.

"Oh my word, this just keeps getting tighter and tighter. These have to be our guys. Did it give the name of the girl?" Johnnie always loved putting the pieces together. "The girl was a minor, and her name was not disclosed. Want to make a bet she has a family tie to Victor." Terry found that she enjoyed the group work on cases.

"Assaulting a member of Andropov's family explains the brutality of Blake's death. It would also explain the far reach for Sonderson." Noah now connected the names on his chart. The top he left blank for the unknown girl. They needed to identify the girl.

"What was the time line on the alleged assault?" Noah was working his chart with details.

"It was several years ago when Colton arrived in Ackers, just after that the girl was allegedly attacked." Terry was watching Noah's growing chart with interest.

"What about Sonderson? Do we know when he arrived in Ackers?" Noah was waiting to add the detail to his chart. So many questions needed answering starting with the name of the girl. It was going to be necessary to explore the family ties, and then maybe the case would no longer be a cold case.

"I think it is just coincidence that these two men, Colton and Sonderson have been tied to Victor. Their crime is unrelated to ours, but just as important. For now we need to get back to the case at hand." Johnnie knew it was important to Terry to resolve the murder of Blake Colton, but they needed to stay on track and not lose sight of Herb and Silva's murders.

"I can put the Colton/Sonderson case aside for now, but when we have solved these other cases, I would appreciate some help. After all, they too crossed state lines." Terry looked at Noah with pleading eyes. Everyone agreed since it seemed like a slam-dunk; they would keep in mind finding the girl or at least her name as the other case moved forward.

***

Johnnie had been at the station for over seven hours. She was always amazed how fast time went when working on an investigation. She was mentally charged, but her body was dreadfully tired.

Just as they were wrapping up the day, putting Noah's chart together with the files, a call came in for Terry. She stepped away from the conference room to take the call.

Returning to the conference room, Terry took a deep breath. "Would you like to start a new investigation file? John Erickson is dead they found him in his hotel room. Mirah went to his room for dinner and when he didn't answer the door, she used her key and found him lifeless."

Noah and Johnnie sat back down. "This is not good. Terry, what do you want us to do?" Johnnie knew in her heart that they should all go to the crime scene. "Let me call Michael and then I will go with you." Noah agreed, and they were soon out the door.

John Erickson and Mirah Anderson had been staying at the Hilton outside of town. It is sort of a draw for people who like to fish or hike, but wanted room service. All three traveled together in Terry's car. Noah wanted to be there since John was an FBI agent.

They pulled into the parking lot by the area surrounded with crime-scene tape. Terry headed up the trio. Before entering the room, she gave Johnnie and Noah gloves and booties from her kit.

Walking into the room, they saw Mirah sitting just staring at the body while the medical examiner was taking the necessary pictures.

Johnnie could not ignore the woman she had seen at the bank these last days. "Mirah, are you okay? Can I get you something?"

Mirah just sat there and shook her head no. She was still in a daze. Terry would be the one to do the questioning. She pulled a chair from the table next to Mirah. "Can you tell me what happened?" Mirah just sat there for a moment with a tear running down her cheek.

"I'm sorry Detective. I have known John for a long time. This is like losing a brother. All I know is that I knocked on his door, but he didn't answer. We were supposed to meet for dinner 20 minutes earlier. We had keys to each other's rooms we never knew what we were getting into when we traveled on a case. So we decided it would be a matter of safety for us to have each other's keys. Guess it wasn't so good on this trip. What does all that salt in the room and on John mean? John he had nothing to do with mining, and he wasn't involved with any of the recent murders."

"Did you hear anything; notice anyone who followed you or always seemed to be present?" Terry hated interviewing people at the scene of a death. "No, we knew we needed to be careful. Our cases were mostly high profile. However, I never saw anyone." Terry suggested that they go to Mirah's room, and let the techs take care of the scene.

Stepping out of John's room, they removed their gloves and booties. If they returned to the crime scene, they would put on fresh booties and gloves, to avoid any chance of transferring fibers or hairs into the crime scene.

Noah, Johnnie, and Terry all escorted Mirah to her room. Mirah sat at the table in the room. Johnnie went down to the café and got some hot tea for Mirah. Upon her return, Johnnie placed the tea in front of Mirah. She felt terrible for not trusting her earlier. Looking at her now, she saw a sad and frightened person.

Terry tried to press on with the questions. "What about strange phone calls? Were there any messages left at the front desk that were odd?"

Mirah responded negatively to all the questions. It did not seem like they were going to get anything tonight. Terry told Mirah that she would station a uniform outside by her door. If she needed something, call room service and have the officer check for identification for anyone making deliveries. It would also be a good idea to have any deliveries checked by the officer as well.

The three returned to John's room putting on fresh booties and gloves. Terry talked to the medical examiner who told her the body was still warm, so it was a recent death. Terry asked if there were any foreign substances on or near the body other than the salt. She told her none that she could see, but the autopsy would provide more details. They looked for any brass casings, but did not see any in the room. John had fallen straight back onto the bed, so he must have been standing at the foot of the bed when shot. "There should be gunshot residue on whoever fired the gun." As they surveyed the room, it was obvious that John was not expecting any trouble. Did he know his killer? Was there someone other than Mirah he would let into his room?

Noah talked to Terry. "I don't care what you need I want this person in custody ASAP. The FBI will be available for any of your needs." Terry knew how he felt. He had to deal with the death of an officer herself, so she knew it was important.

Noah's anger was palpable "I will have the best in our forensic department work on nothing but this until we have all the answers you need. Whoever did this is going to pay. We will find them. We still don't know why John was working with Mirah? I need to contact Leo Links; he has to know why John travels with Mirah?"

Noah was walking up and down the hallway. Doing whatever he could do to avoid the room. As he so often said, too many hands spoil the soup. He needed to allow the technicians space to do what they do best. He needed to get out of the hotel.

***

All three decided to go to Johnnie's house. They had the crime scene photos sent to them on their tablets and they wanted a place to talk openly.

Michael was already home and seemed anxious. He saw the three of them coming up the walk and opened the door. "I guess you heard the news. It didn't happen at the bank did it?" Johnnie assured him that if it was bank related, at least it did not happen on the bank's grounds.

Sitting at the kitchen table, they agreed that it could be a long night. Having had their share of pizza, they ordered Chinese from the take out restaurant at the mini-mall a few blocks away.

Michael sat with them since he was no stranger to these sessions with Johnnie and Noah. Terry was the new comer to the group, but fit right into their style.

Noah started another flow chart to see if they could put some information on the sheet.

Johnnie started. "I did not know Erickson from my days at the bureau, but that doesn't mean a thing. He could have transferred in from another office after I left." Terry agreed saying the only thing she knew was that he traveled with Mirah.

Noah was still visibly angry. "I met John, I believed him to be a good agent. If someone is declaring open season on federal agents, what could happen to the citizen on the street? I need to call Quantico, if Leo has not returned from the field; well, they will just have to find him. It is rare that someone fooled an agent so completely and that point truly troubled Noah."

Noah stepped out of the room to call Leo. "Leo, when did you get back?" Leo was in a rush. "I haven't been in the office for an hour yet. I have been going through my messages. Have you called while I was out?"

Noah calmly explained what had happened that night. "I did call you and it was on a different matter. We have a tragedy in our ranks, and it directly affects your team."

Noah heard Leo drop into his desk chair he was stunned. Leo was a slightly portly man, with gray hair as Noah recalled. "John, what happened, where are you? Who is with you, what is going on?" Leo had been in the bureau for many years, and he had a fear of what he was going to hear.

"Leo, John Erickson works in your team, right?" Noah never liked this part of his job.

"Yes, but he is on special assignment with Mirah Anderson. He only checks in when there is something serious he needs to report. In fact, just listening to the news on TV it would appear he is in Ackers WV."

"Yes, Leo he has been in Ackers. I am here as well. The reported murders here affected the First National Bank of Ackers. Johnnie King works in the bank, the first body was in her office closet. That is what brought Anderson and John to Ackers. We don't know why, but John was found murdered in his hotel room tonight. I know you would want to hear as soon as possible. I have given Terry Nichols, the local homicide detective, access to all of our resources."

"John is more or less an agent for reporting the activity of Mirah Anderson. How did he get involved in the murders at the bank?" Leo didn't want to say too much on the phone. "I need to be in Ackers. How competent is the local medical examiner? Whom do I need to bring with me? I want to be there by the morning, we may have to have others come later." Leo was taking notes at a furious rate.

"Leo, just get here. I will fill you in on everything when you arrive. Maybe we will know something by the morning."

Noah didn't think they would know anything so quickly, but any detail may be helpful. His plan was to stay on target. The murder of Herb and Silva were just going to have to be put aside for now. In finding John's killer it was very possible the other cases would also be resolved.

The food arrived and before getting into the nitty-gritty of the search, they decided to eat and then get started. Still as they ate, they were bouncing all sorts of ideas off each other. Could it be from another case John handled in the past? Who would have gotten into the room without suspicion? Was John involved with Ferns or Andropov? Who knew John's room number, or even where he was staying? Johnnie did not want to think the bank had anything to do with this latest murder.

With the table cleared the group settled down with the files. This was not easy for any of them. The FBI lost an agent, and Johnnie was worried about the bank. Terry took the lead as Michael sat back and observed. In the past, Michael would let Noah and Johnnie toss out ideas, only when he thought of something they missed did he add any comments.

"Well, we can look at his file, but it just might not help. We are going to have to go over everything that the forensic team discovers. Did either of you see anything striking about the room?" Terry asked as she went over the notes she took while at the crime scene.

Noah said that he asked one of officers to check the cars parked in the lot. He wanted to know if any of them were still warm. That would indicate recent arrivals. Maybe the perpetrator was still in the hotel. Noah commented. "I am sure that your forensic team will pull the cameras from the elevators and hallways."

Terry did not take offense to Noah's comments; she knew this was one of his own, and he wanted fast action. "My forensic team will go by the book don't worry. They will take care to follow every procedure. Investigators will canvas the guests in the hotel. They will check the balconies for any potential fibers or tool markings. In the morning, we will go over their findings. For now, let's go over his file."

Michael sat there watching everyone go over the file. He was good at reading body language. When you are in the Navy Seals, they drill in your head to be alert and look at everything. Little nuances can speak volumes and recognizing them can save your life.

Terry read the file from cover to cover. "All I see are good reports and an exemplary agent. I don't see anything in his file that would shed light on the events tonight."

Johnnie agreed. "His file shows he has been in the bureau for five years, joining just after being honorably discharged from the Army. He was assigned to travel with Mirah, but doesn't say why."

Noah had been reading and taking notes. "I would like to know why he was assigned to her. I am just having a hard time understanding why he had the assignment. Was she going to run for some office; governor maybe?"

Noah asked Terry how long it would take to hear from the forensic team. Terry told him she would call the station to see if there was any news.

Terry called into the station and asked if any of the techs had returned from the hotel. She was able to talk to the lead tech. "Yes, we covered all the regular places, even checked the roof and the stairwells and balconies of the hotel with no luck. We did a 100-meter perimeter. With so much yet to cover, we will have to have the second shift continue the canvassing of the guests. We are questioning all the guests as a precaution. Some of them don't like it, but it doesn't matter. We are turning over every stone. Every exit and entrance into the hotel has an officer stationed so that no one will get through without us knowing. Jim Getty will head up the effort for the forensic teams. He is a crime scene expert, and he has been with our police department for the last 15 years. You cannot get better than Jim."

Terry relayed the message from the tech and said as far as she could see there was nothing more to gain tonight. She was going to head back to the office. She asked Noah if he wanted to ride with her.

He told her he just wanted to go through everything one more time. He told her to go on ahead.

Noah, Johnnie, and Michael continued just talking about what they knew of John Erickson. He was a nice guy; nevertheless, the reason for him being with Mirah was an unanswered issue.

Noah said he didn't know who, outside Leo, he could contact in regards to finding why Mirah had her own personal FBI agent. She could have asked for protection for some reason. Wasn't it true that she was taking on some high crime characters? Maybe Ferns or

Andropov was the reasons for their presence, or maybe Mirah knows something about Herb.

Noah was stressing. "I know I am beating a dead horse, but if we need to find out why John was with Anderson, well, who knows what might be brought to light. Hell, it could solve all these problems."

Michael was watching Johnnie and he could see her starting to drag. The adrenaline was wearing off and she was about to crash. "Hey guys, I think we need to call it a night. Johnnie is ready to drop and Noah, you have to be nearing the same point."

Johnnie asked Noah if he wanted to stay the night, or if he wanted Michael to take him to the police station. He decided he wanted to go back to the station and pick up his car. He said he needed to spend some time just thinking about today's events. He told them that John was single, but his section chief would notify the family. He may well have already done so. Noah would also like to know how his team was doing. They no doubt would want answers.

***

Johnnie woke without the alarm. The sun was pouring in through the window and she could smell the luscious aroma of brewed coffee. She put on a robe and headed down toward that heavenly scent.

Michael was sitting at the table with coffee and a cup at her place. He was dividing his time between the TV news and the paper.

"Hi, how's my guy this morning?" Johnnie was in a bright mood. Michael smiled as he poured another cup of coffee for himself. "Well you are in a good mood today considering the events of yesterday."

Johnnie sat down and poured the coffee in her cup. "It isn't a matter of being tired; it is just that I realize how much I miss working with Noah."

"Are you thinking of returning to the bureau?" Michael could read her like an open book and this morning he could speed read.

"I do have to admit, I have enjoyed this work. I am saddened by the loss of these people, but I think I can lend a positive approach to the investigation."

"Well, Noah must think so as well, he is on his way over as we speak."

The doorbell rang as Michael finished his comment. He went to open the door and greeted Noah. Together they came into the kitchen. Johnnie already poured Noah a cup of coffee.

"Noah, I should have gotten dressed already, but I am enjoying my Sunday, besides you have seen me like this before. I enjoy being away from the bank on weekends. But I will have to get dressed for Mass soon."

"What is this I hear about you enjoying this investigation?" Johnnie shot Michael a look. "I was just telling Michael that I didn't realize how much I missed investigative work until now. Banking has limited opportunities for such investigations, outside of what I have been working on recently."

Noah sat down and asked exactly what had she been working on lately. She explained that she was researching every transaction that went through the bank in the last three years on Victor Andropov for the state's attorney general office, Mirah Anderson. She kept it away from everyone's hands and eyes as instructed. Knowing now what she was learning about Andropov's methods; she understood the need for extreme caution. He wanted to know more of what she knew about Victor Andropov.

"Victor is the local merciless hood. People know him for using deadly force to eliminate opposition or perceived threats. I think Logan Ferns has been trying to enter the drug market locally from what I hear. If he is, don't be surprised to find him covered in salt somewhere."

Noah sat his coffee cup back down on the table. "I just came from your bank parking lot. You are not going to guess who we found in a car with several buckets of salt poured inside."

It was Johnnie's turn to put her coffee cup down. "Not another body discovered and in the bank parking lot. Do you know who it is?"

Noah picked up his coffee again. "Let's just say you don't have to worry about Logan Ferns and the hit he put out on you."

Are you saying it is Logan's body? That ends his bid for some of Victor's territory. My life as a banker is suddenly a bit too dangerous. Where did you find the body?"

"A customer for the post office; he was just going to slip a letter in the outside box. Anyway, he saw a car with the window down, and it was drizzling on that side of town. He went over to check to see if the driver was okay or if the car was empty. He said he was going to roll up the window since it was an older car. Needless to say we had a frantic phone call to 911."

Michael put on another pot of coffee as the doorbell rang again. This time Johnnie answered the door not at all surprise to find Terry standing there with a defeated look on her face. Johnnie told her that Noah had already brought the news of Logan's murder.

Michael got down another cup for Terry. "I don't like all this going on in my hometown." Terry looked so exhausted.

Terry sat her files down on the floor beside her. "I have the initial report on John Erickson from the M E's office. I also brought the reports from the forensic team. They are busy now with the Ferns case. Where is all this going to lead?"

Johnnie asked if anyone had talked to Mirah this morning. Terry said she tried, but the hotel said she checked out. She gave the front desk her phone number and said she would be available any time.

"I hope that is a cell phone, because I for one would like to see her back here now." Noah didn't like the idea of her leaving town so soon after Erickson's death. He took the number and called Mirah.

"Miss Anderson, this is Noah Drake with the FBI. I know John's death has been rough on you, but I would like to have you return to Ackers." The others listened in on his side of the conversation. "No, we have not found out anything new yet on John's case; but Logan Ferns was found dead this morning and I think it best if all parties involved were here in town. Besides, if any of this is related to your office, I don't think you should be on the road without a protective detail."

He clicked his phone shut. "She says she will turn around and come back immediately."

"You don't think she is in any danger do you, Noah?" Johnnie was at the refrigerator getting out some orange juice.

"To tell you the truth, I don't know what to think. Is she part of the problem or just someone caught up in the events? Why was she here to start with anyway? Why would the death of a banker involve her office?" Noah just seemed stuck on her presence. If she had stayed in Charleston, John would be alive today. "How does this all relate to Logan's murder? Well, I guess I am assuming it is related. It is possible that these are just untimely happenings."

Johnnie looked at Noah. "Mr. no such thing as a coincidence, you know they are related somehow." Suddenly Johnnie stopped in her tracks. "Mass, how are we going to make it to church?"

Michael looked at Johnnie and shook his head. "I think this is one of those cases where you will be forgiven for this miss at least morning Mass. We will see how the day goes, maybe a 5:30 Mass will work today."

The doorbell rang again, and Johnnie said she was thinking about selling tickets. She went to the door to see Pat Cates standing there with a box from her favorite bakery. "Well, at least you brought something good with you. Everybody else just brought bad news."

"Well, I am here and I don't know if you are going to like me for what I am bringing other than the goodies."

Pat took a seat at the kitchen table, and Michael got down another cup. "Looks like if anyone else shows up, we will need to move into the dining room. I did some checking through some confidential sources in DC and found that Herb and Grammar's murders were definitely drug related. I guess bankers should not live beyond their means, and that includes their recreational activities as well. That explains those two and there are direct links to Andropov. As far as the two older murders, Andropov could have ordered the hit. He has the money and the power to stay protected by a ring of attorneys for the rest of his natural life. Still working on Erickson; his death seemed to have come from out of left field."

Noah pulled out his notebook. "Okay, what exactly do we know about the older deaths?"

Michael put on another pot of coffee. Pat reached for a napkin and a maple doughnut as he answered the question. "The girl who was assaulted was indeed Andropov's niece. Those dumb hicks picked up the wrong girl to mess with that night.

When Blake was murdered, Jim knew better than to stay around. He had taken off from Vienna as soon as word reached that town. Trouble is with Victor, there is no place to hide. Small town meets Russian mob."

"If we know he is in the Russian mob, and we can prove he is responsible for four deaths, why can't we at the very least deport him?" Terry wished she had the power to take down someone like Victor.

Pat spoke up to explain what he knew on the topic. "It is very hard to prove a case for deportation. Besides, Victor seems to be protected by someone powerful; or there is a reason why they don't want to deport him."

Noah looked to Terry. "Topic change. What did your team come up with on John's murder?"

"To start, they checked every camera, but no luck, leaving only the roof to the balcony as an entry point. So they inspected the roof and did find some shoe impressions, they are doing their best to come up with a match. The techs found fibers on the roof's guardrail and on the balcony railing. However, don't be so quick to jump, there are connecting doors, so someone could have come in and out that way."

"Who had the suite next to John's, didn't Mirah have that one?" Noah was determined to find out who was responsible for the young agent's death.

"No, she was actually down about three doors, remember we walked her back to her room. It could not have been through her door. We have a lot to think about on this one."

Terry poured fresh coffee into her cup. "Even if we know that Andropov is responsible for Herb's death it doesn't do us any good if we can't prove it in a court of law."

Pat spoke again. "Proving it isn't really the problem. It is getting through his army of lawyers and their motions that is the problem. Then if he does have a guardian angel, it will make it even harder. Word has it he just wanted to avenge his niece's assault. The dead bankers were a matter of keeping control. It is never a good idea to run a tab with the Russian mob, think you don't have to pay because you think you are someone special, and helping yourself to Victor's product when making deliveries is a definite mistake."

Johnnie could see that would be bad business. "Sooner or later someone will find a way to get him off the streets. I know what you are going to say, Pat. Even if he were incarcerated that doesn't stop him from control. If we can't nail him, can we at least find the primary crime scene? It could answer more questions possibly."

Terry took this time to fill them in on some of the medical examiners reports. "We did find some unique contents in Herb's stomach. It looks like he had eaten a Russian dish called Shashlik. One of our lab techs has a Russian heritage, and she recognized the ingredients. That says Andropov to us. I don't know how we will get a search warrant for his restaurant. It looks like Herb was with Victor before he died; maybe that is the primary crime scene. A judge is going to want more than he ate a Russian dish before his death for a search warrant." Terry was frustrated, and everyone could appreciate her exasperation. Sometimes it just seems like the rules do more to protect the criminal than the public.

"Okay, so as far as he is concerned, we can abandon that avenue. I want to know what happened to John Erickson. Terry, did the M.E. find any foreign substances in his body? I mean besides the salt that was found on his body."

Terry was reading the preliminary report. "Nothing and toxicology reports will take some time. The M.E. said he found a .357 round in John. The first shot got him, but the second went wild. The forensic team found it in the crown molding in the room. I suspect whoever shot it wasn't ready for the recoil. That leads me to think either a frail man, or even a woman; someone who is a novice shot John. Either way I am thinking the FBI could run ballistics faster than my lab."

Noah answered in the affirmative, and said he would go by the police station later and sign out the evidence and have a courier ready to take it to Quantico "We will put it in an evidence bag, and I will have two agents escort it to the lab non-stop. I don't want anything coming back to bite us on a chain of evidence issue. As far as finding anything on a toxicology report, I strongly doubt we will see anything. John was a good agent, he had been undercover and always handling temptation without slipping."

Terry said she thought that would be fine. Noah could come by any time that he wanted, and she would notify the office to have things ready. "Everyone was in high gear on this one. Some of the agents who had been working the bank murders are offering to lend a hand. Some help is good but too many cooks ruin the soup. I do appreciate their feelings. If it were one of my co-workers, I would want in on the case. So Noah, I will let you do whatever you think is best." Terry had lost coworkers and she understood their frustration.

Johnnie had been listening to everything and she had to ask; "We are not going to just drop Herb's murder. I for one want to know where the original crime scene was and how did they get his body into my office without being noticed. What was the real reason for Silva's murder? Apparently, she saw something, but who did she tell if anyone?"

Noah took a deep breath. "I guess we got sidetracked with all the other things happening."

Johnnie sat there hugging her favorite gigantic coffee mug. "Going back to Silva, I hate to say anything that would tarnish her reputation; truth be known, she loved to be noticed by the brass. Maybe she told someone something, perhaps she told the wrong person. Has anyone checked in on Aces, her son? I would hate to think that someone thought he was a loose end. He is a very nice young man."

Terry and Noah were taking notes, and Noah had his flow chart out again. "Would Silva have said anything to her son?" Johnnie said she did not think Silva would have said anything to Aces. She was good about protecting her boys; but with all that in mind, it wouldn't be a bad idea just to have someone watching him on the QT until things are resolved.

Terry offered some help for Aces' protection. "I can alert the officers at the school. In today's world, it was sad but a police presence on any school ground was becoming commonplace. We can have an officer near his various classes. Nothing too obvious or we might frighten the young man. I know his coach on the swim team will be watching out for him. Not sure what abilities he has in the way of protection; but at least he could alert someone. We also have to think about pulling Aces from school to ensure the safety of others."

Michael was obviously deep in thought. "If we get really lucky we might have things under control by the time he was ready to go back to school. It is not as if he is going to rush back. He will want to spend some time with Charleston. The boys are going to need each other until they can cope with the idea of their mother being murdered."

Everyone sat quietly for a few moments; finally, Michael spoke up "Does this mean with Logan out of the picture, that we don't have to worry about why he was following Johnnie?"

Terry said she wished she knew. "He had someone watching his back, but whoever it was I think Victor may have taken the wind out of their sails."

Johnnie looked at Noah. "Do you think that Logan could have been responsible for Erickson's death?"

"I doubt it, his time of death is fairly close to John's. In fact, it looks as though he may have died a few hours before John. Of course, I am only basing that on the cursory look of the medical examiner report, but I don't know. If what your medical examiner thinks is right, then Ferns was out of the picture first. Terry, for a small town it seems like you have some major players."

Terry gave him a sad look. "It has been this way since the big truck stop located nearby, and with the Clarksburg airport is not far away. The airport was small, so the opportunity for drug traffic could be a strong factor. No place is safe from drugs anymore."

Johnnie asked Noah about his flow charts. He said he thought he was making some sort of progress on them until this morning's find. Now he would have to rethink the entire chart.

Noah defended himself while Pat smiled. "I know some of you think this is old school, but I am old school, and it has worked for me. If it isn't broken, don't fix it. I like having it all with easy access. I don't have to back up pages to make changes. I just do it up in pencil. When the case is finished, I do the reports for the file. I put my handwritten charts and notes into the file too. You know old school; document, document, document."

Now Johnnie was laughing. "You don't know how many times I have said that to my co-workers at the bank. Like Noah, I have learned there is no such thing as too much detail."

It seemed as though the group had discussed just about everything, not that it solved anything. They seemed at a loss for the next steps. Noah said he was going back to the hotel to meet with some of the other agents. He would go by the police station first to sign out the evidence and have it delivered to Quantico.

Terry said she needed to see what was happening at the Ferns' crime scene. Michael and Pat decided it would be a good day to check out Andropov's restaurant. Johnnie was going to stay home and work her notes. She said that the restaurant used too many things that she reacted to in their dishes.

Johnnie was up in the study when the doorbell rang. Checking the monitor, she saw that it was Mirah. She went down to answer the door and she and Mirah went to the kitchen. "I didn't know what to do with myself. I really didn't want to go back to the same hotel. I didn't know where to find Mr. Drake, so I came here in hopes that you would be home. I really didn't get a chance to thank you for your kind consideration yesterday."

"Think nothing of it. I am sure you have done the same for people you have dealt with through your career." Johnny, for some reason, didn't know if she should tell her anything about any findings or if Noah should tell her. She decided Noah called her to come back, so, he should be the one to reveal details. Of course, he may not want to tell her anything.

"Have they found out anything about John's killer?" Mirah had said that John was like a brother to her, but Johnnie knew Mirah had a reputation for being blunt. From all the reports she read and what little interaction she had with him, she didn't see the two as a good team. If she treated him like she treated everyone else, he deserved some sort of an award. Sadly, instead he got a bullet.

"I haven't gotten into any details. I know you and he were colleagues, but I really don't know anything that would put your mind at ease. Why don't I call Noah and see if he can help you or maybe meet with you?"

Johnnie was doing her best to side step the issue. She understood how the woman could be feeling. She felt the same way about Silva. However, being a trained observer of human nature, she did not see what she would consider true grief coming from Mirah. Johnnie had to remind herself that there are those individuals that can camouflage their feelings. Johnnie believed in giving people the benefit of the doubt.

She called Noah's cell, and he picked up. "Hi Noah, I have Miss Anderson here at the house, and I think she would like to talk with you. Is there someplace where she could meet you?"

Noah told her where they could meet, and he could have the hotel book a room for Miss Anderson. He asked if Johnnie wanted to join them. She said she could not today, but she would pass the information along to Miss Anderson.

Johnnie relayed the information to Mirah, telling her that she could connect with Noah at the hotel where he and his agents were staying, and he offered to have the desk hold a room for her on the same floor.

Mirah again thanked Johnnie for her help, and said she would meet him at the hotel, and it would be better for her to stay at his hotel instead of going back to the Hilton. She said she just couldn't face that place again.

Johnnie saw her to the door and was somewhat relieved to start a quiet day at the house. She returned to the study with case files, remembering she would have to start one now on Logan Ferns.

Shortly after Mirah left, Noah called Johnnie. "Is she on her way? Don't answer the question if she is still at your place." Johnnie explained that Mirah was on her way to meet up with him.

"Good, I am uncomfortable with her being at your house. I would have thought she would have called me when she arrived."

"She said she didn't know how to reach you, but since you called her on her cell, your number should have been captured on her phone log. Maybe she was just not thinking straight."

Noah said that could be the case, but he wanted Johnnie to lock her doors.

Michael and Pat returned to the house and asked if anything interesting happened while they were gone. "Well, would you call Mirah Anderson stopping by interesting?"

"Are you serious? What did she want?" Michael was not happy to hear of her being at the house. "Was anyone with her?"

"No, she said she didn't know exactly what to do. She didn't want to go back to the Hilton. Besides, she was looking for Noah. He said to have her come over to his hotel and he would arrange for a room on the same floor as the agents. To tell the truth, I don't know why she just didn't call him on his cell. Then to top it off, Noah called back and told me to lock the doors. He was unhappy with Mirah's visit."

Pat sat down in the living room, a room they rarely used except during the holidays. The room was comfortable and sunny but not overly large; it held the furniture in a nice conversational grouping. "We saw the infamous Victor Andropov today. Have you ever encountered him?"

Johnnie said thankfully she never met him and God willing she never would.

Pat said "He was polite and charming and had Sebastian Osis following him around."

"I can't believe he had Sebastian there like family. What would happen if the police came after Osis?" Johnnie asked.

"I don't think the police would go into Andropov's restaurant. I think it would be like kicking a sleeping giant. If they decide they have enough to pick up Sebastian, they would do so when they could find him alone." Pat had experience with such cases and his thoughts were reasonable.

"You know I think it was really strange for Anderson to come here. She had no real reason to do so. I am trying to think what her intentions were by coming to the house. I think I will start carrying my gun in my ankle holster even around the house." Johnnie knew she could take care of herself, mainly because people tended to underestimate her. She had no plans to change their mind. She found out there were times that mindset allowed her to survive.

As they were noticing the clock, it was 3:45. Johnnie spoke up. "I think we can make Mass at 5, to tell the truth, I could use some divine inspiration. Pat you want to call Josie and see if she wants to go with us."

Pat said that he would, and it might be easier if they just met at the church. He told her it might not be a bad idea to use her phone vibrates notification in case something else happened.

It was close to 7 by the time everyone returned from Mass. They were settling in for just a quiet evening.

Terry called Johnnie. "Want some company? I could use someone to help me bounce some ideas."

Johnnie told her to come on over and they could spread out on the dining room table.

Terry must have been on her way because Johnnie barely got the candles off the table before the doorbell rang.

"How many speed limits did you break on your way over, or were you half way here when you called. Do you want some tea or something?"

Surprisingly Terry asked if she had a beer. She got her a beer and asked if she wanted a frosted mug, but she preferred to drink it from the bottle.

Terry sat down and pulled out her case files, ready to layout some of the varying details for them both to review.

Johnnie looked over the files. "Well we know the motive for Sonderson and Colton was revenge. Herb and Grammar appear to be drug related based on the signature. Logan could be a matter of eliminating the potential competition. We still have Silva and Erickson, and what about the attempt on Harrison, and we know that Logan was responsible for his designs on me."

Terry looked at her, "I know that with Ferns gone, it would appear to be safe, but don't let your guard down. All of this is too much to ignore. What if Logan was ordered by someone else to hurt you."

Johnnie wanted to be in on the capture. If they could determine who the guilty parties were in these cases. Taking Victor down would require something more than hiring a bodyguard, regardless of the bodyguard's reputation. Sebastian Osis was the one tied to all the murders, not Andropov.

"If Victor was responsible for Erickson's death, the FBI would utilize all its resources to bring him down. What did using the signature on John indicate? Do you think John's death is related to some other crime he worked in the past?" Johnnie was bouncing questions off Terry as well and listening to Terry's questions.

"Did I tell you that Mirah Anderson was here earlier? She did not want to go back to the Hilton. I called Noah, and he said he would tell the desk to book her a room on the same floor as the agents. Not sure, what her reason was for coming to the house."

Terry looked quizzical. "Most likely she was the one that wanted the background checks done. Maybe it was her way of staying the alpha. Could be that she was just letting you know she knew where you lived. If she knew everyone's secrets and weaknesses, she would play that to her advantage. Of course, I don't know what kind of advantage she would be playing. Noah is right, keep all your doors and windows locked at all times. If Logan was sent to kill you, then someone else might be sent still."

"You know Terry you sure know how to cheer up a person." Terry saw Johnnie smile and knew she was joking.

***

Michael brought Johnnie her morning tea. "Are you ready to start a new week?"

Johnnie took the tea. "Thank you sweetheart, I can smell the Jasmine. I think this is my favorite tea for relaxing. Do you think I will get a chance to relax anytime soon? I am dreading this week. I know Noah will be at the bank today, not sure, where Mirah will be. She may decide to stay at the hotel or she could go to the police station; but I suspect she will be at the bank. If word gets out about John's death, and we know it already has, there will be a media circus wherever she goes. I would think with the FBI in the background could make for a stronger image, she would like that impression. I don't like the bank being in the backdrop though."

Michael sat on the edge of the bed. "Where do you plan on working today? Stay near Noah if you go to the executive floor or stay in your office?"

Johnnie took a deep breath before answering. "I would like to stay with Noah so I can help; but I still have obligations to the bank. So, I will be in my office. If I am lucky, Mirah will stay with the agents. I really need to get some things done. I had put some things in the order of priority when I stopped by the bank on Saturday before going to the police station."

Michael stood up. "You went to the bank alone when it was closed? You think that was a smart move not knowing who might be inside?"

"Don't get upset, I went up by the back stairs and I was in and out in 15 minutes. I can't ignore my job. Besides, with all the agents that have been in and out of there, I doubt there was any danger. There wasn't even a car in the lot. I parked by the drive-in stations so I would not have to walk the lot. Terry knows I am carrying my gun; so I felt perfectly safe."

"Did you have to relinquish your firearm when you went to the station?" Michael was still standing in front of her.

"No, but I was wearing a holster shirt. I love the holster tops. The top works with any suit, or in Saturday's case, I had jeans and my leather jacket. I did buy five of the holster tops when I was still with the bureau. Never thought I would ever wear them again. Besides, Noah kept his so why shouldn't I keep mine with me. I even took my holster purse."

"You are trying to change the subject. Working with Terry or Noah is fine; but you can not go to the bank when it is closed. You still don't know how they got in the bank to stuff Herb in your closet. How could you be so sure it was safe?" Michael was not happy. "Look, I know all about the intense training; but you have been out of the field for three years. It just isn't the smart thing to do, and you know that Noah would agree."

"Okay, okay, I get it. I won't go back in the bank after hours unless I have backup. Does that make you happy?" Johnnie knew Michael was right; but she knew what she was doing. "I plan on wearing my quiet gear for the foreseeable future. I want to be able to protect the staff and myself. Right now I am heading for the shower." She got out of the bed and kissed Michael holding him as tight as she could.

Johnnie knew one of the best things about their marriage was they never had any carry over discussions. Johnnie got downstairs to find Michael buttering the toast and setting it on the table. He had prepared oatmeal and toast to give her a warm breakfast. Johnnie wanted to get out the door but she sat and ate with Michael. As usual, they discussed their plans for the day.

Michael had plans to drive over to the medical center. They were looking for a way to add another layer of protection to their prison ward.

Johnnie was finishing her toast, which she dunked into her coffee before she spoke. "I would like to get some of the bank projects done today. I would not be surprised to find Leo at the bank today. If it had been one of my agents, I would be hot on the case."

***

Noah and his team were back at the Hilton still looking for access points. Yes, they found fibers on the ledges; but they did not find anything in the room that matched the fibers. The fraying of the fibers should have made it easy for transfer into the room.

Noah and his agents were talking about the various happenings. "John's death has upset all of us. We want to clear this situation, and we thought we had a possible scenario going until John's death."

The front desk called Noah's cell phone. They told him he had company. He was not surprised when Leo arrived at the hotel. John reported to him, and Leo wanted to see John's room.

Noah took Leo to John Erickson's hotel room. It was an inconvenience to the hotel and guest, but it was important to retain all the evidence in the room and hallway. The hotel did not like the idea of a murder on their premises but they were cooperating. New guest took rooms on different floors allowing normal operations to continue. Unfortunately, there was nothing fresh to recognize. Terry's people were very good.

Leo had the look of a defeated man. John's death hit him hard. Noah filled Leo in on the events that had surfaced as he sat in the room with the other agents trying to work things through. The two deaths of Blake Colton and Jim Sonderson were easy to explain. The backgrounds of the two victims made for an obvious connection to Victor.

Leo asked Noah how long they wanted to work. Noah said they would be working as late as the job took. Then he asked if they could have access to Johnnie's office. Noah called her and Johnnie said she would call Gary and let him know that the agents would be arriving at the bank shortly after it closed. They wanted to meet up with the agents that were in the boardroom.

When they arrived, Noah called Johnnie to let her know they were at the back door. She said she would be right down. She put the little rubber doorstop in place to leave the tiniest opening so she could get back on the floor.

Noah introduced Leo to Johnnie. "I am so sorry we are meeting like this. From my little contact with John he seemed to be a nice guy."

Leo looked at her with a question. "How is it you had little contact when the murder is what brought him to Ackers?"

Johnnie looked at Noah. "I liked John, but I don't have the same regard for Mirah. I am not a fan of individuals that use tragedy for a photo op. I could be wrong; but I can't help how I feel."

Leo walked into the office and checked the closet that had held Herb's body. "How did someone get a body up here without being noticed? How could it have happened?" Leo then asked if they could go to the boardroom.

Johnnie led the group down to the bank's executive floor via the back stairs. She wanted to stop by Gary's office and introduce Leo. Then they went into the boardroom where Leo met the other agents. Everyone seemed to be less than talkative. Even though the agents at the bank did not work with Erickson, the loss was affecting all of them. No law enforcement took the loss of any officer lightly.

After meeting the team and accepting their condolences, he asked if it would be possible to go back to Johnnie's office. Johnnie took him back the same way.

"Why did you want to come back up? There really isn't much to see. I had Luke McGuire clean the scene when Terry's people were done. His team did an excellent job."

Leo looked at Noah. "Is it safe to talk in here?"

Johnnie nodded and brought out the device that Terry had given her to check for bugs. "It is clear."

Leo asked why she had the device ready to use. She explained that Terry's people had found a listening device in her office, clear back when this all began. "We didn't think about it until Harrison Major was in a near miss accident. Then to be safe Terry insisted that I check the office."

"Sounds like a smart lady, who is she? By the way, is there another access to the bank?" Leo was looking for any possible clue, and talking faster than he was thinking. "Yes, the main door, but it is locked until 9 AM. I don't know who would have a key and as early as it must have been, the door wasn't open. To the best of my knowledge, nobody would have let someone in carrying something as large as a body. Not to mention this is a secured floor. It takes a key code to get up or down from this floor outside banking hours." Johnnie was sure they wouldn't have used the front door. "And as to the 'smart lady' Terry is the local homicide detective we have been working with. I would like you to meet her Leo."

Leo sat quietly for a while then he got up and walked to the closet. He looked over the space and commented that the closet wasn't very large. Johnnie agreed, and said that she would have never expected a body could be jammed into the space.

It looked to Noah and Johnnie that Leo was trying to put himself in the mind of the criminal. Agents do have to think like a criminal. "Leo, I tried the same thing, tried to put myself in the mind of whoever did this, but it is truly hard to accept the events that have happened here. Reviewing it won't help. I know I have done it at least 10 times. I am sure Noah did too, as did Terry." Johnnie wanted Leo to stop torturing himself. This was something beyond their control at least for now.

"Has John or Mirah been up to do the same thing?" Leo was curious.

"I don't think so. John stayed close to the boardroom since that is where Mirah spent most of her time. When Mirah did come up here, it was only to interrogate me."

Noah grinned. "I bet she enjoyed that session…not! She doesn't back down easy this Mirah, but then she has never come up against Johnnie."

"No one saw anyone carrying in a large object? How could that be, and how did they get into the bank in the first place?" Leo had many questions, none of which Johnnie or Noah could answer. "Where did they find the morning computer operator? Noah told me she was on the floor most likely when the act was perpetuated."

Johnnie explained Silva's story stated she turned off the light and hid in the tiny wire room. Because she thought, it was the police coming to get her because she skipped jury duty. Do you know any courts that start at 6:30 in the morning? That story was definitely false."

Leo looked at her incredulously. "John filed a report with me about a window washer with red hair coming onto the floor and that was why Silva turned off the lights and hid. Seems she told two stories, one to the locals and a different story to John. You know she knew something. Could she have tried to blackmail someone?"

Johnnie was a bit sad thinking of Silva. "She was the lady that was murdered the same week. It would seem that she saw something, and someone knew what actually happened. Maybe she told someone the true story, and that someone did not want whatever to be known. We will never know now."

Johnnie took Leo into the confirmation department and they stepped into the computer room. She introduced Leo as an investigator to Karey Cousin. "Karey, Leo would like to see the wire room."

Karey took Leo to the back of the computer room to where the access door was for the wire room. It was a small space not much bigger than the closet in Johnnie's office. He thanked Karey for showing him the location and returned to Johnnie who was checking with the ladies in the confirmation department.

"Can we go back to the boardroom?" Leo seemed satisfied with what he had seen. She wasn't sure exactly what satisfied him. They returned to the boardroom and sat near Noah.

In the bank's boardroom, they all sat quietly with copies of the files in date order. It seemed to Johnnie that they were reviewing the same material over again. She patiently went through the files for Leo's sake.

Terry knocked on the door of the boardroom. "I figured I would find you all in here about this time of day. I called Gary, and he let me in. He is dedicated. Will he stay until we all leave?"

"Most likely he will stay until they are done in the confirmation room and computer room. He takes the employees to their cars to guarantee their safety, well as much as anyone can guarantee at present."

Noah looked at Johnnie. "Have you noticed any behavior oddities considering your knowledge of the staff. Do you have anything that you think could be helpful?" Noah remarked.

"I can understand Herb's vice getting him killed, but Silva. She had to see something and/or say something to someone. Harrison's accident, well, it could have been an accident. To be honest, I doubt it was especially since the listening device was found in my office. As for anyone else, I will keep at it to see if anything materializes." Johnnie was playing over in her mind, the contacts she had with the various personnel in the bank since this all began, nothing exceptional came to mind. Well outside of Kelly's sudden vacation.

The boardroom seemed to be overflowing with folders again. The most recent files for John Erickson and Logan Ferns were merely jackets with basic information about birth dates, place of employment, associates, and the date and manner of the deaths. As time went on, they would gather more information for these files.

Johnnie commented. "Did you notice the viciousness of the deaths of Blake Colton and Jim Sonderson? Ruthlessness is Sebastian's trademark, not just the substance signature. However, these recent deaths just are not the same I don't believe these deaths are the work of Sebastian Osis."

The room sat in silence. Terry was the first to gather her thoughts. "You mean Herb, Grammar, Silva, John, and even Logan all were copycat killings?"

"To be honest, I do believe someone is playing copycat, but they don't have enough information about Sebastian to do the jobs his way. Sebastian is a psychopath in the rawest form. I can tell you, after studying his file, I believe the first two are definitely the work of Sebastian. The remaining ones I don't see Sebastian committing." Johnnie was convincing she had made a good observation.

Noah was considering the idea. "Terry, know anyone who might be angry enough to kill these individuals? Someone is trying to misdirect us possibly."

Terry looked at the files scattered on the table. "Unfortunately, at this point your guess is as good as mine."

Leo wanted to express his thoughts about this new development. "My knowledge of Sebastian is that he is not limited to just the United States. He was on the payroll of drug cartels, gunrunners, and even terrorist cells. This made Sebastian a very dangerous and prolific killer. Who is protecting him? Whoever it is has to be someone in a position of power, and finding out would take a multifaceted task force."

Noah said to Leo, "We are going to be meeting up with Mirah Anderson, let's not say anything about Sebastian's reputation in front of her. She did lose someone she has been working with for the last five years. The same as we did, Leo."

Johnnie made an observation. "You may all think I am being paranoid, but I don't like leaving all this here in the boardroom or anywhere in the bank. Maybe Terry has a space for us at the station; or we can cart it to the house. I have a very secure place to keep it when we are not working with these stacks. What do you think?"

Mirah was on her way to the bank to talk to them about John. She really seemed broken up about the incident. She arrived by taxi. She said she was still shaky and didn't want to drive.

Johnnie could see that she was trying to impress them with her grief. She couldn't help but think about what Mirah had been doing before she came to the bank. "Did your taxi have a problem? I thought you would have been here about an hour ago?"

"Oh you know reporters. They never leave you alone. It was as if I was holding a press conference. I was just coming out of the hotel and they were waiting for me I guess." Mirah gave a diminutive smile.

"Ms. Anderson, I don't know if you should be out and about without a protection detail. Besides we are ready to wrap up here." Noah was looking for an excuse to remove her from any discussions on the case. With her love of the media, the wrong stuff could slip. Noah suggested that one of the agents take her back to the hotel and she could call should she want to go out for any reason. "I think we need to assign you a protection detail. Hey Smitty, how about you take Ms. Anderson back to her hotel and keep an eye on her? Since John's death I am not willing to chance it happening to you, Mirah."

Noah knew that Smitty was a fairly new but good agent, and his hotel room was across the hall from her's. It should make it easier for Smitty to keep an eye on her.

Leo waited until the agent and Mirah left for the hotel before saying anything. "To tell you the truth, these walls feel like they are closing in on me. Johnnie, are you sure you have a secure place to store the files?"

Noah smiled. "I forget you haven't met Johnnie's husband. He is a security expert with intelligence connections. As an expert in his field, he has a state of the art safe room. You might be able to get him to give you a tour. However, don't expect to see the trigger for the room. I haven't seen it and I have known these two for years."

Johnnie wasn't ready to call it a night. "How about we head over to the house and lay all this out in the kitchen and then we can divide into teams, we might have a breakthrough if we switch partners."

"Hey, I am game. Noah, do you want to team up with me? We haven't worked together and I would really like to hear what you have to say." Terry had been working with Johnnie from the beginning and a new angle might help.

"That isn't a bad idea, Leo are you game to work with me?" Johnnie really didn't know Leo, she had heard of him, but had not worked with him.

Noah spoke to the other agents, Rob, Vince, and George. "You three guys could still work as a team, but Smitty is going to be at a disadvantage. If Mirah wants to go out, he needs to take her. Maybe you could give Smitty the capsule version of your findings when everyone is at the hotel or work with Smitty at the hotel."

Vince, being senior among the field agents, assured Noah that they would be working in Smitty's room so they could be close to Ms. Anderson but would not allow her to join them in the conversation. In fact, I think we will work when she isn't near us, just to play it safe."

"Let's not forget Murph." Murphy was standing in the doorway as he reminded them he was still on the case.

"We are not going to leave you out, Murph. Maybe at the house Michael and Pat will be there and they can add their flavor to the pot." Noah was beginning to like this big guy.

The agents needed to get Johnnie's address so they knew where everyone was located. After that, it seemed like a plan to them. They were all ready to head out for Johnnie's when Johnnie's cell rang. Michael was on the phone. "What is your plan for the night?"

"We thought we would bring the notes over to the house and spread out and break up into teams. Is Pat there? Would you be interested in joining our jam session?"

"I am sure Pat would help out. Maybe we could get some subs or something and I can put on some tea or coffee. If you want I could get some wine or beer for when we call it a night."

"That would be great, we shouldn't be too long. We need to gather this all up, get it boxed and we will be home in about a half an hour."

***

On the way over to Johnnie's place Leo asked about the obvious absence of Mirah, and why didn't Noah want her around.

"She is the type to take all the glory on a case without lifting a finger. However, if anything goes wrong with the case, she will point that finger in our direction. Did you catch there just happened to be a crowd of reporters outside the hotel? She likes to play up to the cameras, and we don't want to risk her saying the wrong things." Noah's explanation satisfied Leo.

As they all came in the door carrying the files, Michael was there to greet them. He had several different types of subs ordered and they had arrived.

Noah introduced Leo to Michael. Then looking at the kitchen counter we was pleasantly surprised. "Wow, just like the old days. I need to reimburse you for the subs and drinks."

As Johnnie was taking their coats, she looked at Noah. "How about we wait until we wrap this up, tabs might be a wash by then."

"I take it Mirah isn't a welcome part of the investigation. I don't blame you guys. I saw her impromptu interview. How did they find her and if the interview had been a spur of the moment, how did Mirah know all the reporters? Yes, she could have known the people from the big networks, but the small town reporters from Ackers. She wanted to play the part of the grieving partner, struggling with the death of a friend." Michael didn't care for Mirah anymore than the others.

***

Noah started his flow chart on the white board as they discussed each case. He agreed that Logan had been his choice but now he was back to square one.

Johnnie thought for a moment before she said anything. "What if Ferns was hired to kill the others, but for some reason he had outlived his usefulness?"

Noah smiled. "Now you all know why I missed her in the division. That is a real possibility, but now we have to determine who would have carried out the other murders and why. I doubt Logan went to Virginia to get Jonas. I guess it could be possible. If Jonas died from an allergic reaction, how would Logan know what he was allergic to?"

Terry spoke up and asked if they had details on Grammar's death. "It may be that Herb, Grammar, and Silva were all copycat deaths. What does that say for John and Logan? Who killed them? What are the specifics around Grammar's death and what about the attempt on Harrison? What if the attempt on Harrison was only to misdirect suspicion?"

"I don't see Harrison as the killer type. Maybe Harrison is close to whoever the killer may be, even if he is not aware of the connection." Johnnie didn't want to believe that the killer could be in the bank. Noah started a new graph on another white board. "Let's put together everything we know about Harrison. We have to at least consider the possibility." Noah was not going to give Harrison a free ticket. "Johnnie, what do you know about him?"

"I don't know much about him. He was already working at the bank when I came. He was close to Silva, so I don't think he would have intentionally been a part of any plan to kill her. If he does have a link, it is going to have to be outside the bank. He and Silva were friends. Silva must have seen something or heard someone, there was no other reason that I know, for someone to kill her. I think she was an inconvenient obstacle to someone. I am sure Harrison is close with Aces Silva's youngest. He is the star of the swim team. In fact, if he hadn't left the house so early for practice, he could have been killed as well. He probably is also close with

Charleston, Silva's older son, he was in Iraq, but is home for the services."

Leo said he would like to know more about Herb and Harrison. He asked if Johnnie could get the personnel files. She said she would ask Gary for the files. "I will ask him first thing in the morning. Has anyone thought of something new tonight?" Johnnie was hoping that somebody, especially Leo, would come up with something new. He would be the freshest set of eyes on the cases.

Leo could tell that everyone was hoping he had thought of something. "I hate to break your bubble, but I think the copycat theory is the best going. I guess you should know that John had been assigned to Mirah because of her constant presence in the news. She had a habit of voicing her opinions to anyone who would listen, especially if they had a camera and a microphone. As you all have noted."

"Terry you are right to have been cautious around her. John said that she had interfered with too many cases here in West Virginia, and as a result, alleged killers went free. Now her interference could have been a matter of the publicity hound that she is, or it was intentional. He was more or less her handler. She just didn't see it that way." Leo's comment didn't seem like it surprised anyone.

Terry spoke up. "Actually it was Johnnie that was suspicious first. I just didn't like her. Tell them about your impression of Mirah."

Johnnie was uncomfortable being put on the spot; but Terry was correct. "I have the same feeling about her being a news hound. The idea of her interference in a case that allowed people to go free, that was news to me. I think the grief over John is just an act for her. She has a motive, and I am not sure exactly what it is at this moment."

Pat gave a slight smile. "Word around some circles in DC says that she has put her eye on the US Attorney General job; but some say she is aiming for the Supreme Court. Assigning someone to keep track of her might present the image of her being an important part of the FBI's investigations. If she could use that as an angle, she will."

Leo looked over at Pat. "I have heard those same stories, but if you wanted to move up, would you be so clumsy around high powered cases? What were John's accounts of her like, what did he report?"

Leo sighed deeply. "I am afraid we may never know what he wanted to testify, if anything. Unless we can find his notes, or some kind of journal we are at a loss. It seemed this trip seemed to be important to Mirah, but we don't know why."

Noah was the next to speak up. "I hate to break up this fun fest, but it is just about 10 and I know I want to be back in my room before Mirah gets curious. I prefer not to be seen with her. Poor Smitty, I hated to do that; but she could suffer the same fate as John. I don't want that happening on my watch. Michael, how about you go open your safe room and when you are ready let us bring up the files. Johnnie, are you going to be able to lug this back to the bank?"

"Not a problem, I feel safer knowing they will be in a secure place. If someone is after Mirah, and they find her in the same hotel as your home away from home, they might do some extra searching." Johnnie was already putting the files in date order according to the individuals and the individual files then arranged in alphabetical order.

Michael called down to the dining room so they could come up to the safe room.

Leo was impressed. "This is where you hid out Johnnie?"

Murph and Terry were also impressed. "Johnnie, when you said you had a safe room, I was not picturing something as nice as this room." Terry could not get over all the electronics and monitors in the room.

Murph had to ask. "What about fireproofing?" Michael said it was all part of the package.

"Actually, the other day when the guys Logan sent broke in was the first time I actually used the room. Believe me, Michael has had this set up in every house we have ever bought. The room is entirely self-contained. We even have plumbing installed in the event we are in here awhile. The ambient temperatures and fresh air are on a separate system. Even have a small fridge and an electromagnetic burner should we ever need it. Normally we would have an air mattress in here, but can't have the files and the mattress at the same time." Michael was proud of the work his company did, and it was a definite benefit to get the first of the company's efforts.

***

Johnnie arrived at the bank and asked Gary if it would be possible for the agents to view Herbs and Harrison's personnel files. She explained it might help further the investigation.

Gary tapped on the door bringing the files the group requested. Leo asked if he could add some input that could help them develop some theories.

Gary sat down and handed the files to Noah. He asked who they wanted to know about first.

Noah said. "Did you know Grammar Jonas?" Gary said that they had attended some of the same banking conferences. Noah asked for his opinion of the man. "I knew him mostly through the banking circles, but he also belonged to the same national civic group as I do. Occasionally, we would chat a bit at the national meetings."

Noah asked about the rumors of drug use involving Grammar and Herb. Gary said that he was aware of the fact that both men used recreational drugs. It was one of the reasons the board was planning a special meeting. Herb's work had become suspect where certain individuals were involved.

"Suspect in what manner?" Leo wanted to know all he could in order to get a good feel for the man.

Gary explained. "Herb had a customer suspected of money laundering. This same character was also a friend of Grammar Jonas. The board started looking over the deposit activity at the suggestion of Johnnie. An in-depth study done of all big depositors, and the records seemed to support Johnnie's fears. This gave them all a reason to stop and think. The accounts in question belonged to a real estate developer who also had investments in a few malls throughout the United States."

"I remember doing checks for cash transactions, but that transactions for the Hyde Industries had a waiver status. Maybe it was my background in law enforcement, but I saw it as a possible method for laundering." Johnnie said she wanted to do some additional research when all these events started happening.

Noah asked who owned Hyde Industries. The owner of the entity hides through a maze of shell companies. "We had hoped to get a handle on the ownership, but it ran through so many off shore and international financial powerhouses we could not identify who the owner or owners just might be."

Leo directed his comments to Johnnie. "The investigation you were handling had to do with Victor Andropov, but it is doubtful that Victor had anything to do with these recent deaths. The answer lies beyond Victor. As for Hyde Industries, I doubt they would have been in your office looking through files. Maybe that is where Logan entered the picture. I hate to tell you, but if you are responsible for disrupting their enterprise, well, you could be at risk. Of course, you are not the average banker, with your training and background. I would say you would provide a few surprises."

"You see my concern about this entire deal. If I hadn't brought the organization up for an in-depth look, maybe Herb and Silva would still be alive." Johnnie did not want to be responsible for a lost life. She endured it herself while with the bureau, but never thought she would experience that feeling while working in a small city bank.

Gary asked if they had any more questions for him. If not he would be in his office if they needed anything else.

Johnnie wanted to return to the sixth floor, but as long as the personnel files were with the team, she felt obligated to stay.

Noah finally spoke. "I know we have a lot to concentrate on here, and it is still early, but we can't do it with a tired mind. Let us meet tomorrow at the conference center the hotel has provided for us. I think I have seen too many files and had too many scenarios suggested. I need to step away from this for a bit."

Johnnie spoke up. "Do you have a set time for the conference? Do you want me to attend? If so, can you call me at the bank? Use the cell number please. I need to get some things done at the bank."

Noah told her to expect a call around 9:30. That was going to make it perfect since Mirah never came in before noon. With luck, she would never know Johnnie had been to the bank.

179

***

The next day started like any other day. Michael was up and had Johnny's tea ready. She enjoyed her first cup of the day as they sat in the bedroom.

So what is on your agenda today? Are you going to the bank or to Terry's office?"

"I was planning on working at the bank, but Noah wants to work in the conference room that the hotel has provided. Afterwards I am going back to the bank. I really don't want Mirah noting my absence. I think I need to play banker. Besides, I do have to give some attention to the bank and the employees. I am sure there are several that are feeling nervous. Some may know of John Erickson's death, and since he was in and out of the bank it could cause for greater anxiety."

Michael got up and kissed her on the forehead. He always had the right gesture and perfect timing. "That's my gal, always worrying about someone else first."

Johnnie wanted to dress in a way that would seem approachable. She knew that wearing brown usually kept the employees at a distance. Today, she wore her favorite jewel blue suit. She needed the lift it would give her spirits.

She had a spring in her step as she entered the kitchen. Michael was just finishing the French toast he was making for breakfast. It was an ideal dish to start what she was hoping would be a good day.

As they ate, they talked about their plans for the day. Michael told her he would be working on a bid for a job in DC. He would submit the proposal and do a video conference with the interested party later in the day.

Johnnie said. "I would like to work the entire day at the bank. However, Noah wants some time at the hotel's conference room. Wonder if I take my laptop if I could just Skype. If Mirah should happen to come up to my office, I would not want her to see me in a Skype conference. I will see what Noah says when he calls. I still can't believe that Harrison would be involved with Silva's death. The two found their way into the center ring more often than not, and most likely, it is what got Silva killed. With the signature of the salt in her eyes and her mouth, it gives credence to the idea that she saw something and spoke about it to the wrong person. Harrison was just a matter of being nosy and asking too many questions. I am afraid it has put him on someone's radar."

Johnnie finished her breakfast and second cup of tea then took the dishes to the sink. She gave Michael a kiss and left for the bank.

The employees on the main floor stopped and looked as Johnnie walked into the bank. Harrison was the first to approach her. "Do you have any information about Silva's death? I heard it was murder."

Johnnie sat down at the couch in the lobby. Harrison sat with her and she could see the pain in his eyes. He did care about Silva and her family.

Harrison told her that he had spent the night with Aces. They delayed the services until Charleston could get home from Iraq. Harrison said the services would be the next day and asked if she would be attending. Johnnie assured him she would be there and that they could travel together if he wanted.

Harrison said there were others who would want to attend. Johnnie said she would bring the van so eight could ride with her.

Johnnie went to Gary's old office, her new office, and put her purse on the floor next to her desk. She picked up the accumulated notices and papers on the desk and scanned the various topics. Gary approached her and asked what she knew about the funeral. She told him that Harrison had informed her that the services for Silva would be the next day. She asked him if he would be attending. Gary said both he, and Tom would be there for the services. Gary said there were many people wanting to attend, but somebody had to stay and run the bank. Gary said he and Tom would have to return to the bank after an appearance at the luncheon.

Johnnie told him she was going to the funeral, and would return to her office later if she could. She thought it would be good for the employees. She doubted she would get any work done; but it was more important for the employees to have her available if they needed to talk.

Johnnie went to her sixth floor office and put her items in the closet. She felt an involuntary shiver run through her as she opened the closet door. The most horrifying incident at the bank seemed like it was years ago until she opened the door to her closet. It reminded her that things could change a life in an instant.

It wasn't long before Sarah came into her office. "What do you know about the funeral?

"I heard that Silva's service is tomorrow, who all is going? Do you know what time the service is starting?"

Johnnie said she and Harrison would be there and that Gary and Tom were planning to attend. She did not know about Ernie, and she knew there were many from her departments that wanted to attend, but as Gary said, someone had to remain at the bank.

Sarah sat in Johnnie's office for a while asking questions. It was obvious that she had to put her thoughts before approaching Johnnie.

Sarah left and soon Johnnie had another employee in her office. She could see how this day was going to unfold.

After the visit of the fourth employee, Johnnie returned to her secondary space in the bank. She read a few more notices on the desk and after completing that task, went into Gary's office to discuss how many employees wanted to attend the services. Gary said each department could have two to three people attend, depending on the size and coverage of the department.

Johnnie considered informing Gary of the findings in the autopsy. She did not believe Gary had any ties to the situation, but now she found herself being very guarded as to what information she relayed to anyone. She did not tell him of the salt. She knew that autopsy reports in some states were available as public record, so if Gary wanted details, he could get the report for himself. Besides, she did not want Aces or Charleston to hear through the grapevine the details of their mother's death.

Noah called pretty close to 9:30 as he said he would. He thought they could Skype her side, but she expressed her concern should Mirah find her. Noah said since she was not supposed to go out without her security detail, he would be aware of her timing. If need be he could give her fair warning of Mirah's nearing arrival.

Johnnie returned to her office and reviewed the expected workload for the next day. Luckily, it was mid-month so she could allow three people to attend in addition to herself. She believed it was best to let the individual department heads decide on the attendance.

By the end of the day, it had been determined who would be attending. She told her department heads that she would have her van, and that it would hold six more people as well as Johnnie and Michael as the driver. The individual department heads said they would take their own vehicles, that way they could return to the bank following the services. Johnnie did not know if she would stay very long after the services, but she did want to talk to Silva's sons. She was sure Harrison would want to spend time with the family. In fact, he may want more time than she planned on staying.

Harrison called Johnnie just before closing time and said he would travel on his own as he intended to stay with Aces and Charleston.

***

Johnnie was so glad that the day was over. She went straight home. She needed to see Michael.

As she came into the kitchen from the garage, she could tell he had a good day. "You look like you had a good day."

Michael was all smiles, "sure did, the client agreed to the proposal. I will have to start the review with the installation staff, but not until early next month."

Johnnie asked if he was interested in attending the services for Silva. "Yes, I planned on attending. I am also going to use my mini camera to record the service. I talked to Terry, and she asked if I had a gadget for recording the service. She wants to see who attends, but she did not want to cause a stir by having law enforcement attend. She also said Mirah would be attending. No one seems to be happy about her showing up. That is one of the reasons Terry wants me to record without being noticed. Mirah will be wherever there is a camera."

Johnnie just smiled. "I bet you have a nifty little gadget that will serve nicely for the assignment. I know Noah and the men would like to have a copy of the attendees. So I am glad you will be there as well."

Michael replied that he did have the perfect lapel pin that looked like a microchip. People in the technology fields loved the look. The device had become commonplace and it made a great mini camera. He also stated he had an extra one if she wanted to wear the second one. Johnnie thought this could work well to get better coverage. The item contained a microphone, which would allow for a complete feel for the crowd. Terry would be pleased with the coverage.

The funeral was a sad occasion for everyone. Silva was a vibrant person, and her boys still needed her in so many ways.

Johnnie saw Harrison's emotional state. This was going to be hard on many people. At the bank, Harrison and Silva had lunch breaks together and Silva's laugh carried through the office, as

Harrison would leave the computer room when he did his rounds of good mornings. She was a vivacious individual.

Harrison spent the services very near the boys, who seemed to depend on his presence. Silva's sister and mother were also looking to him for a sense of reason and support.

The services ended in the little church at the bottom of a hill, and then the group ascended to the top of the cemetery alongside the church for a quiet graveside prayer. Afterward, the group went to a restaurant/banquet hall near the bank for the bereavement lunch. Gary and Tom not only attended the luncheon but also picked up the tab and had the banquet hall remain open for the remainder of the day. This allowed employees who could not attend the services to have lunch and visit with Silva's family or at least sign the register. The family no doubt would not stay all day, but at least they could see how people cared.

Johnnie and Michael spent the balance of the day at the hall. Johnnie made sure each visitor signed the guest book. It would be a source of comfort to the boys as they looked back on the day's happenings and a good record to share with Terry.

Nothing looked out of place as Johnnie and Michael made their rounds to the different tables. Mirah floated briefly among Silva's family to express her condolences, then left without approaching Johnnie or Michael.

At the end of the day, both Johnnie and Michael were happy to be home. Johnnie said she would check on the boys in a couple days, but for now, they had the family close and were staying with their Aunt Rayna.

Johnnie sat down in the kitchen and let out a sigh. "You know I had completely forgotten about putting Silva's job up for bid. I am not in a hurry to do so. I wonder if it might be better if we wait a week. I don't like the feeling of just sweeping her life out the window. We have Sarah who can cover for a while."

Michael agreed, saying he had never had to replace an employee in a position because of a death, much less a murder.

Johnnie got up and told Michael she was heading for a long shower. It had been an exhausting day. Michael asked for the mini camera and said he would go edit the results into one file.

After her shower, she went to the study to see what progress Michael had made with the video file.

"Find anything interesting?" Michael was deep in thought when she entered.

"Not really, but I didn't realize Harrison was so close to Silva's boys." Johnnie looked over his shoulder as he moved through the file.

"I knew he made his rounds in the morning and stopped to see her every day; but I am impressed at the level of devotion and care he gave to the boys. Perhaps he is just feeling vulnerable since he had a near miss. Maybe they already know that her death was not the result of the fire. I don't know for sure what they know, and I am afraid for Aces. Charleston has been in Iraq, and he knows what it is like to lose someone close; still it not the same as your mother, especially if the boys know it is a case of murder."

Michael nodded. "I don't know about the death certificate. I think it is different in varied locales. I would think that Terry knows if the boys are aware of the circumstance. You need to stop thinking that this was a banking issue. Most likely Silva just played 'I Got a Secret' with the wrong person. Don't go beating yourself up over something you had no control over. Besides, there is no evidence your Andropov research is at the core of this situation. I know that is what you are thinking."

"I know you are right, but you have to know that I have a guilty feeling nagging in the back of my mind. I guess we need to head for the station. I just wanted to see this town as I did five years ago. Guess this place lost some of its previous luster."

Michael and Johnnie walked up to the front desk to find Will at the desk. "Hi man, guess who we are here to see? Will gave them a visitor's pass but said he would ride up with them. Terry was waiting for them at the elevator.

"How did it go today? Did Mirah attend?"

"It was more emotionally exhausting than I thought it would be. I attended funerals when I was with the bureau, even family funerals; this one was different. I guess it was watching Silva's sons. We have seen families deal with deaths and murder; but to see those boys so young. I know that Charleston has probably dealt with the loss of friends in Iraq, but Aces, he is lucky to have his brother back with him, but I don't know if he has to go back to active service or not. I know their Aunt Rayna will be a wonderful support for them both. Oh Yeah, Mirah did attend, but she did not stay long after the services. She came to the banquet hall, but only expressed her condolences to the family and left."

Terry walked them back to the conference room. "Did you see any surprises at the services?"

"Not really. The only thing we noticed was how supportive Harrison was for the boys. I guess I never saw him in that light. He has been the bank's clown. You know; the one that's always cutting up and playing jokes on people. Maybe he did all that to hide his true nature."

Terry asked if they wanted coffee, but Johnnie requested a soda if possible. "Michael produced a DVD of the pictures we gathered during the service and at the luncheon. I was glad to see the bank step up and handle the luncheon and the banquet hall. Herb was the first employee to be lost due to violence. Now we have another loss to violence. I wonder if there should be a quiet surveillance on their house. Their Aunt Rayna lives about two miles outside the city limits. They have a nice large house, and I think the boys will adapt in time. It will be hardest on Aces, going back to school and keeping up with his activities. Maybe being busy with his swimming will be good for him."

Terry nodded and said that the department would have someone at the school for a few days just to make sure no one attempted anything with Aces. "Charleston may be going back to active duty, if so there is nothing to fear on his behalf. Still for a day or so, we will just keep a mild eye on Aces. We could have an unmarked car go by the house, if you think that is necessary."

Johnnie rethought the situation. "Maybe it would draw unnecessary attention to the family. The school surveillance I think will be enough."

Just as Johnnie and Michael were ready to leave, an emergency call came into Terry. "Johnnie, Harrison was in an accident. He is going to the hospital for observation. I am heading to the scene of the accident."

Johnnie said they would go to the hospital. She wanted to talk to him and see what happened.

***

Johnnie went to the emergency room sign-in desk. She told them she was there for Harrison Magers. As she sat in the waiting room, she could not help but worry about this being an attempt on his life. She and Michael sat in the waiting room for a few hours, and finally, the nurse said that Mr. Magers was in room 317, they would be keeping him a few days for observation due to a concussion.

Johnnie and Michael went up to the third floor and approached the nurse's station and asked if they could see Mr. Magers. The nurse on duty said he was awake and wanting out already, so she was sure he could have a visitor.

"Well, imagine finding you here!" Johnnie did not want to appear to be overly concerned, but she was indeed.

"Hi, didn't I see you earlier today?" Harrison smiled and said to come in, and if she could find his clothes, he would love to get out of the place.

"I think it might be a good idea to spend the night. What happened?" Johnnie took the seat next to his bed, and Michael leaned against the wall.

"I didn't see the car coming. I guess that look left and right then left again, or is it right then left and then right again. Whatever I guess it is something I should have done. I pulled out of the parking lot at the banquet hall, and a car came out of nowhere. I think my car is history. Anyway, the other driver was a woman and her son. I swear I have seen her son before, but I can't place where I met the boy."

"I am sure the police will provide all the information you need. It is important that you rest and relax for a few days. In the meantime, if there is anything you need, call me."

Johnnie was surprised that no one else was in Harrison's room; but he was single and his parents were traveling in Europe. He was alone for the present. His sister Ciara Worls lives in Alaska. Her husband works on a crabbing boat she knew that from reviewing his personnel file.

"I will be fine, I told Ciara not to make the trip. I will be out of the hospital and back in action before she could get a flight. She loves Alaska, and her husband Kevin is out on the boat. I hate it when she travels here alone from such a distance."

"That means you must call me if you need anything. Do you want me to call Ciara and give her an update?"

Harrison gave her the number and said she was normally home all day, but since she lived so far west, the time difference was a hassle. Alaska is three hours behind time. He said for now, she didn't need to call her since he had talked to her just about an hour ago. Harrison also told her he had planned to go out to Rayna's to take the boys shopping. So much of their belongings were lost in the fire.

Johnnie agreed to check on the boys, and Michael said he would take them shopping. Harrison offered his credit card, but Michael said it was the least they could do.

As they left the room, Johnnie gave the nurse her number and said when he was ready for release, to call her

***

Michael suggested that Johnnie go on with her day. Besides, he thought maybe it would be easier on the boys if it were just him.

"I know you lost pretty much all your clothing and things in the fire, so Johnnie and I would like to help you recover."

Charleston was a bit mistrusting. "Why would you want to do that for us?" Michael explained that his mother worked at the bank where Johnnie worked, and they were both upset about what happened and just wanted to make things easier for the boys.

Aces spoke up. "Harrison is taking us shopping." Michael had not realized that the boys had not heard about Harrison.

"I know but I am sorry to tell you, Harrison was in a car accident last night, and he was admitted to the hospital. He has a concussion, and will be there for a few days. In the meantime, I volunteered to go shopping with you guys." Michael could see the boys were concerned, but he assured them it was okay.

Michael finally gained their trust, and the boys agreed to go shopping with him. Neither boy liked going to the mall, so they opted for a few stores in the local strip malls.

***

Johnnie was back at the bank catching up on work that was on her desk. Gary stopped by her office and sat down to talk. "How do you think the boys are going to do with Silva gone? Do you know if Charleston is returning to active duty?"

"I haven't had the opportunity to truly talk with the boys, but Harrison may know since he is pretty close to them." Johnnie asked if he saw how dutiful Harrison was with the boys.

Gary seemed surprised. "I didn't know Harrison was close with Silva's boys."

Johnnie said he and Silva were friends, but his devotion was evident at the funeral. He stayed by the family through the entire afternoon.

"Come to think of it, they did seem to be looking to him at the banquet. By the way, have you heard anything about Harrison's accident?" Gary seemed a tad mystified by the boys dependence on Harrison.

Johnnie recounted their visit to the hospital after she got word of the accident. Johnnie told Gary that Harrison would be in the hospital for a few days with a nasty concussion. She also told Gary about Michael taking the boys shopping. Having lost just about everything in the fire, they needed some clothes now. Waiting for the insurance would take too long to handle the daily needs.

Gary switched from the personal conversation to the business side of things. "When are you going to put Silva's job up for bid?"

Johnnie knew she would have to do it; but she didn't want to seem ghoulish about it. "I thought, considering her service being only yesterday, I just wanted to put a little time between her service and the job up for bid. We don't have any vacations right now, so Sarah can cover. She would have just been working on shredding old records otherwise, so I think I will hold off for maybe a day still, unless you have a problem with the plan."

Gary said it was fine. After a few more comments, he got up he looked across the desk and said good-bye as he took a few of the candies from her dish.

***

Johnnie has a pile of paperwork so she sat down to work through the mounting stack that was before her. A phone call interrupted her work. "First National Bank, Johnnie speaking."

To say she was surprised to hear Mirah's voice would be an understatement. "Is it true that Harrison was in an accident?"

"Yes, he had an accident pulling out of the lot after Silva's memorial luncheon. He will be in the hospital a few days with a rather serious concussion. You sound very concerned, is there something you want to share?"

Mirah's voice was shaky and breaking up. "I need to talk to you; but not on the phone. Can you meet me at the bookstore?"

Johnnie told Mirah that she had several more things she needed to tend to before she could meet her; however, I would be happy to do so after work.

Occupied by her paperwork, she totally lost track of time. Ana popped her head into the office to say good night. Johnnie realized she had to get moving herself; she called Michael and told him she was going to the bookstore and was going to meet up with Mirah.

Michael questioned. "Whoa, what do you mean you are going to meet up with Mirah? I don't think that is advisable. Up to now, you haven't exactly trusted her, why the sudden change and why the bookstore? I know you love that store, but how did she know you loved the store?"

"I know it is a 180-degree turn for me where she is concerned, but she called me, and she said she needed to talk to me. She didn't want to talk on the phone; that is when she suggested the bookstore. I don't know for sure how she knew I would like the bookstore, but I am carrying my Glock, and I doubt anyone would attempt something in public."

Michael was still not convinced. "Again I ask how did she know your love of the book store? Do you have a vest on?"

Johnnie sighed. "She did a background search on me, maybe it came up in her search. I haven't worn a vest since leaving the bureau. Besides it doesn't fit with civilian fashion."

Still being the protective husband, he was not dropping the topic. "Either go home and get your vest first, or I will put a protection detail on you."

"You know Michael I am not a rookie, I can handle myself in a public place. However, to give you peace of mind I will go home and change. How did it go with the shopping today?"

"We can talk about that later, I will tell you about the boys, and you can tell me about Mirah. For now, I love you and will see you afterward."

Johnnie returned home and went directly to the bedroom. She went to her closet and to a box in the bottom drawer of the dresser. Pulling out the vest, she decided to change her clothes in order to hide the outline of the vest. She scanned the clothes looking for a loose-fitting outfit. She finally decided on a tan tunic with a pair of leggings and a pair of ankle boots. As she redressed, she put her ankle holster on and placed her Ruger LCR in the holster. In order to balance the weight of the gun, she placed two extra magazines on the other side of her custom-fitted holster on her opposite leg. She did use her holster purse, and put her Glock in it for easy access.

Two firearms seemed extreme, but she was going to meet the person she was uncomfortable seeing alone. Johnnie had to wonder what part, and if she were involved, why would she call her?

Johnnie grabbed her coat and her holster purse and was on her way. She called Michael to set his mind at ease. "Hi husband. I am heading for my meeting, and rest assured, not only do I have my vest on, I also have my ankle holster and my holster purse." Michael laughed and said he knew she was sensible.

***

Johnnie walked into the store and headed for the magazine rack. Finding a magazine for law enforcement, she took it to the checkout counter, paid for the magazine, and preceded to the café. She purchased a decaf latte and took a seat by the window. Sitting at the table with her latte and her magazine, she waited for Mirah to arrive.

Johnnie started reading and sipping her latte. Before she knew it, she had read every article in the magazine, and her latte was cold. Checking her watch, she realized it was 8 o'clock. Giving up on the meeting, she gathered her belongings and left the store.

Walking in the front door, Michael called for her. "Why are you so late? Hungry? I ordered a pizza."

Johnnie came into the kitchen to find him sitting at the table. She dropped her purse on the spare chair and sat across from him. "My session with Mirah was a waste of time. She didn't show. I waited long enough to read every article in a magazine. I think I will call Terry and see if she has any updates on anything. Well, after I eat. I am starving."

Johnnie retrieved a plate from the cabinet and got a root beer from the pantry; sitting back down again she grabbed two pieces of pizza and took a bite. "Oh boy, I didn't realize how hungry I was."

With her hunger satisfied, she pulled out her cell phone and called Terry.

"Hi Terry. Are you involved with anything right now?"

"I am just getting home and Will and I are going out for a late dinner. You guys want to join us?" Terry asked.

Johnnie was ready to put her feet up for the night. "Thank you, but we just ate. I was wondering if anything odd happened today."

"Well, outside of your odd question just now, nothing happened to the best of my knowledge. Why do you ask?" Terry knew Johnnie had something on her mind.

Johnnie told her of Mirah asking to meet her at the bookstore. Then she said Mirah did not show.

Terry did not seem to be too alarmed. She said Mirah had a reputation of over filling her plate and losing track of time. Therefore, she saw no reason for concern.

Johnnie hung up and told Michael that Terry was meeting up with Will and she had not heard anything of news value.

***

The next morning was uneventful and Johnnie was happy to have a simple workday to distract her from the happenings that had absorbed all her thoughts.

Johnnie stopped by Gary's office and told him she thought it over and would put together a job bid on Silva's position. "I dread this but it is not fair to the rest of employees. We have to consider the cascade effect the bidding process creates. I should have it to you by closing time tonight. I hope it is well received. I am not in the mood for people to be asking questions about her passing."

Gary agreed it was most likely time, and filling the position may take a few days. Following Silva's position, there would be a stream of other jobs affected. This process always took a few days and sometimes weeks to complete. The training and such will be a drawn-out process.

Before Johnnie settled into her office to start writing the job description and requirements, Gary called. "Johnnie, have you heard from Harrison?"

"Not today, is there a problem?" Johnnie heard the concern in Gary's voice. "I called the hospital today, and they said he checked out last night. I didn't expect him to come in, but I thought he would at least let us know he was home."

"I don't like the sounds of this, Gary. Last night, I was to meet Mirah at the bookstore, and she did not show. Do you think the situations are connected? I am going to call Terry and see what she has to say."

Johnnie gathered her papers and returned the materials to her desk then picked up her cell phone. "Terry, remember when I called last night and told you of Mirah's no show? Has anything come to light since then?"

"I haven't heard of anything, what's up?" Terry inquired.

"You are not going to believe this, but Harrison checked out of the hospital last night and is not answering his phone. With two people involved in this investigation being no shows, we should start looking to see what their last known movements were yesterday. I am going to check in with Noah and ask if he saw Mirah last night. I need to tell him about Harrison too."

Johnnie went downstairs to the boardroom where the agents had set up their bullpen.

"Noah, I don't know why I didn't think to tell you this when I came in this morning. Yesterday Mirah called and asked if I could meet her. She suggested the bookstore. I have to admit, due to Michael's insistence; I wore my vest and ankle holster. Long story short, Mirah did not show. Have you seen her?" Johnnie was hoping he had heard from her or saw her at the hotel.

Noah sat down to think when he last saw Mirah. "The agents and I went to dinner last night, and I knocked on her door but she didn't answer. I honestly did not think anything about it. I just figured she slipped away from Smitty and would be in the hotel dining room."

"Maybe her meeting me was a ruse to get me alone; Michael was uncomfortable with the idea of me meeting with her. Still I went to the bookstore and I waited for a rather long time. I don't know why she wanted to meet, and I don't know why she didn't show. I think we should start tracking both she and Harrison."

"What about Harrison?" Noah asked. Johnnie continued with Harrison's situation. "Gary called the hospital this morning they said that Harrison checked himself out of the hospital last night and now he is not answering his phone. After his accident leaving the banquet hall, he was supposed to stay in the hospital a couple of days for observation."

Noah gathered the agents; they needed to divide the group in order to expedite the search.

Noah called the front desk at the hotel and asked for Mirah Anderson's room. She did not answer, but he thought it best to send an agent over to check the room.

Johnnie called Terry and asked her to meet at the hospital. "Sorry, just pulled into the bank lot, why not come down and the three of us will go check it out. Maybe he told someone at the hospital where he was going."

Johnnie told Noah and then Gary, that she, Terry and Murph were going to check the hospital. She would keep them in the loop.

They arrived at Ackers General and together the three went up to the third floor where Johnnie had visited Harrison the night before.

"I don't know what good this is going to do, but I think I just want to see how he was when he checked out last night. Was he agitated? Did someone picked him up like Mirah, or was he forced? Granted he is a decent size man, but he was suffering the effects of the concussion."

Stopping at the nurse's station, they asked if it were possible to see Harrison's attending physician. The nurse on duty pointed to the admitting doctor, but that Mr. Magers checked himself out before the doctors made their rounds in the morning.

Johnnie asked what time and the nurse referred to the chart. "He checked himself out last night about 9 PM" Johnnie thanked the nurse and turned back to Terry and Murph.

"I guess we should head for Harrison's house. Once we locate him, we can see if there has been any news on Mirah. I do find it a bit curious that both are out of touch at the same time."

"Do you know where Harrison lives? If not, we can call the precinct and get an address. It would be helpful to get a description of his car as well. I think it is too soon for a BOLO, but we may want to do that later." Murph unlocked the car as he spoke. Johnnie joined them, riding in the back seat, as Terry called for the information on Harrison as they drove.

"He said his car was pretty much totaled. I know his address. I have looked at his personnel file enough to have it memorized. Oh by the way, I should tell you I do have my weapon with me. I have a license to carry a concealed weapon but I just never thought as a banker I would ever need to carry again. Not knowing what we will find, I didn't want you to be concerned about me."

"Hopefully, it won't be necessary to use it, but at least we know you have it with you. His house isn't far away."

***

"Wow, this is an exclusive area. I didn't even know this area existed. Maybe Michael and I should have checked out this area before we bought. Of course, I think it is a bit beyond our price range"

"Definitely not something a cop's salary could cover." chimed Terry. "How about you, Murph? Do you think Paige would like this area?"

"Do you think I would even tell her about this area? Besides we are comfortable on Jones Street; the neighborhood is perfect for us. It fits our budget, and we have made plenty of friends on the street."

Johnnie smiled. "We found that our street is a great place. We have block parties, and the neighbors look out for each other. Would you believe one night we left the house in a rush and forgot to close the garage door? Finally, the lady across the street called the restaurant where we were eating. She said she wanted to go to bed, but was afraid to leave her window. She had been watching the house for us since we left. I think we are in the perfect place for us as well."

Pulling up in front of the house there was no sign of anyone being home.

Terry knocked on the door and waited for an answer. She tried again. "Ackers police. Open up!" Terry turned to the others and said "Any other ideas?"

"Maybe there is something at the bank that could give us an idea of his habits, possibly a friend where he might be convalescing. I don't recall seeing anything about a local friend to call in the case of an emergency. Let's go to the bank. I want to check with Gary." Johnnie was getting more concerned.

Returning to the car, they were all lost in their thoughts. "Hey, maybe we should check with Silva's sister. I think Harrison would go there to make sure the boys are okay. I know where she lives. Harrison seemed particularly close to the boys. Maybe he feels responsible in some strange way for what happened to Silva. I think it might also be a good idea to talk to Noah and Gary."

Murph was confused. "Why would he feel so responsible? I thought you said they were good friends."

"I truly can't think why he would feel responsible." Johnnie was trying to think of anything she could remember of the two over the years.

The trio continued to chat as they walked in the front door of the bank and walked up the steps to the boardroom.

Noah was at the counter getting a cup of coffee when the group arrived. Johnnie said. "Noah, have you heard any news on Harrison Magers. He is missing. I thought it was best to check in with you before we go out to Rayna's place. We have to pass the bank to get to her place and I didn't want to do it via cell phones. I know he has traits of a leader. That could be the reason the boys gravitate to him. We went out to his home and he isn't there either, if he isn't at Rayna's I am at a lost as to where he would be."

Johnnie sat down with a can of root beer and paged through his personnel file. "Could it be that he took Herb out because he was a tyrant? How could he be so caring with the boys and then just murder someone, and put their body in my office. I just do not see him doing such a thing. This isn't getting us anywhere, reading this file and jabbering about his qualities isn't going to find him. I guess the only negative thing I can say is that he is the comedian in the bank. It is true he jests about several people who are outside his circle. To be honest I have been at the end of his jokes. I don't fit his crowd. I am comfortable with many of them, but as a group, I am out of place. I know he is sending out mixed signals, but none of them say murder."

"You don't honestly think he could be responsible for Herb's death, and put the body in your office because you are not one of his buddies?" Terry's expression said more than her words.

"He isn't a violent person. Maybe he had Logan on his side, until for some reason Logan lost favor. Not sure if he could take out Logan. He definitely could not carry Herb's body. I am thinking aloud and out of the box, as they say. I think we will just go to Rayna's maybe she knows something."

Terry, Murph, and Johnnie returned to the car and started out to Rayna's house. "If he isn't there, I am out of ideas. So you two need to start thinking."

As they drove into Rayna's driveway Johnnie said she dreaded what they might find. She knocked on the door, knowing Rayna would recognize her over Terry or Murph.

"Rayna, I hate to bother you or the boys, but have you seen Harrison?" Johnnie felt as if she was holding her breath.

Rayna looked at Johnnie with a furled brow. "We saw him yesterday at the service. He has been a big help, but I haven't seen him today. Why do you ask?"

Terry thought since it was an accident she should introduce herself and explain the reason for the concern.

"Did you know he left the hospital? As of now, we have not been able to find him. He isn't at his house. We were hoping he came here to do some recovering. Johnnie said he was going to take the boys shopping. We were hoping he had picked them up. He does have a serious concussion. He needs to be resting."

Rayna seemed to be nervous. "I can't say where he would be. I don't like the sound of this, not so soon after, well you know. Promise me you will let us know what you find."

Back in the car Murph seemed suspicious. "Either that was a major blow off, or well, I don't know what. Something isn't right."

Johnnie agreed, but thought she would call Noah again to see what his plans were for finding Harrison and Mirah.

She used her cell. She did not want any of their calls going through the switchboard. "Noah, it was a bust, he is not here, and I think all we did was to make Rayna nervous. What is our next move?"

Noah suggested, "Let's call Pat Cates and see if he has information that can help us. Michael may be able to add some details. It seems like old times, gathering the gang together, your house Johnnie?"

"I will ask Michael to call Pat. Expect a hungry crowd." Johnnie felt like her old self again.

Johnnie could hear Noah address Leo as he was disconnecting the call. "Leo, you ready to go. I think it will be more comfortable at Johnnie's. Have you noticed the employees that come by and check inside this room? I think we need to be able to speak freely without fear of unwanted ears. Thanks to Michael, I know her place will be clear of bugs and unwanted eyes and ears."

Johnnie called Michael. "Hi Love, can you get a hold of Pat. We are going to renew our bull sessions so we need everyone on board and food and probably something to induce relaxation."

Murph spoke up. "Something to induce relaxation? If you're Irish that could mean only one thing."

Terry smiled. "Murph has a habit of inducing relaxation when off duty."

Johnnie rolled her eyes and gathered her coat and purse. "I am going to tell Gary where we will be tonight."

Noah caught her eye. "Don't tell him exactly where we are going or why; just to play it safe." Johnnie frowned. "Okay, I guess."

***

Pulling up to the house Johnnie saw Pat's car pulling into the driveway ahead of them.

"Pat, how did you get here so fast?" Johnnie was surprised, but glad to see him.

"Actually, I was on my way up with some news that was definitely pertinent to your investigation; which makes one ask, how did this become your investigation? I thought this was Terry and the FBI's investigation."

Johnnie kissed Pat on the cheek as she opened the door for everyone. "You know what I mean, it affects the bank, let's just say concerned citizen."

Michael was in the family room with the board set up and had a table full of wonderful Italian delights. "Hey, did I do it right?"

"I guess it's like riding a bike, you never really forget." Johnnie knew that Michael was excellent at setting up a feast.

The group ate and then started talking about the case.

Michael spoke up "The designated driver will be compliments of Tomas. He not only provided dinner, but he also took care of us as if we were at his restaurant except relaxation inducement will come later."

Michael took his position at the board ready to make the notes as they popped up.

Pat cleared his throat and stood up. "This is going to come as a shock, well it did to me; Mirah Anderson the state's attorney general, has also been working on her own project to uncover the source of the drugs flowing through the state. John was more or less her bodyguard. That is why she took off when he was murdered. You see, when Grammar died, we knew his connection was here in Ackers. Then when Herb was found dead it pretty much demanded their presence."

Johnnie was turning pale. "Oh my word, we need to find her. I feel terrible. I have to say I had a hard time being nice to her."

Terry stood up. "No one knew of Mirah's extra activities. Part of her job was to be obnoxious. If she was herself, she would never be believed to be involved in the drug game."

Noah tried to get the team back on track. "Okay, we need to get a BOLO out on Mirah immediately. We will also have to get this session going at warp speed. Where do we start?"

Leo stood. "I hate to disrupt the thought, yes, we need to find her, but we had a different viewpoint. Our unit received a request to keep close tabs on her because she just happened to be at the center of every major case that prosecutors have lost here in West Virginia. I guess the US attorney general isn't sure of her intentions. That is what John was trying to determine. If he had collected any information, it has not been found."

Pat was surprised with Leo's response. "We need to check out Harrison Magers and also Gary Percy."

"Gary Percy? He isn't capable. He is a nice guy with a family. Why do you think he could be responsible for any of this?" Johnnie, stunned by the idea, did her best to think of Gary in such a mode.

Pat said. "We aren't saying he is part of it, but he has been overly anxious about Silva's death."

"He's been overly anxious about Silva's death? In that case I am suspect as well. I am overly anxious about her death, as are 95% of the bank employees." Johnnie could not accept Gary's involvement. "You all have met Gary. Did you see anything in his behavior that would indicate him being involved? We could have judged Mirah incorrectly or we may have been right. We need to find her and Harrison." Johnnie was just amazed that they haven't been able to determine if Mirah was a white hat or black hat.

Leo sat for a second before answering. "I have to say, if Gary is involved, he must be the best actor in the world."

Murph added. "I talked with him at length. He didn't want Herb's job. He was actually leaving the area. He said he had an offer at a bank in Arizona and was going to the job. Then with Herb's murder he had to tell them, he needed to extend his starting time. I agree with Johnnie. He is not the one."

Terry looked bewilder. "When did you learn about his plans to move to a new location with a new position? He has apparently played that close to his vest. I doubt anyone at the bank is aware of his plans. I can tell you for one, I had no idea."

Noah tried to get the team back on track. "There are missing people to be found, several murders, and consider what if Gary had planned everything, and was leaving town at just the right time? Did you check out his story Murph?"

"I may not be FBI, but I am a good detective. Of course I checked on his story and the job offer." Murph felt slighted by Noah's asking about an elementary.

"Sorry Murph, I did not mean to offend. I have seen the work that you, Terry and the rest of Ackers police has been doing and it is excellent. I think I am grasping at straws." Noah felt bad for asking a novice question.

"Okay, back on track let's go with Harrison. What do we know about him?" Noah took the lead. "Johnnie you had a copy of Harrison's personnel file at the bank. What did you find?"

"I have gone through this file more than a dozen times but I didn't see a thing that would indicate anything out of the ordinary. He just doesn't have anything alarming in the file."

Bitter over John's murder Leo was determined to find the culprit. His profiler side kicked in. "That is why they call them psychotic. Johnnie you said that he had a group of people. Were these people impressionable? If so, that would explain why you were on the outside. You are your own person; not easily manipulated; you are not a follower. People like Harrison need a cheering crowd that would laugh at his jokes and accept the stories as funny. They aren't necessarily cruel, but they want acceptance by the person they see as the leader of the fun crowd. The followers, they are not part of his activities. They are good people, they don't use drugs, they are not the ones telling the stories or making fun of others; but they do laugh at the stories. It does give him the perfect image, like you, nobody would ever think he was capable of such activities."

Michael started writing on the board. He put up the Harrison details, name, age, and residence, how long he had worked at the bank.

Johnnie was rethinking what she remembered from Harrison's file again, for what felt like the millionth time and came across an interesting fact. "I hadn't thought of it before, but Harrison was hired by Herb, not by the personnel officer. Now I know Herb liked to rule by intimidation, so it would not be out of order for him to do something like that just to show the personnel department that his word was law. He did the same thing with an employee in my divisions."

Pat spoke up to add how he viewed it from outside the picture. "Harrison came to the bank and maybe Herb thought this was going to make his access to drugs easier. What is the source of the Magers funds?"

"Story has it that bootlegging left the family with oodles of cash back in the day. You know like some other well-known families in our society. However, Harrison's father was an investor, and he invested in the early dot coms; but got out before the crash. Harrison had been away at boarding school, so he stayed in the States. Now it seems as though he is trying to spend the money faster than the dot coms crashed." Johnnie said they would have to consider the story as hearsay since she herself never had a reason to investigate him. Well, not until now.

"How does Harrison feel about the dwindling family funds?" Leo was showing keen interest at this point. Does Harrison have any siblings?"

Johnnie knew of his sister. "He has a sister Ciara Carrington. I think she moved far away from the family. As far as I know, there wasn't a real reason ever discussed in public. But have to remember I am a newcomer to this area. Maybe she just wanted to be on her own, you know like proving herself to her parents. She lives in Alaska and her husband Kevin who works on a fishing boat. When Harrison was in the hospital, he told her not to come because he would be home before she got on a flight. Well, there is another thing to check. If there is all this family money why is his sister living in Alaska with a husband working on a fishing boat?"

"Noah, I didn't have any opportunity to review the background checks that John did, do you remember any of this being mentioned. If not, we have the resources to do some digging on her. Johnnie you said her name is Ciara Carrington and her husband's name is Kevin." Leo felt she was worth checking out.

Terry remained relatively quiet. She was now ready to add her comments. "With what we are suggesting about Harrison, we have not come up with a reason or an ounce of evidence of him being involved. I don't mean to defend him; but his family has big friends, so we had better be solid. If word gets out that, we are investigating him, there will be reprisals, and they will come from some friends in high places."

Pat spoke up again. "I think that is all the more reason to track down Mirah. If she is with us, it might be a bit of a deterrent for any revenge. There may be individuals with powerful connections wanting to defend him; but if we have Mirah on our side with the force of her office it would be better for us and for any citizen who helps us with the investigation."

Johnnie continued. "That could be very true, unless his friends go beyond the state. They could be national or even international. You just never know what rock the snake is under, so we need to proceed with caution."

"That makes sense except so far we have not seen any use of such power. Maybe he keeps that side of him away from his crowd. Herb and Grammar were in the drug scene; but I don't think that Harrison wants general employees to be involved with drugs. Maybe he likes having the control of the big wigs. If they get demanding or something like that, Harrison could have the connections to put an end to the problem. He might have been using his connections to keep both Herb and Grammar in line. From what I have observed, it would take something big to keep Herb under control." Johnnie did not want to believe any bank employee could be involved in any of these things.

Leo added his thought, which was his biggest reason for attending these sessions. "If John was able to collect any information one way or the other on Mirah, we need to find it. Have the techs reviewed the boardroom of the bank thoroughly? Maybe he hid something at the bank. We have to do a search of any place he may have put any notes."

Noah agreed; it was a factor we hadn't considered. "I am not sure how we are going to search the boardroom. What if Mirah showed up or Gary started asking questions. Did John ever mention anything suspicious to you Leo?"

Leo mentioned in a message that Mirah wanted to go to Akers, due to the death of a banker. Nothing more, not even the name of the banker. He felt John wanted to say more but was unable to do so at that time. Later he left a message about a witness and a window washer.

Johnnie spoke up to mention to the group. "Maybe he wanted his ducks in a row first before speaking of any suspicions. Let's just slow the pace, don't get too far ahead of ourselves. Tackle this again later."

Murph spoke up. "I know the layouts and thoughts were supposed to be completed before the relaxation inducement; even so, this is giving me a headache. I need to relax. I am afraid of going over and over the same thing. We need a new angle and I doubt we can do it in our present state."

His comment rather broke the ice. Pat followed suit. "A beer at this point isn't a bad idea, as long as we don't lose sight of our goal. I think we have a lot more legwork to do, before a bull session can determine any answers. I say we find Mirah and find out what she knows. In the meantime, we need to do to some work on Herb and Grammar and then see what we can find out about Ciara. Things like why she is all the way in Alaska. It can't be an easy life. They could be here living a much easier life. Surely Harrison wasn't the only child of the Magers to be benefited from their resources."

Johnnie stood, collected the drink orders. Terry followed Johnnie to the kitchen to help with the drinks. "We have a lot on our plates. I know your work at the bank has to take precedence, but there are things you can help us with from the inside. Everything needs to be checked or rechecked, even Herb and Silva's files."

Johnnie looked up from the drinks she was pouring. "We already checked both personnel folders, do you think we missed something in the files. Since his death, they would have taken it out of the standard files. I will need to talk to Gary, he will have to pull Silva's, I don't know if Gary refiled Herb's file. I do not believe he is involved and most likely frustrated that his job in Arizona is on hold; he may be very helpful. Heck, he probably knows things about Herb that are not in the official records. I can see why Noah wanted him investigated. He did have to work in close proximity to Herb. Maybe that is the reason why he wanted as far away as he could get from him. Herb was toxic, a bully, and that is just in the banking circles. Hard to tell what he was like on the outside the bank. Few people liked him within the banking circles."

The ladies carried the drinks back to the family room. Michael started a fire to make the room cozier. The group needed a break from the earlier discussion and Johnnie needed time to relax and put all these thoughts to rest for the night.

Try as they might, they had rethought and rethought as much as they knew. Noah thought searching the bank and John's room if the hotel hadn't put it back in use, might lead to something. "He may have hidden something he wanted to send to Leo. Or, maybe he knew of someone that was a threat to Mirah. We need to find her." Leo agreed. "I will call my office in the morning and make sure there are no messages that I missed."

True to his word, Tomas called and asked if he could send out some employees to clean up and then take the others to their homes.

***

Another day seemed to drag Johnnie down all the more. Michael brought her tea to wake her and get the day started. "You know Michael, I totally enjoyed last night's bull session; I have missed the work I use to do."

Michael just smiled. "Tell me something I don't know."

"You could pick up on it?" Johnnie grinned.

"It shows on you like red on a rose. I was thinking you would be bringing up the topic soon enough. Let's make a deal, for now we have enough to do. Let's get this behind us and we will see what the future holds." Michael could not help grinning at the idea of Johnnie believing she was keeping her true feelings under wraps. He knew she would want to talk when the time was right.

"I would hate to leave the bank in a bind, with Herb gone. Now with Gary's planned exit, it is going to be difficult for the bank if I make a change of any kind. So for now you are right, we will revisit the topic later." Johnnie truly did care about the bank. Unfortunately, the town had lost its essence of innocence. "Your patience is amazing, how can you just wait for something that could change our lives again?"

"Like I said before, let's jump off that bridge when we get to it. Right now, we had better get moving or we are going to be late today. Just so you know; Pat and I are going to spend the day together. We are going to work with Noah and see if we can find any trace of Mirah. Noah is worried about her. She lost her security detail, as small as it was, and why she got involved with this whole drug thing is beyond me." Michael liked to work things one-step at a time; he did not like speculation. He wanted facts. "Determining why she got involved will help find her."

Johnnie went to the shower to get ready for the day, what a day it was going to be for her. She was to the point where she really hated going to the bank. She never felt like this when she was at the bureau.

She started planning her day as she was dressing, and decided she would first take Harrison's personnel file to her upstairs office. If she found anything of value, which she doubted since she had reviewed it so many times. Of course, she was looking for other things during those previous reviews. If she found anything, she would make notes for Terry. Johnnie had been through Harrison's file so many times she thought she could repeat it word-for-word. She had many different things on her mind. Relaying on her old trick, she dressed in brown, complete right down to her eye shadow. It always had an effect on the employees. Brown is not her color and it always made her look tired or ill. She needed to have time away from the employees today.

As she came into the kitchen for breakfast, Michael commented on her outfit. "I see you want to be left alone today."

"Make jokes if you like, but it works. I am hoping that I can work through those personnel files without anyone coming into my office. I do have to give Ana credit. She does stand guard on the rare occasion when I close the door. So I hope to get a lot done today."

She reminded him that she had her weapon on her person. If what they thought about Harrison was true, she did not want to be unprepared. What if Mirah came to her for whatever reason and needed protection. After all, she did want to meet with Johnnie. What could have happened to Mirah? Now Johnnie felt responsible, but all she could do was research. It was what she did best and it was time to put her talent to work. She told Michael she needed to have transportation, so she would drive herself.

Arriving at the bank, Johnnie went directly to Gary's office. She quietly closed his door. Gary looked at her with a bit of sudden suspicion.

"You know I was in the FBI, and you know that I am working as much as possible with law enforcement on this entire matter. You probably have guessed that I know about your Arizona plans. Can I ask you some questions?"

Gary took a deep breath and let it slowly exhale. "I take it, you talked to Murph. I wasn't ready for it to be announced."

Johnnie could see his discomfort. "You don't have to worry about me knowing. I will not mention it anyone in the bank. The only ones that know are the FBI team, Michael and Pat Cates. I do, however, want to know why?"

Gary took a drink of his black coffee. "I have been looking for something that would work for me and the family. Flagstaff is a beautiful place, and it is serene. I thought Akers was a quiet place, but lately I do not have the same feeling. I have been watching the job listings in the various magazines related to banking. I saw the job opening in Flagstaff come up and I talked it over with Kayla. It turns out; she loves Arizona she jumped at the chance. To be honest, I knew Herb was into drugs. I actually caught him once with cocaine. Herb had some dangerous friends, and I worried about our safety. With this Arizona job, we would have the safety of the new location, and a setting that is perfect for us. I had planned to notify the board once we settled away from here, and safe. I guess if his friends were dangerous it seemed he had enemies that were even more so."

"Gary, this is something that we need to keep quiet for now, and I have to ask; have you ever had reason to suspect Harrison of illegal activity?"

"Harrison? I can't imagine he would actually hurt anyone. The only thing that I have ever noticed is that he lived alone and his parents have been traveling in Europe since I have known him. Beyond that, I wouldn't know. He seems to be a private person."

"Gary, this is extremely important. Harrison has not been located as of yet. More worrisome is the disappearance of Mirah." Johnnie could not lose the idea of Harrison's accident and Mirah's disappearance happening so near to each other.

Gary asked. "Did she go back to Charleston? She was headed that way after John Erickson died."

Johnnie continued. "No, her belongings are still in her room. We were supposed to get together the other night, her suggestion, but she never showed. No one has seen her since. Needless to say after all that has happened I am worried."

"Are you saying something has happened to the two of them? Isn't it possible that Harrison is resting, especially since he should have stayed in the hospital? I think Mirah is just out doing what she does, whatever that might be I am still unsure. Why she even came to Akers in the first place." Gary wondered as she did.

"If you think of anything, please call me on my cell. Don't use the office phones, please."

"Johnnie, I think maybe you have taken this situation a bit too seriously. You have to be careful getting so involved, you don't have a team of agents with you anymore."

"That is true, but once you have the training it doesn't just go away. I am going to do what I have to do in order to keep people safe in this bank. I have another request. I know that Herb's personnel file is not with the active files. I am going to need it to have a starting point to do any sort of investigating."

"You do what you have to do; just remember there is a law enforcement department that can handle this situation. If you think the file will help, I can give it to you. However, I don't want it known that you have the file."

"Believe me, safety is my biggest concern."

***

Johnnie went upstairs to her office. Ana was in the hallway and immediately asked if she was feeling okay. Johnnie felt a bit guilty using her makeup and clothing choice to avoid unnecessary contact with people.

Johnnie smiled at her. "I am just overwhelmed I think. I have several things that need my attention today and I need as few interruptions as possible."

"Not a problem, I will see to it that anyone wanting to see you will go through me first." Ana was like the Swiss Guard with the pope.

Johnnie thanked her then took the files into the office and closed the door.

This was not going to be easy. None of her research calls could be on the bank's phone or the computer in her office. She set out her cell phone and her laptop and started on Herb first.

Looking at Herb's personnel file really did not provide much information beyond what everyone already knew in the bank. Did they fail to maintain information in his personnel file, or did he just remove what he didn't like? He would do such a thing.

Johnnie tried to make notes on what she knew about him from their contact at the bank and the social gatherings the bank arranged.

Herb was divorced, about 52 years of age, three children; physically he was a rather nondescript person. He was approximately five foot nine inches tall and balding. Johnnie could not say if he was a happy person. By all reflections, he was not. That could explain how he got into a drug habit.

Who was his supplier? Did he really deal drugs? Did it get both Herb and Grammar killed? Since they both had the signature of Sebastian Osis, something in their lives got them killed by a determined individual, or maybe some company.

Thinking back on Sebastian, he seemed to be so open whenever he was in public. It seemed everyone knew or suspected what he did; but nobody would approach the topic. That would seem like a sure way to place yourself in serious danger. Still the deaths of Herb and Grammar made her think. The viciousness of Sebastian's reputation was not present with Herb and Grammar's demise. Was he responsible for their deaths or was the idea of a copycat closer to the truth? It was an avenue worth researching. One would think that the FBI maintained a file on Sebastian. She would ask Noah if he could get a dossier on him.

Making notes on her laptop was helpful, and she also kept her casebooks, but those were at the house. She kept them in the safe room. Something she never thought she would be doing in this quiet small-town setting. Crime is present everywhere; she just at no time thought she would be dealing with it here in Akers. At least not to this degree, murdering a FBI agent was not something anyone would expect here in town.

Getting back to Herb Jennings, she needed to find out more about him and his associates. Herb had a few favorite haunts. Maybe she and Michael should have an evening out. She only knew of three places in town that drew Herb's attention.

Picking up her cell phone, she called Michael. "Hi! How is everything going? Are you and Pat making any headway on your projects?"

"We have a few things that we think are worth researching. How's your progress?"

"I am only succeeding in adding to my workload. I also came up with an idea that I thought we could handle. Maybe Pat and Josie would want to join us. I know of the places that Herb had on his social calendar, and I thought we could go out for an evening and just see who we see at these places. It might lead us to connections that will help answer some of the questions."

"That is a good idea, but Pat has already told me he and Josie have plans for tonight. Besides, I am surprised you would allow Josie to be seen with us at some of these locations if you think they can somehow link to his death."

"I was hoping if we went as a group it would not be so alarming to anyone. I am afraid Terry would be recognized. Think Noah would mind being a third wheel?"

"I think it would look more like a social outing with friends, Noah isn't known here in Akers."

Johnnie said she loved him and she hung up. She called Noah's cell. "Noah, I have an idea. I know that Herb had some social hangouts. Nice places in town, but I think they merit a check to see if we spot anyone of interest. Maybe you would want to go with us tonight. We could have dinner and just watch the crowd."

"Sounds like a doable plan. What type of progress are you making on the files?"

"Interesting development, Herb's file is simply his resume. Not even an application. Of course, I guess for such positions they don't fill out applications. I do find it odd that there are no comments in the file for anything. We know he was not the best-liked person, but he did have some good ideas about new projects and clients. That is why I thought we could check out his favorite places and see who we see."

Okay, now that she had Noah onboard she needed to decide which place to go. Remembering Herb's haunts, she noted them on her laptop. One was a large dinner club. Its layout was extensive. It had private dining rooms for parties, another area had the old time pinball games and large screen TVs for sports enthusiast, and the bar area also provided a few booths for casual dinners. The main dining room would not provide any information. It did not allow for viewing the patrons.

So it would seem that the bar area was their best location for an evening out. Johnnie called Noah. "Hi. I think I have the first place picked out for tonight's outing, the bar area of a dinner club. It is casual business and would be the safest bet. Let's all go in one car."

Johnnie made the necessary notes on her laptop and checked the time. It was time for a soda, well maybe this time she would try the flavored water that was in the vending machine. She really had to break the habit of the sodas, even if they were diet.

Walking out of her office, Ana immediately approached her and asked if she needed something. Johnnie told her she was going to the break room for some of the flavored water. She nearly forgot her motive for her day's outfit. It really did work, dressing in this color made her look wiped out. As she entered the break room from the back door, she said Hi to everyone in the room in her own silly way. "Hi Peoples, how is everyone doing?"

She was encouraged to sit with a few of the girls from the customer service area. Sitting down she opened her water and took a long drink.

"When are you going to put Silva's job out for bid?" Marlene Groves was a tall hefty lady who always spoke her mind.

"We will have it out this week. It wasn't an easy one to write up. However, we need to keep the bank going and there will be the cascade effect from the job bids."

Marlene again spoke up. "I would bid but I don't like having to be here so early. Not to mention being the only person in the bank at that hour."

Conversations among management had Marlene pegged as an overly involved person. Johnnie did her best to side step the issue.

"To be honest Marlene, there was some time allotted for healing and for people to handle the grieving process. I need to get back to my office, or I will never get today's work finished."

Johnnie left by the back door, but stopped at the worktable in the corner divided off from the rest of the workspace. She took advantage of the fact it was a good place to listen to conversations. To make it look like she was working, she sat down and opened a file started checking off information on the file. She sat there with the tablet that was always on the table for the convenience of anyone who needed to make notations from the reports. This also gave her the advantage of making cryptic notes of what she might overhear from the break room.

As expected, she heard the employees ask if anyone was planning to bid on Silva's job. Marlene went on to say they wondered if she saw something that morning that lead to her death?

"What do you mean by saying such a thing?" Johnnie recognized the voice of Mary Edgington. Mary worked in the confirmation department. Normally, Mary held her tongue, but she and Silva had gone to school together. Mary was a friend of Silva's, and she did not want to see anyone buzzing about her death.

"I didn't mean anything. I just wondered if anyone was thinking the same thing I was." Having Mary respond so aggressively made the employee back pedal to cover up her comment, or at least she tried. Marlene's reputation was that of a busybody.

Johnnie returned to her office and started looking over Harrison's personnel file for the nine hundredth time it seemed, trying to be open-minded and observant. By this time, she thought a set of new eyes was called for on this topic. She did find one a notation in the file, she hadn't thought much about it before, but with Harrison missing. Herb had recommended Harrison for a position. She read his recommendation letter who identified Harrison as a hard working young man he knew from his church. Okay, that could be the truth, but the church's identity was missing. Johnnie made a note to see if she could check it out some way without drawing attention to the inquiry. To her, it did not seem to be reason for alarm.

Reading further in Harrison's file, there were several commendations in his file from Herb. Another thing to check, did Herb make as many acknowledgments in other employees' files?

Johnnie wondered if she could bounce the idea off Gary. Maybe it would be better if the questions came from Leo. He seemed to have a good relationship with Gary.

Moving on she decided that she would put down her observations of Harrison.

Harrison Magers, age 30, tall, just a tad over six feet, and a rather slight but muscular build, likeable, and single. Of course, in today's world, 30's was the trend to get married.

Johnnie had to admit she was not setting the world on fire with the limited research she could do from her office. She gathered her belongings and told Ana that she needed to see Gary, and then she had an appointment and would be out for the rest of the day.

She went to Marguerite's desk and asked if Gary was in his office. Marguerite, the executive secretary, said he was, and she could go in if she wanted.

"Hi Gary, are you tired of seeing me yet?" She liked Gary, and she was so sorry that he would be leaving the bank. She understood, because she never liked playing politics either, especially when Herb was pulling all the strings.

"I think I will go to see Terry. I have been looking at the files; but I need more in depth abilities. I may be able to use the resources of the police department." She handed him the files that she had been reviewing.

"Harrison! Do you really think you will find something on him?" Gary did not seem to be sharing her concern about Harrison. "You know he has been here at the bank for the last five years. Why would he wait until now, to do something like killing Herb?"

"We don't know if, in fact, he has done anything, but for Silva, someone made sure she was dead. Harrison has had two events and he is still alive. It makes you wonder how he has been so lucky. He hasn't encountered an assailant in person, but Silva did. I am prone to ask why Herb recommended Harrison, so there must be something in common. I can't find any link other than their church affiliation with the few resources I have here in the personnel files."

Gary could only nod and wish her luck.

Gary was one of those people you couldn't help but like, he wanted to believe the best of everyone. It was a great way to live, except it didn't work in police matters.

The trip to the station was a waste. Terry and Murph were out in the field. Unable to gain access to their databases, Johnnie decided to head home.

***

Johnnie arrived home to find Michael on the phone. She never wanted to know about anything he reported to the various agencies. He told Johnnie that those instincts never really went away. Once you are trained with such intensity to be aware you found yourself doing it on a constant basis.

"Did you and Pat have any success on your search today?"

"We did, but some people have a life. Pat needed to get back to his hotel so he could get ready for their evening out. Somehow, I think their evening will not be as focused as ours will be. Besides, I had a bit of information I wanted to check out before our evening. It seems Herb and Grammar would take some time off on occasion and go to the fishing lodge that Ernie owns. We found some pictures online of the lodge. Apparently, they rent it out from time to time. I wanted to review the pictures and commit them to memory, in case we encountered some of the faces tonight. If we did, maybe we could greet them and get their names."

"Sounds like a plan to me. Let me pull up the site on my laptop, and catch up to you. Have you told Noah about the site? We should put pictures on our cell phones too."

"Actually, he is coming over early, we can look over the site together. In fact, he should be here about now." The doorbell rings, as if on cue.

"How do you do that? You always seem to know when the doorbell is going to ring." Johnnie was joking, but it happened more times than not.

Johnnie went to the door, greeted her old boss, took his coat, and they all gathered in the kitchen. Johnnie loved her kitchen, and it seemed like everyone else did as well.

"Hi guy, want to join us? This is going to be very interesting." Michael was concentrating on the screen. He was zeroing in on each face. He also studied the body language. People can change their looks, but the body language always stays the same.

Noah pulled out his laptops and joined the efforts. Johnnie took drink orders; everyone was up for ice tea.

"You know I have been looking at these faces until my eyes hurt. I think it is time to head out on our adventure." Johnnie was glad that Michael made the suggestion, her eyes were blurring.

They started out for their evening. The stop tonight would be at the Flames, Steaks, and Pasta restaurant. Its popularity made it a good place to start. Nobody would think twice about a new face in the place. It was after all a well-known place.

Noah had one more thing he wanted to do. "Give me a minute then I will be ready. I can get someone at Quantico to check the site and run the facial recognition software. I don't know if they are able to get back to us before our evening starts, but they can send it to our phones."

As the group pulled up to the door, a valet came out to park their car. "This is an impressive place, is the inside as well tended?" Noah asked.

Inside it was dark. Some of the features were impressive, but looking past the obvious Michael nudged Johnnie and dropped his eyes to the floor. Johnnie followed suit and noted the carpet was old and tattered. They were shown to a booth in the bar area.

"Noah, Michael noticed the tattered carpet. It definitely doesn't match the image of the swanky place with a valet."

Michael nodded. "Could be financial trouble or just too interested in other things to care for the place."

Noah agreed, they settled in to watch the crowd.

"What would you think if Harrison walked in right now?" Noah was watching the crowd as they entered as he had the seat facing the entrance hallway.

Johnnie thought Noah was making a joke, until she looked in the direction of his gaze "You have to be kidding me. This is just great!" Johnnie hoped she would appear casual, or maybe Harrison would do his best to avoid her. Better yet, he would not see her.

Noah said. "Remember we are just some friends out for the night. I am new in town, so why wouldn't you be showing me the local spots." As he spoke, his phone vibrated.

"Drake." Noah listened with interest. "Thank you, I will share the information."

Noah passed his phone to Johnnie and Michael. "Only one face came up in the review. It matches Stan Albano. He is an undercover agent. Seeing him at the lodge tells us there is something going on there that has caught the attention of somebody."

Johnnie asked if he was local law enforcement or from another agency.

"He's ATF, and is aware of our investigation. I don't know how he learned of our inquiry, especially since we did not know of his. Someone is using the lodge to get an extraordinary number of firearms stockpiled." Johnnie could not hide her surprise.

"Great, first we think we are dealing with a drug ring, and now we are looking at potential gun runners." Johnnie whispered, but could not stifle the excitement in her eyes.

Michael just looked at her. "I can see you are totally upset about working this job." He was grinning and nodding to Noah. "Yeap, she seems to like this temporary assistance as much as she did when she was officially in the bureau." Michael was glad to see a bit of the old Johnnie again.

Johnnie looked at him and then to Noah, "Okay, so I do like or rather appreciate this job more than the bank. Right now, I think it would be a safer job. The only excitement I have had in three years on the job has been the research I am doing for a certain agency. I will admit this is far more interesting, but I think we should be on the lookout for faces from the camp as well.

Their dinners arrived, and they continued to survey the growing crowd. Johnnie was thankful they were in a back booth that had an elevation to it, but no real light. Harrison most likely would never know they were in the building.

They took their time with dinner. They ordered appetizers, salad, and an entree; then finally dessert and coffee. For any eyes watching, it was just a group of friends having dinner.

Just when they thought the night would not produce any other surprises, in came Stan Albano. Harrison approached him, and they settled on a couple of bar stools away from most of the action.

Not long after Harrison and Albano got together, another person joined them in the secluded spot. It was a woman. Now this really raised eyebrows.

There were no pictures of women at the camp. Maybe she is a contact for Albano, or involved in the stockpiling or drugs.

"I can say this entire event has allowed me to see the equipment in the field. Although we test everything, it has never been tested like it has been lately." Michael had equipped everyone with mini cameras just like the ones he and Johnnie wore while attending Silva's services. No need for sound, with the noise in a bar it most likely would be hard to pick up any conversation from a distance. The cameras that they wore could take a decent picture in the low light. The face recognition software did not match her to anyone, but the two men apparently accepted her were waiting for her to show up so they can do whatever.

Their body language led the group to believe this was a regular thing for these three. This was too much to believe. This hometown bank was turning out to be a hotbed of questionable activity.

The three sat at their place unwilling to voice any comments. Noah suggested they make an exit while it was clear and return to the house.

"This is an FBI surveillance outing, so the feds are going to pick this one up." Noah caught the eye of the server and asked for their check.

Exiting the restaurant the valet brought their vehicle around, and they were glad to have made it out without Harrison seeing them. Since he had his back to all of them, it is unlikely he saw any one of the three.

Back at the house, they gathered around the kitchen table. Everyone seemed to realize just how big this case was growing. This was definitely a major situation.

Noah called Quantico asking for everything known about Harrison Magers.

"It is way too late to begin a bull session tonight, besides I am going to try and put things in some sort of order." Johnnie was so glad to hear Noah make the call. She wasn't in the mood to try to figure out answers, when they didn't know what questions to ask.

Were there new surprises yet to discover? Where did Mirah fit into this mess, and where was she?

Johnnie decided that tomorrow she would check with Terry to see if they had learned anything about Mirah's disappearance. Johnnie's plate was going to be overflowing. Somewhere in the middle of all this activity, she had her responsibilities to the bank.

***

The morning was a rush to get to the bank. Johnnie skipped breakfast and arrived at the bank before 7:45 that morning.

Gary always arrived early on a daily basis. This was going to be a difficult conversation. Knocking on his doorframe, she stuck her head in his office and he invited her to come in and sit.

Johnnie knew Gary would be as shocked as she was about what she saw the night before.

"Last night three of us, Noah, Michael and I, went to Flames. We knew this to be one of Herb's hangouts. We went with the thought that we might see someone who caught our attention in this expanding investigation. To be honest the expansion was a surprise. Do you have any details about Harrison besides what is in his personnel file?"

Gary took a deep breath. "I only know he came from a bank in Virginia. He is capable and seems to be reliable."

Johnnie relayed the happenings of the night before. She explained how surprised they all were Harrison appeared and was joined by another man and an unknown woman.

Gary's look was one of confusion and suspicion. "I don't know what is happening. Any idea who these people were that he met? Can this ordeal get any worse? Do you think it has something to do with Herb? More importantly, is it time for you to step away from this investigation. You could be an easy target. If, and that is a big if, Harrison is involved, he could have seen you last night."

"I serious doubt he saw us, he was so involved is whatever he and his group were discussing. It kept them too involved with their own thing to notice anyone else coming or going."

Johnnie told him she wanted to go to the police station. She needed to talk to Terry and see what she may have on the woman's identity.

Before she left, she gave Gary the job bid for Silva's position. She knew people were getting restless about the bid, and she needed to avoid any gossip. Things were bad enough with

Silva's death, and everyone knew of Harrison's near miss and his accident the day of the funeral.

Johnnie left the bank with a question on her mind. What if someone made a comment about her absence, how would Gary reveal her activity or just play dumb?

She arrived at the front desk of the police station asking for Terry. She was becoming a familiar face at the station. Several of the officers recognized her, but never asked questions. Police work is a lot like banking there was an implied confidentially in both occupations. Will was not at the desk this morning Johnnie noticed.

Terry met Johnnie at the elevator again and asked if she had anything new to offer.

Johnnie told her there were plenty of things to discuss. Johnnie was still attaching the visitor's badge as the two went to the conference room.

Johnnie pulled out the papers she had, including copies of the personnel files of the four individuals who were at the heart of the investigation.

"Remember all of our searching for Harrison? Well surprisingly, he showed up last night at Flames. Let me back up here for a minute. Michael and Pat became interested in the lodge that Ernie Compoto owned. Michael pulled the lodge up online. It's often rented to others, so it had a web page. We studied the faces, and Noah notified Quantico and asked them to run facial recognition on the various faces on the page. It turned out that one of the individuals, identified as Stan Albano, is an undercover agent for the ATF. That was a surprise, but the surprises did not end there. Albano arrived heading straight to Harrison. Then a woman arrived and joined Harrison and Albano. I brought a picture of her, and I hope we can identify her. We decided it was high time we left. This is all happening so fast, I don't know where to take the investigation." Johnnie looked a bit puzzled by the turn of events.

"When you bring in developments you really bring in developments! Okay, let me see the picture." Looking at the photo, she immediately knew the face of the woman. "You are not going to believe this; she works undercover in vice. I did not know they had an operation that was active. We can't ignore this and I will call vice and see what is happening."

Immediately Terry called her friend Chuck in vice. "Hi Chuck, I came across a photo of one of the officers in your division. I know she works for you. Do you have a minute, I would like to talk to you and see where our two investigations intersect."

"I'm here for you Terry. Come on over and I'll see if I can help" Terry poked her head into Chuck's office. "Guess who?"

"Hi, to you too let me see the picture. Oh yes, her name is Lisa Ward and she has been working a possible on a possible home grown terrorist angle. It has been going on for some time now. I know that it is extensive, but if we nail this. We can bring an end to a serious drug, and weapons ring."

"Chuck, I desperately need to know all the details of her on going operation. I think it is tying into a case I am working. Has the name Herb Jennings or Silva Ames come up in her reports?"

"Let me pull up what I can. Is Herb Jennings the guy who was found dead in a bank? I think I've heard his name somewhere during the operations. Wasn't he friends with Grammar Jonas?"

"Chuck, you have to come with me and meet the bank officer who is in the center of this mess. Her name is Johnetta King, Johnnie for short. She is former FBI, and this Herb character was the one found dead in her office closet. She is in the conference room right now. We are going over some new occurrences in her 'off the books' investigation." Maybe this would answer many questions.

"Lead the way." Chuck's interest had been piqued.

Johnnie was waiting in the conference room still studying the pictures taken at the restaurant.

"Johnnie, this is Chuck Fields. He heads the vice division. Chuck this is Johnetta King, aka Johnnie."

"Nice to meet you Johnnie. I understand we have bumped into each other so to speak."

"Hi. First let me apologize if I stumbled into your area, but this is very important to me. Not only was Herb murdered, but an employee in my division was also murdered. Things are suspicious to say the least. I know that Herb had a drug connection, and now I have concerns regarding another employee Harrison Magers. There have been a couple of attempts on his life recently. Yesterday we could not locate him, and it was a worry to us at the bank. To further the situation, the state's attorney, Mirah Anderson, also went missing the same day as Harrison. In an attempt to observe Herb's hangouts, we went to the restaurant Flames last night. Much to our surprise, Harrison showed up, Stan Albano who is an ATF undercover agent, arrived and the two of them were joined by your vice officer. The three remained secluded until they had a chance to leave unnoticed."

"Who is we?" Chuck asked.

"Terry did tell you I was in the bureau before I took the job at the bank. My old section chief, Noah Drake, Michael, my husband, and myself went to Flames to see if anyone of interest showed up."

"Why would your husband go on a police matter?" Chuck wanted details before he gave out the information.

"Michael owns a security company he has done this type of work before. This was to look like a social gathering. We wanted it to be low key, making it appear as friends catching up on old times."

Chuck sat down and asked if he could see the pictures. "You stumbled into more than my agent. This Harrison person is a member of the US Marshalls. He is also undercover."

"Hold on a minute, Harrison is law enforcement." Johnnie had many twists in cases she handled over the years, but this was surprising to say the least.

"You landed in the middle of an undercover agent's bull session." Chuck handed back the picture to Johnnie.

"You are telling me, agents meet in public places to discuss their cases?" Johnnie was surprised at not only their identities, their meeting in a public place.

"The group meets on a regular basis. They share information passed on thumb drives. Since they meet regularly, no one is suspicious. They play the part of three friends out for the night. How about I contact Lisa, maybe she could join us for lunch? Although

Harrison and Stan have been working this case for some time, our involvement is rather new."

Chuck called Lisa and asked if they could meet. The group, including Terry, Noah, and Leo agreed to meet at Flames for lunch. Johnnie explained that Noah and Leo had a huge interest in the case. The agent murdered at the Hilton was a member of Leo's team.

Terry, Chuck, Johnnie, and Lisa traveled in one vehicle. Noah and Leo met them at the restaurant. Again, the valet appeared, even for the lunch crowd.

Johnnie was very surprised to see Harrison was joining them for lunch. I can see you were not expecting to see me." Harrison was grinning.

"That is putting it mildly" Johnnie retorted. "I have been informed of your other job. I have to ask is there a reason why you didn't tell me of your true identity? I can understand the need for secrecy, but you knew with Silva's death especially, I would get involved."

"I am sure you have been undercover before, you know you can't break cover. Besides this, situation is complicated. I had to know I could trust you." Harrison answered with a glint in his eye.

"I was the one who was suspicious. I wanted to know of your devotion to Aces and Charleston." Johnnie was also concerned about the boys. "Then you disappeared after your second accident, I didn't know what to think. Your departure was causing me fits."

"I have to admit; I am protective of the boys. I still am angered by Silva's murder and want to find who is responsible. I knew Herb was in over his head. He was, well you know, complex. He was not going to back down from anyone. He chose the wrong people to step on in what he thought was his rise to whatever. The fact that Herb's death may be responsible for Silva's demise makes me livid. We need to work together to resolve this entire situation. I have been in Ackers too long. I have made some friends at the bank, and I am afraid that if someone learns of my identity they could be in danger."

Johnnie had so many questions for him. "Leave the area? Okay, I can understand, but what about your sister and I thought your parents lived here in Akers."

"Believe it or not, that is also part of my cover. My name is not Harrison Magers and Mr. and Mrs. Magers are in Europe with no plans to return. They sold the house lock stock and barrel in an auction. The government is always buying up places for safe houses in unsuspecting locations. This house fit the bill for my created background. The Magers moved to Belgium of all places. They even relinquished their citizenship here in the States; they moved to Belgium. Doing a background on them, we found that they did have a son who died at birth. His name was Harrison, so when this job came up, and it was such a long-term cover, it was perfect. Fact is, I have gone by Harrison Magers for so long, I just might keep the name."

Johnnie found that she was enjoying the layers of his cover peeling away.

They all settled in a large booth. Noah spoke directing his comments to Harrison. "Have you learned anything of value with your undercover task? I think it is the time to share information. This entire case has blown up far beyond what we expected. We know the things on our side, and you know the events on your side, but now is the time to put all the cards face up on the table and see what we all know together."

Harrison spoke up. "Okay, this is going to blow everyone away. I know it did me when I traced the truth. Sebastian Osis, Victor Andropov's hit man is not a hit man, again, another undercover agent. The stories of his kills are greatly exaggerated. Truth; he is Secret Service, and bodyguard for Andropov. No denying Andropov has his faults. However, he is the one who alerted us to a potential terrorist group of some kind."

Johnnie smiled and Noah caught the gleam in her eye. "You find something amusing about this ordeal?"

"Don't you sound like my old section chief? This is serious, you have to admit we had never come across a case like this when we were working together."

Terry spoke. "It seems to me for a banker, you were far happier working in law enforcement. When are you going to tell Michael you want back in?"

Johnnie looked at her. "Right now I'm concerned about finding what is happening in one of America's small town. That is the only thing I want to think about now."

This large lunch group concerned Johnnie. The lunch would be more comfortable if it were in Tomas' private dining room. This seemed too exposed for this meeting.

"Who owns this restaurant?" Johnnie was watching the afternoon faces. She could not help but notice Andropov sitting at the table at the entrance of the dining room where they were sitting."

"Mr. Andropov is the owner, and at this point is sitting guard to make sure no one else ventures into the dining room." How did Harrison have time to collect all the information that rolled off his tongue?

"So all this is somehow tied to a terrorist group. Is it militia, jihad, white supremacist, or a new extremist group with their own doctrine?"

Harrison spoke "This is not a terrorist group as in 9/11. This group is more interested in drugs, money, and power."

Lunch went along very well, and Johnnie was finding that Harrison was far more pleasant when not being the bank's clown. She still had questions for him. "Harrison, yesterday both you and Mirah were unavailable. Where were you? Do you know where she is at this time?"

Harrison put his fork down. "I needed to get to the boys yesterday. I heard from Sebastian. The boys had piqued someone's interest. I needed to stay close. I have no idea where Mirah was then or now. Do we have a problem with her?"

Noah spoke up. "We don't know but she needs to be located, and fast."

***

Lunch was over, and while everyone learned a lot, there were still question. The ride back to the station was interesting.

Johnnie was concerned for this detective she now considered her friend. "Terry, you barely said a word. What are you thinking?"

"I am thinking back to the two guys that we had tied to Victor and Sebastian. That is out the window now, and I have no idea where to go to solve that issue."

"If you ask me, we have a lot of rethinking to do on everything. What are you doing tonight? Are you up for another bull session?" Noah asked, but insisted they were abusing Johnnie and Michael's house; maybe they should meet elsewhere.

"I think we need one too, and I think Tomas' place might be a good location. He has the private dining rooms. We could have him do finger food. Once we get into the meat of the events, we won't want to stop to eat a meal." Terry offered.

"I would like Michael and Pat to come as well. This situation needs a breakdown; we need to hear what the various agents have come up with in their work. Without knowing the results of their work, we don't even know what we are dealing with at this point." Johnnie knew Michael and Pat had earned admittance to this club.

Johnnie was beginning to believe she had lost touch with her former self. How could she have been so wrong about Harrison? She worked with him for years and her perception of him was so off base. Being realistic, she had to admit he had an excellent cover. His performance of the workplace clown did seem to be believable.

At the station, Johnnie told Terry she would be going home to do some work. She needed free access to some delicate research, nothing she could do from the bank.

Terry told her she would be in touch. Johnnie got in her car and headed for home.

Johnnie put the car in the garage. So that no one would know, she was home.

Inside the house, she made herself a pot of tea and went to the study. Sitting at the desk, she started with a note pad. Listing the various characters, she tried to understand these new developments.

Harrison Magers, Stan Albano if terrorists are involved nobody was safe. ATF might become the leader of the joint efforts. Sebastian Osis, undercover Secret Service was a big surprise to Johnnie's group, can't forget Lisa Ward undercover vice. This little 'Norman Rockwell' town is more along the lines of Palermo Sicily. Was this place ever as innocent as she once believed?

In the silence of the study, she believed she heard something. Looking at the monitors, she could not believe her eyes. Mirah was getting out of a car. Why was she here and where had she been? Mirah went to the back door. She did not knock but took something from her purse. Johnnie watched as Mirah jimmied the door.

Johnnie knew this was her cue. Gathering her items, she went to the safe room. She barely had time to secure herself in the room when Mirah came into the study.

Using her satellite phone, she reached Michael. He was with Pat, and he wanted to hear what she was doing.

"Forget what I am doing, the question is what is Mirah doing breaking into our house. She is in the study going through the desk. I am in the safe room, which has had more use than any other items you have tested in any house. I have my laptop with me, so I can just sit here and watch to see what she is doing. She is wearing gloves, so I don't think she is here to take a deposition. I have to go. I want to watch her."

Mirah went through all the drawers and then she started looking at the bookshelves. She still did not appear to be satisfied.

She took out her phone. "Ernie, are you sure there is something here that is worth this risk?" Johnnie could only hear one side of the conversation, and she listened as Mirah started to talk again. "Listen, Compoto, I am taking the risk here; I don't see you doing anything but sitting in your office. You have not even tried to question her on anything. You just keep doing that, and I will take over from this point forward. Things are going to be my way. I was the one who got rid of Erickson and Logan. What did you do? You just stayed out of sight. I am here. I am taking the risks, and I am no longer taking orders or suggestions from you."

Johnnie was stunned. First, she learns that Harrison is undercover, and now it appears that Mirah is dirty, more than just dirty, she is a cold-blooded murderer. Johnnie was glad the recorder was working. No one was going to believe this story.

Mirah cut her conversation off with a hard click and dropped into one of the chairs at the front of the desk.

She was talking to herself. "This lady is a thorn in my ass; I should have gotten rid of her myself. Logan was a lousy contact."

Johnnie was taking it all in. Logan was part of the wrong crowd, but Ernie Compoto. That was a shock, he was too mild mannered. Who would believe there was a different side to him, let alone one that was malevolent?

Mirah made her way back through the house with Johnnie watching every step. She called Michael again.

"Is Pat with you? Put him on please. Pat, I have to ask, where did you get the information that Mirah was working the drug scene to find its source?" Pat said. "I checked her out with some of the DEA guys. Damn, I hate all these alphabet agencies! Why do you ask?"

"Michael told you Mirah was in our house, right? Well, she called Ernie Compoto, the bank's president. She admitted to killing John Erickson and Logan Ferns. She is dangerous, and now knowing she is capable of murder I think we all need to be watching everything said in front of her. Maybe she started out as one of the white hats, but somewhere along the line, she lost her perception. Going to work tomorrow is going to be a challenge knowing Ernie is tainted."

Pat said he was not happy with the news. He wanted to see how this played out to the end.

Johnnie called Terry. "I have a new development everyone needs to hear. I think things are going to move along a lot faster than we imagined. I am going to call Noah and see if we can change the location back to the house. Can you call Harrison? I think he needs to gather all his contacts, and we must meet. This is going to take some sorting out and we need space. Thank Tomas for us, he is most generous to allow us to use his restaurant. I would hate to think of anything happening to him because of our association."

Terry took care of calling Harrison and Lisa, Harrison notified Stan. Noah made sure Leo would be there as well. Terry called Tomas, and told him that they appreciated his offer, but the entire situation was becoming so fluid. She was afraid by the group being there, his other patrons could get caught in a cross-fire or something.

Tomas thanked her for the consideration, he understood. He too wanted to keep his involvement with the police quiet and his other patrons needed to remain safe. He explained that he was still willing to help when things were not so volatile.

***

All the parties met at Johnnie and Michael's place. Out came the white board again. The subject matter required intense attention and the group was not into eating.

Johnnie was in her comfortable jeans and sweatshirt and what she called walkie socks. The socks had become a joke with her and Michael. She changed the words to the song Rocky Top and sang it as walkie socks. The little rubber dots on the bottom of the socks kept her from sliding or falling. Everyone followed suit in the comfort department.

Tonight's meeting brought in some new faces. Stan and Sebastian as well as Lisa and Harrison joined in the bull session.

"I know this is going to hit a few of you as a surprise, maybe for others it is not a big surprise. Today after our lunch, I came home to study the notes on the case. I heard the sound of a vehicle pulling into the driveway. I watched to see who had pulled up and to my surprise, there was Mirah. I know we've been looking for her and she just drove up to the house. I expected her to come to the door. However, she went to the back door and jimmied the lock. Most of you know that Michael uses this house as a ground zero for his product testing before putting any of the features in a client's residence or office. Because of her method of entrance, I decided to gather everything and move to our safe room. Monitors in the safe room cover all the cameras in the house, and on the property allowing me the opportunity to watch her. I not only watched her, but I overheard a call she made to Ernie Compoto."

Sebastian spoke up. "Ernie Compoto, the bank president? Now he is in the picture?"

Johnnie nodded. "Apparently he has been in the background all along. Back to Mirah's conversation, she seemed to be upset with Ernie. Here comes the big shock, she said she was taking all the risk like killing John Erickson and Logan Ferns."

The mood in the room turned silent. Then everyone started talking at once and in distressed tones. Noah took the floor.

"Needless to say, this throws a monkey wrench into the mix. How did we miss this development? I thought she was working with the DEA. Damn! Maybe the DEA partnership was all a ruse to start with anyway."

Al spoke up again. "I am having a hard time picturing Ernie doing anything dangerous. He has never presented himself as an assertive individual. Now he is part of the problem."

Stan spoke up. "I think I know what might be part of the picture. Several major gunrunners frequent the lodge out by the lake. They have a stockpile of weapons at the lodge. I have seen the guns, and we are talking serious firepower. I have the evidence to take care of this side of the equations. Others will make the arrest, just in case I need my cover again, so I will remain concealed for the raid. I can see how Compoto could get Jennings out to the lodge if he killed him out here finding the exact spot won't be found. It is a large area. Having his body taken to the bank shows how narcissistic he is, he no doubt is thinking he can handle any situation. I think he is involved in a lot more, gunrunning is just part of the picture. He owns several pieces of rental property in Ackers. These locations are ideal for drug distribution and prostitution. What better place to launder money, a bank president most of the time does not come under suspicion like this, so it makes for a good cover. No one would believe his involvement. He is good at playing the concerned leader."

Lisa spoke next. "For those who do not know me I work the sordid side of the law. I am an undercover vice officer. Harrison and I have seen Ernie in questionable places. He hangs at a club in downtown Akers known for prostitution and drugs. We never thought he was involved in the activity. He would come in with Herb, we made the mistake of thinking Herb was using Ernie as a pawn. Now it looks like he is bad to the core."

Johnnie looked at Michael and Pat. "This keeps getting better. Okay, let's cover some other things I would like to see cleared away. Sebastian this is one for you. The story about Andropov's niece, is it true? If so, who killed the two perpetrators?"

"The story is part of my jacket. Victor's parents were immigrants; he loves this country. He has his vices. He smuggles things like the extra cargo from truckers, if they know there is an open weigh station on the interstate, well they just lighten the load.

Victor had a guy at the truck stop that helped himself to the items and was splitting profits with Victor. He is not into drugs, guns, or vices. His little entrepreneurial efforts are definitely minor. We had to make him look dangerous so that people would leave him and me alone. The victim and murders are just stories to give me a solid front. Victor's niece is fine; the two individuals as far as I know never existed as we described. The US Marshalls can do a good job at setting up covers."

Stan sighed. "I think the next time I am called to a small town to work I am going to study the town a bit more. This place is a regular hotbed of vices. Noah what is your take on all this?"

Noah just shook his head. "I feel like I came in half way through a bad movie. I had no idea of all the groundwork was already laid out by your efforts. Still, I came because of the death of Herb Jennings that triggered Johnnie's inquiry. Finding out that Herb and Grammar were into drugs, no big surprise; finding Compoto is suspected of money laundering and the death of one of the bureau's agents just pisses me off."

Pat looked to Sebastian. "This signature of leaving some sort of mark on victims, in this case the salt, thought that was your signature, right? How did it show up on Grammar, Herb, and Silva?"

"Apparently, someone is borrowing my signature. Maybe they thought the murders would be on me, and they would be home free."

Harrison asked if they could get back to Mirah's activity. Knowing that she is capable of murder makes her very dangerous. "How do we go about proving her involvement?"

Johnnie waved a computer disk. "She might be vicious, but smart she is not. I have her confession on the disk. She murdered Logan the same day as John. When she broke in went directly to the study, most likely she wanted to be sure I wasn't on to her or Ernie. What we need to do is to draw her out somehow. Ideas anyone? Just throw out anything. We can toss them around a bit to see what sticks"

Harrison came up with an idea. "She was at Silva's services. Once she resurfaces, I tell her my suspicions about Silva's death.

Wouldn't be surprised to find she was involved in it too, because if we come up with one more crime saga I think we will drown in varying scenarios."

"Harrison, what if you voice your suspicions to Ernie. He apparently knows how to make contact with her. We can use him to lure her out of hiding." Johnnie was standing now.

"That is good. What about wearing a wire?" Leo was getting excited. "I want the bitch! She killed one of our agents. It is time to bring her to justice. You know! That justice she is supposed to uphold."

Michael went to the box on the table and pulled out a few of his favorite devices. "These video cams are great. Perfect for today's modern undercover agent, don't leave without one of these little charms."

Terry spoke. "What about the guns that are stockpiling? Do you think Compoto has his fingers in the mix?"

Stan responded that he would just hold off on the arrest at the lodge until they knew all the players and their positions. Considering how many times Ernie had been out to the lodge, it was hard to believe he could be innocent.

By this time, everyone was watching the DVD of Mirah's invasion of the house. Michael called for a selection of Chinese food. He knew it did not take long for the food to come, so it seemed to be good timing.

The group finished reviewing the scene of Mirah's raid on the house when the food arrived. There was enough food to feed an army. Considering their numbers, they appeared to be an army. Michael knew from experience when Noah and Johnnie did these sessions, they always ended up starved when they wrapped up.

"Hey people, today being Friday, we have the weekend to gather our thoughts. When do you all want to do this again? Does anyone have an objection to doing it here?" Johnnie asked.

They all agreed it was a necessity to follow up, and their house was comfortable and relaxed. They planned Monday evening for another session. This would give them Saturday and Sunday to think through anything that might have been missed. Then if they had new developments, they could present them on Monday night.

Noah insisted that at the next gathering the FBI would be supplying the eats.

Suddenly, it seemed that the mood changed from crime fighters to hungry mob.

***

Saturday seemed like a blessing to Johnnie. She decided she would be sleeping in and enjoying a day away from the bank. She and Michael would be doing their own bull session. As she lay in bed, she bounced some ideas around her brain.

Realizing that she would not get back to sleep, she got up and put on her favorite robe. It was floor length, hooded and fleeced, and it was blue of course. She went to the study to gather her notebooks, and she found Michael and Pat going over the recorded events of the day before.

"Hey, look who decided to get up and join us." Pat gave her a hug as he got up to refresh his coffee cup. Michael had a habit of bringing a carafe of coffee upstairs when he was working.

"Hi." She kissed Michael and said she was going to go make her tea.

"What is wrong with our coffee?" Pat loved to tease any woman, well the ones he knew well.

"I like tea, besides I drink decaf even when I do coffee at breakfast. You don't want me going hyper on you do you?"

Pat could not pass up the chance to tease. "You mean this is you calm? Heck no I don't want to see you hyper."

The three of them worked out different game plans. Ernie Compoto was the obstacle. Obviously, he was involved, but murder? What was his motivation? Was he a psychopath or just taken in by the lure of money and esteem? Whatever admiration he had, was gone now. His career was gone, and so was his freedom.

Mirah was a major player and far more dangerous than anyone would have thought. Johnnie was distressed that she didn't catch all the signs before. She was a trained psychologist for heaven's sake. She should have caught on to her. She knew something was hinky with her, but she truly thought she was just a grandstander.

The trio was so intense with their thought process that the phone startled them when it rang.

Johnnie was the closest, so she answered. "Hello."

Josie was calling, and she seemed stressed. "Aunt Johnnie, I think I may have a problem. I have been sitting in the living room, and I realized that a gray vehicle has been sitting in the same place as it was yesterday. It does not belong on my street. Are these some of your buddies watching the house? Someone is sitting in the car, and has been since yesterday, I watched whoever trade off on the watch."

"Sweetheart, you have the house secured? You need to get to your safe room and stay there until we open the room."

"Michael, Pat, someone is keeping an eye on Josie. We need to get over there right now!"

Pat held up his hand to stop Michael and Johnnie. "Wait a minute, if we all three go over it is going to look suspicious. If I go, no one is going to be surprised to see me at her house. Chances are the players in our game will not know who I am. I have been over there a lot in recent times. Since I worked with Michael on the safe rooms, it won't be a problem for me to access the space."

"Call the moment you have her out of there and no one is following you. Oh, tell her to pack for several days. She isn't going back to the house until this is over." Johnnie was twisting a napkin into knots.

Pat just wanted to get over to the house. "Let her know I am coming and I will open the room. I don't want to scare her any more than she already is now."

Johnnie was still worried. She started pacing. The normally cool-headed agent was not so calm when it came to her niece.

"Johnnie, she will be fine. Pat can take care of both he and Josie. He will get her from the security room and out of the house." Michael knew of Pat's ability, and he knew he was armed as well.

"Do you think Mirah is plotting a way to keep us from discovering what she really is? If she hurts one hair on Josie, she had better run to the far ends of the universe. I swear I will make her life a never ending nightmare." Johnnie was furious and it showed in her comments. She normally retained a quiet exterior, but she never made an idle threat.

The phone rang. It was Pat, he had Josie, and all was safe. He got the car's license number and the make and model. He was calling Noah with the details.

Johnnie could relax once she knew Josie was safe. She also was grateful that Michael installed a security room in Josie's house as well. It didn't have all the bells and whistles as the one they had, but it was a comfortable place with a phone and the necessities. It was very serviceable for two people.

Noah had the identity of the car in short order. It belonged to Ernie's wife. He wanted to know who was driving. Pat said it was Ernie sitting there with his newspaper. He was not very good at keeping an eye on the house.

Now Noah knew that Ernie and Mirah were stepping up their activity. Something must be coming to a head. They would need to act soon if they wanted to prevent more trouble and potential deaths.

Pat and Josie left the house and stopped by the bakery on their way over to Michael and Johnnie's house by a distorted route. Josie knew her aunt had a weakness for cheese Danish.

"Hello, we are back, and we brought you some goodies."

Johnnie ran down the steps to greet them. She was so thankful for Josie's safety.

They all sat at the breakfast table. Josie told them how she noticed the car on the street early Friday morning. She didn't think about it until today. It really caught her attention when it pulled up across from her house, and no one got out. She should have called earlier but today it frightened her. She too expressed her thanks for the security room.

***

Sunday morning, after Mass, they stopped for brunch at a local restaurant. It was a nice way to start the day. Josie was much more relaxed. She did not want to impose on her aunt and uncle, but she didn't want to go back to the house alone.

"We don't call it imposing, we call it family. What do you think my sister would say if she knew you went back to the house?" Johnnie knew Josie would not put up a fuss. She had seen how pale Josie was when she arrived the day before.

Michael and Pat settled down to watch the game. Michael recently installed an HD large screen TV just for football.

Josie and Johnnie went to the study so Josie could familiarize herself with Ernie and Mirah. "You need to be vigilant. These people may feel threatened, and that will make them very dangerous. I want you to carry a stun gun. It could be enough to get her to safety. Remember showing a weapon and using a weapon are two different things, if you reveal a weapon you will have to use it. Something she knew Josie would not do with a gun, a stun gun was a better choice." Johnnie just didn't tell her the full power of the stun gun, better she didn't know.

Johnnie sat and explained what she needed to do and watch for in order to be safe. Josie had questions of her own since they found her and apparently knew of the relationship between her and Johnnie.

"Okay, this all started because of what you were researching on Victor Andropov, right? Now you have found out Victor is not the problem. So why was he being investigated?" Josie was doing her best to understand the turn of events.

"What has happened to the research? Is it still important?" Johnnie always did think Josie would make a good analyst for law enforcement. She asked the right questions.

"I think I want to talk to Sebastian. He may have an idea of who started this misdirection. Maybe the Secret Service requested it in order to cement the reputation of Victor and Sebastian." Johnnie was rolling it over in her mind for the zillionth time.

Johnnie kept her investigative books in the security room. After the first break in, she knew it was not safe to leave them in the desk. She would access them later and be sure to make note of the research project. It would be one of her top questions for tomorrow night. She hated to think Gary could be involved in all the happenings, but she didn't want to find a connection the hard way. She decided not to say anything to him about any of the recent happenings.

. "Do you think it is safe to go downstairs? Those two can make more noise than 20 people."

Josie laughed and agreed with the observation.

As the men continued to watch the game, the women decided on supper. Basil pesto was a favorite of everyone; so the women didn't have much to do to have dinner on the table. Fixing a salad with a balsamic, olive oil and a touch of honey made delicious vinaigrette and again an easy choice. Instead of plain bread, Johnnie decided to make her version of croutons out of leftover Italian bread. Cutting the bread in large pieces, enough for the salad as well as the crostini for dinner made it simple.

Johnnie cut the bread and heated olive oil and butter in a large skillet. Combining Jannie spice, she added the bread to the skillet her final ingredients lots of rosemary and finishing with kosher salt. Using tongs, she kept the bread moving so as not to burn. Toasted to a golden brown, she put them on a paper towel to drain.

Josie loved to putter in the kitchen with her aunt. She finally had the opportunity to ask why Johnnie referred to her favorite Italian seasoning as Janie spice. "There was a lady I met a long time ago, it was her mixture, her nickname was Janie. So I call it Janie spice. Just mix of a pinch of granulated garlic, one part oregano, two parts sweet basil, and three parts ground rosemary. See now you have my secret."

Dinner came together as soon as the pasta was cooked and drained. An addition of pesto, a vinaigrette salad and then join the guys in the family room since there was no getting them away from the game. After all, it was football season.

After supper, the men maintained their vigil at the TV, while Johnnie and Josie cleared away the remnants of dinner. The ladies went upstairs to watch a movie on the study's TV with a large bowl of popcorn.

***

Monday morning filled Johnnie with dread. If she had any luck, she would not see Ernie today.

Her reaction to her encounter with Harrison was different. He still played the bank clown, but she had a better understanding of his behavior. To avoid a chance meeting with Ernie, she chose to stay in her office on the sixth floor. Unfortunately, Ernie made an effort to find her. "Hi Kiddo, what are you up to these days?" His attempt at levity was forced.

"I am trying to make sure we haven't overlooked any of the requirements for the morning computer operator. We should have the responses and decision by Wednesday morning."

"How is the investigation going? Learning anything of interest or value?" Ernie was searching for details.

"Somewhat like my old days with the bureau, one step forward...now where do I go?" She knew how to be evasive. She knew the dangers of taking a case personally, but this felt personal. While Silva had her shortcomings, as we all do, she should not have paid with her life.

"I think things are a bit cloudy right now. I had to change my focus, getting Silva's position filled is important. We know what a cascading effect job bids put on the entire bank."

Johnnie intentionally used Silva's name she watched for the slightest tick. She could not help resenting him. Ernie took a few M & Ms from her candy dish, and said he would see her later. She was glad to see him go.

The remainder of the day she filled with the obligations of her banking position. She knew she had been distracted when it came to her responsibilities. It was time to become visible again in the bank. Too much of her time had been away from the job.

Johnnie did her best to make the rounds of her floor, everyone to needed to know that she was still there for them.

The day ended and all she could do was take a deep breath and be glad to be out of there for the day. Her interaction with Ernie made her nervous for the employees.

After she cleared and locked her desk, she called Michael using her cell. He was home and had been in touch with Noah and Terry. Things were set and ready for the night's bull session.

Johnnie asked. "Josie is staying with right?"

"She is staying, but she did not want to be involved in the bull session. She prefers to stay in the study and cuddle up with a good book."

Johnnie was relieved to know Josie would still be at the house, and that she did not want to know any more about the case. All Josie needed to know was that this town might just be better if viewed from the rear view mirror.

***

As promised, Noah and Leo brought enough food to satisfy a football team. From the looks of the spread, dinner was going to be first on the agenda. Josie made ice tea and then joined them for the meal.

Dinner finished, Josie took care of the dishes and then went to the study.

Noah asked if anyone had any questions or comments to share.

Johnnie had a few questions and directed her first inquiry to Harrison. "Is someone on a protective detail for Aces, Charleston, and Rayna?"

"Yes, I called for a special detail. If I wasn't available I wanted them safe."

Johnnie wanted to know how the US Marshalls got involved with the bank.

Harrison said the US Marshalls investigate potentially high levels of money laundering. "First National Bank of Ackers has filed an extraordinary number of exempt accounts from the currency transaction reporting. Ackers is a small town, so the amounts drew our attention."

Johnnie looked at Sebastian and asked how he fit into the big picture?

"The Secret Service works with the US attorney on things of an investigative nature. You are working a research project on Victor Andropov and I believe the investigation was started per request from Mirah Anderson. I think it was to divert any suspicion away from Logan since she was using his outfit for her and Ernie's activities. Since the initial assignment, we have learned a lot from Victor. He brought the lodge to our attention. He was there for a fish outing, when he accidentally found the storage shed filled with the guns. Considering the severity of the find, he reported what he had found to the Secret Service. He did not know where he should report the discovery. As the child of immigrants, he is vigilant when it comes to personal freedoms. When he discovered the cache of weapons, he remembered stories from his parents about why this country was so great. He took it as his personal duty to report the suspicious activity. He was instrumental in getting Stan on the payroll of the lodge. I guess in the end, he has been a huge help. The US attorney has granted him immunity since he has been so helpful in our investigation."

Johnnie listened with great interest. "Were you investigating Victor before his call?"

Sebastian explained. "Victor's activity with the extra cargo had gone unnoticed. It wasn't until he called the Secret Service with what he had found we knew something was up. What have you found in all the work you have done?"

Johnnie spoke. "I haven't found any excessive deposits or any outgoing cash that would require currency reports."

It was obvious that Sebastian considered Victor a flawed decent guy. Once he agreed to discontinue his extra activities at the truck stop, he became one of the white hats from that point and hopefully into the future.

Johnnie had one more question. "Does Ernie pose a threat to any of the bank employees? Was he responsible for Herb's death, or did someone else commit the crime?"

Noah said that was the meat of the session. "Ernie is a behind the scene sort of person. He doesn't want to get his hands dirty. Grammar was involved in drugs and he was buying from Ernie's enterprise, as was Herb. When he found out about Grammar's death, he laid low. He knew they were buying from the same source, which Logan Ferns handled. Logan got Herb to make contacts with other bankers in his travels. Then Herb decided to skim some product, which he sold using the rental property for distribution as Lisa suspected."

"What about Grammar, who killed him?" Johnnie wanted to know it all.

"That was Logan, since Grammar was a contact, he apparently wasn't alarmed when he came to visit. Then while investigating Grammar's death, Ernie's name surfaced. When questioned he said he knew about Grammar's drug habit, and that

Grammar was buying drugs from Victor. Mirah put her name on the approval for the investigation and you know the rest."

Leo told the others why John and Mirah became a team. "Mirah's name emerged in a couple of drug investigations in Virginia and the FBI decided to put John in her office. When Herb died, we suspected she was dirty. The FBI assigned John for her protection; at least, that was her understanding. John was accumulating information that made it obvious she was power crazy. Granted we think all politicians are criminal, but she definitely the worst of the worst. Her only thought is of power and gain. Do not underestimate her, she is dangerous."

Johnnie presented another question. "Who killed Herb, and why put him in my office? Why go through my desk? What was the point of that exercise?"

Terry had been silent up to this point. "This is where we get into the substance of events. Herb like Mirah was power hungry. I guess, Johnnie, you saw that in him in the form of his intimidating nature. He decided that Ernie was a bit too reticent for his position as bank president. Herb did not like the bank's vulnerable position, and wanted to avoid any party's attempt to purchase. As it was, Herb was a big fish in a little pond. In today's market, small fish are meaningless. Herb made the mistake of voicing his opinion to others. Ernie wanted the bank sold. He wanted to get his buyout package and move along leaving Mirah to bigger quests. Ernie heard Herb was trying to garner support for a no confidence vote by the board on Ernie. Ernie was doing his best to weaken the bank, making it easy pickings for an easy sale. Herb believed that with a no confidence vote the position would open up and he was the logical choice for president. Trouble is we have no idea how he found out about Herb's plan."

Johnnie was following the findings but still had a question. "Okay, Herb is eliminated per Ernie's request. I can see that happening, but why my office and why ransack my office?"

Harrison spoke up. "Johnnie, your attitude towards Herb has been noted. People know that you stand your ground. Herb could not coerce you so it made you the perfect patsy. Having your office sacked was more or less a warning. Apparently, you did not catch the threat."

Johnnie continued. "I might have seen it as a possible threat if I hadn't been working on the research on Victor. When I found my office in disarray, my immediate thought was someone was looking for the research project. My next question, did all of you know about the other investigations?"

Noah laughed. "Can you imagine all these agencies working together? If we had put in a request for inter-agency cooperation, do you think the top brass would have seen the significance of a small town? As it is, we all came to rest on this rather serendipitously."

"Okay, who is collecting all the firepower at the lodge?"

Stan spoke up with this one. "We believe it was Mirah's plan. She had Logan do the legwork, but from overheard conversations, nobody pays attention to the guy who schedules visitors. Anyway, I heard by some of the guys bringing in the arms, that Logan would have all the firepower he needed. Didn't say what he planned on using them for, but I can only be visible on a limited basis. If I showed up every time these men showed up, they would get might suspicious. No worries though, I have captured as many as I could, so we will get them."

Johnnie was getting tired of being the inquisitive one. "Does anyone else have any questions? I can't be the only one trying to work through all this stuff."

Michael said he recognized an unanswered point. "We know Mirah killed John and Logan. Even before that, why was Logan shadowing Johnnie?"

Terry said she had a theory. "This is just my thought. Logan had a visible dubious enterprise. Going to him for someone to arrange the fire at Silva's is easy to believe. Who went to him? I think Johnnie could give us a hint. You need to clear the trees from the forest and look at what is truly happening. Put your profiling skills to work."

Johnnie put down her glass of tea. She had to give it a bit of thought. "Silva liked to be noticed by the brass. Previously, Herb was the one that cultured that personality trait. He enjoyed working one employee against another from what I saw. Without him to bolster her, Silva chose to tell John what she saw that morning. John was a good person, but Mirah must have heard, most likely from Ernie, who she had conversations with on a regular basis. Mirah had Logan handle Silva's murder. This set off alarm bells with John. He knew the only one who could know was Mirah. I guess that is why she needed to get John out of the picture permanently."

"Okay, then that more or less caused John's demise. Now to determine why take out Logan?" Terry continued.

Noah said it was a matter of survival. He continued to explain their theory. John being out of the picture put suspicions directly on Mirah; at least with Leo's team. That explained the timing of John and Logan's murders.

Murph sat and listened to all these theories. "With all this presented how do you prove it? You are going to need a boatload of proof to take down the state's attorney. Do you have enough to do that successfully?"

It was Pat's turn to laugh. "At last, a real meat and potatoes man, bottom line please, and hold the jibber jabber!"

Noah assured Murph with the DVD of Mirah in Johnnie's study, they had her for sure, and she no doubt, would roll on Ernie. However, most of the heavy stuff falls at her door. Murdering a FBI agent!"

Noah said his team had developed some ideas; it was time to put them into action. He continued on, saying he had discussed one particular detail with Michael, now it was Johnnie's turn to respond. "Johnnie all of us are involved in law enforcement in some form. You, my dear, are no longer in the bureau. We cannot have you take part in any apprehending activity in your present state."

"Explain what you mean by my present state?" Johnnie looked perplexed.

"I guess you forgot. There is clear danger to civilians; we need to avoid collateral damage. That puts you among the civilians that could be at risk." Noah had to bite his inside cheek to keep from smiling.

"I am not your average civilian. I carry my weapon; I have kept up on the physical training. So what is your point?"

Michael spoke up. "Johnnie, the only way Noah will allow you to continue your involvement is to accept a reinstatement to the bureau."

Johnnie wanted back in, but she wasn't sure of Michael's reaction. "You two have discussed this haven't you? Who else knew this was coming?"

Sebastian spoke up. "Noah gathered us for lunch today at Flames; he presented the idea to us and wanted to know our opinions about your capabilities. We all agree if you want reinstated, we see you as an asset to the investigation."

Noah asked again. "Do you want to be reinstated? We can't have you in the middle of something that is as volatile as this situation."

"I think I should talk it over with Michael. Can I give you an answer tomorrow?"

"You can, just remember without reinstatement, this is the last thing you will do in the investigation."

"Ugh, why not ask me a life changing question on the spur of the moment." Johnnie knew what she wanted. Her eyes were on Michael.

Michael could read her mind. "Johnnie, I haven't said much to you about your working at the bank but I can read you like an open book in large print."

"I guess you all know what my answer will be, but please don't tell Gary. I don't want anyone in danger, and if he isn't suspecting Ernie, he won't say something that could be hazardous to him, and possibly his family." Johnnie was always looking out for someone's welfare. "Oh, to answer your question, Noah, I'm ready to get back in!"

The group gave out a cheer and a round of applause.

Noah stood in front of Johnnie. "I am here to administer the oath of office and to present you with your badge. I also have a service weapon for you, so please stop carrying your personal weapon. I know about the one in your ankle holster, but I am referring to your vested holster and your purse holster."

With the formalities of the job administered, Lisa went to the kitchen and Pat went upstairs to ask Josie to come downstairs for a few minutes.

Lisa and Stan gathered the surprise for Johnnie as Josie entered the room. They followed on her heels.

Pat looked at Josie. "Your aunt has something to tell you."

As if on cue, Lisa gave a bottle of bubbly to Michael. He popped the cork on Johnnie's favorite sparkling wine and handed the first glass to Johnnie.

Johnnie walked over to Josie. "I don't know if you ever expected this turn of events, and I am not sure of your reaction, but I have been reinstated with the FBI."

Josie embraced her aunt. "I have suspected this situation was going to stir a fire that was never going to be extinguished."

Noah took his glass in hand. "I want to be the first one to congratulate me on reinstating a great agent for my team."

This brought about another round of applause. "Seriously, I think tonight has been very enlightening. Leo and I have to go to Quantico tomorrow and lay out our joint findings. Stan, Sebastian, Harrison, and Terry will be joining us so that we will have enough people to keep us straight. How about we call the work end of the evening over?" This again caused an eruption of the group's applause.

The remainder of the night, which was fleeting quickly, was on a more cheerful note. Murph finally could enjoy the libations.

Johnnie circulated among the group. Her FBI career was her most exciting and rewarding work. Her banking career was not able to compare. She expressed this to Harrison, and he certainly agreed.

Lisa was the first to announce that she needed to call it a night and Sebastian said he needed to get back to Victor's place. He left another agent in command of the safety detail, and it was time to return.

The crowd gathered up the glasses and remaining plates and returned them to the kitchen. All of them said good night to the newest official member of the team and left.

Johnnie asked Michael to start a small fire in the fireplace. Together with Josie and Pat the four sat around watching the fire with another glass of wine.

"This turned out to be some evening. I was just so happy to be getting answers to my questions. Reinstatement is the icing on the top. Michael, are you truly good with this turn of events?"

Michael put his arm around her. "I knew you tried to make a go of the bank, but I could see your light dim. I am good with it."

"Aunt Johnnie, how are you going to be able to work tomorrow? You will be chomping at the bit to get back into the investigation."

Johnnie replied. "I guess I will have to approach it as an undercover assignment, and that is not far from the truth."

Talking about the evening and the theories was exhilarating, but soon the excitement gave way to exhaustion, and Johnnie was having trouble keeping her eyes open.

***

Johnnie wanted to be with the group going to Quantico, but it would not be good for her to be out of the bank on a day when so many others were also out of town. Harrison was still missing as far as the bank knew. That could make Ernie suspicious if he knew of Harrison's real identity. She truly doubted he did, and Terry, well as a police officer she had other cases to work. Noah being out of the bank might draw some attention but only with Gary. If he asked, she was prepared to tell him that Noah needed to meet with someone in Clarksburg. That is if he asked. Gary was not the type to ask questions unless he already knew the answers and there was no way he knew the answers to that question.

Noah and Leo left early the next day with Harrison, Stan, Sebastian, and Terry. They had to get to Clarksburg for their flight to Quantico.

The flight was a short one, and he was in his office by 10 o'clock. The four managed to work the timetable of events into a spreadsheet, which made it easier to follow. All the characters in the investigation, not to mention the varied groups of law enforcement, made it vital to keep the details in order.

Terry was looking over the final printout. "I think the only thing that Johnnie did not question was why use the salt."

Sebastian spoke to the question. "My character was known for his signature. I suspect Mirah thought it would be a good way of getting me out of the picture. Sebastian's brutality is well known but salt just wasn't a strong enough signature. I guess she did not research my character very well. That's arrogance for you. However, the salt used is a particular salt mined only in Soledar, a part of the Ukraine. Victor's family lived in the area, and Victor's father had worked in those salt mines. It was another way of tying Victor and me to the deaths."

Stan added another point. "What about the stockpile of arms? We didn't cover that last night. I just need an agenda, so I can have my end prepared on time. To organize and synchronize the take down, everyone needs to be ready."

Noah sat at the desk making notes on all the comments. They still had a big job ahead of them. The needed proof of their theories was going to be paramount before arrests came.

Noah started asking questions to get everyone thinking about the details.

"We have the proof on Mirah. I cannot believe she left herself open by making that phone call in the study. I am just glad that we have it recorded, and it is good that the recording is time stamped and stored on a secured server. It preserves the chain of evidence. When this goes to trial, you can bet the defense is going to try to tear apart the record."

Terry spoke up. "How do we prove our theory of Herb making a move against Ernie?"

Noah nodded. "It is a good theory, but finding substantiating evidence is not going to be easy. If someone did bring Herb's tactics up to Ernie, it is obvious what would happen to anyone who crossed him?"

Sebastian said the fact that Herb is dead just might be enough for someone to approach Noah for protection. It is going to depend on how vulnerable they feel.

Noah sighed. "Wish Johnnie had joined us for this meeting. She could speak to the personalities involved, and that carries weight with the guys from the critical incident response group."

After lunch, the four gathered in a conference room. The room was set up for 10 people. A plasma screen made it easy for all to view the spreadsheet of activity. The hushed earth tones and carpeted walls gave the room a modern high-tech appearance.

Terry was impressed; she appreciated the technology and support given to the agents. Her department would also be impressed. The conference room they utilized was a metal table and four folding chairs.

Chloe Benjamin, Joey Porter, Giuseppe Kemp and Megan Rogers arrived and were introduced as the members of the FBI's critical incident response group. The group engaged in a bit of small talk before settling down to the review. Megan was the first to speak.

"We have all read the review you provided. I have to say, seeing such inter-agency collaboration is refreshing, totally appreciated, and impressive, as is your summarization of the activity. Exactly, how did you discover all of this in a town that is so small?"

Noah took lead. "Herb Jennings was murdered, and his body dumped in the office of Johnetta King."

Before Noah could finish his comment, Giuseppe interrupted. "Our Johnnie King?"

Harrison smiled. "I see she left her mark. Yes, our Johnnie."

Giuseppe spoke again. "I thought Johnnie left to start a family?"

This time Terry spoke. "Johnnie has been reinstated."

Megan spoke again. "How did you arrive at all these details? This took a lot of effort."

Harrison spoke up again. "Hi, I am known as Harrison Magers, and I have been undercover at the bank for some time now. We suspected that the bank might be a major money launderer. Silva Ames was a friend of mine. When she was murdered, Johnnie was suspicious. Then I had two attempts on my life, Johnnie's interest definitely piqued. I tried to get details out of Johnnie by visiting her office for normal chitchat, but she never revealed a thing. I think, or rather I know, she suspected me at some point."

Terry laughed. "Excuse me, at first we thought you were just being nosy, then you were a victim, and then we thought you were the villain. Aren't you glad we found out about the real you?"

Noah was afraid that they would lose too much time. "Look, I know this all looks like it has a ton of loose ends, but we worked with Johnnie. The sister agencies here have shared their findings, and given the timetable and description of each event you can see why we believe we have a good case. We still have a few questions we also want answered. What we need from this group is to assess the situation, and be ready once we tie everything together. I propose we leave our papers with you, and after your review, we would like an okay to proceed. However, in order to proceed, we may need additional agents. Do you believe this to be reasonable?"

Megan said. "I believe it is reasonable on the part of the FBI, but I cannot speak for the other agencies. We will contact the appropriate people and see what they think of their side."

Megan still wanted a question cleared first. "One more question before you all leave, with members from all these agencies who will take the lead?"

Terry answered. "If it comes down the way it looks, there is something for everyone. We all started with our own investigations. Mine being Herb, Silva, and most likely Logan, while John died in my town, he was FBI, so I know Noah and Leo want that one. Harrison has the money laundering, Stan has the arms stockpile and Sebastian, well Sebastian what do you have?"

Sebastian dropped his head to his chest. "I have already had my minute of sunshine. I have Victor Andropov's immunity and the details he provided to get Stan into the lodge. Secret service prefers a low profile. I am fine with it that way."

Chloe also had questions. "How will you coordinate this effort to arrest the alleged guilty parties? You are working from different locations. The bank, the lodge, and still you have your most challenging arrest with Mirah Anderson. Your evidence on her is critical."

Terry spoke to what evidence they had on Anderson. "The evidence on Anderson is substantial. Her own words, and spoken and recorded while she invaded Johnnie's house."

Chloe continued with her questions. "How did you get the evidence of her breaking into the King residence?"

Terry smiled like the cat that swallowed the canary. "Have you met the King's? Michael uses their residence as testing grounds for his security company. As a result, he has cameras and microphones throughout certain rooms of the house. They have a safe room that keeps the occupant secure should there be a home invasion. Johnnie says she never had a reason to use it until recently but twice in the last few weeks. Once when Logan sent his employees to search the house and what brought this entire thing to this crescendo; Mirah actually broke-in and searched the study. Because of the outdoor cameras, Johnnie was expecting to go downstairs and let her in the house. It would have been incredibly dangerous for her. Instead, Mirah went to the back door and broke into the house. The cameras activated by motion and automatically triggered recordings. Johnnie locked herself in the safe room and watched as Mirah went directly to the study. Whatever she was looking for she did not find. She made a call to Compoto and during that conversation, she admitted to the murders of John Erickson and Logan Ferns."

The members of the CIR group were stunned to hear the state attorney was a one of the state's worst alleged felons. They also knew that with the recordings the arrest would be a good one for the FBI. As Noah noted, it is one thing to arrest criminals, it is another to see someone in the judicial system become a criminal.

Joey had one last question. "Can we be sure the evidence is beyond reproach?"

Leo answered this time. "That was my first concern. John was in my unit. We do have a copy of the DVD, but more importantly, the entire incident is on a secured server off site. It is a secured server backed up every night. It is time and date recorded, so yes, the evidence is is going to be difficult to refute."

This case promised to hold a great deal of gratification for the FBI.

Chloe had her last question. "Who killed Herb Jennings?"

Stan was ready with an answer. "It was common to see Herb and Ernie at the lodge together. So best guess, Ernie or possibly Logan. It would have been easier for Ernie to get him away from the lodge. Most likely when I wasn't on duty. Ernie knew Logan was a murderer."

The gathering took a less formal atmosphere. Everyone joined in the casual conversation. Some of the talk included the case, while other talks concerned the various law enforcement agencies present. Noah remarked that knowing individuals in other agencies could be helpful on other cases.

Joey spoke up. "I have one question before you exit. Do Johnnie and Michael still do their bull sessions?"

Stan laughed with a nod. "I see you know them both."

"Oh, I remember those sessions and I am glad Michael still owns his security company. I know he has provided some very valuable information on more than one occasion." He looked at the other members of his group. "You are aware that Michael has a top level clearance. As a civilian, he comes in contact with people who would rather remain invisible, and shares what he finds."

As their flight time grew closer, they started packing up the papers and notes. All believed the meeting was satisfactory. The only thing that the CIR group wanted to do was review the entire time lines and events. They also wanted details as to the arrest plans.

Everyone knew who was to do what and they all agreed to stay in touch.

Everyone was back in Akers by eight o'clock that evening. Terry called Johnnie to see how things went for the day.

"It was a slow day. I wish I knew where Mirah was hiding. She still has not shown. I did leave a message on her phone. I wanted to appear concerned, if I stopped trying to reach her, she could get suspicious."

"I take it, you did not hear back from her." Terry knew the answer before she asked the question.

"I haven't heard a word. Tomorrow will be a busy day. We will close out the bids on Silva's job. I don't know if we have many people wanting to bid. The fact that the position requires an early-morning arrival into an empty bank could be a cause for concern for some. Of course, after we fill that position, we get the torrent of other job openings. How did the meeting go today?"

"Well, you and Michael are well remembered at the bureau. The group seemed pleased with the evidence we had on Mirah, thanks to you. The other points involved the execution of the arrests. The FBI is willing to provide extra support when the time comes if we believe it be necessary. I have to say it went better than I expected." The women took some time to talk on a personal level. Johnnie was going to miss Terry when this was over.

After the call, Johnnie went to the family room where she met up with Michael, Pat, and Josie. "Looks like they had a good meeting, and I believe we just have a few more details to work out. What are you guys watching?" The three had got caught in a comedy marathon. Johnnie joined them for a couple of episodes. Johnnie had a busy day planned for the next day, and she needed to get some rest. She called it a night when the 11 o'clock news was over. Josie followed suit. She was more comfortable in Johnnie and Michael's place than her own house. She resisted their request live with them, but for the present, she felt more secure.

When the ladies departed the men stayed behind and talked. Michael asked Pat if he could plan an out-of-town trip with Josie when the action got closer.

Pat told him he was trying to get her to go to Pittsburgh for a few days. He told Michael of his plan to propose to Josie. Michael smiled and asked him how he felt about taking the plunge. Pat was anxious. Michael told him every guy is nervous when he proposes.

Pat said he was going to head for the hotel and meet with Noah in the morning for breakfast. He also wanted to do a bit of sleuthing himself. Pat reminded Michael that he originally brought the news that Mirah was undercover, only to hear that was not the case. He wanted to find out more about her.

***

Morning again, Johnnie thought. She knew the day was going to be hard. Job bids always made the day draw out to what seemed like an endless barrage of names and job descriptions, except Johnnie worried, this particular job may not have bids.

Michael brought her tea as usual, but found her in the shower. "Hey; you are up early."

"I thought I would get this day over as fast as possible. I just don't know how long this will take to fill Silva's job if no one bids."

Michael wrapped her in a towel as she stepped from the shower. He held her for a moment as he draped the towel around her shoulders and kissed her on the top of the head as he spoke. "Someone will bid; it is the highest paying non-officer position in the bank. Today you should take a break from investigating, and concentrate on the bank."

"I know the bank is the priority of the day, but I can't help but wonder where Mirah is hiding. How does an attorney at her level turn to crime?"

Michael sat down on the bench across from Johnnie's vanity. "She has other motivations. She wants power. This town is a good place to launder money and run drugs. The connection with Herb allowed for the drug game, and Compoto is arranging the money laundering. So just concentrate on the job bid and stay away from Compoto."

"I just hope Ernie doesn't try to insert himself into the selection process. Gary and I have always done these together when it involved my division."

Johnnie decided to dress in a suit with pants rather than a skirt. With all that was happening, she still wanted her ankle gun strapped to her. With the pants, she could wear her ankle boots to hide the weapon. It was hard to say what Ernie or Mirah might try to do, so best be prepared.

Johnnie chose to skip breakfast. The quicker she got to work, the sooner this day would be over. Johnnie pulled into the bank parking lot. She carried her weapon, but she did not want to let Ernie know she was armed. Of course, he had no reason to believe she knew. She was grateful that the bank did not have a metal detector.

Going into the bank through the lobby gave her a chance to see if Harrison was in for the day. It looked as if most of the employees were on schedule, but she didn't see Harrison.

She called Gary. "The bids for the job opening are due in by 10 this morning. Have you heard of anyone planning on bidding?"

Gary said to the best of his knowledge, there were two bids. He was glad to have at least two bids, but he did not know the names of the individuals applying. It would be best if the bidders were capable of doing the job. Johnnie agreed and said good-bye.

In order to make the day go faster, Johnnie tried to occupy her thoughts with the most recent updates on the software changes. Software updates were normally a nuisance, but today they would serve as a distraction. Besides, Sarah was still available to run the computer, and she would help with the update procedure and documentation when Johnnie needed her for the project.

Johnnie was still reading the documentation on the software updates when Gary phoned her at 10 and asked her to meet in his office. She went down by the back stairs, which opened next to his office.

"Do we have more than two bids?" She was hoping this was going to be an easy selection.

"Looks like four bids." Gary said with some relief.

"Well, we have our work cut out for us. Shall we call Denise to come in with all four personnel files? We should look at the background of all those applying for the job."

Gary picked up the phone to call Denise. "Johnnie, how did you make it in the bureau? Your sense of fair play had to get in the way of job performance."

"Things are different when criminals are involved." Denise came and brought all four personnel files. It was interesting to see the bids. The bids required the individual to explain the reason for wanting the job.

Sitting in Gary's office with Denise, they looked over the names. Gary spoke. "Kirk Willis, Drew Bassett, Ginger Lowie, and Kimberly Morgan, anyone want to offer an opinion?"

Johnnie looked to Denise, as personnel manager she should have the insight on the individuals bidding on the job.

"To start, Kirk has been with the bank for a year and in the drive-in tell unit. He has problems dealing with outages; not that he has many, but he becomes extremely flustered when he does. I think being in the bank alone when a problem crops up would not be a workable solution.

Next Drew Bassett also is on the teller line, and he has an air of confidence. He has been with the bank for two years. He is good at his job, and outages are not a problem because he rarely has one.

Ginger Lowie is in the loan department, length of employment four years. She has had computer experience, but it is limited to personal computers. I don't believe that relates to the job upstairs. It is different from running Excel or Word.

Last person, Kimberly Morgan employed here for three years. Great with customers, currently working in customer service new accounts. She often requires direction to keep her on course. The computer operator will need to be able to work without supervision for a few hours in the morning. This could be a problem for Kimberly."

Gary looked at Johnnie. "Any of the candidates sound like a possibility?"

"Well, we are going to have to look at everything, especially their reason for wanting the job. I would rather have someone who is interested in the job, not just the pay scale."

Denise started again with Kirk. "He gets nervous when there are outages. He is interested in the higher income. He wants to take more college courses, so he needs money for his education."

Gary asked what kind of classes was he interested in taking.

Denise said he wanted to continue with his accounting studies.

Gary was impressed. "My thought, the bank does pay for continuing education. I don't think this job is right for him; but tell him of the educational opportunities. In the long run, that just might be best for him."

Denise went to Drew Bassett. "Drew is very capable. His outage record is good. He is looking for something more challenging. He is a good contender."

Next Denise addressed Ginger's bid and her explanation as to why she wanted the job. "Ginger works in the loan department, but she has worked in several other positions. She says she wants to learn as much as possible. She is another good candidate.

Finally, we have Kimberly Morgan, currently in customer service. She likes the earlier hours since it would allow her to be home when her kids got home from school. She is okay in her current position."

At this point, Johnnie commented. "Kimberly is very pleasant. Problem is she makes a great number of mistakes that affects the work down the line. I think we need someone in the position that makes fewer mistakes. Remember this position requires accuracy, and we can't have the entire bank affected by simple mistakes."

Gary sat back in his chair. "I hate musical jobs. Johnnie, who do you like for the job?"

"The way I see it, Drew Bassett is the one I would choose. He is confident, and he likes a challenge. This is definitely a more challenging job."

Gary turned to Denise. "What is your input?"

Denise flipped through the pages of the four candidates. "I have to agree with Johnnie. Drew is the best candidate for the job."

Gary agreed and told Denise to write up the announcement and put Drew's job up for bid. "Like I said, I hate musical jobs."

The group broke up and each went to handle their own responsibilities, Denise would write up the announcement and then post the next job opening up for bid.

With the job decided, Johnnie wanted to see Noah. He was still in the bank's boardroom. "Noah, how did it go yesterday?" Johnnie asked.

"Hi Johnnie, we had some enlightenment. The CIR is going to give us the backing should we need extra resources. The varying cases seem to have the appropriate law enforcement to take care of the arrest. Terry will take Herb, Silva, and Logan's cases. We need proof to tie Logan to Herb or Silva's death."

Johnnie reminded Noah. "Remember what you and Terry said. I would like to venture a suggestion on Logan's death. Mirah and Ernie could not have pulled it off all this by themselves. They are too reputable to be dealing in drugs and money laundering in the open. They needed someone behind the scenes. I think, that was where Logan fit in the picture. I suspect he is the one responsible for both Herb and Silva. Maybe he approached Mirah for a bigger cut of the deal."

Noah listened with interest. "Possibly, but Mirah isn't going to give up anything without a fight. I see you still have your skills."

Johnnie smiled. "It's like riding a bike, you know how that goes."

After leaving the boardroom, she sat in her office thinking about the idea of Mirah. She started writing out every thought that came to her mind about how Mirah could be at the center of Logan's death.

The day moved along as expected until Ana interrupted Johnnie's work announcing that Mirah Anderson was in the building and wanted to see Johnnie.

***

The sight of Mirah made Johnnie's blood boil. She needed to play this encounter with a blank slate and finesse and close her notes on Mirah.

Mirah closed Johnnie's door. This had the feel of a showdown.

"Hi Johnnie, you look surprised to see me." Mirah was waiting to see Johnnie's response.

"Mirah!" Johnnie came around the desk and gave her a hug. "Are you okay? Where have you been?"

Now it was Johnnie's turn to watch for a reaction. This was going to be like two fighters circling each other in an opening round looking for an opportunity.

"I sort of went into hiding. I think I liked it better back in my office in Charleston. Is this what it is like being on a case? Too much adrenaline just wore me out." Mirah was evasive, but Johnnie expected such behavior.

Johnnie watched every tick of every muscle in Mirah's face. "It would have been better if you called and let someone know. The police were running wild trying to find you."

"Really, who exactly was trying to find me? I know your friend Noah was at Quantico, along with several others, including Detective Terry Nichols. Why did they leave you out of the visit?"

How could she know? Who gave it away?

"I don't have a pulse on everything Noah or Terry do. Yesterday we were gathering the bids for Silva's job. To do that, I needed to be here. Higher paying job openings create many questions. I was not privy to any meeting." Johnnie had to find out how Mirah knew, but this could be dangerous. She decided she would play the dedicated bank employee.

"The bank has been through a lot of jolts. I have to concentrate on getting things back to normal. People are still jumpy about the murder and Silva's death."

Mirah raised her perfectly arched eyebrow. "I thought Silva was also murdered. Do the employees know the details?"

This was a chess game, and Johnnie knew how to play. "Details like that, should they be true, are part of a police record. I don't know how it would have been divulged."

"Oh come on Johnnie, I know you and Terry and Noah have been thick as thieves. If Terry knows something, you know it too. Noah being your old section chief, I bet you know what the FBI knows."

"You have a very high opinion of me. I am paid by the bank, not the local law enforcement." Johnnie pointed to a chair, and she returned to her place behind the desk.

"I told Ernie you were a problem, with that Noah guy coming to the bank when Herb turned up dead in your office. Of course, you have some sort of pull with the FBI." Mirah was enjoying this too much.

"I am a bit overwhelmed by your presumption of my standing. The bureau does not share their investigations, even with retired agents."

"We know you know what they are doing every step of the way. Nice to have such a golden reputation that your old section chief would keep you informed." Mirah was grinning as she spoke.

"Again, you presume a lot." Johnnie was rerunning all her conversations in her head.

A knock at the door interrupted their conversation. Mirah got up to open the door.

Johnnie knew things were coming to a head, and the rest of the team did not know it was going down.

"Mirah, has she acknowledged anything?" Ernie took the other chair in front of Johnnie's desk.

"She is trying to play it as the bank employee." Mirah gave Ernie a sideways glance with a smile.

Johnnie knew they knew, but to what extend was still a mystery. "Ernie, what are you two suggesting? I have been busy with the job position that was filled today."

Ernie's countenance broke and now his face became that of a psychopath. It was a look she had seen from others many times before, but never expected to see it coming from Ernie. Johnnie knew she was in danger. That was not her concern she needed to protect her coworkers. Psychopaths never concerned themselves with who is hurt or killed, as long as they get what they want. Right now, it appeared they wanted information or they wanted Johnnie out of the picture.

"You two think you have something figured out, and it appears as though you think I know something. I have to say this entire conversation has me unnerved."

Mirah and Ernie both smiled. "Ernie, can we tell her now?" He nodded.

"It is like this; the boardroom had a recording camera installed over the weekend. The board thinks the installation is to record the board meetings. Nice thing about the setup; all the conversations were recorded. Ernie has a record of everything. We knew by the various talks you had, that you and your friends pieced the picture together."

Johnnie could only think of how to protect her coworkers. She could not allow another death.

Ernie stood up and moved his jacket back far enough for Johnnie to see the gun. "I think we should all go to lunch." The head nod meant now.

Johnnie came around the desk and went to the closet. She was trying to act as normal as she could. She believed she could take them both, but not here and not now, if she failed too many innocents were in the way.

Walking out the door, Mirah said for the benefit of the employees. "Do you like that Italian restaurant over in the plaza? They open for lunch don't they?"

Johnnie tried one more ploy. "Have you ever been to Tomas' restaurant? It is great I would really like to take you there to see for yourself. I think you will like the place."

Mirah played along with the suggestion. "Sounds great, I have not been there before."

Johnnie said the back stairs was an easy exit if they didn't mind the steps.

Mirah said she could not do the steps because of her knee. That only left the elevator and more exposure for the employees. They exited by the elevator and the front door. They went to Johnnie's car, and Ernie took the keys saying he was driving.

"Did you really think we were going to go to a restaurant of your choice? Your attempt to tell Ana where we were going has failed. We prefer Flames. It has a dark atmosphere, and we know that Victor is not coming to your rescue."

Johnnie gave a silent sigh, maybe Victor would remember her, or if Sebastian is there he may be able to help. This could work out favorably still. Of course, there was always the possibility that they would go to lunch and she would go to the bottom of the river.

During the drive, Ernie and Mirah talked in hushed whispers. Johnnie was in the back seat with the child safety lock on the doors that guaranteed Mirah and Ernie that Johnnie could not escape. Mirah took Johnnie's purse, which lead to the discovery of her gun.

Johnnie was relieved to see that they were going in the direction of Flames. At least, this meant the river landing wasn't immediate.

Once they pulled into the restaurant, the valet came to get the car door. After he opened it for Mirah and Ernie, he went to the back door to let Johnnie out. The valet was unfamiliar with the child lock, and it took him an extra second to realize he had to hit the unlocked button. Johnnie took the moment away from Ernie and Mirah to say. "Tell Sebastian that Johnnie is here with Mirah and Ernie. In case he would like to join us." She did so with a hushed tone and her eyes lowered. The valet was unaware of the circumstance and nodded as he looked back to the pair waiting for Johnnie to catch up.

"We didn't think you would try to run. You are not the type to endanger people. Interesting things you learn about people when you read their psych profiles." Johnnie saw the malicious look in Mirah's eye. This was not good.

Johnnie had to wonder just who it was that gave Mirah her file. Or was she guessing to throw her off? The three walked into the restaurant with Johnnie in the middle. Her only hope was that the valet would not make a big fuss when he spoke to Sebastian. She wondered if he spoke to Sebastian yet. Hopefully Sebastian would be in the restaurant?

Once seated in one of the elevated booths, Ernie gave the lunch orders for all three, although he did ask if they preferred a specific drink. Mirah suggested chardonnay while Johnnie indicated water was fine.

"Very good Johnnie, play the part of the luncheon guest. It will keep you alive a bit longer." In the three years Johnnie was at the bank, she never saw anything that would indicate Ernie was a psychopath. Then again, his office was next to Herb and she did everything she could to avoid Herb. Not to mention psychopaths have a talent for the impression of normalcy.

Johnnie saw Sebastian come through the hall she prayed he could tell she was not at ease. If he was a good agent it should be evident, at least she prayed it was obvious. Sebastian disappeared up the stairs, and was out of sight.

Victor came down the same steps and approached the table. He greeted the table. "Ernie, it is so good to see you again. May I ask about your lovely luncheon party?" Victor was as smooth as silk. He bowed slightly as Ernie introduced the two women. He called over the server and said to put the lunch on the house, and he bid his farewell.

"So this is the kindly old man you have been investigating. Johnnie, don't you feel terrible? He is just an old world gentleman." Mirah's voice was dripping with honey. Too much honey, sickly sweet.

Johnnie remained silent. Her conversation at the table consisted of thanking the server when the meal arrived.

Mirah looked at Ernie. "Can we now tell her why she is doing the research?"

"Go ahead, it doesn't matter anymore."

"Victor has a reputation in this town. However, he is content to be a minor player, and we know this is the last place anyone would look for our specialized activity. You see Johnnie, Logan was doing very well supplying us with certain services. That is until he got greedy. Good thing Ernie heard you talking to Noah this morning. I knew when Ernie called it was time to do some work myself. Two things I don't like, a greedy underling, like Logan, and a has-been fed who thinks she can still play the game."

Johnnie finally spoke. "You killed Logan, did you do it the same day you killed John?"

"Oh yes, John, I am rather sad about that job. I think he got wise to me when Silva became a problem. I do believe we should have put some distance between her telling John what she saw in your office and the fire. I made sure we didn't have connecting doors. No one would believe I had anything to do with his death. I can play the part of the devastated partner quite well. It fooled you and that Terry."

"Yes, you both fooled everyone. I would like to know how you know about me." Johnnie was playing to Mirah's narcissism.

"You are not an agent anymore. I was able to get into your house with so much ease it was ridiculous. Logan's men told us of the study, so I wanted to check it out for myself. Nice place, but I didn't have time to do the tour, but I liked what I saw. Too bad it is going to burn down tonight with you and your hubby inside."

Johnnie's eyes went black, her tell for when she was enraged. "You won't fool Michael. He knows about people like you. He will read you for what you are, and he isn't going to let you waltz into the house and take over."

Ernie sneered. "Oh didn't we tell you, your niece Josie is going to be in an accident. Michael will of course respond."

Johnnie's eyes were beyond black now they took on the look of fire. "You go near Josie, and I will make sure you two rot in prison."

"Come now Johnnie, did you think your world would remain intact? We did not get to our positions because we are shy. You will be an example to anyone else who thinks they can take down what we have been building all these years. Besides you are not going to be around to do anything about anything."

Johnnie could not believe the venom that spewed from Mirah. She seemed to be angry at the thought of a normal life and family. Johnnie took the chance to throw her off her game.

"Mirah, why do you hate so much?"

"Let me tell you, while you and your husband were busy having your lavish life, I worked deep into the night. I saw this so called justice system turn loose so many criminals, I decided to do something about the matter."

"What, by becoming a criminal yourself? Oh no, you are a psycho. The two of you are both psychopaths. I will tell you what you are, evil; there is no other word for it. You are both simply evil." Johnnie was controlling her breathing. Never let them hear your voice crack. Stay in control. "Our life style is not lavish, we had to work our tails off as well. Michael had to see an ill-used military run by people who had different agendas; but he did not go out and become a murderer."

Mirah spoke again. "Yeah, you could be right. Truth is, I will be the US Attorney, and you will be ashes."

Johnnie needed to pace her reactions. She learned a long time ago, if you don't control your expressions and reactions; you will never make it in this business. She slowed her eating, hoping that Sebastian had an idea.

Sebastian came back down the stairs and took a seat at the far side of the bar. He had a nice spot to watch the trio. He watched all the faces. Mirah and Ernie seemed very pleased with themselves. On the other hand, Johnnie appeared to somewhat stiff from what he had observed previously. He decided to call Noah and see if he had any thoughts on the matter.

"Noah, Sebastian here. Johnnie is having lunch with Mirah Anderson and Ernie Compoto. She looks angry. The valet let me know she was in the restaurant, per her request. I had Victor do one of his famous walk throughs. He told me she was not talking, just listening, and nodding only. This is not like our Johnnie."

Noah sat and listened. "Is she okay? Did you perceive a threatening situation?"

Sebastian told him that she was sitting between Ernie and Mirah, to the casual glance, no problem. Knowing the situation, he said it could only be bad news.

"Okay, let me call Michael and get Harrison up there. Can you call Terry? What about Stan, we wanted this all to go down at the same time. If we miss our opportunity, we could lose the upper hand on the activity at the lodge."

Noah knew Michael needed to know, and he wanted to talk to Terry and Harrison. "Michael, Noah here, we have a problem. Is Pat with you?"

"Yeah he is here, do you want to talk to him?"

"Please put him on." "Hey Noah, what's up." "Pat we have a situation, Compoto and Anderson have Johnnie. They are having lunch at Flames, and she asked the valet to let Sebastian know she was having lunch there with Ernie and Mirah. Sebastian spotted her, and had Victor do one of his greet the customer walk through visits. He said she looks angry, and she is sitting between the two. Do you think this is a problem?"

Pat didn't know what to think at first. "Do you think they know what we know?"

"I don't see how they could not know. But I can't imagine how they found out. We need to think of a way to get her out of there if possible, or we need to ready a take down. Talk it over with Michael and get back to me ASAP." Pat handed the phone to Michael and said. "We need to talk."

Michael stopped his writing and looked at Pat. "Something is wrong. What is it?"

Pat knew that Michael was aware of Johnnie's capabilities. "Noah wanted to tell me that Johnnie is with Ernie and Mirah at Flames for lunch. She had alerted the valet to tell Sebastian she would be having lunch with those two. I can only think that was to let someone know she was at this point a prisoner or hostage. Sebastian is ready to do something, but he wanted us to know and to see if we wanted a full-on assault. We weren't planning anything this fast, but it just might be necessary."

Michael stared out into space with a determined expression. "We have to do something, and we are not going to have much time to plan. Have Sebastian keep an eye on the three, if they appear ready to leave, is there some way he or Victor could delay their departure? I think we need to call Stan and Harrison as well. We need Terry with us. This is her jurisdiction."

Pat said he would call Noah back, and see if he could make contact with Harrison. He would also call Stan. He suggested that whoever is available should meet at the diner near the bank.

Soon the group gathered at the diner. Stan did not want to leave the lodge, so he stayed there; but requested backup. If Compoto and Anderson were on to them, they probably would try to move the weapons. He knew he could not take on the men who he had seen at the lodge, not alone..

Sebastian continued to sit at the bar in the restaurant to keep an eye on the trio reading his newspaper. Ernie knew of the reputation Sebastian had cultivated, well he thought he knew. Sebastian had his blue tooth ready to report without anyone noticing.

Harrison came to the diner to meet up with Pat and Michael. Noah, Leo, Terry, and her partner Murph arrived shortly afterward.

Michael cleared his throat. "You all know Johnnie can take care of herself, but without backup, she will not risk a situation where collateral damage could happen. I called her office to see what Ana knew. All she could provide was that the three were behind closed doors, and then came out saying they were going to lunch."

Sebastian is aware of the three of them being at the restaurant. By the mere fact that Johnnie had the valet notify him could mean she was asking for backup." Noah nodded in agreement. "I worked with Johnnie for some time. I know how she thinks and how she protects. Michael is right. So I would agree that she would look for backup, without it, she would delay her move."

Harrison was taking it all in, and he was thinking the entire time. "We have been using Flames as a meeting place for several years. Since we came to town, we made constant use of the place, so we would be part of the regular crowd. I could go in to offer additional backup."

Noah said that would not work, reminding Harrison that he had been out of touch for several days. Harrison said it was a good point, so he would be willing to go wherever they needed him.

Michael's cell phone rang. Ana was calling him with something she remembered. "Michael, I just remembered something. As they were leaving, Johnnie was talking about going to Tomas' place. I thought if you were looking for her, that is where you will find them."

Michael closed his phone. "I am certain that she is requesting backup. When the three left her office, she was talking about going to Tomas'. We have been there with Terry, and we know he is particularly helpful on police matters."

Terry agreed, and she stated that they needed a plan now.

"Okay, I am going to call the CIR team and let them know we cannot wait for additional backup. If we don't do something now, we could lose too many major players. We know that the lodge is stockpiling weapons, whether those were for the militia or for Logan's antics, we can't be sure. Especially since Logan is gone. Terry, do you know anyone who could go out to the lodge and not be suspicious. Stan is going to need help. Once that place is secure, then we can make sure we have our sights on Ernie and Mirah."

"I could send someone. He works the front desk, but a good cop. Will Hastings was an active detective until he took a stray bullet. He knows how to handle himself. He most likely would have made captain by now hadn't been for that stray bullet. He took the desk job because he didn't want to endanger a partner due to his bad shoulder. I will call him and tell him to go out to the lodge and introduce himself to Stan. He is the perfect image of a hunter, so he will fit the bill." Terry was already dialing Will's cell.

"Do we know why Herb was targeted? Why would they do something so blunt? Something changed and it would be nice to know before we go into action."

Michael responded. "We don't have every loose end tied up yet, but we will. That is a guarantee."

Sebastian continued to watch the booth that held Mirah, Johnnie, and Ernie. He watched for any opportunity to remove Johnnie from the other two. He was staying alert for any possibility, when Pat Cates arrived. "Hey man, what are you up to today" Sebastian recognized him from the bull session. The two men did not get much time to chat, but they knew they were in for action. He sat down beside him. "Can you see them?"

Pat wanted Sebastian's take on how things were developing. "What is happening? Terry has an extra guy heading to the lodge to assist Stan. We were hoping that we could get Johnnie out of here without incident. Something tells me, they are not going to let her get up for even a restroom visit."

Sebastian perked up. "I have an idea, if we could get her to go to the ladies' room, we know that Mirah would go. Maybe we could take Mirah by surprise."

Pat spoke out. "I bet Johnnie has her weapon? She has a built in holster in her top, blouse, tank whatever you call that piece. Plus, lately she has been carrying her ankle gun as well. She is very proficient with hand to hand. If she can make a break and get away from Ernie, I suspect she can take Mirah."

The men did their best to let her know, she would have the backup she needed.

The meal was over, and the trio started to stir. Pat walked to the far side of the bar in hopes that she would see him.

It worked! Johnnie made direct eye contact with Pat. Now if Pat and Sebastian could delay Ernie, she was more than an even match for Mirah. Johnnie could only hope that Mirah would not get a shot off in a struggle.

Johnnie turned to Mirah. "I am going to the ladies' room; I assume you wish to accompany me."

Mirah smirked. "Not a chance of going on your own, I can tell you that for sure."

Johnnie knew the lay out of the restaurant. The ladies' room was near the private party room. Mirah followed her into the restroom. With lighting speed, Johnnie did a roundhouse kick, and Mirah hit the wall then fell to the floor. Her head had a gash in it from where eyebrow to hairline. Mirah was seething. "So you think you can take me? You are soft; been out of the game too long."

Johnnie could not kick off her boots, but still she could stand her ground somewhat bouncing on her toes. "You think so? Whose head is bleeding? Just so you know I was watching you in my house. Everything you did and everything you said is securely in the hands of the FBI. Oh, in case you are wondering, I am an official agent of the FBI. I was sworn in Monday night. So not only can I kick you inside out, I'm going to arrest your ass!"

Mirah was in a rage, the thought of Johnnie being able to arrest her definitely destroyed her composure. So many thoughts went through her mind. As a cold-blooded psychopathic killer, she would fight Johnnie to exhaustion or worse. Her fingers took on the appearance of talons. They curled, and she hissed. Johnnie knew the more Mirah let her emotions take over, the easier it was going to be to take her in hand to hand.

Johnnie was ready for any move Mirah attempted. Michael utilized the basement of their house as a gym, and he took her to the gun range at least once a month. She was ready, and her stare down made Mirah seethe even more.

Mirah pushed herself up off the floor. Mirah attempted to kick her shoes off, but Johnnie's moves were too fast. Mirah did her best to take her on one to one, but Johnnie's training in Wing Chun allowed her to block just about every kick. Johnnie's defense only enraged Mirah more. Blocking strike after strike continued to exasperate Mirah. Her attacks became more violent and less precise.

Mirah was swearing and screaming as she came straight at Johnnie, and again, the blows were blocked. Johnnie took one blow to her forehead, which did split the skin. Still she fought on. The blood ran down her face, but she simply swept it away without flinching.

Johnnie had her weapon, but she did not want to introduce it into the ruckus. She wanted to take Mirah in a hand-to-hand. Too many times innocent civilians get hurt when guns are in the picture. Johnnie was not going to chance a civilian being hurt. Besides, there was going to be a great deal of personal satisfaction in taking Mirah down.

Sebastian and Pat knew that the trip to the restroom was a ploy on Johnnie's part. She was ready for action. Pat decided to stand by the wall of the ladies room, but slightly out of sight of Ernie.

The sounds escaping the restroom amused Pat. He had lost to Johnnie's training on occasions. He had no doubts about Johnnie's ability to take Mirah in this scuffle. Mirah may be a cold-hearted killer, and being a woman allowed her to take her victims by surprise. Johnnie knew her crimes and her abilities, which usually came from a gun. It is one thing to be in control with a weapon, but depending on your own physical ability to take down a perpetrator, it was different. Mirah was barely standing. Her stance was unsteady. For extra measure, Johnnie performed a beautifully executed ankle sweep, a defense technique she had mastered. Her boots turned out to be a decent weapon. The added weight of her ankle gun worked in Johnnie's favor, and she never had to display the firearm. It allowed her to hit Mirah with a more solid strike. Mirah hit the floor with such a crack it echoed throughout the restroom. Her head had another split on her forehead and Mirah was down and dazed. Johnnie smiled. "And that was for even thinking of threatening my niece, Josie."

Pat, no longer hearing a commotion, opened the door. "I see you haven't lost your touch."

Johnnie touched her bloody forehead. "I have to admit, defending against a real felon does come with bumps, bruises, and blood. Do you have any flex cuffs?"

Pat handed the cuffs to Johnnie and enjoyed the look on Mirah's face. He knew the best was yet to come. Johnnie cuffed Mirah as she announced; "Mirah Anderson, Ms. Attorney General for the state of West Virginia, you are under arrest for the murder of John Erickson and Logan Ferns. Oh yes, and we cannot forget the assault of a federal officer." She then Mirandized her, and handed her over to Leo as he entered the room. He smiled and took her from Johnnie leading her to the private dining room, and Victor closed the door to the room.

Victor came rushing over to Johnnie. "You need medical attention. I'll call 911."

Johnnie smiled at the elderly gentleman. "I am fine, a bit of glue, and I will be good as new."

"Glue, what kind of glue?" A surprised look appeared on Victor's face.

"The medics use something like a super glue to seal wounds. The bumps and bruises will heal without a problem."

Victor looked at the banker with a new appreciation for her.

Johnnie asked Pat, "What happened to Ernie, did he get away?"

"Not to worry, Sebastian is entertaining him. Leo on the other hand was too anxious to get up here so he headed here first. Noah and his people are coming to take them into custody. Noah and I thought it might be a good idea to have them incarcerated in another city. We want all the arrests completed without alerting the others. Harrison's at the bank. Noah informed Gary of Harrison's identity. There should not be any problems at the bank, but we are playing it safe. As far as we know it was Ernie that had organized the money laundering so it should be okay."

Pat sat at the nearest table in the gaming room. "Our next exercise is to secure the lodge and confiscate the gun stockpile. No one attempted to move the arsenal. Terry called Will, he was with Stan holding the lodge, and playing it safe until the ATF arrived. It will be a cinch to shut them down. With Logan out of the picture, the place is nearly empty, except for the elderly woman who cooks at the lodge. Her son is the caretaker, and Stan knows he is okay."

Johnnie was feeling good about the day. "I am interested in the plan for the weapons. We have Ernie and Mirah, Logan's dead and Victor, well Victor is smiling like a police commissioner on his best day."

Sebastian approached the table where Ernie sat waiting for Mirah and Johnnie. His demeanor changed only slightly. Ernie was doing his best to look as though he was in total control. The truth of the matter was Sebastian scared Ernie who visibly shrank in Sebastian's presence. Ernie might have been the organizer, but he was strictly back room. Sebastian decided that keeping him off center was a good thing. He started a conversation concerning Herb.

"Ernie I have to know, was Herb murdered because of drugs? Where do you think, he was murdered? It is obvious it wasn't in that office in the bank."

Ernie swallowed hard. "What makes you think I know where he died? I would have thought he was in King's office when he died."

Sebastian continued. "See, in my position, I learn a lot about what happens in this town. I even heard that your bank has been the center of several illegal activities. Did you know there is a stockpile of weapons? Story is the arsenal was financed by the bank. They are at the sports lodge you own I believe. I heard the weapons were for Logan and his guys. Then, of course, we can't forget the money laundering, that takes us to drugs and last but not least, murder."

Ernie was losing his composure. He was great at giving orders for illegal activity, but to put them at his doorstep was different. "I have no idea what you are talking about. I don't know what Herb was up to; any illegal activity he was into was his own doing, not the bank's."

Sebastian enjoyed the verbal cat and mouse game. "If that is the case, why was his body left in the bank? It looks like some unsavory types at the bank. Why bring his body to the bank? Was it meant to be a warning to someone?" Sebastian decided to bait him a bit more. "Do you think that Johnnie King is the one involved with drugs?"

The last comment allowed Compoto to regain some composure. "Well, we know that she and Jennings were at odds. Maybe the drugs were the center of their trouble. After all, he did hire her. She must have been his connection."

Sebastian had one more jolt to give Compoto; one more shock. "I heard she was FBI, been reinstated and everything."

Ernie's composure evaporated. "You mean she was FBI, for all I know she was into drugs while in the bureau. Maybe that is why she left the bureau."

The smile on Sebastian's face had a sinister nature. "No, I heard she has been reinstated. I guess she was bored with banking. Of course, your bank is not your typical bank. Still she decided she wanted to catch the bad guys instead of working with murderers."

Ernie looked like he had gone 12 rounds with a gladiator. If Sebastian read him right, he was ready to give up at that moment.

Noah arrived after the flurry of activity. "Hey Noah, guess who is all done up in a pretty package?"

Sebastian whistled catching Leo's attention. "Leo, do you want to cuff him? I think you should have the honor.

"The FBI is escorting them to Pittsburgh. Their crimes crossed state lines, so it is FBI jurisdiction not to mention the murder of an agent and let's add assault of a federal agent, Johnetta King. I think we need to get these two out of here, what do you say Leo?" Noah was so pleased to see this went off without a hitch. Not a shot fired, just some blood.

Leo was smiling for the first time in days. "I want to ride with the agent taking them to Pittsburgh."

Soon it seemed like the place came alive with many new faces. Michael went directly to Johnnie. He embraced her and held her tight for a wonderful warm and loving moment. They were even swaying as if they were going to start dancing.

Terry broke off their personal moment. "Before we start celebrating let's make sure we have those guns secured. Will is with Stan and they are awaiting the arrival of the ATF. I will feel better when everyone is safe."

***

Out at the lodge, Stan and Will were sitting at a table inside the shed that held the armaments. Will and Stan were talking as if they were old friends. "I was a Ackers detective until a stray bullet found my shoulder. It messed me up so now I work mostly at the front desk, but I can go out on calls if I choose. That is why I am with you. When Terry told me what was happening out here, I was furious. I use to come up here and stay during hunting season. I would like to see this place continue with its intended purpose before Compoto bought the place.

"I came here because Victor Andropov found the weapons stash by accident. He might have had his fingers in some small deals; but he didn't like what he saw." Stan commented.

Outside they heard several vehicles pull up to the lodge's front. Stan opened the door and recognized the team exiting the vehicles.

"Hey Carson, over here, big guy." The tall African-American man with shoulders like a linebacker waved to Stan.

"I see you are sitting down on the job." Carson was always joking.

"Well Carson, Will and I would like to make it to town and check out the rest of the activity. I am going to leave you with securing these things for shipment. Being the nice guys that we are, we did the inventory for you. You are welcome to take it from this point. I don't want my face associated with the arrest. You never know, I might have to come back here someday."

Will and Stan got into Will's vehicle and headed for town. Will asked. "Do you have any idea what has happened in town?"

Stan already had his cell phone out. "I will call Noah and see what is happening."

Will waited while Stan talked with Noah. "This turned out great and a bit embarrassing. You know Johnnie King, who worked at the bank? They reinstated her the other night, and once again, she is an FBI agent. Anyway, she took the state's attorney down in a hand-to-hand assault. Sebastian detained Ernie Compoto, and they are now in custody. Noah said everyone was going to the bank's boardroom. They have some things to explain to the bank officials. Leo and one of Noah's team will be taking the captives to Pittsburgh. They don't want the arrest known just yet."

***

Josie was waiting at the house. She was upset when she saw Johnnie's injuries. "Someone by the name of Jasmine called for Uncle Michael. She said to tell him, she was coming home. She said visiting family is fun, but she missed her own place. Oh and there is a lady by the name of Kelly in the family room. She is very upset, and in tears. I think she needs to talk to you." Johnnie thanked Josie and went to the family room.

Kelly was tearing a tissue apart and crying almost uncontrollably. When she saw Johnnie, her cry intensified. "Is it true, about Mr. Compoto? It is my fault entirely. I am responsible for Mr. Jennings' death."

Johnnie was trying to be as soothing as possible. "How did you find out about the arrest?"

Kelly explained. "The valet is my cousin he knew I worked at the bank he called. I was already on my way back to town. I was going to give my notice and get out of town for good. But I owed it to you to let you know I was leaving."

Johnnie was interested in Kelly's explanation she wanted to know how she thought Herb's death was her fault. "Tell me what you mean about Herb's death being your fault."

"I knew that Mr. Jennings was going to try to force Mr. Compoto out of office. You know Silva had lunch with Mr. Jennings, and they must have been as thick as thieves, because he told her about his plan to have the board do a no-confidence vote against Mr. Compoto. Silva told me about Mr. Jennings's plan. She liked to share things from her lunches with Mr. Jennings. I guess it made her feel important. I went to Mr. Compoto and told him. I was just trying to do the right thing. So many people didn't like Mr. Jennings, and if he became president, life would be miserable for everyone. By me telling Mr. Compoto, Mr. Jennings died. I feel so terrible. I don't know if I can ever stop crying. When Silva died, I thought I could be next. That is why I asked for my vacation time, I was afraid and didn't want anything to happen to my family. So I thought out of sight, out of mind. I made such a horrible mess of everything."

Johnnie assured her that the events of the last several days would have eventually happened because of the personalities involved. "In this situation with Herb, Logan, Silva, Ernie, and Mirah, something had to give. Not everyone can be the alpha. Silva was the innocent one in this, but it was her desire to play 'I've got a secret' that cost her life. Eventually it would have ended the same way. By you setting things in motion, and I know you did it innocently, we found out many things about Ernie and even our state attorney. I am so glad I didn't vote for her. Silva told John Erickson about what she had seen the morning they discovered Mr. Jennings body. Ernie or Mirah found out that Silva told John that she had seen a tall red headed man with a window washer harness carrying something large into the office. The man she saw was Logan Ferns, we never know the things people do for attention."

She told Kelly that things had already started to unravel for Herb, and it didn't have anything to do with her telling Ernie of Herb's plans. Johnnie asked Kelly if she wanted to return to the bank.

The look of relief was evident on her face. She started crying again, and choked out that she did truly want to return. Johnnie said to come back on Monday. It would all be okay. The fact that Kelly told Johnnie what had happened answered some of the last questions about the events.

Johnnie was walking Kelly to the door and comforting her as much as possible when the guys returned.

"Hey, guess what, I know why Herb was killed. He planned to have the board do a no-confidence vote on Ernie. That would leave the presidency open for him to waltz in and take over the bank. Silva told Kelly about the plan, and in turn, Kelly thought she was doing the right thing by warning Ernie. She did not want Herb to become the president. So ends... As the Bank Turns."

***

Johnnie was in no hurry to get to the bank in the morning. She knew the questions would be nonstop. There was no way to hide the bruise on her face, so she just did not try.

She came up from the back stairs and stopped in Gary's office. "Well, how do you feel?"

He laughed. "How do you think I feel after all you people dropped on us yesterday? I had a lot to talk over with Kayla last night. We decided to stay here in Ackers. Someone has to stay and help Tom run the bank."

Johnnie smiled. "I am glad to hear it; this bank needs you. I am going to take a few days off. I would like to give you a bit of insight; when the time comes I suspect Ana will take over in my position, she is very capable. However, please consider Sarah, she deserves a chance at advancing as well. She is a smart girl."

Johnnie went up to her office, and as she opened the back fire door, the room erupted with cheers and whistles. She could not help but blush. Everyone came to greet and talk to her. She sat in the large open area of central processing. She took the time to tell her coworkers as much as she could about the events. So many details had to remain under wraps until the trials of Ernie and Mirah. The news reports were extensive, but it only talked of Ernie and Mirah's arrest. She just used different words to say the same thing.

As far as work was concerned for the day, it was another lost day. It seemed that everyone, including some of the board members made an effort to come to her office.

Finally exhausted by the day, she left early.

***

Upon arriving home, she found Michael, Pat, and Josie all waiting for her. "Please, no more surprises. You all look like you have a secret."

Pat spoke up. "We do. We are all going to Pittsburgh for a couple of nights. We know you told Gary you were taking a few days off, so we can just go and enjoy the city."

She looked at them in disbelief. "You want to go for a mini vacation when I look like this, my head black and blue and with a glued seam. Are you crazy?"

Michael took her by the hand. "We are not crazy, and we are going. Let's get you packed. We are waiting. You need to move it!"

Her bag packed, she settled into the back seat of the minivan with Josie. The trip was rather enjoyable. They pulled up at the Hilton, and a valet helped unload the vehicle and took the keys. He parked the van and the group went inside to check into their rooms. They had a very large suite of rooms. Three bedrooms each with its own luxurious bath and a living room with a wet bar, everything a person could ask for was provided. All Johnnie wanted was to go to sleep. It did not take long for everyone to decide on a nap. It had been one of the most active weeks since Johnnie left the bureau. Later they would go to dinner at the top of the Incline.

Johnnie slept so pleasantly she hated to get ready. It would be dinner then back to the hotel.

The restaurant was beautiful and they had reservations, which surprised both Johnnie and Josie. It would appear as though the guys had everything planned out for the night. The reservations were for a secluded table near the window overlooking the night-lights of downtown Pittsburgh.

Josie had never been here before. "I don't know what could make the night any more perfect. I am so glad we have you back safe Aunt Johnnie. I was so scared for all of you."

Pat said he had one more thing to bring up before the entire episode was over. Johnnie and Josie were confused, that is until he dropped to one knee in front of Josie.

Somehow, through the tears, she said yes and Pat put a beautiful ring on her finger. "Now it is perfect." Johnnie said. "Yes, now it is all perfect."

About The Author

Jan O'Kane grew up in a small coal-mining town just outside Wheeling WV. She worked in the local bank for 21 years before retiring. During Jan's tenure in the pecuniary world, she received tributes in
Who's Who in the South and Southwest.
As well as
World's Who's Who of Women.
In 1995, she and her husband, Michael, moved from Wheeling WV to Durham NC. Together they started a mailing service, which is still in operation today. The company was awarded the
Micro Business of the Year
award by the Durham Chamber of Commerce.
Jan has written for magazines and newsletters both on-line and in print. She also has a blog
http:// janokane.blogspot.com.
Jan now devotes the majority of her time to her writing.

Watch for more Johnnie King adventures.